Praise for *New York Times*
bestselling author

FAYE KELLERMAN

and

justice

"One of my favorite authors . . . Mystery
lovers have much to be happy about. . . .
Faye Kellerman does not let us down."
Omaha World-Herald

"A virtuoso."
Sue Grafton

"This series . . . just gets better and better."
Atlanta Journal-Constitution

"[*Justice*] will likely increase her
constituency. . . . Surprising twists and
engaging subplots will keep readers turning the
pages to the satisfying conclusion."
Publishers Weekly

"Kellerman is splendid."
Milwaukee Journal-Sentinel

"She does for the American cop story what
P.D. James has done for the British mystery,
lifting it beyond genre."
Richmond Times-Dispatch

"No one working in the crime genre is better."
Baltimore Sun

P9-CRL-331

By Faye Kellerman

ATTENTION: ORGANIZATIONS AND CORPORATIONS
Most Harper paperbacks are available at special quantity discounts
for bulk purchases for sales promotions, premiums, or fund-raising.
For information, please call or write:

Special Markets Department, HarperCollins Publishers,
10 East 53rd Street, New York, New York 10022-5299.
Telephone: (212) 207-7528.   Fax: (212) 207-7222.

FAYE KELLERMAN

justice

A DECKER/LAZARUS NOVEL

HARPER

An Imprint of HarperCollins*Publishers*

Grateful acknowledgment is made for permission to reprint from the following copyrighted work: "Mary Jane's Last Dance," by Tom Petty. Published by Gone Gator Music copyright © 1993.

This is a work of fiction. Names, characters, places, and incidents are products of the author's imagination or are used fictitiously and are not to be construed as real. Any resemblance to actual events, locales, organizations, or persons, living or dead, is entirely coincidental.

HARPER

An Imprint of HarperCollins*Publishers*
10 East 53rd Street
New York, New York 10022-5299

Copyright © 1995 by Faye Kellerman
ISBN 978-0-06-199936-9

All rights reserved. No part of this book may be used or reproduced in any manner whatsoever without written permission, except in the case of brief quotations embodied in critical articles and reviews. For information address Harper paperbacks, an Imprint of HarperCollins Publishers.

First Harper premium printing: August 2011
First Avon Books mass market printing: August 1996
First Avon Books mass market international printing: March 1996
First William Morrow hardcover printing: September 1995

HarperCollins ® and Harper ® are registered trademarks of Harper-Collins Publishers.

Printed in the United States of America

Visit Harper paperbacks on the World Wide Web at
www.harpercollins.com

10 9 8 7 6 5 4 3 2 1

If you purchased this book without a cover, you should be aware that this book is stolen property. It was reported as "unsold and destroyed" to the publisher, and neither the author nor the publisher has received any payment for this "stripped book."

To my own teenagers, my tweener,
and my toddler.
Please G-d, just keep them safe.

justice

❧ Prologue

He saw the flash before he heard the pop. The percussive *ppffft* that almost drowned out the moan. The head snapped back, lolling from side to side, then finally found a resting place slumped over the right shoulder. As blood dripped from between the eyes, he wondered if the bastard had ever felt a thing, he'd been so dead drunk.

The thought didn't quell the shakes, his hands clay cold and stiff. For a while he heard nothing. Then he became aware of his own breathing. He crept out from his shelter and swallowed dryly. Tried to walk, but his knees buckled.

He melted to the floor.

Stayed that way for a long time. It could have been minutes, it could have been hours. Time was a black hole, a stupor of sleep and restlessness. Everything was shadowed and fuzzy.

Slowly, things came back into focus. The room, the floor, the bound body, the hole between the eyes. Blood had seeped onto the carpet, pooled around his shoes.

He stared, hoping tears would come. But they didn't. They never did.

With great effort, he hoisted his gawky frame upward, nearly tripping over spindly legs. The curse of being tall at such a young age: He was all height, no muscle. Light-headed, sick from the smell of gunpowder, he let go with a dry heave.

He tried to walk but again fell forward.

He needed air—*clean* air.

He crawled on his hands and knees out the back door, pushing open the squeaky screen. Wrapping his hands around the porch column, he raised himself to his feet. His bicycle was still resting against the apple tree, leaning against the trunk because it didn't have a kickstand.

He knew he had to tell someone. Even though she hated the jerk, Mom would still freak. That left only his uncle. Joey would take care of him. He had to get over to Joey.

He straightened his spine and inched his way over to his transportation. He gripped the handlebars, swung his leg over the seat. Pressing down on the pedal. Propelling himself forward.

Down the driveway and out onto the street.

Faster and faster, harder and harder, until wind whipped through his platinum hair.

He did a wheelie. He felt all right.

🦢 1

Pages 7 and 8 of the paper were missing. National news section. Specifically, national crime stories. Decker laid the thin sheets down, his stomach in a tight, wet knot. "Rina, where's the rest of the paper?"

Rina continued to scramble eggs. "It's not all there?"

"No, it's not all there."

"You've checked?"

"Yes, I've checked."

"Maybe Ginger got to it," Rina said casually. "You know how the dog loves newsprint. I think she uses it for a breath freshener—"

"Rina—"

"Peter, could you please distract Hannah from the dishwasher and get her seated so I can feed her? And take the plums out of the utensil basket while you're at it."

Decker stared at his wife, got up, and lifted his pajama-clad two-year-old daughter. She was holding a plum in each hand.

"You want a plummer, Daddy?"

"Yes, Hannah Rosie, I'd love a plum."

"You take a bite?" She stuffed the fruit in her

3

father's mouth. As requested, Decker took a bite. Juice spewed out of the overripe plum, wetting his pumpkin-colored mustache, rills of purple running down his chin. He seated his daughter in her booster and wiped his mouth.

"You want a bite, Daddy?"

"No thanks, Hannah—"

"You want a bite, Daddy?" Hannah said, forcefully.

"No—"

"You want a bite, Daddy?" Hannah was almost in tears.

"Take another bite, Peter," Rina said. "Eat the whole plum."

Decker took the plum and consumed it. Hannah offered him the second plum. "Honey, if I eat any more plums, I'll be living in the bathroom."

Rina laughed. "I'll take the plum, Hannah."

"No!" the baby cried out. Her face was flushed with emotion. "*Daddy* take the plummer."

Decker took the second piece of fruit. "Why do you keep buying plums?"

"Because she keeps asking for them."

"That doesn't mean you have to buy them."

"As if you can resist her requests? I noticed the other day she was playing with your gold cuff links—"

"She likes shiny things," Decker interrupted. "I like how you skillfully changed the subject, darlin'. What happened to the newspaper?"

Rina set a dish of eggs in front of Hannah and poured her orange juice. She shrugged helplessly. "What can I tell you?"

Decker felt nauseated. "Bastard struck again."

Rina nodded.

Decker said nothing. But Rina could see his jaw working overtime. She said, "Cindy called this morning. She asked me to hide it from you. I shouldn't have done it. But she sounded so desperate for an ally. She couldn't handle you and her mother's hysteria at the same time. Besides, there's nothing anyone can do—"

"What do you mean, 'There's nothing anyone can do'?" Decker snapped. "*I* can do something. I can bring her back home *out* of that hellhole."

"LA's not a haven from crime—"

"It's better than New York."

"Not all of New York is like the area around Columbia, Peter."

"Well, that's just fine and dandy except Cindy happens to go to Columbia." Decker got up from the dining-room table and walked into the kitchen, staring out the back window at his acre's worth of ranchland. The riding corral was now a foot-deep mud pit; the stables had been battered from the recent storms. Behind his property line stood the foothills bleeding silt. His house was fine so far, the gunk at least five hundred yards away. But who knew? He had plenty of garbage to deal with here. He didn't need problems three thousand miles away.

"Did you talk to her at all?" Decker asked.

"For a few minutes," Rina answered.

"How's she doing?"

Rina glanced at Hannah. "You want a video, muffin?"

The little girl nodded, licking egg-coated fingers. "Mickey Mouse."

"You've got it." Rina slipped the tape into the VCR, then walked into the kitchen. To her husband, she whispered, "How's she doing? She's shaken up, of course."

"Goddamn *police*! This is the third one and they don't seem one ounce closer to finding this maniac. What the hell are they *doing*?"

"That's an odd thing for you to say."

"I know incompetence when I see it."

"So what do you propose to do, Peter? Go out to New York and handle the investigation yourself?"

"I've seriously thought about it. I was in sex crimes for over a decade—"

"Peter—"

"Maybe I'll call the principal investigator—"

"You don't have enough work at home?"

"It's been a slow month."

"*Baruch Hashem*," Rina said, blessing God.

"*Baruch Hashem*," Decker repeated. "Besides, this is *my* daughter we're talking about. I want to make sure everything possible is being done."

"I'm sure they're working overtime. Just like you'd be doing."

"Right. Overtime on doughnuts." Decker grimaced. "I know I'm not being fair. Frankly, I don't care."

Rina sighed. "Peter, why don't you go visit Cindy? I'm sure she'd be thrilled to see her six-foot-four detective father. She and all the other girls in the dorm. But go out as a protective *father*, not as a cop."

Decker drew his hand across his face. "Son of a bitch! Preying on young girls like that. God, I swear, Rina, if I come face-to-face with that sucker, I'm gonna shoot off his you-know-whats." He looked at his wife. "Was the latest one hurt? Of course she was hurt. I mean, was she beaten or anything?"

"No. Same MO."

The MO. Bastard sneaked up on the girls, brought them down from behind, placed a large paper bag over their heads, and raped them from the back. The victims had described the violation as strong and painful but mercifully fast. Before they could utter boo, the monster had been upon them. Equally quickly, he seemed to vanish into the miasma. Cindy was a big girl, almost five nine, and in good shape because she worked out. But a five-nine girl could easily be bested by a five-six man in equally good shape. Daughters. Thank God his other two teens were boys—Rina's sons. Not that he didn't worry about them. At nearly fifteen, Sammy had height but he was still thin. Jake still had some growing to do, but he was just thirteen.

Decker's head hurt. Thinking about his kids always gave him a headache. "I need to go out there, Rina."

"I understand. I love Cindy, too. I think it's a great idea."

"Come out with me."

"It would probably be better if she had you all to herself."

"So go out and visit the relatives in Borough Park. The boys haven't seen their grandparents in over a year."

The boys' grandparents, Rina thought. Her late husband's parents. It was always a heartache to see them. But the boys meant so much to them. And then there were Peter's recently discovered half siblings. "Everyone's going to want to see you. At least to say hi."

"Scratch the thought from your mind!" Decker paced. "You'll just have to explain why I'm not there. I can't handle Cindy and your little religious crowd at the same time."

"They're your relatives."

"But they were your friends before they were my relatives. Don't push me on this, Rina. Oh, just forget the whole thing. Stay home!"

Again, he glared out the back window, hands leaning against the kitchen tile. Welcome to Decker's mud baths. He should sandbag the ground again, anything to sop up the moisture. On top of that, the sky looked threatening.

Seven years of drought followed by two years of floods. Not to mention earthquakes, fires, and riots. Decker wondered what plague was next. City was getting too damn biblical for his taste.

Rina walked up to her husband, slipped her arms around his waist, and rested her head on his back. "What do you want, Peter? Tell me."

"Make it stop raining."

"No can do. Next?"

He turned around. "What do I want?" He took his wife's hands and kissed them. "I want you to come with me. I miss you terribly when I'm away from you and long plane rides make me depressed. So come with me to New York. But once we get there, leave me alone so I can deal with my daughter and my own anxiety."

"So I'm to be your therapeutic escort."

"And a damn pretty one, at that."

Rina laughed. "I'll come with you."

Decker said, "Thank you. And . . . if I'm up to it . . . if I have the energy . . . I'll come visit the relatives."

"You look like you just sucked lemons."

"It's been a rather sour morning."

Rina stroked her husband's cheek. "I'm sorry you have to go through this, that we have to go through this. I'm very concerned, also. Kids. A life sentence in terror if you think about it. I'll be happy to help you out. And yes, it has been a while since the boys have seen their grandparents. It's very considerate of you to think of them."

"I'm just a saint."

"I believe the appropriate response to a compliment is a simple thank you."

Decker smiled. "The boys can miss school?"

"Of course. How about we leave next Wednesday? I can still get discount tickets if I buy them a week in advance."

"Fine."

"You'll call Cindy?"

"Yes."

"And phone Jan, too," Rina said. "Just to let her know you're going."

Decker looked pained. "Is that *really* necessary?"

"Peter, she's Cindy's mother. She's worried sick about her."

"I know, I know. She's very angry I haven't insisted that Cindy come home. As if she's insisted. She just

wants *me* to be the bad guy. Well, screw that! If she
wants a—"

"Peter—"

"All right, all right. I'll call Jan. I'll even be civil."

"A big stretch for you, dear?"

"A very big stretch for me, darlin'."

❧ 2

The red Trans Am was following me. I'd known something was up from the look Chris had given me in orchestra. We'd been in the same class for over a year, and today's stare had been a first. Only one reason why boys like him were interested in girls like me. Guess this one didn't want to approach me in public.

The car slowed and honked. I stopped walking. Since parked vehicles were occupying the far right lane, the Trans Am was blocking traffic. The Jeep on Chris's heel blasted its horn. He turned around, threw the impatient driver a dirty look, then sped up and pulled the car curbside a half block up. I jogged over. He rolled down the passenger window, told me to hop in.

"I'm not going straight home," I said. "I've got to pick up my little sister."

"Last I checked the car's not a two-seater." He waved me forward. "Come on."

I opened the door and got inside, dumping my backpack on the floor. "Thanks."

"You're welcome. Where are we going?"

"Just go straight." My eyes were fixed on the front windshield.

11

Cars were bumper to bumper. Since the '94 earthquake and the recent flooding by overzealous rain clouds, the West Valley had become a snarl at rush hour. Chris waited for a nonexistent opening. Headbanger music was screaming from his car stereo. It suddenly seemed to annoy him. He punched it off.

A Jetta stopped and waved Chris in.

"Thank you, sweetheart," he said to himself. To me, he said, "How far are we going?"

"'Bout two miles up."

"And you walk that every day?"

"It's good exercise."

"What do you do when it rains?"

"I take an umbrella. Sometimes, if it's convenient, my stepmom will let me have the car."

Chris paused. "You live with your dad and stepmom?"

"Yes."

"Where's your mom?"

I hesitated. The question was way too personal, but I answered anyway. "She died when I was born."

Chris waited a beat, then raised his brow. "Your dad's a good Catholic, huh?"

I looked at him, stunned. His face revealed nothing.

"The unbaptized before the baptized." He pulled a crucifix from under his T-shirt. "Takes one to know one."

I didn't answer. In this city of religious nothingness, it was rare to find an overt Catholic boy, let alone one who looked like Christ.

He said, "What about you? Are you a good Catholic girl?"

"Good enough to feel guilty about my mother's death."

"The nuns must have had a field day with you."

"Mostly my father."

"What'd he say?"

"It's what he didn't say."

He turned quiet. I stared at my lap.

"You still go to Mass?" he asked.

"Sometimes."

"I go sometimes, too. Old habits are hard to break."

I smiled and nodded. He was determined to talk. That being the case, I steered the conversation from myself. "You live by yourself, don't you?"

"Yep."

"So where are your parents?" I asked.

"They're dead."

"*Both* of them?"

"Yes, both of them."

I felt my face go hot. "That was stupid."

"No such thing as a stupid reaction." He tapped on the steering wheel. "My mom died of breast cancer when I was thirteen. My father was murdered when I was almost ten. A gangland thing. I was hiding in the closet when the hit went down, witnessed the whole thing—"

"Oh, my God!" I gasped. "That's *dreadful*!"

"Yeah, I was pretty scared."

The car went silent.

"Only the upshot of the mess was I hated the son of a bitch." He scratched his head. "So after the shock wore off, I was kind of happy. My dad was a two-fisted drunk. He'd get soused and pummel anything—or anyone—in his way. That's why I'd been hiding in the closet. Lucky for me. Otherwise, I wouldn't have made it into double digits."

I didn't answer. I couldn't think of anything to say.

"I don't know why I'm telling you this," he said. "Must be your confessional aura. How far is this school, Terry?"

"Oh, gosh, I'm sorry. We passed it." I looked over my shoulder. "Turn left at the next light."

Chris inched the Trans Am forward. "Distracted by our stimulating conversation?"

"I think the operative word is morbid."

Out of nervousness, I started to laugh. So did he. He turned on the radio, switching to a classical station. Mozart's Jupiter Symphony—good commuter music.

"So what's your middle name?" he asked. "Mary or Frances?"

"Anne."

"Ah, Teresa Anne. A respectable Catholic name."

"And you?" I asked.

"Sean. Christopher Sean Whitman. A respectable Irish Catholic name. Is that the school up ahead?"

"Yeah. You'll have to pull over. I have to fetch her."

He parked curbside and I got out. In all fairness to my stepmom, Jean treated her biological daughter with as much apathy as she displayed toward me. Poor Melissa. I worked my way through the school yard until I spotted her. Usually when I arrived, I was tired, anxious to get home. But with Chris driving, I had the luxury of observing her at play.

My sister was attacking a tetherball, dirty blond pigtails flying in the wind. She had an intense look of concentration, little fists socking the leather bag, turning her knuckles red. Her opponent was a second-grade boy and she was clearly outmatched. But she put up a valiant struggle. After her defeat, she shuffled to the back of the line. I called out her name. She looked up and came running to me.

"You're *early*!" she shrieked

"I bummed a ride home. Come on."

"Will we be in time for *Gornish and Narishkite*?"

Melissa's favorite cartoon show. It was off-limits by my stepmom and not without logic. The characters were a fat crow and an over-plumaged macaw. They had nothing better to do than peck out each other's body parts.

I checked my watch. "If we hurry."

"Yippee!" She jumped up and down. I picked up her backpack—an amber thing emblazoned with Simba from *The Lion King*—and slipped it over my shoulder.

She took my hand, half skipping as we walked, tugging on my shoulder. But I didn't mind. Her hand was soft and warm. She smelled sweaty, but it wasn't an unpleasant odor.

"I can't *believe* I get to see *Gornish and Narishkite*. You won't tell Mom?"

"I won't tell Mom."

"Who's taking us home? Heidi?"

"Someone else," I said. "This way."

I led her over to the car, opened the door, and got her settled into the backseat. "This is Chris," I said. "He was kind enough to offer us a ride home. Say thank you."

"Thank you."

"You're welcome," Chris answered.

"Is he going to pick us up tomorrow, too?"

"Don't press it, Melissa." I closed the door. "Besides, you have gym class tomorrow. Put on your seat belt."

"I can't do it. It's too hard."

I turned around, hanging over my seat as I looped the belt around Melissa's waist, securing the metal into the latch. As I straightened up, I accidentally brushed against Chris and felt him immediately stiffen. I sat back and scrunched myself in my seat.

"Excuse me," I said.

"What for?"

"I accidentally . . . never mind." I looked out the window. "You need tutoring, Chris?"

"Yeah."

"You could have just called."

"I've got a unique situation. I'll explain when we get to your house."

I was quiet and so was he. Mozart, however, was working himself up into a lather. Chris parked the car in front of my two-story claptrap. It wasn't a bad house, just in need of repair. The siding needed paint, the stucco was chipped, and the roof was old and leaky. We'd gone from two buckets last winter to five the last time it rained. The roof upgrade was supposed to be my father's weekend project. Instead, he opted for hooch and sports on TV. My father was a passive lush—the kind who'd drink himself into a coma, gradually slipping away until Jean's nagging became elevator music.

Chris helped Melissa out of her seat belt. Liberated, she sped to the front door, then raced upstairs as soon as I undid the lock.

"Uh, excuse me, young lady," I called out to her. "The dishwasher is still full."

"I'll do it later," she shouted from the top of the stairs.

"Famous last words," I muttered. I shouted back, "Never mind. I'll do it." I turned to Chris. "Have a seat at the dining-room table. Can I get you something to drink? Juice? Soda? You know, I can even make you coffee I've got so much time."

"Coffee would be great."

I marveled at my good fortune, having gained the better part of an hour. I put up coffee, then looked in the fridge. Jean had prepared a chuck roast. I took it out.

"This'll be shoe leather if I cook it now," I said to myself. "Maybe I'll turn down the heat and roast it slowly." I said it into the oven and turned the temperature to 300 degrees. Then I went into the laundry room and threw the wet clothes from the washer into the dryer. I came back into the kitchen and took out lettuce and tomatoes from the vegetable bin. I washed them under the tap, shook them dry, then started making the salad. I glanced up and saw Chris staring at me from the dining room. I was so caught up in my routine, I had forgotten about him.

I put down the lettuce and dried my hands. "Coffee's almost done."

He came into the kitchen. "Do you do this every day?"

"Do what?"

"The cooking, the laundry . . . child care?"

"They wrote a story about me. It's called 'Cinderella.'" I fetched down two coffee mugs. "Tell you one thing, though. I'm not waiting for Prince Charming. I'd rather have a maid." I turned the coffeepot off and took out some milk and sugar. "How do you like your coffee?"

"Just black."

"A *real* man."

"Very macho."

I loaded my coffee with the accoutrements, went back into the dining room, and took my datebook out of my backpack. "I've got an opening on Monday at eight. Or I can give you an hour on Thursday at eight—"

"Terry, why don't you sit down and let me tell you what's going on?" He showed me the chair. "Please."

I sat, then wondered why I was listening to him. It was my house, but he was playing host.

He took a sip of coffee and looked at me earnestly. "If all goes well, I'm slated to go to the Eastman School of Composition in New York next fall. I squeaked by my junior year. This time I don't know what's flying. I'm not a great student, but I can pass tests if I concentrate."

I nodded.

He flipped a chunk of blond hair out of blue eyes. "Also, I'm away a lot. I play gigs."

"Gigs?"

"I do fill-ins for ensembles, orchestras, small chamber groups. Once in a while, I even do solos in some of the smaller towns for special occasions. It's usually for only one or two performances. But my time away includes another day or two for practice beforehand. So I can be gone as much as a week at a time. I miss a lot of class."

He sipped more coffee.

"I talked to Bull Anderson. He says you charge fifteen an hour."

"That's right."

"Then you're going to make out like a bandit from me. 'Cause I figure I need five days a week, 'bout two hours a day. I need a teacher as well as a tutor. Are you up for it?"

He stopped talking. I stared at him. "That's one hundred fifty a week."

"You can add."

"Classical music must be a high-growth industry."

"Money's not a problem. You save your dollars, Terry, you can earn yourself a fine set of wheels by spring break. What do you say?"

I paused. "Sounds great in theory."

"The money won't be theoretical." He stood. "We can start tomorrow. I'll pick you up at ten to seven, take you to my place, and have you back here by a little after nine."

"That's a big commitment for me, Chris. I need time for my other students. Plus there's my own studying."

He sat back down. "How about this? I'll pick you and your sister up from school every day. That'll save you five hours just like that."

"I still have other students—"

"Terry, why don't you open your appointment book and we'll go through it together. Find a schedule that suits both our needs."

I was being pushed, but the money was too tempting to protest. I opened my datebook. With some rearranging and haggling, we decided on four days a week—two hours a day, with Wednesday our day off.

"Mondays and Fridays I can come to your place at seven," I said. "But Tuesdays and Thursdays it would be better if you just came here right after school. Melissa goes to gym so we'd have privacy. Sound okay?"

He took a pen and a sheet of paper from his backpack. "Tell me the schedule you want."

I dictated. He wrote. "You're left-handed," I said.

"Yeah."

"Don't you play cello right-handed?"

"Yeah."

"Isn't it hard?"

He looked up from his writing. "I don't know any differently. I play all my instruments right-handed."

"What else do you play?"

"Anything with strings."

"Violin?"

"Yep."

"Are you a prodigy on violin like you are on cello?"

"Why? You want to exchange violin for French lessons?"

"No, Chris. I think I'm hopeless."

He studied at my face. "Violin's a hard instrument."

"You're diplomatic. What else do you play?"

"Viola, bass, mandolin, guitar. I started guitar when I was about twelve. Picked it up like that." He snapped his fingers. "But then my mother died and I was taken into custody by an old-fashioned aunt. She thought electric guitar was a very rude invention. I was instructed to find a more suitable instrument. You want to do Tuesdays and Thursdays here?"

"It really would be more convenient. Are you still in contact with your aunt?"

"Nope. She died two years after my mom." He looked up. "Natural causes, Terry. She was in her sixties."

"I didn't say anything."

"You had a look on your face."

"Just because a sixty-year-old woman seems old to be your aunt."

"Yeah, she was old and old-fashioned." He flipped his hair back again. "But she wasn't without her good points. She fancied herself a real classy lady. I was a punk when I went to live with her. She reinvented my life. Sent me to private school, taught me about music and art. She even gave me *diction* lessons. I useda towk like a real Noo Yowkeh."

I smiled. "You should have given your accent to Blake Adonetti."

That got a laugh out of him. Encouragement. I was on a roll. I said, "Yeah, Blake's trying very hard to be the resident street guy. Someone should tell him that street guys don't drive Porsches, they don't have neurosurgeons for fathers, and they don't live in ten-thousand-square-foot houses. They also don't mousse their hair."

He said, "How do you know Blake?"

"I tutored him for a couple of months—chemistry. His dad harbors hope that Blake'll be a doctor."

Chris said, "You tutored him, you tutored Bull."

"Yeah, also Trish and Lisa for a while. I went through most of your group—"

"They're *not* my group."

His vehemence took me by surprise. I looked

away. "Sorry I pigeon-holed you. It's just that our class is so large, one is more or less defined by one's clique."

He said nothing.

I kept blathering on. "I mean everybody has to hang out with someone. Being a B.M.O.C. is infinitely better than being president of the nerd squad, the honored post occupied by yours truly."

He was still stone-faced. I gave up. "I'll need your backpack . . . to see what classes you're taking."

He dropped his knapsack to the floor. "Funny how we see ourselves. Guys I know don't find you nerdy. Matter of fact, they think you're very pretty. Just a little . . . frosty. But that's okay. It's good to be picky."

I felt myself go hot. He told me he'd see me tomorrow. I nodded, keeping my eyes on my shoes. I knew he'd left when I heard the screen door slap shut.

🐦 3

In school, Chris stayed with his crowd, I stayed with mine. I'd have liked to talk to him, but one never crosses party lines unless invited to do so. And Chris didn't hand me the scepter. So I looked on from afar, seeing him laugh with the beautiful people, Cheryl Diggs giving him neck rubs. A righteous-looking troop—both girls and guys being lean and lovely—typecast for a syndicated TV school serial. I guess I would have played the odd girl out. Because that was what I was.

The dismissal bell rang and he made it to my locker before I did. He waited as I rearranged my books, then carried my backpack as we walked to his car. I reminded him that we didn't have to pick up Melissa today. She went to gym with a friend whose mother drove them both. Jean did the pickup.

By six in the evening, I was expected to have finished the laundry, set the table, and prepared dinner. Afterward, Jean would load the tableware in the dishwasher. Unless, of course, she and my father had plans for that evening. Or Jean had a date at the health spa. In that case, my stepmother assigned cleanup to Melissa. Which meant she assigned it to

23

me. When Jean yelled at me, I shined her on. But I hated it when Jean yelled at Melissa.

As talkative as Chris was yesterday, he was quiet as we rode to my house. Last night, I had gone through his backpack, scanned his textbooks, and flipped through his spotty notes. He wasn't much of a student, but he was a great artist. His sketches seemed to be a cross between Matisse and Picasso. Just a few well-placed lines and there was an image. Amazing to me because I couldn't draw a straight line.

I also discovered that he smoked and believed in safe sex, judging from the loose packets of condoms. He might be a practicing Catholic, but he was practicing other things as well.

As soon as we settled in, I made coffee. Sipping Java, we went through his subjects one by one. He was way behind in his classes, and it took me some time just to find out his level. Once I did, we started with Geometry. My gift was numbers. I'd already completed advanced-placement calculus for seniors, and was doing studying on my own. His level of math was a cakewalk for me.

Chris wasn't a terrible student. His attention tended to wander, so we took frequent breaks, but at least he was *methodical*. After two hours, he thanked me, paid me, and left.

The next evening I drove to his apartment. I don't know what I expected, but I didn't expect what I saw. His unit was on the top floor of a four-story building. He had a balcony that looked out on a one-hundred-and-eighty-degree view of the Valley. It was something out of an uptown movie set.

In actual size, the place was compact. The living

area was a small open pocket separated from the kitchen by a bar-top counter. Under the counter were two high leather stools. The place had white carpeting and was furnished with a five-foot black leather sofa, a glass coffee table, and one skinny-looking modern red chair. The walls held two large, abstract canvases—one was minimalist, the other was covered in color. In another world, I might have asked about them. But I wasn't here in that capacity. I came to do a job.

As he put up coffee, he gave me spare details of his life. He had moved out to Los Angeles a year and a half ago. Initially, his guardian had helped him financially. But now his work was enough to support him. He was completely independent, having turned eighteen around six months ago.

We studied at the countertop, sitting on stools. He asked me if he could smoke while we worked. I told him yes and thanked him for his consideration. He not only smoked, he also drank. Not much, just a couple of shots of Scotch over a two-hour period, but it bothered me. I didn't like it, but it was his house. I was only hired help.

The next week went smoothly. He was always on time and always respectful. I would have liked more, but it was obvious he didn't. That might have been painful, but rejection was nothing new to me.

A couple of times, I somehow got sidetracked, found myself telling him my dreams. I wanted to be a doctor, do top-notch research. I wanted independence and respect. He was a good listener. He'd missed his calling as a shrink.

After a few weeks of tutoring, he called me, saying

he had a gig, he'd be away for a few days. When he came back, we were back to square one. Two weeks later, he was almost caught up with his classes and I was three hundred and sixty dollars richer. Five more sessions passed and my earnings topped the five-hundred-dollar mark. Chris placed three tens on my dining-room table.

I pocketed the money and thanked him. He stood and stretched. He was not only very tall, but also long-limbed. Fully extended, he could palm my eight-foot ceiling with little effort.

He said, "Tomorrow's our free day, right?"

"Right."

He gathered his backpack. "Then I'll see you on Thursday."

"Chris?"

"What?"

"I need a favor."

He looked at me. "Shoot."

"Can you keep the money you give me? Hold it for me at your place?"

He stared at me.

"I have my money hidden upstairs," I said. "I'm afraid Jean's going to find it and start asking me questions."

"She doesn't know you're tutoring me?"

"She doesn't know you're here on Tuesdays and Thursdays. On Fridays, I've been telling her that I'm out with friends. She thinks I'm tutoring you once a week. Like I do with most of my students."

"Why the subterfuge?"

I rubbed my hands together. "I'm afraid she'll hit

me up for some of the cash. You know . . . family obligation. I'm trying to save as much as I can for college."

"She'd ask you for *your* money?"

I looked at the ceiling. "My father was laid off from work a couple of years ago. He started drinking heavily—"

"This sounds familiar."

"No, no, he's getting better," I said, defending him and not knowing why. "He has a job now, but it doesn't pay much. Jean's as nervous as a cat."

"So what does that have to do with you?"

"You don't understand my stepmom. She won't *demand* it. But she'll . . . you know . . . the guilt. Look, if it's too much—"

"Why don't you just put it in the bank?"

"They'll send the statements here. If I don't get to the mail before she does, she opens my stuff."

"Jesus!"

"Look, Chris. I don't like her. But she takes care of my dad, keeps him sober enough to be respectable. So I don't want to anger her. If it's too much of a problem—"

"Give me the money. I'll keep it for you."

"Thanks." I ran upstairs, retrieved my wad, and handed it to him. I laughed nervously. "One of the reasons why I never took drugs. I knew Jean would find my stash."

He stared at me.

"I'm *kidding*!" I said. "I don't do drugs. Actually, I don't do *anything* except study. I'm a grind. It's pretty pathetic."

He kept staring at me.

"Look, just forget it." I made a grab for my money but he pulled it out of my reach, then pocketed it.

"You want to go out for a hamburger or something, Terry?"

I became aware of my heartbeat.

"Just as friends," he amended. "Nothing else."

Crushed, I averted my eyes before my blighted hope slapped him across the face. "I have to make dinner." I turned to walk away, but he held my arm.

"Believe me, Terry, it's not you. It's me. I can't. I'm engaged."

My eyes met his baby blues. "You're *what*!"

"I'm engaged to be married."

"You're eighteen years old!"

"I know that."

I couldn't find my words. Finally, I managed to ask him who the girl was.

"Someone I've known forever. She lives back east."

"And you're *serious*?"

"Am I ever *not* serious?"

This was true. Chris had a good sense of humor, but he was a grave boy. Always organized and completely controlled. Just like me. Two hyperadults— had turned out that way because our families were nests of insecurity.

I threw up my hands. "I appreciate your honesty." I bit my lip. "I guess I also admire your loyalty. That's unheard of in this day and age. You must be deeply in love."

"She's okay," he said.

"She's okay? That's *it*? She's *okay*?"

"She's okay," he repeated.

"Chris, why are you marrying a girl that's just *okay*?"

He shrugged.

Suddenly, it dawned on me.

Chris caught my look. "No, she's not pregnant." He patted his pocket. "I'll keep your bread safe. Bye."

He left before I could ask another question. And maybe that was good.

As usual, he was waiting at my locker after school. We walked to his car, neither one speaking. But he didn't drive to my house. Instead he drove to the bank. He pulled into the parking lot and shut the motor.

"I feel funny keeping your cash. What if you need it and I'm not home?"

"I told you I can't put it in the bank."

"We'll open up an account together. I'll make sure the statements come to my house."

I paused. "How cute. Like playing house."

"Terry—"

"I still don't understand why you'd marry a girl you don't love."

"I didn't say I didn't love her."

"Do you?"

"No."

I slumped in my seat. "This is none of my business, right?"

"Right." He opened the car door, but I held his arm. Instantly, he stiffened. I jerked back my hand.

"Sorry."

He closed the car door, looked at his arm, then looked at me. Without embarrassment, he said, "I have a problem with being touched."

"I've noticed."

"I'd like to go into the bank now. How about you?"

I didn't move.

He raised his eyebrows. "Would you prefer to wait out here, Terry?"

"You're very polite."

"I was trained with manners—yessir, nossir. I wasn't polite, I got the shit kicked out of me." He started the car. "Bad idea. Let's forget the whole thing."

I started to place my hand on his arm, but caught myself and pulled it back.

"Sorry. I'm a touchy person."

He killed the motor. "Terry, anyone touches me, I tense. It doesn't mean I'm mad. As a matter of fact, it doesn't mean much of anything anymore. It's just a habit. So don't worry about it, okay?"

"Doesn't it get in the way?"

"What do you mean?"

"I mean with your fiancée . . . if you don't like being touched . . ."

He stared at me. I should have cut my losses and shut up, but I didn't. "I noticed you carried . . . stuff . . . in your backpack."

"Stuff?"

I felt my face go hot. "Never mind."

"Do you mean condoms?"

If the earth had opened up, I would gladly have jumped in.

Chris said, "Are you asking if my peculiarity about being touched gets in the way of sex?"

My face was on fire.

"The answer's no."

I covered my face. "God, I am such a *jerk*!"

"You want to go into the bank now?"

I opened the car door and so did he. We sat at a desk titled NEW ACCOUNTS. The woman in charge wore a crepe wool suit of deep purple, with contrasting black velvet collar and cuffs. It was beautiful and I wondered if I could remember it well enough to copy it. I was very handy with pattern paper and a sewing machine.

She handed me an identification card. I started to fill it out. It had been at least eight years since I opened a bank account. By now, I had a driver's license number as well as a Social Security number. I felt very important.

I was racing through my personal data when my eyes suddenly blurred. Small typed letters mocking me. I blinked hard, then moved on, but with less bravado. I handed the card back to Ms. Beautiful Suit, hoping she wouldn't notice.

But she did.

"You forgot to fill out your mother's maiden name," she told me. She poised her pen, ready to catch my pitch.

I sat paralyzed.

Chris looked at me. "What's wrong, Terry?"

My eyes darted between him and her. "I . . . don't know it."

Ms. Suit stared at me.

My eyes suddenly filled with tears. "I forgot it."

"Forgot it?" Ms. Suit asked.

I felt so stupid. Chris said, "Can we phone it in?"

Ms. Suit was still staring at me. Finally she returned her eyes to Chris. "Certainly."

Chris gave her the cash. Ten minutes later, she handed him a bank book. Transaction completed. I got up slowly, feeling like a fool.

Once seated in his car, I found my voice. "Thanks."

"You're welcome." Chris waited a beat. "Maybe we should call it quits for today. You look upset."

"Her first name was Amy," I said. "And I really did know her last name."

"Terry, she died a long time ago. It's only natural—"

"No, you don't understand. I *really* knew it. I just forgot it!" I stared out the window but saw nothing. "There were grandparents. I don't know what happened to them."

"Why don't you ask your dad?"

"If I ask him anything about my mother, he gets weird. And if Jean overheard . . ."

I turned to face him.

"I was five when he met Jean. Soon after, he went through the closets and threw my mother's stuff out—pictures, clothes, mementos, anything that reminded him of her." My eyes widened. "Except . . ."

"What?" Chris asked.

I didn't answer. We rode back to my house in silence. When we got there, I leaped out of the car and dashed into my father's den. Chris found me rummaging through the drawers like a bag lady sorting through garbage.

"What are you looking for, Terry?"

I barely heard him, kept digging until I hit success. The brittle newspaper clipping had yellowed with age, but it was still legible.

"It's *Reilly*. Her name was Amy Reilly." I showed

him the obit. "It's such an easy name, I can't *believe* I forgot it."

I read aloud. ". . . survived by her husband, William McLaughlin, infant daughter, Teresa Anne, and parents, Mary and Robert Reilly of Chicago, Illinois." I stopped reading. "I wonder if they still live there."

Chris said, "Why don't you call and find out?"

"Oh, no, I couldn't do that."

"Why not?"

"I just couldn't." I searched my brain for images to match the names. None came. "They must have had their reasons for breaking off contact with me."

"I doubt that, Terry. I'm sure they'd love to hear from you."

"I'm not going to call them." My eyes settled back onto the obit. With shaking hands, I held it out to Chris. "Can you keep this for me, too?"

He took the clipping. "Are we on for tomorrow night?"

I took a deep breath, then let it out slowly. "I can work now if you want."

Chris studied my face. "All right. I'll get my books from the car."

"Chris?"

"What?"

"What's her name?"

He rolled his eyes. "You ask a lot of questions. It can get you into trouble."

I said nothing, continued to wait him out. Finally, he said, "Lorraine."

❧ 4

The next evening, as soon as I walked inside Chris's apartment, he handed me a slip of paper— the name of my grandparents with an accompanying phone number. He closed the door, beckoning me forward with a crooked finger. He pointed to the countertop.

"I found the number, but *you* make the call. There's the phone."

My eyes returned to the slip of paper. "I can't do it."

"Terry, just pick up the phone and punch in the numbers. Underground cables will do the rest."

I couldn't move.

Chris blew out air, then snatched the number from my trembling hands. "It's a good thing you're smart. Because you'd never make it on aggression."

He lifted the receiver, but I ran to the phone and depressed the hang-up button. "Please don't." My voice cracked. "It's probably too late over there anyway."

"It's nine in the evening Chicago time. I'm sure they're up."

As soon as he started pressing the numbers, I

tried to grab the phone again. But this time he held it above his head, out of my reach.

My stomach was suddenly a wave pool of acid. I could hear the phone ring, I could hear someone pick up. Chris started talking and I started dying.

"Hello, my name is Christopher Whitman, and I'm a friend of your granddaughter, Teresa McLaugh— Hello?"

"She hung up?" I whispered.

Chris waved me off. Into the phone, he said, "Yes, I'm still here . . . you can ask her yourself. She's standing right next to me. Would you like to speak with her?"

Chris held the receiver out to me.

"She'd like to speak with you."

Slowly, I took the handset. My hand was cold and clammy and I almost dropped the phone. I leaned against the counter for support and cleared my throat. "Hi."

"Teresa?"

The voice on the other end was frail and choked with emotion.

"How are you, Grandma?"

"Oh, my God!" She paused. "You sound just like . . . excuse me . . . I think I'm going to cry."

I beat her to it. Tears started streaming down my face. My past had been closed for so many years. And suddenly, without warning, the door had swung wide open. We both started talking at the same time, then we both started laughing, then crying.

I heard a beeper go off. I looked up. I hadn't realized that Chris carried a pager. He put on a leather jacket.

"I'll be back."

"What?" I suddenly started shaking uncontrollably. "Wait. Don't leave."

"Teresa, are you all right?" my grandmother asked.

I spoke into the phone. "Grandma, can you hold for a moment?" I covered the receiver and said, "Chris, don't leave me alone."

Chris walked up to me and held my face, wiped my tears with his thumbs. "I've got to go. I'll be back. Talk as long as you like. Good-bye."

He was out the door.

I put the receiver back to my ear. Actually, it was good that he did leave because the conversation became very emotional. We laughed, we cried; I asked questions and so did she. Then my grandfather got on the extension and soon we were all talking so fast, it was hard to understand anyone. But it didn't matter. Because within minutes, I was talking to family. Eleven years of emptiness vanquished in a single stroke, all because someone had cared enough to make a phone call.

I gleaned a history of what had happened to them. They had faded into the breeze at my father's request. He had felt that as long as my mother's memory was kept fresh in my mind, I would never develop a close relationship with my new stepmother, Jean. They had wanted only what was best for me, so they had pulled away. They related my history, defending my father at every twist and turn. But I could feel only anger and resentment.

Did I ever receive the Christmas cards and presents they had sent me?

I told them I hadn't.

How about the birthday cards and presents?

Not them, either.

I told them I would write. I told them I would send pictures. I told them I would call whenever I got the chance. If they wanted to send anything or write back, I told them to address the letters in care of Chris, then gave them his address. After forty-five minutes of nonstop dialogue, I finally relinquished the line to a dial tone.

I was so exhausted, I sprawled out on Chris's leather couch and closed my eyes. He came back ten minutes later. His face looked drawn, his eyes looked dead.

I stood up. "Are you okay?"

"I'm fine." He brushed hair out of his eyes. "How'd it go?"

I smiled. "Great . . . it went . . ." The tears came back. "I don't know how I'm ever going to thank you." I moved toward him, then stopped.

He laughed. "Come here."

I ran to him and hugged him tightly. It was like embracing granite. His arms wrapped around me, his fingers in my hair. He kissed my forehead. "I'm glad it went well."

I burrowed myself deeper into his chest, listening to the steady beat of his heart. After a few moments, I became aware of something hard pressing into my hipbone. I adjusted my position in his arms, then went warm with embarrassment when I realized what it was. I giggled out of nervousness.

Chris whispered, "Yes, I have an erection."

"At least I know you like me."

"I like you very much."

My eyes found his. "Then why—"

"Not now, Terry. Please." He broke away and took off his jacket. Poured himself a shot of Scotch and drank it in a single gulp. "We're going to have to forgo the lesson. I have a gig lined up. I have to pack."

His voice was calm but his posture was tense.

I clapped my hands once. "If you need help, I'm a really good packer. I do all of my stepmom's packing whenever she goes out of town."

He smiled but it lacked warmth. "I'm fine."

"Okay." I shrugged. "Thanks again. I'm going to owe you money for a very long phone conver—"

"Forget it."

"I also told them to write to me in care of you. I gave them your address. I hope that's okay—"

"It's fine, Terry."

He was very anxious for me to leave. But I couldn't get my feet to move. "When will you be back?"

"Don't know. Maybe Thursday or Friday."

"Where are you going?"

"Back east."

The room turned quiet. I said, "Are you going to be seeing your fiancée?"

Chris raised his brow. "You really like to torture yourself, don't you?"

"I feel very comfortable on a cross."

"Yes, I'll probably be seeing her."

"You'll be seeing *Lorraine*?"

"Probably. It's getting late."

Actually, it wasn't, but he wanted me out. I said, "I'll leave now. Thanks again."

"Take my books."

"Why?"

"Because I'm going to fall behind and you'll need to prepare lessons to catch me up." He reached into his pocket and pulled out three fifties. Showed them to me. "For the week I'm gone. I'll deposit them in your bank account."

"Christopher, it won't take me ten hours to prepare your lessons."

"Think of it as a retainer." He brushed my nose with the corner of the bills, then pocketed the money. "You're now in my employ."

"You say that with such glee." I laughed softly. "Must be nice to be rich."

"I wouldn't know. I work for every dime I have."

I turned hot, glanced at him, then averted my eyes. "God, that was an awful thing to say. Of course you do. I'm very sorry." I picked up the books. "Thanks for everything, Chris."

He held my arm. "Terry, look at me."

Quickly, my eyes swept over his face.

"Nuh-uh," he persisted. "*Look* at me."

I managed to meet his eyes.

Chris said, "You didn't offend me. I knew what you meant."

"You don't need to pay me—"

"Terry—"

"All I'm saying is, I'd tutor you for free." I felt my eyes get wet and looked away.

"I know you would, Terry. And that means a lot

to me. But it's not necessary." He kissed my fore-head. "Go home."

A very good idea. He'd been full of them this evening. Quietly, I shut the door behind me. I thought my grandmother had taken away all my tears. But I was wrong.

5

The trips had become so routine, he wondered why he didn't keep a prepacked valise. Same inventory every time. Two white shirts, two black shirts, two pairs of black pants, couple of ties, underwear, socks, shoes, and a suit in case he decided to see Lorraine. Her daddy liked things nice and formal. Proper. He didn't want things to get out of hand before the wedding. Not a problem for him. But daughter had undergone a severe case of hot pants over the past year.

She had detested him when they were first introduced. And she had taken every opportunity to tell him so. He was immature, ugly, stupid, unmannered (that was a lie)—and worst of worst, he was a mick. It had been an insult to her intelligence that her father had ever agreed to the arrangement. She'd go through with it because she knew she had to. But he shouldn't ever, *ever,* expect *anything*!

Her words had stung his cheeks like a blustery day. But eventually he had learned to tune them out, just like everything else. His apathy to her had been so complete, it took him months before he realized *her* change of attitude.

At first, he had wondered why. *He* hadn't changed. *He* was the same person. Until he looked in the mirror one day for a self-portrait. His cheeks had been thick with grizzle, toughening the flawless skin that had once been speckled with teenage blemishes. His eyes had deepened in color and in intensity; his mouth had turned sensual and hungry. His body had hardened from pumping iron. His forearms were developed from hours of cello playing. Suddenly he realized what had happened. Hormones and genetics had finally worked in his *favor*. They had turned him into a man.

A vengeful person might have reacted with hostility. But since emotions weren't part of his equation, he reacted as he always did. With control and calculation.

He regarded himself through her eyes. It must have been hard for a rich, spoiled Italian princess to accept a gawky fourteen-year-old mongrel three years her junior. Her former boyfriends had been older than she—nineteen or even in their early twenties, with deep voices and developed muscles. He must have looked like a worm in comparison.

So he decided to be gracious with her. Kind but never attentive, closed but not cold. Physical affection, of course, but only the obligatory kind if you please—a peck on the cheek, his hand on her arm as they strolled through the family's vast country acreage.

She knew something was off, but she couldn't call him on it. Because he behaved like the perfect gentleman that Daddy had ordered. They played tennis together. He always won, but not by too many points.

They went to the symphony together. He knew the pieces by heart, could have conducted them if push came to shove. She had a hard time staying awake. He teased her about her strong New York accent, but it was always in good humor. They went to Mass together. He prayed fervently as she sneaked him sidelong glances, her leg rubbing against his thigh.

He jerked her around like a rag doll, kept her off balance. After the official engagement had been announced, she waited . . . and waited and waited. Finally, she came to him. To his amazement, she was still a virgin. So he'd been gentle with her. Gentle but dispassionate. Their first nighttime tryst, which she had arranged to cement their relationship, had only served to increase her anxiety.

What was wrong?

Nothing, it was fine.

What could she do to please him more?

Nothing, he was fine.

What could she do to make herself better?

Nothing, she *was fine.*

He had finally gained the upper hand.

He pulled a suitcase down from his bedroom closet. He didn't feel like packing, so instead he lit a cigarette.

What he really wanted was another *drink*.

But that was the *wrong* thing to do.

It was time to use logic, analyze why he wanted the drink so bad.

Was it the gigs? After all these years was he finally getting performance anxiety?

No, he never was anxious about anything.

Was he worried about failure?

No, he was a pro.

Was the thrill gone?

He sucked on his smoke.

That was part of it. Just wasn't as thrilling as it used to be. Truth be told, he was just going through the motions. So what? That was life, buddy. Everybody had to earn their keep. Besides, he needed the bread now more than ever because he was doling out so much of it to her.

Her.

Still the same thrill every time he thought about her. At least that much hadn't changed. How she'd slipped by him in orchestra was still beyond his comprehension. He chalked it up to the way he was. He never went after girls. They had always come to him.

Just like Cheryl.

Not that he hadn't noticed Cheryl. How could he not have noticed Cheryl? And yeah, he had wanted her. But Cheryl had been business as usual. He'd sent her "the vibes" and she had responded quickly ... satisfyingly. . . .

Terry had been different. He hadn't noticed her because she'd been buried in the back of the second violin section. They'd been playing Rossini's *William Tell* Overture. The beginning of the piece, Hedding purposely dragging the tempo, milking the cello solo—his solo, of course. Then Hedding had stopped the orchestra. Apparently, someone had been making loud snoring noises in the background.

Lack of sleep, Miss McLaughlin, or do you have a problem with the tempo?

Lots of giggling now ... at least, two or three girls.

No, sir. Sorry, sir.

The voice had been sultry. He had craned his neck, but hadn't been able to make out the person.

Perhaps you'd like to come up and conduct the piece at a tempo more to your liking.

By then the entire orchestra had gotten into the act. Egging her on. Red-faced, she stood up. But she did it. Conducted the entire piece. Did a pretty good job of it, too.

All he had remembered was his heart pounding out of his chest. Good thing he was such a natural, because he hadn't known what he'd been playing. His mind racing, his thoughts a jumbled mess.

Where the fuck had she *been hiding?*

So mind-boggling gorgeous, and best of all, she didn't even know it.

Immediately, he started sending her "the vibes." But they hadn't worked and he figured out why. She was a good girl. Well, that wasn't so bad. Because he knew all about good girls. They weren't hard to catch, but you had to do it indirectly. Then she walked by one day, and Bull made some lech comment. They had all laughed about it. Bull also mentioned that she'd been his tutor.

The opening he'd been waiting for.

But it wasn't working out as planned. She was supposed to be a blow and go. Instead, something got messed up in his head.

He closed his eyes, allowing his brain to flash up her image. He studied the purity of her oval face, the arch of her cheekbones, the liquid in her exotic, amber eyes, the sweep of her long, auburn hair.

Though he tried to fight it, he knew he was going under.

He was falling in love.

His groin ached. He realized he was rock hard.

So that's why he had wanted to drink. He had wanted to suppress his arousal. God, he wanted her.

But that was out of the question.

He grabbed his rubbers, a handful of old neckties, and headed for the streets.

🌿6

Rina realized the bed was empty. Not an infrequent occurrence of late. Ever since Peter had returned home from New York, he'd been hit with bouts of insomnia. The nightstand clock read two A.M. Stomach still awash in sleep-laden nausea, Rina rose slowly from the bed, donned her robe, and slipped her feet into mules. Moving slowly through the darkened house, she found Peter seated at the kitchen table, fingers running through his mop of red hair, his shoulders hunched over the Formica top.

"What are you doing?"

Startled, Decker pivoted around to face her. "I didn't hear you get up."

She sat next to him. Immediately, Decker began stacking papers in front of him. Once they were piled up, he covered them with his elbows, hiding them from Rina's eyes as if she were trying to cheat off him.

"Peter, what are you *doing*?"

"Just going over loose ends."

"What loose ends?"

"Just business stuff. Not important." He scooped up the papers and stood. "Come on. We'll both go back to bed."

Rina pointed to his chair. Decker sat back down. "Tell me the truth. Are you working on the shopping-bag rapist?"

Decker didn't answer.

"Peter, just what do you hope to accomplish from three thousand miles away?"

"So what *should* I do? Sit by while this asshole picks off women? He got another one—"

"I'm aware of that—"

"Rina, I sat with my daughter and her friends for two friggin days. Hearing them cry . . . they may be women on the outside but inside they're frightened little *children*. I spoke to Cindy this afternoon. This time, *she* wants to come home."

"So she's coming home?"

"I told her no." Decker began to pace. "I told her, give it a little more time. Because if she comes home, the bastard wins. And what will that do to her psyche? Chased away by a phantom. Know what, Rina? He *is* winning!"

"It's wretched, but—"

Decker blurted out, "You ask me what I can do three thousand miles away? The sad truth is nothing. But if it makes me feel better reading some detective's case notes, then *indulge* me!"

Abruptly, he threw the papers across the room and looked at Rina.

"Do you think I did wrong by telling her to stay?" Decker began to pace again. "As her father, I really want her home. But I don't want her to leave because someone is chasing her away. I raised her to feel she was strong enough to conquer the world.

Now this SOB . . ." He sank back in his chair and rubbed his face. "I think I'm going *nuts*!"

Slowly Rina got up and began assembling the papers. She set them in front of her husband, then placed a kettle of water on the stove. "Do the police have *any* ideas?"

"They think it's someone on the inside because he knows the secluded areas of the campus. *College!* Perfect breeding grounds for weirdos and perverts. You've got hyper-hormoned kids with poor judgment thrown together unsupervised. Bastard rapist. He knows they're easy fodder."

"Cindy's twenty-one."

"When she cries in my arms, she's a kid. I can't stand this. Screw it! I'm sending her a plane ticket tomorrow—"

"Peter, you did the right thing by telling her to stay. You can't protect her forever."

"So I'll protect her as long as I can."

"If the monster strikes again, then you and she can reevaluate. In the meantime, if she can stick it out until he's caught . . . handling this situation will give her a sense of mastery. That this maniac *didn't* scare her away. Believe me, I know what it's like to live in fear."

The kettle began to boil. Rina brought out two mugs and made tea. Decker was quiet, remembering how they'd met. Rina had been a witness to a rape, Decker had been the cop assigned to the crime. During the course of the investigation, they had found out that Rina had been the intended victim. Even with that knowledge, Rina had held firm, refused to be scared away by a madman's perversions. In the end, she had come away the better for it.

But this was his *daughter*.

"So you think I did the right thing?" Decker asked.

Rina placed a cup of ginger tea in front of her husband. "I think so, yes. Drink."

"Okay, you're a smart person." Decker sipped boiling tea. "I'll trust you."

"Thank you."

"I trust you, you trust me. Isn't that what this whole thing's about?"

"You mean love?"

"Yeah, love and the whole nine yards."

"The whole nine yards?"

"You know what I mean. Love, marriage, kids, dogs, mortgages, responsibility, life—"

"Poor Peter. You're feeling so burdened."

"I'm not *feeling* burdened, I *am* burdened."

Rina took his hand. "You want to go out to New York again?"

Decker shook his head no. "What does that say to Cindy? That every time there's a crisis, Daddy'll come to rescue her? No, I've got to let her deal with it and just pray for the best." He looked at the kitchen clock. "Is it too early to say *Shacharit*?"

Rina thought a moment. There were entire sections of Talmud written about the permissible times to say the morning prayers. Rina looked at the kitchen clock. A little before three A.M.

"It's never too early or too late to pray. And Peter, add your own private wishes at the beginning of *Shemonah Esreh*. Ask Hashem specifically to look

after Cindy, to watch over her and keep her safe.
Make your requests as detailed as you want."

Decker smiled. "I can do that?"

Rina smiled back. "You can do that."

❧ 7

In the dead of night, I wrote letters to my grand-parents, all the while growing even more aloof from my father and stepmother. Jean tried to cut through my secrecy with insipid stabs into my personal life. It became clear that she thought I was sequestering a boyfriend. I answered her politely, but revealed nothing. My father never even picked up on my change of attitude. To him, I was a house pet. As long as I was healthy and didn't pee on the carpet, I was left to benign neglect.

The school week rocketed by. With Chris gone, I was back to walking home. On Tuesday, Bull—né Steve—Anderson met me at my locker after school and offered me a ride. The school's star halfback, as did Chris, ran in the fast lane of booze, drugs, and sex. Steve was handsome and buffed with a con-man smile. He'd been cordial to me the year I'd tutored him. But beyond that, he had never given me a second glance.

On the lift home, I sensed a change—the wolfish way he looked at me. I sat rigidly in the passenger seat of his Camaro, showing scant interest in his conversation. When he parked in front of my house, he told me I needed to loosen up and have some fun. He invited me to a party that night. I declined, citing schoolwork. When I closed the door to my house, I turned the deadbolt.

The next day, when Steve saw me in the halls, he acknowledged me with the barest of courtesy. I was relieved.

Chris called me up the following Friday morning. Hearing his voice sent ripples of pleasure down my spine. He wasn't coming to school but he told me to come to his place tonight at the usual time.

I was weak-kneed when he answered the door that evening. He wore a black silk jacket over a black tee and faded jeans. His hair had been stepped in back, but it was long and loose in front. A gold crucifix hung from his neck. He took the lead-filled backpacks I was carrying.

"Welcome back," I said.

"Thank you." He hefted the book bags onto his kitchen counter. "These are heavy. Next time, just leave them in the car and I'll get them for you."

He poured me a cup of coffee and told me to take a seat. I pulled up a stool. "How'd your gig go?"

"Without a hitch," he said. "I never have any problem with work. How've you been?"

"Fine. A little nervous actually."

"Why's that?"

"Mr. Hedding announced an orchestra test this Monday."

"Which piece?"

"Brandenburg Number Two. I'm embarrassed to play in front of you."

"Why?" He poured himself a shot of Scotch. "I've heard you play before."

"Yeah, but now it's different. I know you."

"You see me struggling in my studies all the time. I'm not embarrassed. You shouldn't be either."

"But this is different."

"Why?"

I leaned on my elbows. "Because my bad playing is so . . . visceral. It's so . . . out there . . . public."

"You never cared before."

"Because I never had to look you in the eye afterward."

Chris held a finger in the air, disappeared, then came back a moment later with a violin case. He took out the instrument, tuned it, then motioned me up from the stool. "Play for me."

He offered me the fiddle. I regarded it as if it were an evil talisman. "I don't have the sheet music."

He sat on his leather couch and sipped his drink. "Play what you know by heart."

"I don't know anything by heart."

"So just draw the bow across the strings. Get a sound from it, all right?"

I sighed. I got As in orchestra only because I showed up on time and took all the tests. It was no reflection of my skill as a musician. Red-faced, I started bowing open strings. My hands were shaking. I made sounds akin to a strangling cat's. I stopped and giggled, but Chris kept his expression flat.

"Keep going."

"I know how sensitive your ear is. How can you stand it?"

"Keep going."

I played the test piece as best I could by heart. I made mistakes. I sounded terrible. I was almost in tears. I kept waiting for him to grimace, but he sat stoically.

"Play it again."

"Chris—"

"Play it again."

"This is torture—"

"Play it again."

I did. I sounded a bit better and Chris gave me a compliment to that effect. "Can I please stop now?" I asked.

Chris got up from the couch, took the violin.

"It's a beautiful-sounding instrument," I said. "I wish I could do it more justice. Why don't *you* play the piece?"

He shrugged, tucked the violin under his chin, and came up with a concerto that was note-perfect as well as sound-perfect. I told him I hated him.

He smiled, put the violin away, then patted his jacket pockets. "Where'd I put . . . ah, here we go." He pulled out a small wrapped package. "Maybe this'll make you hate me less." He handed it to me.

I looked at it, then at him.

"For *me*?"

"Yes, for you. Open it."

I ripped open the paper. The box held a set of pearl studs for pierced ears. My eyes went from him, to the earrings, then back to him. "I don't know what to say."

"Thank you is fine. Try them on."

I replaced my gold hoops with milk-white orbs. "How do they look?"

"They look beautiful. Rather, you look beautiful in them."

"I don't understand . . ." I lowered my eyes, then raised them to his face.

"What can I say, Terry?" Chris spoke softly. "You know I'm engaged to someone else. But the heart has a mind of its own." He walked over to me and slipped his arms around my waist. "Do you love me, Terry?"

Without hesitation, I told him I did.

"I love you, too. So now what do we do?"

I leaned against his breast, soothed by his heartbeat. "I don't know."

He said, "Usually, when two people love each other, they express their love in intimate ways. But I can't ask you to sleep with me. Because I'm going to marry someone else."

"Do you want me to tell you that it's okay?"

He held me tightly. "Is it okay?"

I didn't answer him. He said, "Since we last saw each other, I haven't been able to get you off my mind. And that's saying a lot. Because I'm usually very good at compartmentalizing. I don't want to sleep with you because it will hurt you in the end. But there are other ways we can be intimate with each other."

I lifted my head and met his eyes. He read my confusion.

"Let me draw you," he said. "Completely."

Completely. As in the nude. My heart started racing. I closed my eyes and buried myself in his embrace.

"Look at me, Terry," he said. "Do you trust me?"

I opened my eyes but said nothing.

"Do you?" he repeated.

I smiled weakly. He picked up my hands and kissed my fingers. "Terry, I know what they've taught you, so I know what you're feeling." He placed my hand on his cheek. "Embarrassment, shame—"

"I'm not that pious anymore, Chris." I pulled my hand away. "I haven't been to confession in over six months."

"But the crap's still there, right?"

"It's not crap."

He waited. When I remained silent, he drew me close and said, "You know the Italians have it over the Irish in their Catholicism. I mean the guilt's still there in the Italians, but they're more . . . flexible. God, even my aunt Donna, who was an old, old-fashioned Catholic woman, could look the other way. She once caught me drawing these pictures."

He smiled at the memory.

"Real explicit pictures . . . of guys and girls. . . . Anyway, I was thirteen and suicidal over my mother's death. What else was I supposed to do?"

I hugged him hard.

Chris said, "The lady was smart. Know what she did?"

"What?"

"She took me to the Met. The art museum, not the opera house. We covered the place from top to bottom in a week. Mostly we concentrated on the religious art . . . lots of nudes in religious art, believe it or not."

I nodded.

Chris whispered, "Terry, it changed my whole . . .
image of what a human body was. From something
hidden and shameful to something incredibly beautiful. My body is beautiful. Your body is beautiful.
And I *want* it."

I didn't respond.

"Look, I'll take you through it step by step. Anytime you want to stop, just cut the phone wires. I
swear I'll stop. Please do it for me."

I bit my lip. "I'd do anything for you."

Chris traced my profile with his left index finger—
a preamble to his sketching. "I know what you're
giving me. Thank you for trusting me. I promise I
won't let you down." He broke away and looked
around the room. He rubbed the back of his neck.
"Light's probably better in here with the spots and
all." He faced me. "But I'd rather draw you in the
bedroom. More personal that way."

He took my hand and led me into his sleeping
quarters. It also had a city-lights view and lots of
built-in cabinets. Not a thing or an item appeared
out of place. Not surprising. Because Chris was
compulsive.

He hung up his jacket in his closet and pointed to
his king-sized bed covered with a black quilt. "Just
sit there for a moment. The cover will make a perfect
backdrop. I want to get some auxiliary light."

"Are you going to take photographs?" I asked.

"Nope. Just me and my charcoals."

"What are you going to do with them?"

"The sketches?" Chris broke a smile. "Ah, little
girl, what you don't know. I'm going to *look* at them

whenever I'm alone and lonely . . . which is often. Rest of the time they'll be locked up and stowed away. I swear they're for my eyes only. I'll be back."

He came back a minute later toting lamps, an easel filled with paper, art supplies, and a bottle of Chivas. He set his equipment down on the floor and poured himself another drink. "Will Jean have a fit if you're not home by a certain hour?"

"No," I said. "My parents are out for the evening. Melissa's sleeping over at a friend's house. You can take your time."

"Good." He took about a half hour to set up. "Would you like some music before we start?"

"That'd be nice."

Chris opened a drawer and pulled out a CD cartridge. "Let's see what I've got loaded—Pearl Jam, Spin Doctors, Metallica, Crash Test Dummies, Greenday, Eric Johnson, Joe Satriani, Nicholas Gage, Yo Yo Ma, Jacqueline DuPres, Vivaldi's *Four Seasons* . . ." He looked up. "That's nice and light. How about that?"

I nodded. He put on the music and told me to move to the middle of the bed.

"Keep your clothes on for now. Just sit there like you're doing, Terry. With your knees pressed to your chest and your shoulders hunched over like that. But keep your head up and look at me . . . to the left . . . perfect. Hold that position, all right?"

This was easy enough. He studied me, then started making swipes at his easel.

"Can I talk while you draw me?" I asked.

"Absolutely." He looked at me, then back at his paper. "Say whatever's on your mind."

"Did you see Lorraine while you were back east?"

Preoccupied, he didn't answer. He flipped over his preliminary sketch and started anew. "Yes, I saw Lorraine."

"Were you on good terms with her?" I asked.

"Good terms?" He squinted at the paper. "Are you asking if I slept with her? Yes, I slept with her."

I didn't say anything.

"Look at me, Terry."

I did.

"Ah, such anguish in those beautiful eyes." Chris started on a fresh piece of paper. "I did it because it was expected. Closed my eyes and imagined you. She means *nothing* to me. I'm not marrying Lorraine, I'm marrying her family. My uncle arranged the whole thing when I was fourteen." His eyes went from me to his drawing. "Believe me, I'd get out of it if I could. But you don't mess with my uncle without good reason."

"But you don't love her."

"That's not a good reason." He stood back and studied his work. "It's chilly in here. I'm going to turn up the heat. Give you a chance to strip down to your bra and panties without me staring at you. And sit in the same position. If your feet are cold, leave your socks on."

He disappeared. Slowly I took off my sweater, jeans, and shoes. Barely clad, I rubbed my arms and shivered. When he came back in, he glanced at me, saw me shaking. Keeping his eyes averted, he draped a comforter over my shoulders.

I know what they've taught you so I know what you're feeling.

He knew *exactly* what I was feeling. Doing everything he could to make it easy on me, to make me feel beautiful. All the guilt, the shame . . . he was right. It was crap. I had to get past it. I couldn't live with myself if I let him down.

"You can take the cover off whenever you want to." Chris rubbed his hands and reviewed his pictures.

"Can I see?"

"When we're done."

I slowly let the comforter drop from my torso until it rested over my legs.

Chris took in my bare shoulders with his eyes. "Nice." He began a new sketch. "That's real nice. Look up, Ter."

I raised my head. There was nothing lecherous in his eyes and that made me feel good. I said, "Why isn't 'you don't love her' a good reason?"

He started shading with his thumb. "You ever hear of Joseph Donatti?"

I scrunched up my forehead trying to attach the familiar name with an event.

"His murder trial made the national papers about four years back." Chris's fingers were black. "Before that, he'd been arrested for racketeering, extortion, bribery . . . uh, pandering and pushing . . . money laundering. Nothing ever stuck. Evidence got lost."

I stared at him, openmouthed.

"He was acquitted in his murder trial, by the way. Witnesses either changed their stories or mysteriously disappeared."

I remained silent, wondering if he was putting me on.

Chris spit into his hand, rubbed his palms together, and began working the moisture into the
paper. "My uncle's mob, Terry. And I don't mean
small-time hoods who're cute movie characters.
I mean *real* mob. Lorraine is a daughter of the mob.
She's from a rival family. Our engagement has
bought both families a truce and lots of money. If
you're warm enough now, toss the comforter on the
floor."

Mechanically, I did what he asked. I was still dumb-
founded by his recitation. It was his demeanor—as
casual as an afternoon sail.

Flipping over his sketch, Chris attacked the clean
paper with renewed vigor. "I want you to know that
I have *nothing* to do with my uncle's activities. All *I*
want is a nice, quiet life as a classical cellist. Unfortunately, what I am is a pawn in a wargame played
by two dangerous men. I screw with this engagement, heads'll roll. Namely my own."

I stammered out, "Your uncle would . . . *kill* you?"

Chris continued drawing. "Nah, you're right. He
wouldn't kill *me*." His eyes bored into mine. "*I*
wouldn't be the problem."

Slowly, my brain absorbed his words. I felt myself
go light-headed. Chris stopped drawing, placed the
comforter over my shaking body, and stuck Scotch
in my face. "Drink."

"I don't want—"

"*Drink!*"

I took a sip and immediately started coughing.
He patted my back. "Take another sip."

"It makes me sick—"

"Drink it, Terry."

I sucked the smoky liquid into my mouth. I could never figure out why people drank to clear their heads. Alcohol only made me queasy. I wrapped myself in the comforter, resting my pounding head in my hands.

"Are you all right? You're white."

I whispered that I was all right.

He let out a small laugh. "Guess honesty isn't always the best policy. Terry, *nothing's* going to happen to you. My uncle doesn't care what I do just as long as I show up at the altar. You know, I could tell my uncle about you, right now, at this *moment*—"

"*Please* don't do that."

"I won't, but I could." He put his arm around me. "He'd probably feel sorry for me. Loving one girl and marrying another. He'd know how much it hurts. Because he loved his mistress very much." He removed the comforter from my shoulders. "You want another sip of Scotch?"

"No."

"Can you take your bra off for me?"

I closed me eyes. "Chris, I don't feel very well."

"You want to stop?"

I opened my eyes and peered into his—unreadable. "No." My voice was shaky. "No, it's okay."

"Are you sure?"

I answered him by slipping off my bra. He stared at my chest for a long time before going back to his easel. "Hunch over like you were doing before."

Gladly, I did as I was told, my knees hiding most of my nakedness.

He began a new drawing. "You're very, very beautiful."

"Thank you."

"Don't ever be ashamed of what God gave you, you hear me?"

I nodded.

He drew one sketch, then another, then another. We didn't talk as he worked his way through one pad, quickly replacing it with a new one. He wiped sweat from his brow.

"I'm hot," he said. "I'm going to take off my shirt."

I shrugged. He worked bare-chested. His body was hard and developed, but not overdone. Not an anabolics user. Too much chest hair, and he was more sinewy than inflated. I remembered Bull Anderson parading around the halls in his swimming trunks one day after school, his oiled, hairless barrel chest reddened by patches of acne.

Chris stood back and fingered his crucifix, his eyes on my face. "Your color's back. You must be feeling better."

I nodded.

"Good."

I said, "You used the past tense when you spoke about your uncle's mistress. What happened to her?"

"She died."

"Did he kill her?"

Chris jerked his head up. "In a sense, I guess he did."

I waited for more, but he didn't explain. He sketched furiously. "You can take your panties off now."

I froze.

Chris said, "If it's too hard for you, Teresa, we'll forget the whole thing. The purpose of this is to make us closer, not to put up walls."

He spoke smoothly and soothingly, as if my feelings were his only concern. At that moment, I would probably have drunk poison for him. Instead, I slipped off my panties, keeping my knees up, legs soldered together.

Chris walked over to me. Looming over my smallness, he must have sensed how insignificant I felt. He knelt down and spoke very softly. "Give me privilege, angel. I swear I won't ever let you down."

I still couldn't move.

"Let me help you."

He put his hands on my knees and opened my legs, positioning them about two feet apart. His face was so close I could feel warmed air on my inner thighs. His skin was flushed, his eyes had dilated, and his breathing had become audible. He remained in the same position for what seemed like an interminable period.

Finally, he let out a breathless laugh. "I swear to Jesus, I can't get up. I can't *move*. I'm . . . too weak."

I smiled.

He closed his eyes, crossed himself, and finally stood up. He threw back his head and burst into unrestrained laughter. "Well, that was a first." Slowly, he made his way back to his sketch pad. "Just keep that position."

He laughed again. It was infectious and I started to relax. After a while, my eyes traveled down his body, landing on the noticeable bulge in his crotch.

I felt tingling below, wondered if he noticed. A moment later, he gave me a knowing smile.

"You dirty girl, keep your eyes up and off my groin."

"You can look, why can't I?"

"I don't mind you looking," he clarified. "But I need to see your beautiful eyes."

"You're not looking at my eyes, Christopher."

Again Chris smiled. "You're *nasty*, Teresa. Of course I'm looking at your eyes." He flipped to a new piece of paper. "If you're that curious, I can take my pants off."

"I'll pass. My heart's only good for a shock a day and I'm still dealing with your uncle's death threats."

"Terry, *nothing's* going to happen to you." He studied me, then his drawing. "I'd . . . *kill* myself before I'd let anything ever happen to you. You may be little in size, but you've got a six-four, one-hundred-eighty-pound killing machine at your service. More reliable than a pit bull and I don't have bad breath. Hold still."

"Chris?"

"What?"

"How did your uncle's mistress die?"

He didn't answer me. I didn't press it. He sketched in silence for half an hour. Finally, he set down his charcoal, put on his shirt, then picked up the comforter from the floor. He draped it across my shoulders.

"She died of breast cancer. She had it for a long time, but was afraid to go to the doctors. She was afraid of losing her breast, disfiguring the body he loved so much. She just let it go until it was way too late. Stupid. He later told me the sexiest thing about her chest wasn't her breasts but her heartbeat."

He traced my jawline with his finger.

"You would have liked my mom. She was beautiful, but real down to earth. Just like you."

"Your *mom*?" I looked at him, wide-eyed. "So your uncle Joey isn't really—"

"No. After my dad was murdered, my mom took a job at Joey's place as a housekeeper. He took an instant liking to her; they became lovers. Joey's wife—the woman I call my aunt—was always the refined lady. She just . . . looked the other way. After my mom died, she and my uncle adopted me. They never could have their own kids, so this seemed like a good solution."

He stopped talking, his eyes far away.

"My aunt got her revenge on my mother. She co-opted me. I never talked about my mom after she died. My aunt wouldn't have allowed it. I was no longer my mom's kid. I was my aunt's child. Only remnants of my former life are some scars and my name."

"It must have made you angry."

"More sad than anything. I knew what she was doing but was still grateful to her. Both she and my uncle could have sent me packing. Which would have meant five years in foster homes. After my mom died, I had nowhere to go."

I said, "Now I understand why you agreed to marry Lorraine."

His laugh was bitter. "I didn't *agree* to anything, Terry. I *obeyed* an order."

The room fell quiet.

"Only thing I ever bucked Joey on was school," Chris continued. "He wanted me to marry Lorenza as soon—"

"Lorenza?"

"Lorenza's her given name. He wanted me to marry her as soon as I turned eighteen. I told him it made more sense for me to finish up my schooling out here, then go back east and get married. He finally gave in, but he wasn't happy about it. He won't be happy until I'm tied for life with a couple of sons under my belt . . . common grandchildren."

He kissed my hand and brought it to his cheek.

"Can we do this again next Friday night? Make it our special evening?"

I told him yes.

"Thank you." He kissed my hand again, then let it go. "Terry, listen to me. Everything we've said is very private. We go back to school on Monday, it's like before. You stay with your friends, I stay with mine. You understand why?"

"You don't want your uncle to find out about me."

"Yes. Also I've done stuff in the past—a couple of drug convictions and some B and Es. Stuff I did to prove myself to my uncle. All I got for my efforts was beatings. But I didn't care. I wanted my uncle to see me as tough."

"I understand."

"Joey spent lots of money on me, Terry. He bribed the right people. Now I've got a clean record. Matter of fact, that's why he sent me out here in the first place. A fresh start. But I'm still known as Joey Donatti's kid. If my uncle ever goes down, I drown with him. It's better if people think you're only my tutor. It's late. Get dressed and I'll follow you home. Make sure you get in all right."

"You don't have to do that."

"Yes, I do," Chris whispered. "You have a treasure, you guard it with your life."

❧ 8

And it was exactly like before. Chris stayed in his group, Cheryl Diggs giving him neck rubs, outwardly oblivious to my distant longing stares. Nothing passed between us, even when we were alone. I simply tutored him. As if he had locked up his feelings for me and put them in cold storage.

His apathy confused me, then angered me. In the end, he had cut me to the quick. I felt embarrassed and ashamed by what I had done for him, for falling for his glib talk and sweet words. By Friday, I decided that I didn't want to see him anymore. When I came to his place that evening, he threw open the door, pulled me inside, then shut it with a slam.

He was short of breath and paced his living room. "I'm running a little late. My uncle. Effing pain in the ass, excuse my language. Gotta put everything on hold whenever Joey calls. Jerk was in a panic. He's always in a panic. And me, his effing errand boy. God, I hate that man."

He suddenly stopped moving and faced me. "I'm almost done setting up. I made coffee. Have a cup while I finish up."

I stared at him. "Setting up what?"

His eyes went wide, then he smiled. "You're putting me on, right?"

I shook my head no.

"Terry, c'mon." His smile lost some wattage. "This is our night, remember?"

"Ah," I said. "I see. I get Friday while Cheryl Diggs gets Saturday through Thursday. Thank you, but I'll pass."

His face fell. "What are you *talking* about?"

The best defense was an offense. I wasn't about to be taken in. "Chris, I don't feel well. I'll see you Monday. Oh, good going on your math test. Farrell told me you did well."

I turned to leave, but he came over and gripped my arm. I averted my eyes but didn't resist his hold.

"Terry," Chris whispered. "Cheryl means nothing—"

"Oh, please!" I interrupted. "Cheryl means nothing, Lorraine means nothing. What do you do? Surround yourself with girls who mean nothing to you? So what does that say about me, Chris? And let go of my arm."

Slowly, he dropped his hold on me. Without looking at him, I told him I'd see him later.

"I wrote a composition for you," he blurted out.

How convenient. I turned around and looked at him as best I could. Because my eyes were in the back of my head from rolling them.

"No, really. I'm not lying." He held up a finger, indicating that I should wait. Then he went inside his hall closet and returned holding a sheaf of paper. He handed it to me.

My eyes slipped down to the title page.

A poem for Teresa

With special gratitude to Our Lord Jesus Christ, thanking Him for giving me a true spiritual love. May God forever protect her and keep her from harm's way.

In the left-hand corner was a small drawing that could have been lifted from a fourteenth-century wood-panel painting. A young girl in a red dress, the crown of her head illuminated in gold pen by the spirit of God. Long chestnut hair, eyes closed, her hands folded in prayer, head bent modestly toward her breast.

The face was mine.

My eyes went moist as I scanned the pages. Six sheets of musical notation with lots of cross-outs. Chris took the music from me. "It's done but it isn't refined yet. But with the mood you're in . . . I figured I'd better bring out the heavy artillery."

I laughed through my tears. He lifted my chin until my eyes met his. "Let me play what I have so far, okay?"

I nodded. His smile was brilliant. "Okay, sit down." He led me to his couch. "Okay. Sit. Wait."

He went to his bedroom and came out carting his cello and stool. "Okay." He sat down directly across from me and placed the instrument between his knees, burying the spike in his white carpet. "You never heard my Rowland Ross. It is one bitchen instrument. Okay. Okay. Now you gotta remember that it isn't polished yet, all right?"

I smiled. "All right?"

"And I may make a few mistakes. I don't have it all down yet. So cut me slack, all right."

"No, I'm going to critique you," I said, wiping my tears.

"So you're happy now?"

"Yes. I'm happy now."

"Good. 'Cause I'll do better if you're happy."

"I'm delirious with joy. Play it already."

His smile was edible. Then he closed his eyes a moment, started to breathe slowly. When his bow made contact with the strings, I closed my eyes.

The room filled with a sound so pure and sacred, it brought an ache to my heart, chills. Because he wasn't playing music. He was praying. Soft, plaintive pleas of repentance answered by the all-encompassing embrace of God's mercy. When he had finished, I couldn't see, I couldn't talk, I couldn't move. Emotion had paralyzed me.

"Do you like it?" he asked me.

I opened my eyes and swallowed dryly. "It's . . ." Tears had been running down my cheeks. "It's positively . . . sublime."

"Like you."

"Hardly."

"Look at me, Terry."

I did.

He said, "What Beethoven did for Elise, that's what I want to do for you. I want to *immortalize* you."

My heart stood still. I couldn't answer him.

"That's why I wrote this for you; that's why I draw you." He placed his cello on its side rib and came over to me. His lips brushed my forehead, his touch as gentle and spiritual as baptismal waters. "You are holy to me. Our relationship is holy to me. Do you understand?"

I nodded.

He handed me the title page. "Keep it. And whenever you doubt me, look at this. Because it's the way I really feel. I love you, Teresa. More than you ever could know." He paused. "Will you let me draw you tonight? Completely?"

I dried my eyes and nodded yes.

He whispered, "Go into my bedroom, take off your clothes, and put on one of my robes. I'll be there in a minute, all right?"

I got up and did what he asked of me. He came back in, set up for around five minutes, then turned to look at me. I regarded his eyes. I was looking for a window to his soul. All I got was leaded glass. I cleared my throat. "You want me to take the robe off now?"

He nodded yes.

Slowly I untied the belt and let the garment fall from my shoulders. "Should I sit the same as last time?"

He shook his head no. "I want something different tonight."

"Different?"

"I want to tie you up."

Involuntarily, my fingers wrapped around my throat. *"What?"*

"I want to tie you up."

The room went silent. I started shivering. *"Why?"*

He extended his arms out from his shoulders and slumped his head to the side. "You are my artistic vision of Our Lord Jesus on the cross. I can't crucify you. So this is the next best thing."

I was too stunned to talk.

"Say no if you're squeamish."

"Chris, I'm not squeamish—"

"So do it." He came over to the bed and draped his robe around my shoulders. "Please, please, Terry. It's very *important* to me."

I looked at the ceiling. "You are absolutely the most wonderful, but *weirdest* boy I have ever met in my entire life."

He smiled sheepishly. "Call it artistic temperament." His eyes met mine. He lowered his head and kissed my feet. "I'm *begging* you. *Please*?"

I fell backward onto his mattress. "I must be crazy—"

"You'll do it?"

"Yes, I'll do it."

Without ceremony, Chris got up from the bed, went to his closet, and pulled out a dozen neckties. I felt my heart beating wildly. I stuttered out, "You've *done* this before?"

He didn't answer.

"Just swear to me that you're not a serial killer."

"I'm not a serial killer. Lie down." He waited, I waited. Gently, he pushed down on my shoulders. "Please."

As I lay on his bed, he pulled off the robe, took my right arm, and secured it to his headboard with one of his ties. Then he did the left. I felt as powerless as a deboned chicken. I wiggled my fingers.

"Too tight?" he asked.

"No . . . I have circulation . . . barely."

"Your limbs start to tingle, let me know. I don't want to hurt you."

"Well, that's comforting."

His face became flat. "Terry, I could snap your neck as easily as taking a breath. I don't want to do nasty things to you. I draw you as an expression of my love for you. Do you believe me?"

"Of course, but—"

"Good. Then cross your ankles."

"You're tying my feet, too?"

"Jesus was bound and constrained when he died. *Cross* your ankles."

I crossed my ankles. He tied them together, then took another tie and bound me to his footboard. Completely immobilized, I started to shiver. He threw the blanket over my body and started arranging my hair.

"You want to paste a false beard on me?"

He didn't answer, smoothing out loose strands of hair. He moved my head to one side, then to the other. He told me to look up, look down, close my eyes, open my eyes, smile, frown, then look beatific. Finally, he stood and removed the blanket from my body. Chris studied me for a long time.

He went to his easel and drew for twenty minutes, then stopped. "The angle's not right. It's too much an aerial view."

"Perhaps you'd like to construct a cross and we can try it again next week."

His voice turned harsh. "Don't make fun of me."

I was quiet, felt tears in my eyes. He stared at me for a moment, then threw his chalk across the room. "*Fuck* it!"

He stomped over and began untying my arms, angry and frustrated. I felt as if I'd failed him. Worse yet, I felt as if I'd failed art.

Freed of the binds, I shook out my limbs as he sat dejected on the edge of his bed. I blanketed myself with his comforter, sat next to him, and reached for his hand. He tensed at my touch. I withdrew my fingers.

I said, "It's early, Christopher. Let's try it again."

He looked at his watch. "It's almost nine. How much time do you have?"

"As much as you need."

He ran his hand over his face. "God, I'm being a selfish pig. You're pale. You must be hungry. Let me take you out to eat."

"No, it's okay. Let's just keep going."

"Not until I get some nutrition into you." He stood and began to pace. "Put on one of my robes and I'll make you something. While you're eating, I want to look at some religious art books. That sound okay?"

"Yes, it sounds ducky."

He bent down and kissed my forehead. "You're a great sport."

"Thank you," I muttered. "You can put it on my tombstone as an epitaph."

He left without answering me. I shuddered. I was sorry I'd made the wisecrack.

After the break, Chris became very mathematical about his proportions. He measured distances and angles—from my shoulder to my hand, from my hand to his headboard. He struggled with many positions until he found a couple of poses he liked. By the time he actually began drawing, it was close to eleven. At one in the morning, Chris ripped up his current work.

"I'm fading." He paused. "You looked tired, too."

I was exhausted. I never realized that modeling was such hard work. He untied me. I shook out my limbs, feeling numb and drained. He placed the comforter around my shoulders, then told me to put my clothes on.

He didn't see me when I walked into the living room. I watched him play back his answering machine messages, the last being a girl telling him to get his butt over to Tom's because he was missing a terrific party. I knew the voice. She was pretty and loose—two traits that made her very popular. Short blond hair and bright blue eyes. The sex goddess of Central West Valley High.

"Cheryl Diggs," I said.

Chris turned the machine off and pivoted to face me. "You've got a better ear than I thought."

"For some things." I rubbed my eyes. "What's the story with you and her? Why is she always giving you neck rubs?"

"What are you *really* asking me, Terry? You want to know whether I've slept with her? Yes, I have."

I looked away. Chris said, "You want me to treat you like I treat her, Terry?"

"No, but . . ."

He waited for me to complete my sentence.

I sat on his sofa. He sat next to me. I didn't look at him. "I'm not a nun, Chris. I have sexual feelings—"

"I know that—"

"I also have human feelings. I get jealous."

"And that's precisely why I'm not sleeping with you. I don't want to hurt you."

And what could I say to that? "You don't mind hurting Cheryl?"

"Cheryl's been around the block. I walk away tomorrow, she couldn't care less."

"How do *you* know?"

"I know."

"Yeah, you're a mind reader."

"No, I'm not. I know she doesn't care because she's promiscuous. Terry, I'd rather be with you. But you're complicated. Cheryl's easy. So that's why I'm with her. Any other questions?"

I didn't answer. He blew out air. "Look, we're both real tired. How about we try this again next week?"

Finally I kicked the words out. "I don't think so. I'm a tutor, Chris, not a model. I don't feel comfortable doing this, even for immortality."

"But you're a *great* model."

"Thank you, but it's irrelevant—"

"Let me show you some of the drawings. Maybe they'll change your mind."

He started up, but I held his arm. At least he didn't tense. I said, "It won't change my mind."

He tapped his foot. "Look, you're making fifteen an hour as a tutor, right? I'll pay you fifty an hour to model for me." He glanced at his watch. "Tonight's haul would be two hundred and fifty just like that. That's great bread by anyone's standards."

I glared at him. "You think I'm holding out for *money*?"

"No, of course not. I was just trying to motivate you—"

"By offering me *money*? I'm not a nun, Christopher, but I'm not a whore, either."

The room fell quiet. Something wasn't right.

I said, "You know, Chris, you're doing okay in your work. Maybe it would be better—"

"No, no, no, no, no." He smiled weakly. "I'll behave myself. Forget about this whole modeling thing. I shouldn't have . . . let's just go back to the way it was."

My head was reeling. "Chris, that isn't possible—"

"Sure it is." He began to pace. "It's just perspective, Terry. That's all it is. I can view you this way. Or I can view you that way. You can be my girlfriend. Or you can be my tutor. Or you can be my model. It's just perspective, compartmentalizing. You know what I'm saying?"

I stood and slipped the strap of my bag over my shoulder. "No, I really don't."

"Terry, please don't leave." He grabbed my hand. "Just sit a moment, okay?"

With great reluctance, I sat back down. He sat next to me. Calmly, he said, "Just tell me what you want."

"I don't want anything, Chris. Everything's okay."

"Then if everything's okay, we'll go back to the way it was. You're my tutor, I'm your student. I'll see you on Monday then."

I kneaded my hands. "I think . . ." I cleared my throat. "It really would be better if you found another tutor."

The room turned silent and cold. I started shivering. He rubbed my arms.

"Is that what you want, Teresa?"

My eyes became moist. "I don't know."

"We're both too tired to make decisions. Let's talk on Monday."

"Chris, this past week has been real intense. I need a break. How about if you call me in a week, okay?"

He stared at me for a long time.

"Please, Christopher. If it's love, it can wait a week."

His eyes never left mine. Staring me down. Finally he shrugged. "Sure, I'll call you in a week."

Suddenly, I could breathe. "You're not mad?"

"Mad at you?" His smile was wide but off. "I could never be mad at you. Sure, I'll call in a week."

We both knew he'd never call again. He dropped my hands and scratched his head. "In the meantime, I've said some things to you in confidence."

"You know I'm very trustworthy." I laughed nervously. "Besides, you have some pretty detailed drawings of me. In the leverage department, you've got a clear advantage."

He laughed out loud. "Yeah, you're right about that."

"Can I have the drawings, Chris?" I gave him as earnest a look as I could muster. "Please?"

But he shook his head no. "Don't worry. I'll keep them locked up. No one but me will ever see them." He crossed himself. "That much I swear."

"Why can't I have them?"

He smiled slowly. "Because they're mine."

9

Over the weekend I had second thoughts. By Monday, I was determined to talk to him. I spotted him before first period. He was with his friends, Cheryl Diggs on his lap, his hands traveling her body like ants on a sandhill. She was equally demonstrative. From a distance, it looked like he saw me. He paused, then brought Cheryl's face to his and devoured her mouth.

Something snapped inside as I walked away, a long-buried aching that surfaced as a ravenous need for love and affection.

I became moonstruck and boy, did Chris *know* it! For the next three months, he drew me into a horrid game of "I told you so." And the more he tortured me, the more I lapped it up. I knew I had reached rock bottom when I found myself flirting with Steve Anderson just to get close to Chris. Next thing I knew I was going to the parties.

The parties.

There was always some house available, somebody with out-of-town parents. The drugs were plentiful, the booze flowed like tapwater, and sex was open and often. Chris sprawled out on the floor, one hand up

Cheryl's blouse, the other down her pants. Her hands on his crotch, teasing him to a massive erection.

I looked away.

But I always came back for more. The only thing I can say in my defense is that I never let Steve touch me in public. In private, though I guarded my virginity like a chastity belt, I had no choice but to give him something if I was to keep him. And I needed to keep him because he was my link to Chris. I *hated* doing things with him. I wondered if he told his friends about me. I wondered if he told Chris. How I despised myself.

But I kept going back because I needed to see Chris. In fact, what I saw was an alcoholic in the making—my former student packing away shots without breaking a sweat. Drinking made Chris gregarious—a foreign entity to my eyes. He'd smile, he'd joke, he'd become a good ole boy with lots of fans. *Lots* of drinking also made him amorous. After an hour of raging, he'd disappear with Cheryl into a back room.

Always making sure I saw him go with her.

My grades started slipping. I became despondent. Lying like a lump in bed, listening to Vivaldi's *Four Seasons*, thinking suicidal thoughts. Out of desperation, with no one to turn to, I turned to prayer—to my obligation of confession. Dense as I was, it finally hit me. It wasn't that I had posed nude for Chris. Had he loved me as he should have, I would have died for him. It was debasing myself for a boy who regarded me as dirt.

I unburdened my soul, asking Jesus for forgiveness and acceptance. For me, confession had always been a painful process even when I did it on a regular basis. But a yearlong neglect of my spiritual duties made me feel even more shameful and guilty. But I forged ahead, seeking penance from God. After it was over, I felt better. But guilt continued to gnaw at my bones. Because my heart still ached for Chris.

But righteous actions first. Maybe the thoughts would come later.

I went cold turkey. I broke up with Bull Anderson. No more parties, no more torture. Then I started *avoiding* Chris. The hardest period was orchestra. He always had a crowd around him and was very good at catching my eye.

Then one day something drew my eye away from him. Perhaps it was Jesus guiding my soul. Or maybe it was the scent of another wounded animal just like me.

His name was Daniel Reiss. Besides being in orchestra with me, he was in my math class. He was a computer junkie, an almost nerd with glasses that often fell down his nose. He was skinny but at least he was tall. He was staring at Chris, a piece of his flute in each of his hands. His eyes weren't resentful. They were simply perplexed, saying: *Why would God who made a Chris also make someone like me?*

Violin in hand, I walked over to Daniel. "It won't work unless you put it together."

Slowly he turned, amazed that I was talking to him.

"You've got to put the pieces together." I smiled briefly. "Then you've got to blow."

I walked away.

He followed.

Daniel was wonderful in his simplicity. He was sweet, and gentle, and didn't expect a thing sexually. So anything I gave him was met with unbridled excitement. He gave me back my sense of self, and because of that, I wanted our senior prom together to be extra-special.

With my tutoring money, I could have afforded almost any dress I wanted. But store-bought wasn't good enough. I wanted something unique—handmade.

Which meant made by me. Every day after school, I rummaged through fashion magazines. Once I settled on the design, I started my hunt in the fabric stores. I found a bolt of teal-blue taffeta woven with gold thread that cost a fraction of its original price.

I cut, I snipped, I sewed. I adjusted and pinned until my eyes gave out. But when I was done, I had my one of a kind—a backless and strapless bodice attached to a form-fitting miniskirt that gave my body a sexy embrace.

But something was missing.

It needed trim. It needed a bow. But not just any bow. A monster-sized bow that I tacked on just below the waistline. It swayed when I moved. It gave me kinetics. With the rest of the fabric, I made a matching stole. I accented the entire outfit with a black lace bag, matching lace gloves cut off at the fingers, and black garters and stockings. I kept my jewelry simple—a cross around my neck and Chris's pearl earrings—a nice, ironic touch.

On prom night, I felt as desirable as a courtesan. Yet inside, I was pure . . . well, maybe not totally pure. But at least I came away from high school still a virgin.

Daniel was speechless. His hands shook as he pinned a corsage onto my bodice. I took his arm as we walked to his car. He had wanted to rent a limo, but I told him not to waste the money. His six-year-old Volvo would do just fine. I felt cocky as I made my entrance into the gym.

I could feel the eyes on me—male and female. The girls looking at my dress, the boys eyeing what was inside. I could hear a buzz as Daniel and I walked over to the picture line. I kept my expression genteel but inside I was flying.

All these years of keeping a low profile. But not tonight. Tonight was *my* turn.

Casually, I glanced around the room.

I saw him before he saw me. He was absolutely gorgeous—completely at ease in formal wear. I figured he must have attended a lot of weddings in his day. He was talking to his friends, Cheryl at his side. But there was a distance between them. No body contact.

Then she took his arm. He stiffened. She looked upset.

I felt bad.

He turned and looked in my direction.

I caught his eye.

Abruptly, his face turned into something inanimate—cold and emotionless with the eyes of a dead fish. I looked away and moved closer to Daniel. When I glanced up again, he was gone.

I pretended the interchange never happened. I

danced, I laughed, I flirted, I drank punch and ate cucumber sandwiches. Midway through the affair, I saw him again, moving through the crowd, heading for the side door.

Without a nod to rational thought, I excused myself from Daniel and gave chase. I found him alone under a tree, knees up against his chest—same position I'd modeled for his sketches. I sat next to him, hugging myself because I was cold.

"Stuffy in there," I said.

He didn't answer.

"Like my earrings?"

He didn't move.

"Look, Chris . . ." I tried again. "I'm sorry it ended so badly. I'm sorry that things got so messed up. You were a very important person in my life. I feel very deeply about you and—"

"Are you wearing garters or panty hose?" he asked me.

I waited a beat. "What?"

He looked at me for the first time. His voice was calm. "I asked if you were wearing garters or panty hose."

I stared at him.

He shrugged. "If I'm gonna fantasize about fucking you, I want to be accurate."

I opened my mouth, then closed it. Without a word, I got up and went back to the gym. Daniel found me, asked me where I'd been. I didn't answer. I'd been subdued.

Another hour going through the motions.

Someone put Tom Petty on the PA.

Oh my my. Oh hell yes.
Honey, put on that party dress.

My head began to throb.

Last dance with Mary Jane,
One more time to kill the pain . . .

I asked Daniel to take me to the restaurant now. I knew it was early, but I had to get out of there.

He told me, anything I wanted.

We were at his Volvo, almost inside, when we heard Chris call Daniel's name. We turned around.

"Hey, Reiss," he said loudly. "Can I have just five minutes with your girl before you whisk her away?"

I felt anger overflow. "Why are you asking *him* for permission to talk to *me*?"

He turned to me, his face bathed in sweat. Jumpy eyes. An emotion in him I'd never seen before. He was nervous.

"Just five minutes, Terry. After that, I'll leave you alone, I swear."

I rolled my eyes, looked at Daniel. He gave a sheepish smile. "Maybe I'll go grab another cup of punch."

"Thanks," Chris told him.

We both watched him walk away. When he was out of sight, Chris wiped his face with a handkerchief, then stuck his hands in his pockets and rocked on his feet.

"I'm sorry."

I shrugged.

"Terry, I've been a real jerk. Not only tonight but

these past months. I was angry at my situation and I took it out on you. But I'm not making excuses. I acted like a total and complete *asshole*."

I shrugged again. "Who noticed?"

He was breathing audibly. Then he rubbed his neck and laughed. "That was real rich, Terry."

"You want absolution, Chris, go to confession."

"You know, Terry, we really deserve each other. I may be a motherfucker. But deep down inside, you're a real bitch."

Then he pounced on me. He shoved me against the Volvo and attacked my mouth with feral hunger. I could have protested. And I knew he would have stopped. But I didn't.

Because I wanted it.

I clutched his neck and drank in his juices. His tongue wrestling with mine, moving down my neck until his mouth was between my breasts. He slipped his hands inside my dress, liberating my flesh, drawing my nipple to his mouth. He licked and moaned and so did I.

He hiked up my dress, picked me up, and sat me on the hood of the car. His mouth ravaging mine, he opened my legs and pressed himself on top of me. My back felt the chill of the Volvo's cold steel, but my insides were scalding hot. I coiled my legs around his hips and drew him closer. He rocked against me, bringing a sweet ache to my loins. Our warm breath mixing as his lips danced with mine.

"Be with me, angel," he whispered. "I'll ditch her, you ditch him—"

"Chris—"

"We'll make love until the sun comes up."

He dipped his hand under my panties. I was sopping wet. "I'll take you away, baby doll. I'll take us both away *forever*! Out of reach of your parents, out of reach of my uncle, out of reach of everything except each other's arms."

"Chris—"

"Now or never, Terry."

"Oh, God—"

"Say yes!"

"Yes!" I shoved him away and tried to catch my breath. I sat up and closed my legs. "Yes. Okay?"

He stared at me, flush-faced and panting. "You mean it?"

"I mean it." I was breathing hard. "Do you mean it?"

"Yes."

"What about Lor—"

"Screw her. Screw everyone except *us*! I can't live without you, Terry. I don't want to live without you. God, I love you so much I'm in *pain*. Baby, tell me you love me."

"I love you." I took a deep breath. "I love you, love you, love you. Help me down."

He put his arms around my waist and swung me from the car. I attempted to tidy my appearance. I tugged on my skirt, smoothed out my hair, and re-did my lipstick. He came toward me, but I whacked him back. "Daniel'll be back any minute."

Chris rubbed his neck. "What are you going to tell him?"

"I don't know. God, he's been so *good* to me." I looked at him beseechingly. "Can you just give me tonight with him? It's so cruel . . ."

My voice faded.

Chris took a deep breath and blew it out. "What the hell! Give the guy a break. Have dinner with him. We've got a lifetime together."

My heart took toward the sky. "You really mean that?"

His smile was dazzling. "Yes, I really mean that!"

He'd imitated my tone of voice. My laughter was mixed with tears. I erased lipstick from the corner of his mouth, then touched his cheek. I was hopelessly in love.

I said, "Besides, I'm sure Cheryl could use a break, too."

"Yeah, she could use something." He rotated his shoulders. "She'll never die young because she's getting old too fast."

"At least you got your answer," I said.

"Pardon?"

"You know if I'm wearing garters or panty hose."

He laughed. "A lot of good it'll do me." He waited a beat. "That's not what I wanted from you. I mean I wanted that too, but . . ." He shook his head. "I can't believe all the time I wasted. Playing stupid mind games. I'm much better at revenge than I am at love."

"It doesn't matter now."

"That's good of you to say." He looked at me. "Did you know, after you blew me off, I used to break into your locker?"

I stared at him. "Why?"

"Just to smell your jacket or your lunch or your books. I saved every page of notes you'd ever given me. Every pen or pencil, every . . ." He laughed. "Every *eraser* shaving you ever left at my place. You left a sweater in my closet. I used to sleep with it, that's how *obsessed* I was with you. I still am obsessed with you. I've never, ever stopped looking at you, Teresa Anne McLaughlin. Even when you stopped looking at me."

"I'm glad you're obsessed with me. Because I'm obsessed with you." I paused. "How'd you break my padlock?"

"Ain't a lock around that I can't pick," Chris said. "Courtesy of my dad, mind you, not my uncle Joey. That's why I got into so much trouble with B and Es back in New York. I was too good for my own good." He kissed me again. "I ache for you, angel. You really want to be with *Reiss* tonight?"

"No, I don't. But I owe him something, Chris."

He shot me a chilly look. I ignored it and glanced up at the inky sky. "Should I call you when I get home?"

"Let me call you," he said.

I paused. "Will you? This isn't a game with you?"

"Good God, no, Terry! This *isn't* a game! This is the most honest I've ever been in my entire life!"

"What about your uncle?"

"Good old Joey." He raised his brow. "I don't know. But I'll think of something." He kissed me on the forehead. "I'll call you around one."

"Swear?"

He crossed himself. "Swear."

I got home at twelve-forty-five and waited.

At four-thirty in the morning, my resolve weakened. I picked up the phone and called him. The line connected after the third ring. He mumbled a sleepy hello. I couldn't find my voice.

He muttered an obscenity under his breath, but into the phone he calmly stated, "Terry, don't hang up. Let me explain—"

I slammed down the receiver, then took it off the hook. At sunrise, I went to sleep.

❦ 10

Stepping across the door's threshold, Decker caught the photographer's flash. Swell. Just when he needed his eyesight for detail, he'd be seeing a dancing moon for the next few minutes. Officer Russ Miller was trying to get his attention. Taking his notepad from his jacket, Decker detached the pen from the cover and clicked the nub at the end, bringing up the ballpoint.

"Backtrack for me, Russ."

Someone shouted, "Anyone in fucking *charge* here?"

Decker looked up. Benny, the lab man, was irritated, sweat dripping from his forehead. Swaddled in his white lab coat, he swiped at his face with his arm, making sure not to contaminate his latex-covered hands. He caught Decker's eye.

"Sergeant, I can't do a goddamn thing with all these feet and hands flying in the air."

"I just walked through the door, Ben. Let me get my bearings, okay?"

"It's in your best interest to clear the bodies out." Benny paused. "The live ones."

The flash went off again. Decker shielded his eyes. Sticky moisture was coating his armpits. He took off

94

his jacket and draped it over his shoulder. Then he did a head count. Ten officers—way too many people crammed into the double-occupancy hotel room.

Aloud he said, "Everybody freeze for a second. Who was first on the scene?"

"Crock and me," Miller said.

"Then you two stay here." Decker started pointing. "Howard and Black, you two canvass rooms on floors one and two. Wilson and Packard, this floor and the one upstairs. Be polite and be careful. Also, do a little crowd control. There's a group of looky-loos that's a potential fire hazard. Officers Bailey, Nelson, Gomez, and Estrella, back in the field. Go."

As the room emptied, clearing the area around the bed, the victim came into Decker's view. He started making notes—not much more than first impressions but sometimes they were valuable.

Nude, white female—late teens/early twenties.

He stopped.

Cindy's age. And the bastard was still at large.

No, don't even think about it, Deck. Because once personal crap starts interfering with work, you're a goner.

He shook away his daughter's image and went back to the victim. Her head was slumped to the side, her hands had been bound to the headboard by a bow tie and a stocking, her feet were untethered but crossed at the ankles. No visible gunshot or stab wounds, but fresh, deep bruises colored her neck. No distinct ligature marks: She'd probably been strangled by someone's hands. Decker took in the silky ashen face, the silvery gray skin, the full but cyanotic lips. A pretty girl—a Picasso painting in his blue period.

Her eyes were closed. Made it easier to digest the horror.

She was so damn *young*!

His eyes traveled to her hands dangling in the constraints. Graceful hands with long, tapered fingers. He wondered if she had ever played an instrument— piano or maybe violin. The nails were bright red as were the fingertips. Lividity. Blood pools to the low spots.

"I got *room*!" Benny, the lab man, stretched. "You want me to bag the hands and feet first, Sergeant? Or do you want to wait until the coroner cuts her down?"

"Do the bagging first," Decker said. "Don't want to lose any nail scrapings. Coroner will work around you. Lynne, you almost done?"

The police photographer looked up. "Just a few more snapshots and I'm out of here."

Decker returned his attention to the lone pair of uniforms still in the room. Russ Miller was tall with broad features. His partner, Billy Crock, was a recent southern transplant who'd joined the force a week before the earthquake. His apartment building was now a vacant lot. Everything he owned had been buried under rubble. Crock had shrugged it off. Decker figured this was a guy with a future.

His eyes went back to his notepad. "Shoot, Russ."

Miller cleared his throat. "Call came through dispatch at eight-oh-eight; Crock and I arrived on the scene at eight-twelve. First one we talked to was Dave Forrester, the front-desk clerk. He directed us to the room, and to Adela Alvera, the maid who found the body. She discovered it around eight this morning, doing routine cleaning."

"Opened the door and wham." Crock slammed his fist into his palm. "First thing the lady did was throw up. Then she called the front desk. Forrester called nine-one-one."

Decker scribbled notes as he looked around the room. Typical cheap hotel room—a queen bed, a TV equipped with pay-per-view channels resting in a particle board dresser stained to look like wood, a small writing table and chair, two flimsy nightstands and a house phone that charged an arm and a leg for a local call. There was a menu on one of the nightstands. The place had a coffee shop downstairs. Evidently it provided room service.

Decker rolled his tongue in his mouth. "Does the victim have a name yet?"

Crock said, "No personal belongings found in the room. So it looks like we got a robbery/murder."

"What about registration cards at the front desk?"

"No cards, nothing on computer," Crock answered. "Forrester doesn't understand how that coulda happened."

Decker wrote: *No reg card or computer entry. Clerk took bribe? Why? Victim young girl—Affair? Prostitute?* "Did Forrester work the desk last night?"

Crock shook his head. "No, that would be Henry Trupp. We've called him, Sarge. Guy isn't home or isn't answering."

"Either of you pull the cards for the rooms adjacent to this one?"

"Sure did," Crock said. "A Mr. and Mrs. Smith to the left. Mr. and Mrs. Jones on the right."

"Terrific," Decker said. "I'll call Vice. Find out if this place is a hooker palace."

He gave the room another sweep with his eyes. Something pink and shiny lay crumpled in the corner. He walked over, gloved his hand, and picked it up. A sequined party dress. He thought a moment.

First Saturday night in June.

Prom night.

Man, did that kick in a few buried memories. Especially since Saturday had ceased to be a day in his vocabulary. Saturday had turned into *Shabbos*. On his pad, Decker wrote down the names of the three local high schools—West Valley, North Valley, and Central West.

"Mr. and Mrs. Smith, and Mr. and Mrs. Jones." He raised his eyes. "I think we had some after-prom festivities here last night. Kids getting a head start on being sleazy adults. Something went awry. They all probably panicked and fled."

"I'll second that theory," the lab man said. "Lookie what I found under the covers." With a pair of pincers, Benny held a condom aloft, then slipped it into an evidence bag. "Guess she believed in safe sex."

Decker regarded the body. "Up to a point."

Crock drawled, "A lot different from my prom night back home."

"Mine, too," Decker said.

Not that he'd been a paragon of virtue. After the party, he and his buddies had taken their dates to an isolated park for a night of petting and binging bar vodka. Afterward, he had thought he'd been doing just *fine*! Then he had turned on the motor of his dad's truck, smiled at his girl, and proceeded to heave his guts inside the cab. His date had joined him for the barfathon. Lyle Decker's punishment had been simple but effective. Decker remembered all too well scrubbing tuck and roll with a toothbrush, cleaning scraps of detritus stuck in God-awful places.

He checked his watch. Eight-fifty-two. "Anyone check Missing Persons to see if a parent has called, wondering where the hell his or her daughter might be?"

Crock said, "I'll call Devonshire."

"Call Foothill, Van Nuys, and North Hollywood as well. And while you're on the horn, Billy, find out the names of the principals *and* the girls' vice principals of the three major high schools out here."

"West Valley, Central West, and . . ."

"North Valley. Call them all up, tell them police need to meet them at their respective schools within the next hour, maybe two hours tops." Decker turned to Miller. "You go back to the maid. Get her story again, along with her name, address, and phone number. And search her purse. She may have vomited initially, but after the shock wore off, she may have lifted something from the room."

"Anything else?"

"Yeah, go down to the clerk and have him check the phone records. Maybe someone made calls from this room."

"Got it," Miller said. Then he and Crock left.

Decker ran his hand through thick, carrot-colored hair, stroked his chin and felt grizzle. Wakened from a rare morning of sleep, he hadn't had a chance to shave. He had said a shortened version of his morning prayers, then rushed off to work, throwing a kiss to Rina and the boys. Hannah was still sleeping.

Little Hannah. At that age, they were easy because your eyes never let them out of your sight. Not so with the big one. Please God, just keep Cindy *safe*!

Again he studied the victim. The poor kid hadn't had a chance to grow up. Decker felt low, wished Marge was here. But he was glad his partner finally had taken some time off. He hoped the Maui sun was being kind to her, hoped her new friend Roger was being kind as well.

The police photographer closed her camera case. "I'm all done, Sergeant. Meat wagon's outside. You want me to call in the boys for you?"

Decker nodded. "Snap me a couple of Polaroids of the face, Lynne. We don't have a name. I'll need them for ID."

"Certainly." Lynne took out a camera and aimed. "Pretty thing, wasn't she? Natural good looks, but not a natural blonde."

Decker looked at the body, at a dark bush of pubic hair. He wrote: *Condom in sheet. Sex. Good pubic comb.*

Lynne handed him four photographs. "Is this enough?"

"Great. Thanks, Lynne."

"Tell the boys to come in?"

"Please."

She gave a wave and left. Again, Decker studied the surroundings. The room was on the third floor, the window barred, the escape lever untouched. Whoever did this walked in and out the door. He tore put a clean sheet of paper, dividing the space into four sections. Later he'd add the furniture.

Benny took out a fingerprint kit. "I can't dust

until the stiff's out of here. Powder'll screw up the autopsy. Where's the men from the coroner's office?"

"Lynne went to get them." Decker frowned and went over to the bed. "I can't stand it. I'm going to take her down."

He gloved up, then slowly undid the knots on the bow tie and stocking that bound the victim's wrists to the headboard. Her arms remained extended, as stiff as a cardboard cutout. He lowered the T-shaped girl to the bed, then dropped the bow tie into one plastic bag, set the stocking in another. He examined the neck.

A voice behind him said, "Rather large bruises. I'd say our perpetrator had large hands."

Decker looked up. ME office had sent Jay Craine. He was a thin, good-looking man in his mid-thirties. Heavy with the affectations but a good coroner. Today, his face looked exceptionally drawn. His nose was Rudolph red.

Decker asked, "Allergies or a cold?"

Craine sneezed, then slipped on a mask. "A tad of both, I'm afraid. Oh my. Terrible. Was she tied to the headboard?"

"Yeah." Decker made room for Craine to work. "I couldn't look at her anymore like that. I took her down."

"Obviously rigor has started." Craine leaned over and started examining the body. "She's not ice-cold. I'll take a rectal temperature as soon as I've checked out her anus for sexual penetration."

He attempted to flex her arms, then bent her legs at the knee.

"Rigor's not totally set. Lividity's evident." He

looked at Decker. "Perhaps we're working within a range of three to eight hours. When was the body discovered?"

"Eight in the morning."

"So that's more or less between the hours of twelve and eight. Rigor is somewhat advanced although physical exertion prior to death can speed it up." Craine opened his leather bag, took out a swab kit. He snorted, coughed, sneezed, then began his examination. "Semen in her vagina."

Decker paused. "Are you sure? Ben found a condom in the bed sheets."

"And another in the garbage can," Ben broke in. "Someone was having a good time."

Decker regarded the rigor-laden girl. "And someone wasn't. Why would she have semen in her vagina if her partner was using a condom?"

"Perhaps he ran out and they got careless," Craine postulated. "Or she had more than one partner."

"What about her anus?"

Craine examined her rectum with watery eyes. "Appears clean from a visual." He took several swabs and sealed them in vials. He sneezed ferociously. "But one cannot tell . . ." Another sneeze. "Until one puts it under a microscope."

Craine continued on. "First impression, Sergeant . . ." A pause, then a sneeze. "The girl might be pregnant . . . thickening of the vaginal tissue, vascularization. Either pregnant or it's her period. But I don't see any menstrual blood."

Decker ran his tongue along the inside of his cheek, then wrote down the word—*pregnant*. "How far along?"

"Early. I'll tell you more specifics when I get her on the table."

"Now there's a switch," Benny said. "Someone was using a condom even though the girl had been knocked up. The power of the virus."

"But she had semen in her," Decker said. "Maybe Doctor C. is right. We're working with more than one man."

"We'll know for certain once the tests come in." Craine stood, then sneezed so hard he rocked on his feet.

Decker said, "You sure you should be working, Doctor?"

"On the contrary, it's the best time to work," Craine sniffed. "The nasal mucosa is so inflamed, it virtually blocks out all odious olfactory sensations. I can't smell a thing. Shall I remove her so Ben can dust thoroughly?"

"Great idea," Ben said.

Decker said, "Take care of yourself, Doc."

"Oh, yes, indeed. Rhinoviruses are persistent little creatures. Bed rest is essential."

As soon as Craine left, Officers Crock and Miller walked back into the room. Crock said, "Got hold of the principal at Central West Valley and West Valley. They'll call the girls' veeps and meet you down at the schools whenever you come. I haven't hooked up with anyone from North Valley yet. Also, no frantic parents have called any of the station houses."

Decker nodded, then turned to Officer Miller. "What about you, Russ?"

"Maid seems on the level as far as I can tell. So

does the desk clerk, Forrester. You want to interview them?"

"I'll introduce myself before I leave for the high schools. What time did the maid go on shift?"

"Six."

"And the desk clerk?"

"Six, also."

"So at six, we had a changing of the guard at the desk—Forrester came in and . . ." Decker rotated his shoulders as he checked through his notes. "And Henry Trupp went off duty. Phone calls from the room, Russ?"

"Two calls to room service downstairs. One at twelve-oh-six, another at two-fifty-six." Miller rubbed his hands against his pants. "That should help narrow down the time frame."

"If she was alive when the calls were made. Who was on duty in the coffee shop last night?"

Miller cleared his throat. "Seems room service is brought up by the busboys. They come and go . . . paid in cash. Everything is off the books."

"Illegals?"

"Probably."

Decker said, "I'll take it from here. Thank you. You two can go back in the field now."

He looked at his room map and started on the first quadrant. After an hour search, Decker had a collection of carefully marked plastic bags containing hairs, buttons, two beer-bottle caps, a butt of marijuana, specks of white powder, three bathroom towels, all the bed linens, discarded underclothes, a pair of pink sequined shoes that matched the dress, and one wilted orchid corsage that said it all.

He pocketed his survey notes and left the room, yielding the final check to Benny and his lab men.

A brief talk with the maid and Forrester revealed no new information. Neither one saw or heard anything. He used the lobby phone and dialed Henry Trupp's phone number. It rang and rang and Decker hung up. He found Officer Mike Wilson, who had just finished canvassing the first floor. Decker called him over.

"Anything?"

"Nothing."

"Why am I not surprised?" Decker shook his head. "Mike, go into the coffee shop. I want a list of everyone who was working last night. If they hassle you about giving names of cash-only employees, tell them we're not interested in calling either the INS or the IRS. But we'll call both if we have to."

"I understand, Sergeant."

"Yeah, make sure they understand as well. Be back soon."

Decker slipped on his jacket and headed for high school.

❧11

North valley was a bust.

Central West was a different story. Decker took out the Polaroids and laid them on the principal's desk. The rotund black man winced distastefully, but there were no sparks of recognition in his eyes.

Not the case for the girls' vice principal, Kathy Portafino. One glance turned her a putrid shade of olive. She was about Marge's age and height—early thirties, around five ten and hefty, with a square jaw and a no-nonsense face that said, "I've seen it all." But there was something uniquely ugly about post-mortem photos. A cold finality combined with clinical sterility brought out emotions in even the most jaded.

"Who is she?" Decker asked.

The woman covered her mouth. "I think it's Cheryl Diggs."

"You think?"

"No, it's her. She just looks so . . . different." She wiped her forehead and swallowed weakly. "Excuse me, but I'm not feeling—"

"Go," Decker said.

The woman fled the room. Decker turned his attention to the principal. He was staring at the top of his paper-piled desk.

Decker said, "Do you know this girl, Mr. Gordon?"

The principal ran his hand over his close-cropped salt-and-pepper hair. "Now that Kathy has identified her, I know who she is." He sat down in his chair. "This is just . . . terrible."

Decker took out his notepad. "Did the school hold its senior prom last night?"

The man nodded, rubbed his forehead. "All of a sudden that seems like years ago."

"And Cheryl Diggs was there?"

"I suppose."

"Do you know who she went with?"

"No, I couldn't tell you that."

"Then tell me about Cheryl."

"Ms. Portafino would know more."

"What do you know, Mr. Gordon?"

"What do I know?" His pause told Decker he didn't know much. "Cheryl ran with the wild crowd. Wild over here doesn't mean homeboys mowing each other down. This is still a predominantly white, middle-class, gang-less school. But we have guns here." He took a deep breath. "We have guns, we have knives, we have drugs, we have pregnancies, we have diseases, we have suicides and overdoses. We have every urban problem you can think of, including violent crime—theft, robbery, rapes, assaults. But *this*?"

"Never any murders before?"

"One in the five years I've been here. Two boys fighting over a parking space. One of them just pulled out a thirty-two and shot the other in the head. You don't recall that?"

"I wasn't in Devonshire five years ago," Decker said.

"I thought we'd hit rock bottom then." Gordon sighed. "Even though we beefed up our security afterward, it took a long time to calm jittery nerves. Lord only knows what this is going to do."

"Tell me about Cheryl's crowd."

"Cheryl's crowd . . ." He hesitated, trying to formulate his thoughts. Just then, Kathy returned to the room. Her face had been splashed with water. She was pale but no longer green. Gordon turned to his ally. "Kathy, who were Cheryl's friends?"

"Lisa Chapman, Trish Manning, Jo Benderhoff—"

"Boyfriends," Decker interrupted.

"She hopped around." Kathy sat down. "Steven Anderson, Blake Adonetti, Tom Baylor, Christopher Whit—" She stopped talking. "I think she went to the prom with Chris Whitman. At least I saw them there together. I remember them because they made such a beautiful couple." The VP tapped her foot. "You know, I think something was wrong. Cheryl looked upset."

Decker wrote as he spoke. "Is that hindsight talking or was there some definite incident you remember?"

"Nothing precise. She just looked . . . sad. I noticed it because it marred her otherwise stunning appearance."

"Did the boyfriend seem upset?" Decker asked.

She shrugged. "Chris is always hard to read.

Also I'm more tuned in to the girls. All I remember about Chris is that he looked great. He always looks great."

"He's a handsome boy," Gordon added. "A gifted cellist."

"More than gifted," Kathy added. "He was professional quality."

"He didn't belong here," Gordon continued. "He should have been in Juilliard."

"Then why was he here?" Decker asked.

Both Gordon and Kathy shrugged ignorance.

"Don't tell me," Decker said. "He's a quiet boy. A loner with social problems."

"Not at all," Kathy said. "He has friends. As a matter of fact, he's quite popular. Very well liked with the boys as well as the girls."

An ember ignited in Decker's brain—a familiar profile. He said, "You said he was hard to read. What did you mean by that?"

Kathy thought a moment. "Chris is very . . . even-tempered. A trait like that stands out when you're dealing with a thousand hormonally unbalanced adolescents."

Decker said, "More adult than the rest of the kids?"

Kathy nodded. "Yes."

Gordon suddenly spoke up. "Kathy, isn't Christopher an emancipated minor?"

"I think he's eighteen now, Sheldon."

"But he came in as an emancipated minor," Gordon said. "I remember that clearly. Despite all the divorce and broken homes, very few kids have their own apartments."

Bingo! In his notepad, Decker wrote: WHIT-MAN, CHRIS. NARC? CALL VICE. "So Christopher Whitman has his own place?"

"I believe he does," Gordon said.

"Is he a druggie?" Decker asked.

Gordon looked at Kathy. She said, "I don't recall him ever getting busted, but he hangs out in the druggie crowd."

"But as far as you know, he isn't a user."

"As far as I know, yes."

"And you saw him with Cheryl at the prom last night," Decker said.

"Yes. I couldn't swear he came with her. But he and Cheryl were hanging out together."

"And she looked sad. Any idea why?"

Kathy shook her head no.

Decker was quiet. According to Jay Craine, the coroner, Cheryl was probably pregnant. If Chris Whitman, her supposed boyfriend, was a narcotics officer and knocked her up, he'd be finished as a cop.

Talk about motivation for murder.

"I'll need Chris Whitman's address," he said. "Cheryl's address as well. I'll also want all the addresses of her friends—male and female."

Gordon looked at Kathy. She stood up. "I'll pull those for you right now."

"I'd like to come with you," Decker said. "Take a look at Whitman's transcript."

Kathy eyed Gordon. He waved his hand. "Let him see it."

Decker followed Kathy into the registration room—a long, cavernous hall filled with banks of metal files. She went to an area marked CURRENTS, sifted through the ws and pulled out Whitman's file.

"Here you go."

Decker studied the particulars. According to the files, Whitman was almost nineteen—old for a high school student. He had transferred as a junior from St. Matthews High in Long Island, New York. All that was listed from his prior education was about a year's worth of mediocre grades. Nothing written in the space reserved for PARENT OR GUARDIAN. Though he had provided the school with his current address and phone number, there was no emergency listing. He showed the papers to the girls' vice principal.

"The vitals are incomplete."

Kathy took the transcript. "He came as a junior, mid-semester. Sometimes the schools just send a partial. The rest of the transcripts usually follow."

"Anything else in his file?"

Again, Kathy plowed through racks of folders. Finally she shut the file and shook her head, a troubled expression on her face. "There's nothing else listed under his name."

"In other words, the boy's a cipher."

Kathy gave him a sheepish smile. "We have lots of kids here, Sergeant."

Decker said nothing. He went back into Gordon's office and gathered up the Polaroids still resting on his desk. The rigor-laden corpse had turned into a person named Cheryl Diggs, a victim snuffed out by a madman. Since she could no longer speak for herself, Decker would have to be her voice.

He regarded Sheldon Gordon. Elbows resting on his desk, the principal sat with his head in his hands.

"This is going to be so traumatic for the kids." He raised his eyes. "It's going to scare the wits out of the girls here. Every single boy is going to be seen as a potential rapist/murderer."

Decker thought of his daughter. For a decade plus, Decker had worked juvenile and sex crimes in the Foothill Substation of LA's San Fernando Valley. Every so often, he had unwittingly exposed his daughter to the horrors of angry, unbalanced men. He often wondered if he had skewed her perception of the male gender.

He glanced at a Polaroid of Cheryl Diggs. At the moment, with Cindy being alone in New York, a campus rapist on the loose, he wondered if her skewed perception wasn't an asset.

Whitman lived on a nondescript side street populated by twenty-year-old apartment buildings that had made it through the earthquake. Sundays were usually quiet, but to Decker's eyes, the neighborhood seemed exceptionally sleepy—perfect camouflage for a secret narcotics agent. After giving Whitman's door a firm knock, Decker waited a beat, then pounded the sucker until his fist turned red.

Either no one was home or Whitman wasn't answering. Decker left a business card with his phone number, instructing Chris to call the station house immediately. Then he rode the elevator back to the first floor and studied the place's directory.

No on-premises manager, just a small-print phone

number that had been inked out and replaced with a set of new digits that were written in barely legible pencil. Decker copied the phone number down, called and got no answer.

He took the staircase down to the apartment's underground parking lot. Whitman drove a red Trans Am. Ten minutes of searching produced no such animal.

He left the building, walking over to his unmarked Volare, cramming his legs under the steering wheel. Left hand drumming the dashboard, he put in a call to Devonshire Detectives. Luckily, Scott Oliver answered the Homicide desk—working Sundays to avoid his wife.

"Hey, Rabbi," he said. "I hear you bagged a good-looking babe."

"Good-looking but dead, Scotty."

"Bring her over anyway. She couldn't be any worse than my last girlfriend."

"I need you to run a name through department files for me. Christopher Sean Whitman. Find out if he's working Vice. If nothing pops, see if he has a yellow sheet. If you still draw blanks, run the name through NCIC."

"Why are you running a name through Vice, Pete? Was the stiff a hooker?"

"Whitman was the victim's boyfriend. I think he might be a narc. Also, do me a favor and put a lookout call for Whitman's red Trans Am." He gave Oliver the license number. "Call me if you come up with something. If not, I'll call back later."

From his jacket, Decker pulled out the address

list of Cheryl's friends. He'd check them later. Unfortunately, there was dirtier work to be done first. Though no one had called in to ask about Cheryl Diggs's whereabouts, the girl wasn't an orphan.

It was time to pay the dreaded call to her mother.

❧ 12

The apartment house was an iffy—one of those buildings that suffered cosmetic cracks from the earthquake but was still structurally sound. Unfortunately, the landlord didn't think enough of the place to give it a face-lift. It was coated with dingy brown stucco, large chunks missing at corners and window frames. The planter boxes held more weeds than flowers. The directory was posted on the outside of the building, but Decker knew Cheryl's unit number. He took the staircase up to the second floor, knocked on the corresponding door. He heard shuffling, but that was all. Someone was taking their own dear time.

Weekends. Everyone slept late except him. On *Shabbos*, it was up early for *shul*. Since he worked his schedule around his Sabbath, he picked up the slack on Sundays. Which effectively meant he worked six days a week.

Not that he minded his job. In fact, he got antsy if he stayed away too long. But everyone needed a break. Especially from dreaded things like grievance calls.

He knocked again. Finally, someone answered.

As soon as he saw her face, he knew what had caused her delay. She was either newly drunk or nursing a bad hangover. Watery blue eyes, puffy lids and mouth, and a nasal drip. She sniffed, then rubbed her nose. Medium-sized, voluptuous build. Not unlike her daughter except Mom had gone to seed. She wore loose cotton shorts and an oversized T-shirt that did little to hide her unbound pendulous breasts.

He took out his badge. "Police, ma'am. I'm looking for Mrs. Janna Diggs."

"Gonzalez," the woman answered. "Janna . . . *Gonzalez*! You got the name wrong."

"I'm looking for Cheryl Diggs's mother. Would that be you, ma'am?"

"Depends on what you want."

Decker said, "May I come in, Mrs. Gonzalez?"

" 'Pose so."

Janna cleared the doorway; Decker stepped inside the living room. Though he kept his face impassive, his stomach did a back flip. It was almost impossible to see furniture because it was covered with garbage—dozens of empty beer bottles, squashed aluminum cans, crumpled newspapers, rotting food, discarded paper plates and utensils, and heaps of dirty clothes. The couch had been opened into a bed. The pillowcases were uncovered, sheets wet and stained. The woman scratched her cleavage.

"You want some coffee, Mister . . ." She looked confused. "Or is it Officer?"

"No coffee, thank you, ma'am."

Janna pushed aside the unwashed sheets and sat on the open mattress. "Okay then. Whattha little bitch do?" She sniffed deeply. "How much is it gonna cost me?"

Decker tried to keep his voice gentle. "Ma'am, early this morning, police discovered the body of a young teenaged girl. We have reason to believe that it might be your daughter, Cheryl."

Janna froze, then blinked but didn't speak. Decker waited for another reaction but nothing came. He said, "Mrs. Gonzalez, if there's someone you'd like to be with, someone you'd like to call, I can do that for you."

Janna remained silent. With great effort, Decker forced himself to park his butt on the dirty bed. "Is there something I can do for you right now, Mrs. Gonzalez?"

She still didn't answer.

"Maybe pour you a drink?" Decker offered.

The woman nodded mechanically.

Decker went over to a small card table. Among the scattered debris was an open bottle of Wild Turkey. He held it up. "Is this all right?"

Janna looked in his direction but said nothing. Decker found a dirty cup, rinsed it in a food-encrusted porcelain sink, and poured her a shot of bourbon. He brought it over to her. She took it, then raised it to her lips. She wiped her nose on her T-shirt.

"Howchu . . . you know it's Cheryl?"

"Someone has initially identified your daughter from photographs taken at the crime scene. When you're ready, and feel strong enough, we'd like you to come down and make a definitive identification."

"You want me to look at the body?"

"Yes," Decker said. "We want you to look at the body."

Janna rubbed her nose. "From pichures, you could tell it was Cheryl?"

"Somebody thought it was your daughter, yes," Decker answered.

"You have the pichures?"

Decker kept his face flat. "I think it would be better if you witnessed the body in person. Less chance for a mistake."

"But you have pichures."

"Yes, I do."

"You have them on you?"

Inane to lie. Decker said, "They're in my pocket."

Quietly, Janna said, "Lemme see."

Decker paused. "Mrs. Gonzalez, they were taken at the crime scene. They're hard to look at even for a veteran like I am."

"That bad, huh?" Janna rubbed her eyes. "I'm stronger than I look. Lemme see."

Decker hesitated, then reached in his pocket and pulled out the Polaroids. Janna stared at the first one. Instantly, tears ran down her pallid cheeks. She went through the snapshots one by one, her eyes over-flowing each time she studied another pose. Finally she blotted her face with her T-shirt and handed the pictures back to Decker.

"It's her . . . Cheryl."

"You're sure?"

She nodded, her lower lip quivering.

"Can I get you a glass of water, Mrs. Gonzalez?"

"Nothin'." Her voice had dropped to a whisper.

She touched her mouth, then pulled her hand away. "Is that it?"

"I'd like to ask you a few questions."

Though she shrugged indifference, her face had set in a mask of grief. "Go ahead."

"Do you know where your daughter was last night?"

Janna shook her head no. "I haven't talked to Cheryl in . . . 'bout a week."

Decker took out his pad. "What do you know about your daughter's friends?"

"Not much anymore. Cheryl and me haven't been getting along so hot." She blinked rapidly. "Not that I didn't try, but . . . you do the best you can, you know? Sometimes it's not enough."

"Has Cheryl been living with you, Mrs. Gonzalez?"

"In and out." Again, the tears started flowing. "She'd eat my food, steal my booze . . . then she was gone. Sometimes, when I would go away or be with my boyfriend, she'd bring her friends over. Cheryl had lots of friends."

"Tell me about her friends."

"Wild like she was." Her chin touched her chest. "Wild like I am. The fruit's the same as the tree or somethin' like that."

"Do you know her friends by name?"

"Some. Lisa and Jo and Trish. Trashy girls. I think Lisa got caught shopliftin'. Jo was picked up once for turning tricks."

"Did Cheryl turn tricks?"

"Wouldn't put it past her. Anything for money. But if she did, she never got caught. Least she never had me bail 'er out."

"Tell me about boyfriends. Did Cheryl ever talk about her boyfriends?"

"Oh, she had *lots* of boyfriends, Detective."

Decker wasn't sure if he heard jealousy or disapproval in Janna's voice. "Ever meet any of her boyfriends?"

"A couple. I remember one of 'em. An ape of a guy with big tits. Not real tall but real pumped."

"Chris Whitman?"

"No, I never heard that name before."

Decker took out his list. "Blake Adonetti, Steve Anderson—"

"That's the one. Stevie, she called him. She went with him for a while, but he wasn't the only one."

A look of anger spread across her face.

"She liked the boys, Officer. She saw something in pants that pleased her eye, she took it. Even if it belonged to her mother. First time, I forgave her. After I caught her with another one of my friends, I kicked her out."

The room became silent.

"Course I'm not good at being mad. Truth was I missed her. So I said she could come back. And she did whenever she needed a place to crash."

Her mouth turned downward.

"She was a very pretty little baby. And smart, too. Could do the ABCs forward and backward at three years old. Isn't that something?"

"Yes, it is."

"So damn smart. Too smart for her own good."

Janna laid her head on Decker's chest and wept openly. Decker enclosed her heaving body and patted her back gently. But that wasn't enough comfort. She threw her arms around his neck and pressed her chest deep into his.

"Hold me," she whispered as she sobbed. "Hold me, please."

Decker continued to pat her back. "Who can I call for you, Mrs. Gonzalez? You mentioned a boyfriend. Can I ring him up for you?"

The woman kept him locked in a bear hug. "Hold me please . . . *love* me please."

As Janna raised her mouth, Decker jerked his head back and broke her hold. The rejection caused her to weep even harder. She sobbed into her hands, her shoulders bouncing with each intake of breath. Decker stood, trying to keep his posture relaxed, but inside he was a bundle of coiled nerves. "May I use the phone?"

She didn't answer. Decker took that as an affirmative. He called the station house and asked for a cruiser, requesting that one of the uniforms sent over be a female. Then he just waited it out. Five minutes later, Decker answered the loud, distinct police knock at Janna's door—Linda Estrella and Tony Wilson. That was good because both had been to the hotel this morning. They had seen the body; hopefully, they could empathize with Janna's misery.

He whispered, "This morning's victim was Cheryl Diggs. This is her mother, Mrs. Janna Gonzalez. I think she has a boyfriend, but hasn't given me a phone number to call him. Let her compose herself, then if she's up to it, take her down to the morgue for the definitive ID."

Linda said, "You don't want to be there?"

"Not necessary." Decker smoothed his mustache. "We know the victim. Let's get the perp."

Using the unmarked radio mike, Decker called the station house. Oliver was still manning Homicide.

"I can't believe you're working this hard on Sunday," Decker said. "Your old lady must really be pissed off."

"It ain't easy living with a junkyard dog."

"You might try throwing her a bone now and then."

"You mean a boner." Oliver laughed over the line. "Actually, she's out of town. Just my fortune that my girlfriend's down with a bad case of herpes. What's a poor pussyhound to do?"

"It's a cruel world out there, Scotty. Did you get a chance to run Christopher Whitman through the computer?"

"I did do that, Pete. The guy has no sheet locally or nationally. I've also checked with Narcotics in Devonshire and the other Valley divisions. They deny having a mole at Central West Valley."

"I don't buy it."

"Could be you're right. You know how Narcotics can be. Codespeak. Getting info outta them is like using a foreign dictionary. You're speaking the same words, but not talking the same language."

Decker opened his thermos and drank lukewarm coffee. "Whitman didn't happen to call in by any chance?"

"Nope. You need anything else, Rabbi?"

"Got some time on your hands?"

"What do you need?"

"In the abstract, it would be nice if someone could pull Whitman's tax forms—state and federal for the last two years. Kid's an enigma. He's hiding something. He's got an apartment, he's got to pay rent. I want to know where the money's coming from."

Oliver paused. "I'd like to help. But we all know that hacking his papers on-line would be an invasion of Whitman's privacy."

"Of course," Decker said.

"Still, if I were you, I'd check your mail in an hour. Never know what could show up unexpectedly."

Decker smiled to himself. "Today's Sunday, Scott."

Another long pause. Then Oliver said, "There's always special delivery."

❧13

Running down the list of Cheryl's friends, Decker underlined the name Steve Anderson, the ape of a guy with big tits whom, according to Mom, Cheryl had dated. He fit the description of a steroid popper, and anabolic users were notoriously unpredictable in their behavior.

Unlike Decker's old haunt of Foothill, the West Valley was a predominantly white middle-class area. Apartment streets like the one Whitman lived on weren't unusual. Nor were blocks of sensible, one-story houses. But the eighties land boom had given the area a new face—gated housing developments composed of million-dollar estates meant to attract a more desirable—i.e., moneyed—population.

Anderson lived in a two-story colonial set on a sweeping mound of rolling lawn. There were a Mercedes, a Jaguar, and a Ford Explorer stacked up in the long sloped driveway. Decker parked on the street and walked up the herringbone-brick pathway lined with white impatiens and pink begonias. The entrance was double-doored, the bell on the right. Decker pressed the button and deep chimes could be heard from inside the house. A female voice asked who was there. Decker identified himself.

There was a pause. The woman said, "Just a minute."

Clacking sounds inside—heels reverberating against a hard surface. A moment later, the door opened, giving Decker a view of a man with a tanned face, dark, curly hair, and uncertain eyes. Behind his broad shoulders, Decker could make out a petite form with styled platinum hair. The missus had faded into the background.

"You're the police?" the man asked.

Decker took out his badge and ID. "Detective Sergeant Peter Decker, Devonshire Homicide. Are you Mr. Anderson?"

"Yes, I am. Did you say *Homicide*?"

"Yes, sir, I did. May I come in?"

"Do you have a warrant?"

Decker stared at him. "No, Mr. Anderson, I don't have a warrant. Do I need one?"

Anderson rubbed his hands together, his frame still blocking the doorway. He wore gray designer sweats and running shoes with no socks.

Decker said, "I'd like to talk to your son, Steven."

The woman gasped. Anderson crossed his arms in front of his chest and rocked on his feet. "What about?"

"Do you want to continue talking in the doorway, Mr. Anderson? Neighbors might think it's kind of funny."

Slowly Anderson ceded space, allowing Decker entrance into the large marble hall, then leading him into the living room. It was as light and cold as vanilla ice cream. The carpeting was spotless. Decker checked the bottoms of his shoes. The missus caught it. She was neat and nondescript.

"Don't worry, Sergeant. The Berber is Scotch-garded."

"Susan, why don't you bring in some coffee?" her husband suggested.

"No thanks on the coffee." Decker took a seat on a cream-colored modular sofa. "Is Steven home?"

Anderson remained mulish. "What do you want with Steven?"

"Bring him down," Decker said. "You'll find out."

Anderson kneaded his hands. "Is he going to need a lawyer?"

"I can't tell you that until I've talked to Steven."

The man turned to his wife. "Get him down here."

She obeyed without question. A minute later, a compact boy entered the room. He wore a tank shirt and shorts, the muscles and veins of his arms and legs inflating the skin like stuffed sausages. He wasn't bad-looking—dark curly hair like Dad, square face and a strong chin. But his complexion was bad, acne pitting his cheeks.

"Sit down," Anderson ordered his son.

The boy rubbed his nose and sat.

"I'm Detective Sergeant Peter Decker—"

"He's from Homicide, Steven. What the hell is going on?"

"Homi . . ." The boy's eyes grew wide. "Dad, I . . . I . . . I . . ."

Decker said, "Mr. Anderson, please sit down and let me ask the questions."

Reluctantly, Anderson sat down. Decker thought a moment, wondering how to play it. Straightforward came to mind. Eyes on Steven, he took out the Polaroids and spread them on the glass coffee table. The boy took a look, jerked his head back, and turned white. The missus gasped. The old man froze.

Decker said, "Do you know this girl, Steve?"

In the background, Decker heard a dry heave. Susan had run out of the room. Decker returned his attention to Steve. The boy had his massive arms wrapped around his barrel chest. "It's . . . it's . . . Cheryl, isn't it?"

"Cheryl who?"

"Cheryl Diggs."

Decker regarded the boy. "Do you need a glass of water, Steve?"

He nodded. Anderson screamed out, "Susan, Steve needs some water. Make it two."

She didn't answer. No one seemed perturbed by her lack of response.

Decker took out his notepad. "When was the last time you saw her, Steven?"

"Don't answer that," Anderson interrupted.

"Dad, I didn't *do* any—"

"Shut up!"

"But I didn't do—"

"I said *shut up*!" He turned to Decker. "We want a lawyer."

"I don't need a lawyer," Steve protested. "I didn't *do* anything."

"Go to your room, Steven. Right now!"

"But—"

"NOW!" Anderson bellowed.

The boy stood, walked a couple of paces, then turned around. "No."

Anderson stood up. "Steve, get out of here—"

"No, Dad, you get out of here. *You* get out of here. What the hell do you know about *me*? Or my friends or my *life*, you goddamn *prick*—"

"Steven—"

"Don't you *Steven* me! You were never around. Only around to put me down—"

Anderson moved closer to the boy. "If you don't shut up—"

"You shut up! I'm over eighteen, Dad. I don't need your permission to talk. So *you* shut up!"

The boy gave his father a slight shove. Decker moved quickly between them and held out his arms. "BACK OFF NOW! BOTH OF YOU! BACK OFF!"

The room fell quiet except for heavy breathing. Decker seized the moment. "I need your help, Steven."

The boy seemed suddenly deflated. He glanced at his father. That was all the room the senior Anderson needed to horn in. "You don't have a warrant, Sergeant, I don't want you in my house! Now, you do what you have to do, but my son isn't talking until I've talked to him."

Decker gathered up the Polaroids. "Fine. I'll cart him down to the station house and Steve can wait in jail while you contact a lawyer!"

Steve screamed, "I'm not going to *jail*! I didn't do a fucking *thing*!"

A small, birdlike voice piped in, "Can everyone please be sensible—"

"Susan, get out of here!" Anderson yelled.

The woman put down a tray holding three glasses of water and scooted away. Decker said, "Come on, Steven—"

"Wait!" Anderson interrupted. "Talk here. Steven, sit back down and let's get this over with."

Decker wished he could isolate son from father. And since the boy was eighteen, Decker had the legal grounds to do it. But these days, lawyers entered weird pleas with kids charged with capital crimes *if* they were still living at home. Despite all the talk about personal responsibility, it seemed that whenever a problem arose, there was no such thing as adults anymore—only grown children.

Decker said, "Have a seat, Steven. Please." Slowly, the boy returned to the couch. Decker took out his notepad and said, "You saw Cheryl last night?"

Steve nodded.

"When was the last time you saw her?"

"Don't answer that," Anderson broke in.

"Mr. Anderson, if you don't stop interrupting, I'm going to hit you with an obstruction of justice—"

"You can't do that."

"*Watch* me, sir." To Steven, Decker said, "When was the last time you saw Cheryl Diggs, Steve?"

"I . . . don't remember."

"You don't remember?"

"Not . . . really, no. I can't believe . . . this is like *surreal*!"

"Have some water, Steve."

The kid gulped down the cool liquid. Decker said, "Okay, let's back it up a moment, Steve. When do you *first* remember seeing Cheryl last night?"

"Somewhere at the prom. The Central West Valley's senior prom."

"Was she your date?"

"No, sir."

"Who was your date?"

"Trish . . . Patricia Manning."

"Do you know if Cheryl had a date?"

"Yes, sir. Christopher Whitman."

"She went to the prom with Christopher Whitman?"

"Yes, sir."

"What time did you leave the prom, Steve?"

The boy blew out air. "Around . . ." He covered his face and looked up. "Oh, God, I'm afraid I'm gonna make a mistake."

Decker said, "Just answer me as best you can, Steven. When did you leave the prom?"

The boy looked sick. "A little after midnight maybe."

"What did you do after that?"

"Hopped around."

"What does that mean?"

"We went to a couple of parties."

"How many parties?"

He looked at his dad. "Maybe two . . . yeah . . . two."

"Was Cheryl at these parties?"

"Yes."

"You saw her at both parties?"

"Yes."

"Was she with her date?"

"She was with Chris, yes."

"What time did *you* leave the last party?"

Again, Steve looked at his father. He closed his eyes. "Maybe one-thirty, two."

"Did you go straight home?"

His voice fell to nothing. "No."

"Where did you go, Steve?"

The room fell quiet.

Decker said, "Where did—"

"I heard you." Steve scratched his face. "A group of us went to a hotel—"

"Jesus!" Anderson stood on his feet, flushing and sweating. "You *what*!?"

Decker said, "Take some water, Mr. Anderson."

He did. It seemed to cool him off. Decker asked, "Which hotel did you go to, Steve?"

"Grenada West End."

"You rented rooms there?"

"Sort of. I didn't exactly rent a room. We had rooms, though. I think Cheryl got us all comped. She knew the night clerk. I think she got a special deal from him because she had done him some favors."

"Favors?"

"I think she . . ." He moved his hand up and down.

"She had relations with the night clerk?"

"Something like that. Cheryl got around."

"Do you remember the night clerk's name?"

"Henry Tripp or Trupp. Something like that."

Decker wrote DIGGS AND TRUPP? Again, he made a mental note to call Trupp. "And you saw Cheryl at the Grenada West End."

"Yes, sir."

"Do you recall the last time you saw Cheryl?"

The boy shook his head, then covered his face. "Man, this is a *fucking nightmare*!"

Anderson was about to speak, but Decker held up the palm of his hand. "Steve, do you remember the last time you saw Cheryl?"

"Trish and I—"

"Uncover your mouth," Decker said. "I can't understand you."

Steve started again. "There were a lot of us in this room—in Cheryl's room."

"Who was in Cheryl's room?" Decker asked.

He started ticking off his fingers. "Trish, Cheryl, Jo Benderhoff, Lisa Chapman, me, Blake Adonetti, Tom Baylor, and Chris were all in Cheryl's room."

"What time was that?"

"I guess right after we got there—around two."

"You remember seeing Cheryl alive at around two?"

"To the best of my recollection, yes."

"What were you doing in the room, Steve?"

"We were drinking a little."

"Meaning they were guzzling from the bottle," Anderson muttered.

Decker pushed on. "You were drinking, Steven. What else?"

"Doping a little, maybe."

"Maybe," grunted Anderson.

"What else were you doing, Steve?" Decker pressed.

He looked down. "Fooling around."

Anderson blurted out, "I work my ass off so you can go out and have an orgy—"

"We weren't having an *orgy*, Dad. Just . . . like fooling around. Nothing big. We were having fun. It was no *big* deal."

"No *big* deal?" Anderson orated. "Is *murder* a big deal, Steven?"

The boy suddenly shuddered and looked to Decker for support. Decker remained impassive.

The teen said, "All I'm saying is we weren't outta control. We didn't do anything that the girls didn't want."

"What the hell does *that* mean?" Anderson boomed.

"Mr. Anderson—"

"I know, I know. I'll shut up!" Anderson paced, then sat back down. "You don't understand how *hard* this is for me."

"Sir, I assure you I understand." Decker meant it. "Just let me do my job as a detective, then you can do your job as a parent." He turned back to Steve. "Let me see if I have this right. You, Trish, Cheryl, Jo, Lisa, Blake, Tom, and Chris were all hanging out—drinking and doping and fooling around. Groping each other—"

"Nothing sick, Dad, I swear . . ." He blew out air. "Just some stupid fun. Except Chris wasn't into it."

Decker paused. "Why do you say that?"

"I mean he was drinking and everything. But I could tell he was anxious for us to leave."

"You know Chris Whitman pretty well, Steve?"

"No one knows Chris well. Because the guy doesn't

talk. But you know how guys are when they want to be alone with a girl. He didn't say anything, but he was anxious for us to get the hell out."

"How did he act?"

"I don't know. He acted like Chris."

"Was he nervous, angry, hostile?"

Steve took another drink of water. Talking about Whitman made him relax. "No, Chris doesn't get nervous or hostile. He doesn't get much of anything. He's kinda flat."

"Then how could you tell he wanted you to leave?"

"I don't know. He seemed . . . annoyed. Kept checking his watch. I was trying to prod Trish along, but she was having a good time. I didn't want to . . . get her out of the mood."

"What kind of mood was Cheryl in?"

"Cheryl was Cheryl. A free spirit." He paused. "Except last night . . . she couldn't keep her eyes off Chris. She was so . . . *hot* for him. It was almost embarrassing."

"Was he hot for her?"

"See, you don't know Chris. You can't tell what he's thinking. I've never seen him mad or amped or upset, even when he raged to the max." Steve looked at his hands. "Once, after this party, we all were feeling kinda good. So we piled into Tom Baylor's car and went for a ride. Trouble was we'd been drinking and Tom was pretty blitzed."

The boy looked at his father. At this point, the man was beyond words. Disappointment had replaced outrage.

Steve continued, "We got stopped by the cops for speeding. Chris pulls out the keys from the ignition, pushes Tom out of the driver's seat, takes the whole rap. They have him walk the line. They have him take a breath test. Guy's totally cool." The boy raised his eyes in wonderment. "Course they gave him a speeding ticket, but he got out of a DUI."

Decker nodded as he wrote. "But he didn't join in the fun last night?"

"Nope. Just drank and watched."

"Cheryl didn't ask him to join in?"

"No, she wouldn't do that. Because when Chris gets in his . . . annoyed moods . . . he gets spooky. Real quiet . . . cold. You keep waiting for him to blow, but he never does."

Or maybe he did, Decker thought.

Steve said, "Anyway, we were maybe fooling around for a half-hour, maybe forty-five minutes tops in Cheryl's room. First Jo and Blake left, then Tom and Lisa. Trish and I went to our room about five minutes after Tom and Lisa."

"So that was around . . . what time?"

"Maybe three. That was the last time I saw Cheryl, I *swear* to God. I'll take a lie-detector test, I'll do *anything* you want."

Decker said, "How long did you stay at the Grenada?"

"I don't remember," Steve said. "I was home by five in the morning. The place is like maybe twenty minutes away. Course I had to drop Trish off first. So maybe I left the Grenada at four-thirty." He shrugged and smiled weakly. "That's it. I swear."

"You didn't see Cheryl when you left?"

"No, sir."

"Did you knock on the door to Cheryl's room?"

"No, sir."

"Did you see Christopher Whitman when you left?"

"No, sir."

"Did you see Jo Benderhoff or Lisa Chapman or Blake Adonetti or Tom Baylor when you left your room to go home?"

"No, sir. No one. Ask Trish."

Decker said, "What was Cheryl wearing last night, Steve?"

The boy squinted. "Some kind of party dress. I don't remember exactly."

"What was Trish wearing?"

"A red-sequined minidress."

"What were you wearing last night?"

"A tux."

"Bow tie and cummerbund?"

"Sure."

"What was Chris wearing?"

"A tux, also."

"Did it have a bow tie and cummerbund, too?"

"I guess."

"Was Chris wearing his bow tie and cummerbund when you saw him in Cheryl's room?"

"I don't remem—" He closed his eyes. "You know, he was wearing his bow tie, but it was undone, like draped around his neck."

"You have your tux from last night?"

"Yeah."

"Can I see it?"

"Sure."

The kid was up and down in a flash. Sure enough, the tux was complete with bow tie and cummerbund.

Decker looked over his notes—a good start. If the kid was to be believed, Cheryl died after three but before eight. "Anyone see you come home, Steve?"

"My mom," Steve said. "She always waits up for me."

"Goddamn overprotective," Anderson muttered.

"I don't ask her to do it," Steve said. "She just does."

Decker stood. "Don't go anywhere, Steve. You're still not out of the woods."

Anderson got up. "My son cooperated fully. What more do you want from him?"

Steve said, "I'll do *anything* to help. Believe it or not, Sergeant, I *liked* Cheryl. I feel . . . sick that this happened. She liked to live on the edge, but she didn't deserve *this*."

Indeed, Decker thought. He folded his pad. "Steven, you keep real *quiet* about this interview. You start talking, you'll mess yourself up, you hear me?"

"Loud and clear."

Decker put his pad away and said, "Go upstairs. I want to talk to your dad for a moment."

The kid retreated. Decker put his hands in his pockets. "I've got kids myself, Mr. Anderson. I don't know if I would have reacted any differently from you."

Anderson stared at Decker, then nodded.

"You know your boy's on steroids," Decker said. "Does he take them with your approval?"

Anderson didn't answer.

"Don't tell me. He's your only son and you didn't want him to grow up a wimp. For *his* sake, not yours of course. Well, you don't have a wimp, Mr. Anderson.

Now what you have is a loose cannon. I don't want to be back here, six months from now, in an official capacity because somebody's temper blew up, you understand what I'm saying?"

"Yes."

"Get some help, all of you."

Anderson said he would. Decker didn't believe him.

❧ 14

From the Volare's radio, Decker heard his unit number and picked up the mike. A moment later, Scott Oliver was patched through the line.

"How's the case coming?"

"It's coming. Why?"

"If you're pressed for time, I'll be happy to interview the victim's friends—the females. I'm good with girls, Rabbi. They cry on my shoulder, tell me their life stories. It's because I'm sensitive . . . just a P.C. kind of guy."

"What's *really* up, Scotty? Or are you just killing time until the hookers come out?"

Oliver laughed. "No. Christopher Whitman called, left a message at the desk."

Decker paused. "You're *kidding*!"

"Nope."

"What message did he leave?"

"Just returning your call."

"When did he phone the station house?"

"About forty-five minutes ago."

Decker scanned through his notes. "I've got his number. I'll do it from my radio."

He hung up the mike, was just about to return

Whitman's call, then changed his mind. He turned on the ignition and drove to Whitman's apartment. He parked, climbed up the three flights of stairs, and knocked hard on his door. A moment's pause, then it swung open.

Decker kept his expression neutral, which was not an easy feat. Because the face staring back at his was reptilian cold. He took out his badge and identification. "Detective Sergeant Peter Decker of the LAPD. Devonshire Homicide. Are you Christopher Whitman?"

"Yes, I am."

"Thanks for calling back. May I come in?"

Whitman continued to study Decker's credentials. When he was done, he looked at Decker. *Looked at*, Decker realized. *Not up.*

Because the kid was at least his height, but long-limbed and lanky. Decker must have outweighed him by some forty pounds. Whitman was neat and clean, wearing a black T-shirt tucked into jeans. Model handsome, he had thick blond hair, a sharp jawline, a solid chin. His skin held no remnants of adolescent acne. An exceptionally good-looking boy except for the eyes. Nothing wrong with the bright blue color, just with the expression. They had none.

Whitman said, "You're from Homicide?"

"Yes," Decker said. "May I come in?"

Whitman stepped aside, Decker walked through the portal. He started to walk around the room, but Whitman reined him in. "Have a seat." He pointed to a black leather sofa. "Do you want some coffee, Sergeant?"

"Nothing, thank you."

Decker sat and so did Whitman.

The boy said, "Who died?"

Decker stared at him. Whitman didn't flinch. Slowly, Decker took out the Polaroids and laid them on the glass table. Equally slowly, Whitman closed and opened his eyes. His gaze then went from Decker's face to the snapshots.

Something registered in Whitman's eyes. Could have been anything from horror to excitement to relief. But his facial muscles remained fixed, so he was hard to read. He studied the pictures closely, moving them into his line of vision with his pinkie nail. Then he looked up and waited.

"Do you know the girl, Chris?"

Whitman didn't answer.

Decker said, "Simple question, guy. Yes or no, can you identify the girl?"

"It's Cheryl Diggs." Whitman paused. "What happened?"

Decker said, "I was hoping you could tell me."

Whitman was silent.

Decker said, "Where were you last night, Chris?"

Whitman stood. "I need a cigarette. Okay?"

"Sure."

The boy walked over to the kitchen counter, pulled out a pack of smokes and an ashtray, and came back to the living room. He sat back down and held out the pack. Decker shook his head.

"I don't mind talking to you." Whitman lit up, waved the match in the air, and blew out a plume of smoke over his shoulder. "But I want my lawyer to be present."

Decker waited a beat. "That's fine. Give him a

call. Tell him to meet you at the Devonshire Sub-station as soon as possible."

"It's Sunday. I doubt if I can get hold of him."

"You don't know unless you've tried."

"He won't be available until tomorrow."

Decker thought about the calling card he had left at Whitman's door. It had mentioned he was from Homicide Division. "You've already called him, haven't you?"

"He won't be available until tomorrow."

"Not a problem. We can appoint an attorney for you, Chris. We won't even charge you."

"Thank you, but I'll wait for my own lawyer."

"Then you'll wait in jail."

Whitman rubbed his neck. "How about this? My attorney and I will meet you down at Devonshire station tomorrow at five in the afternoon. I'll answer any question my lawyer says it's okay to answer—in regard to Cheryl." He tapped a nail on his glass table. "I'll even take a polygraph if you want. Does that sound reasonable?"

Decker rolled his tongue in his mouth. "Are you trying to cut a deal with me, Chris?"

Whitman sucked hard on his smoke. "I'm trying to do what makes sense."

"All I want to do is ask you a couple of questions."

"I know that. I'm not trying to be difficult. But I am trying to be careful."

"You need to be careful about something?"

"Once you say something, Sergeant, it's impossible to take it back. So I'll see you tomorrow at five?"

"No, Chris. You'll see me today at booking and arraignment."

Whitman took another puff, letting smoke escape passively through his nostrils and mouth. Decker felt his mouth water.

"I'm asking for twenty-four hours," Chris said. "Believe me, I'm not a flight risk. If I were going to run, I would have done it already."

"We'll just let the judge at your arraignment decide your risk factor. You're going to need a lawyer for that, Chris. Unless you want to represent yourself."

"I guess a public defender'll be good enough for a bail hearing." Whitman paused. "You know you're making extra work for yourself. I'm willing to cooperate."

Decker stood. "Let's get going. I've got other people to talk to."

Whitman stood. "Are you going to cuff me?"

"You're a big guy. I like to play it safe."

Whitman reached under his shirt, pulled out a gold crucifix, and laid it on his coffee table. Then he took off his belt and untied his designer running shoes. "I'm going into my bedroom to get a pair of slip-ons. Is that all right?"

"As long as I come with you."

"Fine."

Together they walked inside Whitman's bedroom. Chris pulled back sliding closet doors and examined his shoe rack. His clothes were meticulously arranged. Jackets, pants, and shirts were color-coordinated and all facing the same way on the hangers. Decker thought about his sons' closets—legally declared disaster areas. Chris pulled out a pair of black Vans, slipped them on his feet, then slid the closet door shut. They both walked back into the living room. Whitman finished off his cigarette, smashed it in the ashtray, then cleaned the ashtray and put it away.

Taking off his belt, removing his necklace, getting shoes without laces. Decker said, "You've walked this road before, haven't you, Chris?"

Whitman didn't answer.

"Nothing local popped out on our computers," Decker said. "And nothing showed up on NCIC. Must have been as a juvenile, probably when you lived back east. Maybe they've sealed the records. But maybe they haven't."

Whitman's expression was flat. "You did homework. I'll make it easy on you. I don't have a record. How long do you think this will take? I'm hungry."

"I'll buy you a burger on the way over."

"Hard to eat with handcuffs on," Whitman said. "I've got a couple of leftover pieces of chicken in my refrigerator. Do you mind?"

The boy was a suspect in a gruesome murder, yet he had an appetite. Pretty damn good. It could have been a ploy, also. It was clear Chris knew the ropes. If Decker had refused him food, Whitman might claim at some time that he was subjected to inhumane treatment.

"Go ahead."

"Thank you." Whitman took out a plate of chicken, wrapped a paper towel around a drumstick, and bit in. He leaned against his kitchen counter as he ate. "Want a piece? It's good."

"No, thanks." Decker glanced around the room.

"Man, I would have killed for a place like this in high school."

Whitman licked his lips and stared at him. "It has its merits."

"How do you pay your rent?"

"I manage."

"You did it up very nicely."

"Thank you."

Decker walked around, looking for something to zero in on. But Whitman was just too damn neat for the room to be telling tales. The front room was open space, so the living room gave an impression of being larger than it was. Not a speck of dirt on the white carpet, not an iota of dust on the tables, not a thread of a cobweb lurking in the corners. Decker turned to the oils on the walls.

"Abstract expressionism," he said. "Never saw much to it myself."

"It has its place."

"Not your signature on the canvases," Decker said.

"No, they're not mine."

Decker's eyes went to Whitman's face. "You draw then."

The boy closed his eyes and opened them. Decker said, "You have any samples of your work? I bet you're good. You look like you have a sharp eye."

Whitman didn't answer.

"Modest guy, huh? Don't like talking about yourself."

"I just don't talk when my mouth is full. It's called good manners." He started on a second piece of chicken.

"What do you like to draw?" Decker asked.

"That's like asking, what do you like to eat?"

"Whatever suits your fancy." Decker smiled. "Whatever speaks to your soul. Isn't that the way the critics talk?"

Whitman poured himself a glass of juice. "I wouldn't know."

"I hear you're also a gifted cellist."

The boy drank, shrugged, and attacked a third piece.

"Is there any money in that?" Decker asked. "Being a classical musician, I mean."

Whitman stopped eating. "Why? Is it a fantasy dream of yours?"

Decker let out a small laugh. "Just making harmless conversation, Chris."

Again Whitman closed and opened his eyes. Third time he'd done that. Decker realized the mannerism was Whitman's alarm. Something Chris did when he felt he was talking too much or showing too much emotion.

Whitman wiped his mouth on a napkin. "Is there money in being a classical musician?" He washed his dish, dried it, and put it away. "You work hard enough at anything, you pay your bills." He faced Decker. "This trek is unnecessary. I'm *not* going to run."

"You're careful and so am I," Decker said. "Who's your lawyer, by the way?"

Whitman paused. "I suppose you'll find out soon enough. McCaffrey, Moody and Sousa. I don't know which one will be dealing with me tomorrow."

Decker felt his heart thump against his chest, but kept his expression even. He knew the firm well.

They were shrewd defense lawyers for the type of people who drove race car imports and hauled cocaine bricks in refrigerated semis. Astronomically expensive, they dealt with clientele who had lots of cash and lots of unreported income.

"Very high-powered," Decker said.

"Yes, they are."

"How'd you come to use them?"

Whitman rubbed his neck. "Guess you'll find that out, too. They're my uncle's lawyers."

"Who's your uncle?"

Whitman met Decker's eye. "Joseph Donatti."

It was Decker's turn to think before he spoke. Without emotion, he said, "You're Joseph Donatti's nephew?"

"Yes, I am."

Decker waited a beat. "Donatti's short and dark and compact."

"And I'm tall and blond. The wonders of genetics."

Decker said, "Something's hinky with you, Chris. What are you doing out here? Setting something up for Donatti?"

"See, Sergeant, that's why I like to have my lawyer present. You'd start out by asking me questions about poor Cheryl, next thing I know you're pumping me about my uncle. You're a cop. I realize it's natural. But it is annoying."

Decker stared at cold eyes. He heard Steve Anderson's words.

Chris gets . . . annoyed.

It was obvious that Whitman had called his uncle as soon as he saw the police business card stuck in his doorframe. What was his reason? To protect his uncle or to protect himself? And what *was* he doing out here? He was old for high school. And both the principal and the girls' VP at Central West Valley had stated that Chris didn't belong.

Decker said, "Your uncle doesn't like you talking to cops, does he?"

"My uncle's very cooperative with law enforcement. He expects me to be cooperative as well."

"As long as his lawyers are around."

Whitman said, "A cop with a clue."

Decker grinned. "Hey, Chris, I guess being a professional cellist means you need *all* your fingers."

Whitman stared at Decker, then a hint of a smile appeared on his lips. "I love my uncle dearly, Sergeant."

"I bet you do, son. Turn around so I can put these on."

Whitman slipped his hands behind his back, ready to be cuffed. So Decker cuffed him.

❧ 15

Since crime didn't work a forty-hour week, the Detectives squad room at Devonshire Substation was rarely devoid of people. But on nights and weekends, the confines had considerably more breathing area. Though Decker loved the space, he missed the buzz. At two-thirty, Sunday afternoon, the place had become a crypt of empty desks, blank computer screens, and idle phones and fax machines, all of it minimally lit to conserve energy.

Apparently, Scott Oliver had found it a refuge. Either that or he had nowhere else to go. He had hunkered down for the afternoon, feet propped up on the desk, soft music wafting from his boom box. Devonshire's desks, like most D-squad rooms, were arranged in a capital I configuration. Oliver's place was at one of the crosspieces. When Decker walked in, Oliver was folding several sheets of glossy fax paper.

Decker headed for the coffeepot, took down a filter, and started a fresh brew. "Get you a cup, Scotty?"

"Thanks."

Oliver was dressed in an imitation Armani three-button jacket over a pair of black chinos. Nice-looking guy, Decker thought, but disheveled today. A day's growth of beard had charcoaled his cheeks and chin; his dense crop of black hair, usually tamed by mousse or gel, was sticking out at weird angles. The guy needed a woman to keep him hygienic.

Oliver finished his origami airplane and sailed it over to Decker. "You will *never* believe who Whitman's legal guardian is."

"Was. He's eighteen now."

"Guess."

"Joseph Donatti."

Oliver plopped his feet to the floor. "You must be a gas at surprise parties. How'd you find out?"

"He told me."

"Did Whitman get in your face about it?"

"Actually, he was reluctant to tell me—one of the reasons I believed him." Decker paused. "Although I'm sure he's a seasoned liar. He's too calm and controlled not to be."

"Where is he?"

"Van Nuys. Bail hearing set in a couple of hours."

"You had enough to book him?"

"No, but I have enough to hold him. He's recalcitrant. Won't answer anything without Uncle Joey's lawyers protecting his ass. Since he had a relationship with the victim and I have a witness who put him at the scene around the time of Diggs's death, I have grounds for keeping him locked up until his lawyers come to his rescue. I put him in the drunk tank. Whitman's fastidious. I'm hoping the stay will imbue him with the spirit of cooperation."

"You think he did it?"

Decker said, "Seems logical. You got a sex crime murder, you look at the primary partner. But I'm not ruling anyone out." He bent down and picked up Oliver's aerodynamic creation. "Creepy sucker. Big, too. Whitman's as tall as I am."

"The battle of the giants. I brought in your mail for you, Rabbi. It's on your desk."

Decker went over and scanned the loose fax pages—Whitman's tax forms. He smiled at Oliver. "I won't ask." He gave the records a closer look.

A year and a half ago, Donatti was listed as Whitman's legal guardian, giving his charge five hundred dollars a month for living expenses. Whitman had augmented the income by two hundred fifty a month from working as a professional musician. He was a card-carrying member of the union.

Decker moved on to his current records, sifted through the pages. "Whitman's income rose considerably this year. Almost two thousand a month from his cello playing. Not a fortune, but Whitman's expenses were minimal. Even figuring the cost of rent, food, and basics, he was left with some pocket change." Decker paused. "Actually, that's much more than pocket change. That's two thousand a month from playing the cello—*part-time*."

"Maybe the kid's real good."

"I've heard he *is* really good. But you want to know what I think, I think Whitman's been playing a lot of cello for Uncle Joey."

"He's dealing for Donatti?"

"He's doing something for Uncle Joey."

"So what does Donatti have to do with the Diggs murder?"

"Could be something, could be nothing," Decker said. "I just spoke to Jay Craine from the ME's office.

Diggs was pregnant and Whitman was her boy-friend. I don't know if that's the motive. But it's as good as any for a starting point."

"What kind of physical do you have?"

"At the scene? Usual hairs and fibers, plus a cou-ple of used condoms." Decker poured himself a cup of coffee, poured Oliver one as well. He walked over to the detective's desk, plunked down a mug of java, and took the empty seat next to him. "The condoms may not have belonged to Whitman. Diggs was also full of semen."

"Maybe Whitman ran out of protection." Oliver blew on the hot liquid. "Either that or two guys, Rabbi."

Decker sipped coffee. "Could be. Diggs liked the boys." He recapped Steven Anderson's recitation. "I have appointments with the other kids from Whit-man's group. See how much of Anderson's story they can corroborate. Anderson put Whitman with Diggs at three, three-thirty in the morning. Last time he claims he saw Cheryl alive. But he could be lying."

"You need time, Rabbi, I'll do a few interviews."

"You must really be bored."

"It's a big case," Oliver said. "I like seeing my name in print."

Decker smiled. "I'm scheduled to see Patricia Man-ning and Lisa Chapman. You get the guys—Blake Adonetti and Thomas Baylor. That leaves Josephine Benderhoff. I'll pick her up later." Decker gave Oliver the addresses, then checked his watch. "I've got to get back to Van Nuys. Hopefully, the judge'll hold Whitman overnight . . . give me enough time to pull a warrant for his place."

"Wasn't Diggs strangled?" Oliver said.

"Yes."

"The murder didn't happen at the kid's apartment. So you can't be looking for a weapon. What are you looking for?"

"A tux." Decker looked at his watch again. "I'd better call Rina. I'm not going to make it home for dinner."

Oliver broke into a wide grin. "If you want, Rabbi, I'll drop by your place and deliver a *personal* message to your wife."

Decker winked. "Make you a bet, Scotty. If you can talk to my wife without your pants getting wet, you can even stay for dinner."

"How about this?" Rina said over the line. "I'll take a snack now and have dinner with you when you come home."

"It's going to be too late, Rina. Eat with the family. I'll just grab a pack of frozen bagels and couple of cans of tuna fish."

"Why don't you just skip the food and swig Thunderbird out of a paper bag."

Decker laughed. "Yeah, it does sound depressing."

"Why bother getting married if you're going to eat like a bachelor? Come by the house and I'll lunchbox some ribs for you."

"Ribs?" He realized his stomach was growling. "You made *ribs*?"

"I'll put the cole slaw in a Tupperware tub, fill up your thermos with fresh coffee, and even give you some wipes for your hands. A truly complete domestic meal for the man on the go, packed personally by his long-suffering wife."

"You're milking this."

"Homemade barbecue sauce, Peter. You're missing out."

The growl had evolved into a roar. He looked at the wall clock and knew he couldn't swing it. "Keep them warm in foil. I'll devour them at one in the morning and get heartburn."

"One in the morning?" Rina paused. "*That* late?"

"Maybe a little earlier. I'll call you in a couple of hours and let you know how it's going."

"You've got the Prom Queen Murder, haven't you?"

"The *Prom Queen* Murder?" Decker echoed. "What in blazes is the *Prom Queen* Murder?"

"Central West's prom queen was found this morning, bound and strangled in a hotel room. You were called out early. I figured it was your case."

"They said she was a prom queen?"

"Yes. Sherrie Dickens or something like that."

"Cheryl Diggs."

"Oh, Peter, what a horrible thing!"

"It's a difficult case . . . especially when people talk to news personnel before it's cleared with the principal investigator. Who'd they interview?"

"Lieutenant Davidson."

Good old Loo, Decker thought. Thomas "Tug" Davidson was an icy bastard who detested the media. Decker was sure that nothing crucial had been leaked. He wondered why Captain Strapp had called Davidson instead of him to handle the mikes. Tug was ill at ease with reporters, viewing them as adversaries instead of stiffs just trying to do a job. He was often abrupt and rude, doing a disservice not only to himself but to all of the LAPD. Tug sure wouldn't win any congeniality awards. But the man had a reputation as a hardworking cop.

"How'd you know Diggs was a prom queen?" Decker asked. "Did Davidson mention it or did the newspeople?"

"One of the reporters brought it up. Davidson was very uncomfortable with the whole thing. You have much better television Q, Peter."

"Call my agent, we'll do murders. Did they mention any names, any suspects?"

"No names," Rina said. "Just that police were conducting an intensive investigation."

Decker wrote in his notepad: *Cheryl—Prom Queen*? Ironic, he should learn it from the idiot box. "Rina, I've got someone in custody right now—"

"Wonderful!"

"We're a *long* way off from celebrating. We're just holding him. The kid hasn't even been charged with anything yet. I've got to go back to court and wait for the suspect's bail hearing. Then I have several interviews to do after that. Plus, I'm trying to pull a warrant."

"Another all-nighter," she stated. "I'll keep your dinner warm."

"The meat'll probably be buckskin by the time I get home. Did the boys feed the horses?"

"Yes, they did. And they took Ginger out for a full hour walk. Hannah and I stayed home, putting plums in the dishwasher. By the way, Cindy called. Don't panic. Everything's all right. She just wanted to say hi. I think she wanted to thank you for telling her to stay at Columbia."

"I'll give her a call right after I hang up with you." Decker swallowed dryly. "I hope she hasn't let her guard down just because the rapist has been lying low."

"She assures me she's still ultra careful. She's never alone in the reference stacks, she never goes into secluded areas, and she never, ever walks alone at night. If she needs a walking partner because she studied late in the library or in a lab, she calls up the student walking service. They send a guy out to escort her back to the dorm."

"A *guy?*"

"Peter, there are nice guys out there. I'm talking to one right now. Call her up. It would mean a lot. She loves her daddy."

Decker felt his chest swell with pride. "I'll call her. Give the other kiddies a hug and kiss for me—a big kiss and hug. And tell them I love them."

"I'll relay your message with emotional content."

"Rina, I love you very much. Please be careful."

"*You* be careful, big guy. You're the one carrying the gun."

It was Erica Berringer on offense, Brandon Krost on defense. Decker had had only minor dealings with them because both were relatively new. Erica was in her late twenties with curly hair and big eyes magnified by round, tortoiseshell glasses. She wore a gray knit dress. Krost was also in his twenties, neatly pressed in a basic black suit. He had thin blond hair that looked even more diaphanous when compared to Whitman's thick gold mop. Both were standing, pleading their cases to the bench. While standing on the sidelines, Decker observed Judge Helen Strong. She looked tired, deep pouches underlining skeptical green eyes.

Berringer's voice had become strident. Not good to show frustration in public, Decker thought. But at least the prosecutor sounded earnest.

"Your Honor," Erica said, "we're talking about a particularly gruesome crime—"

"Your Honor, my client has not been *charged* with anything," Krost countered.

"Your Honor, Mr. Whitman is Mr. Krost's client in only the broadest of terms. The suspect has consistently refused to cooperate with law enforcement personnel even with counsel present—"

"Mr. Whitman has stated repeatedly that he will cooperate fully as soon as he receives the specific representation that he deems proper."

"Are you telling the court, Mr. Krost, that you are deemed improper representation?" the judge broke in.

Decker smiled inwardly. Krost turned red. Strong rolled her eyes.

"Let's keep it simple, gentle people," the judge spoke. "It is my understanding that State is asking the court to hold Mr. Whitman until five o'clock tomorrow afternoon. At that time, Mr. Whitman and his lawyers will meet with law enforcement personnel. Mr. Whitman intends to respond to any and all questions deemed fit to answer by Mr. Whitman's private counsel. Are we all in agreement so far?"

"Yes, Your Honor," Krost answered.

"Prosecutor?"

"True, but—"

"Since no charges are being formally entered at this time, this session is tantamount to a bail hearing," the judge bulldozed on. "It is simply a matter of whether the defendant is trustworthy for the next twenty-four hours. Comments, Ms. Berringer?"

Erica took a deep breath. "Currently State is still amassing evidence against Mr. Whitman. Since he has chosen to take a rebellious stance, State considers him to be a highly probable flight risk."

"Your Honor," Krost countered. "Mr. Whitman has no prior record. There is no indication to support his being a flight risk. State's claim is highly prejudicial—"

"Highly prejudicial, Mr. Krost?" Strong interrupted. "He has been brought in for questioning as a possible murder suspect. Where is the bias?"

Krost said, "State has fears that he will flee based solely on his relationship to Joseph Donatti."

Strong zeroed in on Krost. "Your client is related to Joseph Donatti?"

"Yes, Your Honor," Krost said. "Mr. Donatti is Mr. Whitman's father."

Decker's ears perked up. Now Donatti had been elevated to Whitman's father. Before he'd been an uncle. According to the IRS, he was a legal guardian. Just what was the story? Decker regarded Strong as her eyes swept over Whitman's face.

To Erica, Strong said, "And just what—if anything—does Mr. Donatti have to do with this case?"

"Nothing so far," Erica stammered out, "but Mr. Donatti's history is one rife with—"

"I'm not interested in Joseph Donatti, Prosecutor." Strong cut her off. "He's not on trial here."

Krost jumped in. "Your Honor, Mr. Whitman hasn't ever been charged with so much as a . . . speeding ticket, let alone anything remotely criminal. As you heard, their claim is highly prejudicial."

"Excuse me, Your Honor," Whitman interjected.

Strong stared at Whitman. "Do you wish to say something, Mr. Whitman?"

"Yes, Your Honor."

"What?"

"I have had a speeding ticket."

The court burst into laughter. Even the judge chuckled. Decker hadn't taken his eyes off Chris. The boy's half-smile was perfect, charming but not cocky. His posture was relaxed. Four hours in the hole had had no appreciable effect on his demeanor.

"But I did pay it," Whitman added. "On time, too."

Again, the court tittered.

"Thank you, Mr. Whitman," Strong said, dryly. "Records will indicate your good citizenship. Since your reluctance to be interviewed seems to be the focal point of this fracas, sir, I'll address these words to you as well as your counsel. Your counsel has stated that you *will* appear willingly and without coercion tomorrow at five o'clock at the Devonshire Substation. At such time, you will, willingly and without coercion, answer all inquiries deemed appropriate by your counsel concerning the police's ongoing investigation regarding the death of Cheryl Diggs. Is that a correct assessment, Mr. Krost?"

"Yes, Your Honor."

"And how about you, Mr. Whitman?" the judge said. "Did you understand what I just stated?"

"Yes, Your Honor," Whitman answered. "That was an accurate evaluation."

"Accurate evaluation," Strong repeated. "You know some vocabulary words, Mr. Whitman. Do you fully understand them?"

"Yes, Your Honor. Completely."

"Mr. Whitman, do you also understand that if, for any reason, you fail to show at Devonshire tomorrow at five P.M., you forfeit bail and *will* be arrested immediately?"

"Yes, Your Honor."

"Very well. Defendant is released on his own recognizance until five o'clock tomorrow afternoon, at which time he will meet with police investigators at the Devonshire Substation of the LAPD."

Strong banged her gavel to indicate dismissal of the hearing. Krost broke into a grin and moved to congratulate Whitman. But the boy was already at the door. At the last moment, he looked over his shoulder and met Decker's eyes.

Not a word was exchanged, not even a hint of an expression passed between them. In Decker's mind, that was telling.

❧ 16

The error was so egregious, he couldn't understand how it got past him. But if his eyes had noticed it, it was certain that the cop's eyes had seen it as well. Only a matter of time before the warrant was pulled and they came in and tore up the apartment.

Okay. He knew they had the condoms. That was fair game. It wasn't great, but he could explain them away. Plain and simple, he'd had sex with her like he'd done many times in the past. Having sex with her didn't mean he had killed her. So right then and there, he knew he had to admit he did her.

Sitting at his kitchen counter, he poured himself a half glass of Scotch and took a healthy swig.

Why in Jesus' holy name had he *done* her? His mind ran down the list of flimsy excuses. Because he'd been buzzed, because he'd been hornier than a goat after seeing all those skin flicks, and Cheryl had a drop-dead body. Lying on the bed spread-eagled, begging him to do her one last time . . .

And because he'd been furious at Terry because she hadn't immediately run off with him into the sunset. Choosing Reiss over him, even if she had meant it just to be nice one last time. Cheryl had been his last bit of revenge.

Better at revenge than at love.

He lit a cigarette, let the smoke slowly drift out of his nostrils. Excuses didn't hold squat. He did Cheryl—not once, but twice—because he was a fucking *moron*!

But all that was past now. Don't look back, just forward. Nothing he could do about the damn bow tie. The Polaroids had shown it as clear as daylight, securing poor Cheryl's left arm to the headboard. It would be a bitch to explain. He knew he couldn't pull it off. That was the key to being a pro—to know the limitations.

He took another drag on his cigarette.

He'd simply have to approach the problem another way. If he couldn't make the bow tie disappear, he'd have to lose the tux.

Too bad, because it was a nice one, a designer original with a shawl collar. Hand-tailored because nothing off the rack ever fit his long legs. Joey had dropped over two thousand dollars for it and was going to be pissed. He knew he'd have to make it up, which wasn't a problem. There was always a favor one could do for Uncle Joey.

He took another swig of Scotch.

Most sensible thing was to chuck the threads in the Pacific Ocean. But tides that carried stuff away could also bring stuff back. Besides, he had the feeling that the red-headed cop had placed a tail on him. That being the case, it made more sense to stay put and hide the thing in the house.

But where?

A tux wasn't exactly a nickel bag of drugs. It was a big article, hard to hide. He knew all too well what a good search could uncover. Nothing was safe. Not bed mattresses, not ceiling tiles, not floorboards, not locked cabinets, not holes in the wall, not *anything*.

He thought about cutting the monkey suit up into strips and dissolving it in acid. Rejected the idea. It wouldn't work because he couldn't get 100 percent results. All the cops needed was a *single* thread for fiber analysis.

He thought about cutting it up into shreds and burning it. But again, a fire wasn't foolproof. If Decker sorted through ashes, he'd find something. And also, with that much scissors work, there'd be too many loose threads.

No, he had to hide the thing *in toto*.

Slowly he got up from the kitchen counter and started looking around for a spot.

Living room had nothing. The cushions of the couch would be opened, the entire frame would probably be checked. The chair was a no-go as were the floorboards under the carpet. He looked up, regarded the spotlights recessed into the ceiling. The holes were too small to accommodate something that big.

He opened the front door, spotted a potted banana plant.

He could plant the damn thing under the tree's roots. But then the dirt would be freshly turned. And he knew he'd spill dirt while he was doing the transplanting.

He closed the front door and walked into his bedroom. He searched through his closet and removed the tux, laying it on the bed. Initially, he'd been going to drop it off for dry cleaning first thing in the morning. But instead, he had elected to leave the tux for later and drive by Terry's house, hoping she'd be up . . . explain to her what had happened. That Cheryl had waylaid him. But she'd been dealt with, he was going to say. Now they could run off together. But Terry's shades had been drawn and he hadn't wanted to wake her. Hadn't wanted to arouse suspicion in her bitch stepmother. . . .

He snapped back to the present, to the formal wear resting on his quilt. He picked it up and sniffed. It smelled strongly of marijuana, booze, and cum. Shaking his head, he walked onto his balcony and laid it over a chair, hoping to air it out.

He went back inside, into the second bedroom that doubled as a practice room. He rooted through the closet where he kept his instruments and his weights. No sense hiding it there. Closets would be the first places the cops would look. His eyes fell on his cello case—worth about a thousand dollars because it was custom-made. But he'd sacrifice it if it would do him any good. He took it out, opened it, and removed his Rowland Ross. His fingers palpated the padding. The insides had been specifically designed to accommodate his cello. Any increase in the padding and the instrument wouldn't fit. Besides, it would be nearly impossible for him to open and resew the lining without leaving telltale signs. If Decker had any sort of an eye, he'd know the case lining had been tampered with.

Don't push it, he thought. Something will come up.

He sat on his stool. Picking up his cello, he placed it between his knees, setting the spike into the right groove. He brought the instrument to his body and drew the horsehair bow across gut strings, sustaining sweet notes with a gentle vibrato. The sound box emitted soft moans like a woman in the throes. His hands fingered automatically as his mind took to fantasyland. The music was so pure, it hurt.

Wondering what Terry would have been like, if she would have made any sounds. When he kissed her, she had responded with body as well as soul. He knew that given enough time for the virginal rawness to dissipate, she would have been a beautiful lover. Sadly, he also knew that now she'd remain a mystery to him. The realization cut deeply.

He stopped playing, touched his fingers to his forehead. Despite his calm, he knew it was bad. He was going down and there wasn't a thing he could do about it. He picked up the bow and again started playing. Then he abruptly stopped and clipped his left thumbnail with his incisors.

Only a matter of time before Decker charged in with the warrant.

Like the commercial said—just *do* it!

He laid down his cello, went to the hall closet, and sorted through the art supplies he stored there. Thank God he was organized. He easily found his round-tip putty knife and, with his fingernails, picked off scabs of dried paint. Once it was free of debris, he wiped it on his T-shirt and pocketed the clean implement. He lugged out both cellos—the Rowland Ross as well as his cheap knockabout—and brought them into the kitchen. Carefully, he placed them on their side ribs.

Next, he retrieved his tux from the balcony and sniffed it deeply. It didn't smell wonderful, but it was decidedly less odiferous than it had been twenty minutes ago. He laid the shawl-collared jacket and satin-striped pants on the kitchen counter, spreading them out like a dead body.

Shit, this was going to *hurt*!

He pulled a sharp scissors from a kitchen drawer, carefully snipped off the sleeves, then cut the trunk of the jacket into two pieces. Next he bisected the pants at the crotch. Carefully he scanned the countertop, picking up even the most minute piece of thread. Because under a microscope, minute pieces looked very large. When he was satisfied that everything was clean and perfect, he turned his attention to his instruments.

First, he loosened the strings of his Rowland Ross, carefully depressurizing the tension until the bridge was movable. He took off the strings, then removed the bridge and unscrewed the tailpiece from the body.

Now the hard part.

He turned on the front burner of his stove top.

Take your time. Take your fucking *time!*

He heated his putty knife until it nearly glowed red, then picked up his stringless Rowland Ross. Deftly, he inserted the searing-hot knife into the glue joint between the soundboard and the instrument's side rib, meticulously moving the blade through the space, carefully following the cello's curvature. The smell of sizzling glue assaulted his nostrils. Hot glue but not burning wood.

Thank you, Holy Mother, for a steady hand.

It took many reheats of the knife and several trips around the circumference, but eventually the glue had become soft and sticky and the sound-board loosened. A little bit of jiggling and the top popped off.

He breathed a deep sigh of relief and repeated the procedure on his knockabout. Then he studied the insides of the instruments. The easiest way was to tape the fabric to the backs of the instruments, but he immediately discarded that idea. Better to line the upper side ribs and upper top *just in case* Decker shone a light through the f-holes.

Probably an unnecessary precaution. Because who but a select few knew that most classical-stringed in-struments were held together not by mechanical joints and screws but by glue specifically meant to be soft-ened for ease of repairs. Maybe Decker was aware of that fact. But he was betting the sergeant wasn't.

Not even a day old and the Diggs file already took up half a drawer's worth of space. Decker had sheets of paper with details that he'd probably have to re-view at least fifty times before the case was over. Listed first were names and statements of Whit-man's friends at the hotel. On superficial glance, the kids' accounts seemed to agree with Steve Ander-son's story. But that didn't mean much. Tomorrow, he'd go over all the statements line by line. If every-thing made sense, he'd progress to his analysis by constructing a "time and place table" for every major player in the show.

Decker rubbed his eyes. Eleven-thirty at night. Yet he wasn't quite ready to crash. Push, push, push. He flipped through the paperwork. More lists—the names and statements of the hotel personnel. The officers had done a decent job. There were the desk clerks, the bellhops, the maids, the workers at the hotel coffee shop, as well as the patrons unlucky enough to be rooming at the Grenada West End when the murder occurred. He'd leave those for tomorrow when his eyes were fresh and his brain had been recharged.

Finally, there was the preliminary autopsy report. Decker picked that up, scanned the findings.

Most probably, Cheryl had died of asphyxiation consistent with strangulation. Deep bruises encircled her neck, those on the left side of her neck slightly more pronounced than those on the right. Her vagina had been full of semen, but there was no indication of the typical bruising usually associated with rape. There was no indication of anal or oral intercourse. And yes, Cheryl had been pregnant, the fetal age about eight to ten weeks.

He read further, forcing his lids to remain open. Fluids extracted from the condoms found in the room as well as from Cheryl's vagina had been sent to the lab for analysis. At present, he couldn't find any lab work that compared the two samples. He made a note to ask Dr. Craine about it in the morning.

He skimmed through the rest of the pages. The pubic comb . . . blond hairs not associated with the victim found in pubic/genital region . . . black hairs not associated with the victim also found in the pubic/genital region.

Just as he had thought. It looked like Cheryl had been involved with two separate men. Whitman was blond and probably a natural one. Decker put him down as the owner of the blond hairs. All the other boys in the group had dark hair, so it was anyone's guess. At a glance, it looked like the party that Steve Anderson had described had gone beyond simple fooling around. It might indeed have been an orgy.

Call Craine in the morning. Decker paused. What the hell. Why should he be the only dedicated soul in this ordeal? Besides, the deputy ME was already sick. He ran down his Rolodex, found the number, and dialed. Jay wasn't happy to be awakened at midnight. But he was coherent.

"I thought you might call." Craine sneezed into the receiver. "However, I had hoped it might be earlier."

"Just got back from doing some interviews. I want to go over something with you."

"You're wondering about the two different types of pubic hairs, am I correct?"

"You are correct."

"Both samples went straightaway to the lab. The blond hairs are consistent with a blond male Anglo, the black hairs are consistent with a black male African American—"

Decker suddenly sat up. *"What?"*

"Yes, I was quite surprised by the results, in light of the population of your area. But it does appear as if our Cheryl had sex with a black man. Having said that, I can't tell you if the black pubic hair . . . excuse me."

Craine sneezed.

"I can't say if the black pubic hair matches the semen taken from the condom or from the vagina. For that, we'll need to run additional tests. And that will take time, Sergeant."

"Do it."

"Perhaps a DNA blueprint might be in order." A pause and a sniffle. "Yes, that might be just the trick."

"Sounds great, Jay."

"Also, let me posit this to you. To the naked eye, the vaginal sex appeared to be consensual, based on the lack of vaginal bruising and microscopic hemorrhages usually associated with physically forced rape. But despite that observation, sex still might have been nonconsensual. She could have been too drunk to resist. Did you notice her blood-alcohol level?"

Decker flipped to the fluids. BAL was 1.7. He whistled into the phone. "I wonder if she was even conscious."

"Anyone's guess. I did order her fluids through gas chromatography to bring up the regular battery of common recreational drugs. If she had mixed drugs with *that* level of alcohol, she might even have been close to death, perhaps even unconscious, before the murderer got his hands around her neck. Still, it is my belief that she was alive when she was strangled. Lung analysis is quite consistent with death by asphyxiation."

"Has anyone matched up the condom semen with the vaginal semen to see if it's from the same person?"

"Not yet. All the fluids are still . . . excuse me . . ."

"Bless you," Decker said.

A sneeze. "Thank you. All fluids are still under analysis at the lab."

Decker was quiet. "Are you sure the black hairs were from an Afro-American man?"

"Secure enough to state it in court."

Well, that sure threw a monkey wrench into the investigation. All of Cheryl's friends were white.

Decker said, "Can you tell which sexual activity came first—the condom sex or the unprotected sex?"

"Am I able to date the age of the semen? No. I can tell you that there were fewer live sperm in the condom semen. Which makes sense since the vagina is a protective environment. Sperm deposited inside would on the average probably live much longer. Especially because the particular condoms used in this case had also deployed a spermicide. Even if the condom user had been the first one to have sex with Cheryl, his sperm might still look older and deader than the sperm deposited inside her vagina."

"So there's no way to know."

"Not unless someone had a video camera inside the room."

Decker blew out air, wondering exactly how hinky the group might have been. Maybe someone took pictures, although he couldn't imagine any of them callous enough to sit by idly, watching Cheryl get trussed up and strangled to death.

"An African American," Decker said into the phone.

Craine said, "Yes, Sergeant, the pubic-hair pattern is consistent with those of black descent."

Decker's lids were dropping despite his iron will to stay awake. It was time to call it quits. "Thanks, Doc."

"Any other questions you might have, Sergeant, feel free to call me." The doctor paused. "In the *morning*. Shall we get some sleep?"

"Indeed," Decker said.

Sleep sounded like a dandy idea.

❧ 17

Arriving before sunrise, Decker had free access to the computer. He managed to enter all seventy-six names that had come up during his investigation of the Diggs case. The first list was arranged in alphabetical order. The second roster was fashioned in order of importance, Christopher Whitman at the top. Printouts in hand, he took the papers to his desk and proceeded to mark the race of each name known to him. Not surprisingly, all the knowns were white. But there were still fifty-odd unknowns—clerks, bellhops, restaurant personnel, and the other guests at the hotel.

He started making phone calls. By eight-thirty in the morning, he had identified three blacks out of thirty-five names. Five minutes passed and Lieutenant Davidson walked inside the squad room, taking an empty seat next to Decker. He was big and broad, his scalp freshly mowed into his favored crew cut. He placed his beefy hands on the table and leaned back in the chair, nearly breaking it with his weight.

"There's another crew outside from the networks, Pete. Get rid of them."

Decker continued marking his papers. "Sure you

173

don't want to field it, Loo?" He grinned. "I heard you did a bang-up job yesterday with the media."

Davidson snarled. "Go."

"Can I just finish what I'm doing?"

"What's that?"

Decker turned serious. "Jay Craine did a pubic comb on Diggs. Two different types of foreign hairs were found—one type was blond, corresponding to a white Anglo male—"

"Whitman," Davidson interrupted.

"No doubt," Decker agreed. "The other type corresponded to a black male. I've gone down the names and marked the black males on the list. As soon as I've got the entire list completed, I'll call up all the blacks and ask them for a sample. See if we can't come—"

"You're going to ask the black males on your list for a pubic hair sample?" Davidson interrupted.

"Yes," Decker said. "There are only three so far. It should be easy."

"And what if they don't comply?"

"Then that tells us something, doesn't it?"

"Maybe."

Decker paused. "What do you mean?"

"It may tell us that they have something to hide. Or it may tell us that they don't want to cooperate with the honky white-ass police in crackerville valley." Davidson faced him. "Are these blacks also friends of Cheryl Diggs?"

Decker regarded the names. "No. One was a bellhop, one was a guest, the last one was—"

"You can stop right there," Davidson said. "Since they're not friends of Diggs, you can't single them out *unless* you're planning to get a pubic sample of *every* male on your list. Otherwise, your investigation could be charged with racism."

Decker paused. *"What?"*

"You're asking for blacks, why not whites?"

Decker said, "If I can't get a match from the obvious white males—that is, Cheryl's friends—I will go through all the whites on the list. I'm doing the easiest first."

Davidson rubbed his nose and dropped his voice. "Pete, there are intervening factors here. You start accusing blacks in what looks like a white murder, you don't just have a homicide, you have a loaded situation."

He swiped a quick glance over his shoulder.

"And after *you-know-who*, last thing the city wants or needs is another loaded situation. Look, Diggs had an orgy in her hotel room with a bunch of white male friends—all of them out of control. So I'm just suggesting you concentrate on them as suspects first, starting with the mafioso boyfriend."

Decker stared at Davidson.

Davidson fidgeted. "Now, Whitman's coming in today at five, armed with his lawyers, right?"

"If he doesn't jump, yes."

"So make sure he doesn't jump. Put a tail on him." Davidson shook a finger. "Because I think Whitman's the guy. He's the boyfriend, he won't talk without lawyers, and let's face it, scum breeds scum." He sneered. "Donatti's kid. What the hell is he doing out here anyway?"

Decker shrugged.

Davidson said, "You concentrate on him and forget

about the black pubic hairs, which probably were lab error."

"Craine was positive—"

"Yeah, yeah, I've heard it all before. Labs never make mistakes, right?"

"Lieutenant, I don't think the black hairs were a result of lab error." Decker smoothed his mustache. "I can't disregard evidence."

Davidson's eyes were sheepish, but his tone was hostile. "Decker, I am not requesting you to disregard anything. But I am *ordering* you to prioritize. *Get* it?"

"Oh, I get it, sir."

Davidson ignored the sarcasm. "Did you pull a warrant for Whitman's apartment?"

Again Decker paused. He still couldn't get over Davidson. Tug was breaking a *cardinal* rule of Homicide investigation. The evidence should lead to the perpetrator, not the other way around. Finally he said, "I've asked for a warrant, yes. Both judges wanted me to specify what I'm looking for and why."

"And?"

"I told them I wanted to confiscate Whitman's tux for fiber analysis. See if it matches the bow tie found at the crime—the one that'd been used to bind Cheryl. Both benches said that since I haven't talked to Whitman yet, they didn't believe I had enough probable cause to justify a warrant at this time. They told me to try again after Whitman's interview."

"Assholes," Davidson yelled. "And in the meantime, Whitman could have destroyed the damn thing."

"He might have," Decker said. "Except, at this point, he doesn't know I'm looking for it."

"You haven't asked him about it?"

"I haven't questioned him at all since he immediately asked for his lawyers."

Davidson drew his hand over his near-shaven head. "I'll try to get us that warrant. Let's meet by . . . ten. Go over the way you're going to question the bastard."

"Fine," Decker said. "Also, Whitman offered to take a polygraph. I've set one up with Reuter."

"Now, that's good. Reuter's the best in the business." Davidson stood. "So we'll meet at ten."

Decker paused. "How about around noon?"

"Why?"

"You're wondering what Whitman's doing in LA and so am I. I'd like to look into it. The kid's a cipher—incomplete transcripts at his school, no real paper trail, no criminal record—"

"Now, that don't mean nothing. Donatti could have bought someone off."

"Possibly," Decker said. "I'm just saying that since I'm going to question Whitman, I'd like to know something about him. If that's not possible, maybe I can check up on Donatti's activities out here since Whitman arrived."

"Donatti sent him west to set something up." Davidson nodded. "I like it. Sure. Look into it. More you know about this scumbag's family, better off we are. See you at noon."

Decker waited a beat. "And what should I do about the evidence staring me in the face, Loo?"

Davidson gave Decker a long, hard look. "You've got a *lot* of evidence staring you in the face, Sergeant. Like I said before, there's nothing wrong with prioritizing!"

"For the record," Decker said, "I'm doing your priorities, not mine."

"And for the record, I'm your superior. So you're doing the right thing by doing it *my* way."

Decker looked straight into Davidson's hard eyes. "For the time being."

Davidson gave him a mock smile. "You want to feel self-righteous, Pete, go ahead. In the meantime, go get rid of the media. We'll deal with one cancer at a time."

After checking in with the Organized Crime Intelligence Division of the LAPD, Decker discovered that Donatti's activities on the West Coast had been kept to a minimum. Most of the talk had been centered around his involvement in the film and recording industries—two areas known for wealth and excesses, the nutrients that fed Donatti's voracious appetite. Beyond a few rumors in gossip columns and the occasional arrest of an underling, Donatti hadn't been much of a headliner. Either he had kept his business private or hadn't been deeply interested in the Big Orange.

Decker thought a moment.

It could have been that Whitman was sent out here to start something up for Donatti. But if that was true, Donatti's influence should have increased since Whitman's arrival. In fact, it had *decreased*.

So what *was* Whitman doing out here?

Decker checked his watch. Only ten-thirty. He was still doing okay on his time. He doodled as he thought.

Maybe the boy hadn't been sent here to do something. Could be the other way around, that Whitman did something bad back east, requiring Donatti to ship him out west. Going on that assumption, Decker needed to look into Donatti's and Whitman's activities *prior* to Whitman's arrival in LA.

So a trip to the library was in order.

By eleven, Decker was at the computer, using the Astrolab Database information system, asking it for old *New York Times* articles containing Donatti's name. It spit back twenty-seven pieces, the majority of them having to do with Donatti's murder trial around four years ago. He'd been accused of setting up a hit-and-run of a high-powered Grocers' Union leader who'd been talking about reforms. After Donatti's acquittal, there were several columns covering his subsequent return to private "business." Donatti's occupation had been listed as "local entrepreneur."

One of the articles showed a picture of Donatti's house in upstate New York, describing it as a Federal-style thirty-room brick manse that sat on ten manicured acres surrounded by thirty-five acres of forest. The house was reported to be filled with antique furniture and original works of art, his collection considered to be top-notch.

Decker sat back in his chair.

Forty-five acres and a top-notch art collection.

Where was the friggin justice here?

Don't even try to figure it out. All it will do is aggravate the hell out of you.

He moved on to Whitman. When he asked the Astrolab system for articles containing Whitman's name, it gave but one and from the society page of all things. It had nothing to do with any nefarious activities back east. But Decker suspected it might have much to do with nefarious activities out here. He asked for a printout of the entire article, then stuffed it into his briefcase.

❦18

School let out at two-thirty today, ostensibly to give us time to study for finals. But everyone knew the real reason. Nobody could concentrate on anything except the news. Rumors circulated and everyone had a different opinion. As for me, I spoke little and revealed nothing. When the dismissal bell rang, I gathered my books and left the campus without joining the fracas of the spin doctors.

Melissa was at a friend's house so I went straight home. The place was eerily quiet. Maybe it was in contrast to the buzz of the school. My ears were ringing, my head was throbbing. I scooped up a handful of textbooks from my backpack and went up to my room.

Chris was on my bed.

Immediately, I retreated, taking several giant steps backward until I banged into the corner of my desk, dropping several of the textbooks I'd been clutching. They fell with a crash on my hardwood floor, one bouncing off my toe. I felt pain but didn't react. Because I couldn't move.

"You've got a good deadbolt on your back door,"

he said. "Actually took me some work. I just picked it, I didn't break it."

I was silent.

Slowly he stood up, appearing massive to my eye. He looked around the area, never having been up in my bedroom before. It was tiny—a shelving unit with a built-in desk, a bed, a nightstand, and no space for anything else. I'd tried to spiff it up with home-made lace curtains and lots of fresh potpourri. Right now the sweet smell was making me sick.

He studied my books as he spoke, his voice calm and low. "Where's Melissa?"

I thought about lying, but what purpose would it have served? It took me awhile to find my voice.

"She's . . ." I realized I was still hugging my lone math textbook. I clung to it like a life preserver. "We're alone."

He looked at me, his eyes unreadable. Then he reached in his pocket, pulled out something thick and folded.

"Your tutoring money," he said. "I closed the account this morning. It was something like eight hundred and eighty-six dollars and change. I made it an even thou." He proffered me the wad of bills.

I remained rooted to my spot.

He kept his arm extended for a moment, then threw the money on my bed. "Here are also some letters from your grandparents." Three envelopes were dropped on top of the money. "I've had them for a while. Sorry about that."

He slipped his hands into his pants pocket. His eyes never left mine.

"You're spooked, aren't you?"

I shook my head no, but my stance told him differently.

He continued to study me. "Yeah, you are. I know it's natural . . . but it hurts." He shut my door, then said, "Go ahead and ask me, Terry."

I said nothing.

He bit his lower lip. "It's what you want to know. It's what everybody wants to know. So I'll give you an exclusive."

I opened my mouth but nothing came out.

"What?" He took a step toward me and immediately I backed away. But my desk served as an immobile barrier. Pressed against the hard wood, there was no more room to retreat. He moved close to me. I could hear his breathing, could see the beads of sweat on his forehead.

"You want to know if I did it? Just *ask* me, Terry."

I stumbled over my words, then finally got out a sentence. "I waited and . . . waited for you to call me. Why didn't you?"

His face registered surprise. It wasn't the question he had expected. He inched backward until he hit my wall. Spine pressed against the plaster, he slowly slid to the floor, dropping his head between his knees, his hands cradling his temples. He sat rocking himself for a long time. Finally, he ran his hand over his face and looked up at my ceiling.

"Because Cheryl told me she was pregnant."

He waited for me to react. I had already heard rumors, but there was nothing like words from the source. I thought I was too numb to feel pain. But I was wrong.

He spoke haltingly. "Rationally . . . I knew it wasn't

mine. I always used protection. But when you hear the word *pregnant* . . . you don't think rationally. An adrenaline rush just takes over." He looked at me. "I couldn't leave and ride off to Neverland with you until I found out her story."

He rubbed his neck.

"Cheryl knew it was over between us a long time ago, but she chose to play charades because she liked me. Prom night, when I told her we were a done deal, she got *real* upset. So she said the one thing she knew would get my attention."

He scratched his head.

"And it got my attention. I kept trying to get her alone. But she kept dragging me to parties afterward. After all, she was the prom queen." He let out a bitter laugh. "Papers have her framed like she was the celestial virgin. You know how she got the title, don't you?"

There had been talk about Cheryl and Mr. Gobles, the English Lit teacher. Mr. Gobles had headed the committee that selected the prom's queen and her court.

"Anyway, Ms. Virgin Queen had been doping like crazy," Chris continued. "Flying in the stratosphere. Anything to drown me out. Because she really didn't want to talk about it. I decided to just wait her out. I was going to call you, but I didn't know what to say. I figured the best thing to do was to get Cheryl squared away first and deal with you later.

"We eventually reached the hotel . . . and I thought, 'Great. I finally got her *alone.*' Wrong! Suddenly Bull and Trish popped in with a bunch of porno flicks.

Then came the rest of the gang. Suddenly, everyone was raging all over again. By then we were all strung out. You know how the parties can be."

He rubbed his neck again.

"I'd been drinking all night just to pass the time. So by then I was pretty buzzed. I should have just walked away. Should have walked away a long time ago."

He bit his lip.

"It's not that I minded Cheryl. I just didn't have any . . . *use* for her anymore. See, when you blew me off, Terry, I blew her off. Basically, I stopped sleeping with her. Cheryl was my weapon against you. And when she couldn't make you jealous, I didn't want her anymore."

I said, "What do you mean you *basically* stopped sleeping with her?"

"It's gonna come out anyway." He blew out air. "Terry, I slept with Cheryl . . . that night. Actually, I did it twice."

I stared at him, feeling something between disgust and horror. "After what you *said* to me, after what we said to *each other* . . . you had *sex* with her?" I felt my eyes get wet. "You're a much better liar than I gave you credit for."

"I'm a pathological liar, but I wasn't lying that night. I meant everything I said—"

"God, *stop* insulting my intelligence!"

He looked up and caught my rage. Something eerie set into his eyes. I suddenly became frightened and tried to curl inward. His voice became soft and soothing.

"I know you're scared of me, Terry. Like I said

before, it's natural. But please don't be. You can tell me anything. I would never hurt you. Okay?"

I didn't answer.

"You want to know why I slept with Cheryl?" Chris spoke softly. "I did it because I'm self-serving and spineless. Whatever feels good, that's my motto." He bit his nail. "I don't have any character. Never interested me to develop any. Cheryl wanted me. I was aroused . . . so why not?"

I looked at the Brontë novels resting in my bookshelf. "You certainly never had any trouble controlling yourself with me. Or was I the Madonna and poor Cheryl the whore? Lord, spare me from Catholic boys."

"You know, first time I ever laid eyes on you in orchestra, I had it in mind to seduce you." He looked at me. "There was never any school of music back east. Whole tutoring thing was a ruse. A way to get near you so I could make my move."

"Your *move*?"

"To get you on your back, Terry. I was supposed to *nail* you . . . chalk up another point for the stud." He looked at the ceiling. "Instead, I fell in love with you. Yes, even pathological liars have feelings. Believe it or not, I was trying to behave myself 'cause I didn't want to *hurt* you. I knew I had to go back to Lorraine . . . but I thought at least we could ride out the year together as close friends or something or other. When you blew me off, I was destroyed."

"I didn't blow you off."

"Of course you blew me off. Man, I was a *basket case* that weekend. Must have dialed your number like a hundred times. But I always chickened out. Then I don't know . . . I suddenly got real pissed off. Putting me through all this shit when I loved you so much. I wanted to make you pay." He paused. "For what it's worth—and that's not too much—I really am sorry." He checked his watch. "I'm late."

"For what?"

"I'm supposed to meet with my lawyers at three-thirty . . . go over things. I'm supposed to see the fuzz at five. They set up a polygraph for me. That should be interesting."

"Are you nervous?"

He looked at me. "Of course I'm nervous."

Softly, I said, "Are you going to pass it, Chris?"

"That's a nice way of asking me *the* question." He closed and opened his eyes. "The crucial stuff I'll pass. But if they ask me . . . related stuff, I may not do so well."

I waited.

He said, "If they ask me if I ever killed anyone, I may not do so hot on that."

We locked eyes. With sudden insight, I realized what he was talking about.

Only upshot of the whole mess was I hated the son of a bitch. So after the shock wore off, I was kind of happy.

"You killed your . . ." I covered my mouth, recoiling from the horror.

Chris nodded. "Yes, I killed my father."

It all made sense. Why he was so indebted to his uncle. I said, "Donatti set it up like a professional hit, didn't he? He took the blame for you."

"He was willing to take the fall, but luckily it never came to that. Technically, it's still an open file on the books—unsolved. But there isn't any statute of limitations on homicide."

"You were a kid," I told him. "He was abusing you. It was self-defense."

"Except it really wasn't self-defense. He'd been chasing me with a knife, but he'd given up. Got himself smashed and passed out dead drunk on the couch."

There was a long pause.

"Whole thing was . . . surreal," Chris said. "I got out of the closet, sneaked away real quiet so not to wake him up. I meant to just . . . walk away . . . like all the other times before. Instead . . . I began to feel real . . . real . . . *weird*. Next thing I knew I was holding a gun . . . not sure how it even got into my hands. My dad was . . . handcuffed. Don't know how that happened either. I took the gun . . . placed it between his eyes."

He cleared his throat.

"There was this flash . . . then a loud pop . . ." He looked up. "I must have fainted. When I came to, I got my bike and fetched Uncle Joey. My dad used to do some odd jobs for my uncle. Joey thought he was a jerk, but he had a thing for my mom, so he kept him on. He won't admit it, but I did him a favor when I whacked my father. Saved him the trouble of doing it. Because Joey never messed with married women. It was a point of honor with him."

He checked his watch again.

"You'd better go," I said.

"I'm fucked up already. Another ten minutes won't make a difference." He looked at me. "He was a real horrible man, Terry. He . . . did things to me."

I nodded, but he shook his head no. "You don't know. How could you?" He paused. "You ever been with a guy, Terry? I know you didn't do much with Bull . . . much to his chagrin. But maybe you and Reiss . . ."

I didn't answer him.

Chris said, "I'm just trying to find out if you know your way around the male anatomy."

He was leading me somewhere. I said, "I know the sensitive parts."

He tapped the floor next to him, asking me to sit.

Up until then, I hadn't realized I was still backed up against my desk, clutching my book. I had been a coiled wire for over half an hour. Suddenly, I gave myself permission to relax. Uncurling my shoulders . . . unclenching my jaw. It felt good. I went and sat beside him. My fear had vanished, but not my apprehension.

Quickly, he undid his zipper and pulled his jeans and Jockey shorts down to his shoes. He was wearing a long T-shirt that hid most of his nakedness, but not all of it. I looked away.

"Give me your hand," he said.

I complied.

He placed my hand under the warm folds of his scrotum. I could feel skin tighten under my touch . . . see him growing hard. He noticed how nervous I was.

"Just a reaction 'cause you're touching me. I'm not going to do anything." He gently wrapped my fingers around one of his enormous testicles and spoke softly. "This one's legit." He brought my hand around his second testicle and forced my fingers to give it a hard squeeze. I tried to pull away but he wouldn't let me. "Obviously, this one's a prosthesis."

He curled my finger around the shaft of his erection.

"I have a rep for having the biggest balls in the school." His voice was deep and melodic. "It's probably true. First off, I'm a big guy and lucky enough to be proportional. But because I have only one testicle, when I reached puberty it grew twice the size of normal to make up for my loss."

"Hypertrophy," I said.

"Exactly," Chris whispered. "It hypertrophied. I've had two operations to replace the prosthesis . . . to even things out. I've finally settled down. But for a while, I was pretty lopsided."

"You weren't born that way, were you?"

"No." His eyes met mine. "My dad injured me in one of his drunken rages. Held me down and repeatedly kicked me between my legs. I had a massive hemorrhage."

I flinched, tried to bring my hand to my throat. But he kept my fingers around his erection. I hadn't realized it—his hypnotic voice had kept me spellbound—but we'd been stroking him together. I moved my eyes downward. He was fully extended. Quickly I averted my eyes.

"They surgically removed the worst one and used it to repair the better one. I don't know if my dad meant to hurt me like he did. He claimed he was just trying to teach me a lesson. And he was all apologetic afterward. But that didn't stop him from getting drunk a week later and coming at my mom with a butcher knife. Nice, huh?"

He let go of my hand, pulled up his pants, and

zipped himself up. Without thinking, I reached out to him. He blinked, then melted in my arms, my breasts a pillow for his head, his arms hugging me tightly. He lowered his head to my lap and looked at me with soft eyes. I stroked his hair, wondering who this boy really was.

"No one knows. Not my uncle, not Lorraine, not anyone. My mom knew about it, of course. So did my aunt Donna—Joey's wife. Now it's just you."

"I hope there's no connection," I said. "Your mom and your aunt are both dead."

His laughter was genuine. I said, "You have a doctor?"

"Of course. Yeah, he knows about it, too. Which is another reason why I knew that Cheryl's baby couldn't have been mine. Every time I go in for a checkup, they take a sperm count. I'm not totally sterile, but it's pretty damn low. I don't know if I'll ever be able to sire kids. That's all right. I'd make a lousy father."

"Did you use condoms with Cheryl that night?" I asked.

"Yeah. Not that Cheryl had a *no glove, no love* rule. She played it loose. It was me. I didn't trust her."

"Did you leave the condoms at the hotel?"

"Unfortunately, yes. I didn't expect Cheryl to die."

"So the police have evidence against you."

"I wouldn't call it evidence *against* me. Yes, I fu . . . I had sex with her. So what? They still have to develop a case against me. They don't have a motive."

"Cheryl's pregnancy."

He kissed my crotch over my jeans. "It wasn't mine—"

"Chris—"

"I know, I know. It looks bad."

"You have to see your lawyers. You're in trouble."

"Yes, I am." Again, he kissed denim between my legs. "I have to go. But I don't want to go. Because once I leave here, I'm never going to see you again."

"I don't know about that."

He sat up. "Teresa, I'm going down for this. No matter what the truth is, they'll find a way to screw me. Because of my uncle. And when I go down, I don't want your name associated with me, do you understand?"

"Chris—"

"*Listen* to me, Terry. *Listen* to me because I know what I'm talking about. It's unlikely that the police'll link me and you. We haven't been together in months."

He took my face and kissed me hard on the mouth.

"But if they do . . . talk to you . . . you were my tutor, I was your student. Nothing more. I told you in earnest that I never wanted you grunged by any of my dirt. I mean that now more than ever. Don't call me. Don't come to my place. Don't write. Don't try to contact me. Don't do anything on my behalf. Just forget I ever existed!"

"I don't know if I can accept that," I said.

"You've got to accept it, angel, because you're *dead* to me! It's got to be that way!"

Chris ravaged my mouth, then let go of my face.

"You start . . . trying to defend me . . . defend a *Donatti* . . . if you do that, the authorities'll turn on you like rabid dogs and drag you over concrete with razor-sharp teeth. All your hard work, Terry . . . all your *dreams*'ll be flushed down the crapper just because you had the bad luck to be loved by a bad boy. That's the *last* thing I want. I'd rather do time than have them ruin you."

"How would they *ruin* me?"

"Believe me, Terry, they have *ways*!"

❧ 19

The elevated view room was separated from the larger interview room by a darkened one-way mirror. As Decker made final adjustments on the tape recorder and video camera, Scott Oliver stepped inside, closed the door, and took a seat at the table.

"The secretary from the McCaffrey *et al.* law firm called. They're going to be late."

Decker stopped fiddling with the controls of the camera and looked at his watch. Fifteen past five. "They're already late. Is Whitman with them?"

"She says Whitman's with them. The car just got stuck in rush-hour traffic." Oliver took out a comb and ran it through thick, wavy hair. "Hope she's telling the truth. Because if she's jiving me and the kid bolted, I'll bring her down along with the shysters who're supposed to be the kid's keepers."

Decker smoothed his mustache. "It's a well-established firm. They'd know better than to cover for Whitman."

"Joseph Donatti's a very big guy."

The room fell silent. A moment later, Davidson and Elaine Reuter, the polygraph administrator, came in. Elaine was tall and slender with an attractive but somewhat equine face. She sat down at the table, but Davidson leaned against the wall, peering into the empty interview room. Suddenly the area felt cramped. Decker broke into a sweat.

"Where the hell are Whitman and his legal eagles?" Davidson asked.

"Stuck in traffic," Oliver said.

The lieutenant looked at his watch. "It's twenty after. I don't like it. We'll go another ten minutes. Then we execute the warrant."

Oliver said, "The secretary swears they're on their way."

"With Whitman."

"With Whitman."

"They're hotshot lawyers," Davidson said. "Their car must have a cellular phone."

Oliver said, "I'll get them on the horn."

Decker said, "Might as well plan some strategy as long as we're all here."

Davidson looked at Oliver. "What's he doing here?"

"He interviewed some of Whitman's friends for me," Decker said. "When I interview the kid, I want him around to make sure I don't misquote his notes."

"You want to do the polygraph before or after you question the kid?" Elaine asked.

"Before," Decker said. "Get his initial reaction to the key questions on paper."

"I got the cellular number." Oliver started dialing. "Hope this sucker connects through."

"Some people like to do the polygraph first," Elaine said. "Other dees I've spoken with think it ruins the element of surprise during the interview."

"I'm not pulling rabbits out of my hat," Decker said. "I'm just using it as a gauge."

Elaine said, "Since it's inadmissible in court, it's not good for much else. Too bad. In the hands of an experienced operator—like *moi*—you've got a real useful tool."

"Unless you've got a psycho," Oliver piped in, phone tucked under his chin. "Damn, another *busy* signal!"

"Do you have any problems with the questions I gave you?" Decker asked Elaine.

"No, they're fine."

Davidson said, "Lemme see the list."

Elaine handed him a copy.

"How come you only got forty questions?"

"That's all the firm's allowing us," Decker said.

"Including the basics," Elaine said.

Davidson skimmed the questions. "So why are you asking Whitman about previous arrests? Isn't his sheet clean?"

"According to the files, yes," Decker said. "According to *me*, he's been on the wrong side of the law before."

"His lawyer'll object to the questions. Write something else."

"We're testing Whitman's reactions, Loo," Decker said. "Even if the kid doesn't answer the question, we'll still get a reading on the graph when he *hears* it. Let the lawyers object."

Oliver mimicked, "The cellular customer you are trying to reach is currently away from the mobile phone. . . ." He slammed down the receiver. "I don't like this."

Davidson regarded the room clock. "Another minute."

The phone rang. Decker picked it up, told the operator thank you. "They're here."

Everyone breathed a collective sigh of relief. The place fell silent. A moment later, uniformed officer Latimer escorted three figures into the interview room below.

Elaine's eyes widened. "Who's the big blond in the black silk blazer?"

"Christopher Whitman," Decker said.

"He's only eighteen?" Davidson said.

"According to his records," Decker answered.

"I don't believe it," Elaine said.

"He looks older," Davidson answered. "In his twenties."

"Up close, he looks younger," Decker said. "It's his expression."

"Yep," Oliver agreed. "It says: *Done it all, seen it all.*"

"A genuine stud muffin," Elaine answered. "He looks too good to be straight."

Decker raised his brow. "Maybe he isn't."

"Homosexual panic," Davidson nodded. "He couldn't get it up. She teased him. He got pissed. No more teasing. I like that."

Oliver said, "Weren't there two used condoms in the room?"

"Not to mention the semen inside the victim," Decker said.

Davidson said, "Who said the fluids belong to Whitman?"

Oliver asked, "Do they?"

"We haven't asked Whitman for a sample yet,"

Decker said. "Until now, I haven't been able to approach him."

"He likes classical music, doesn't he?" Davidson said.

"He's a classical cellist," Oliver said.

"Loo, lots of people like classical music," Decker said.

"Not eighteen-year-old red-blooded males," Davidson pronounced. "They like that heavy metal shit. Gets the hormones pumping. I'm telling you he's queer."

Elaine frowned. "Another one bites the dust."

Davidson said, "Elaine, ask him if he's ever had a homosexual encounter."

"You're over forty questions."

"Throw it in anyway. And if you can get away with it, ask him if he's homosexual or bisexual."

"Got it," Elaine answered. "Who's the silver fox in the gray Armani suit?"

Decker studied the figure below—six one, one-eighty, medium build, alert blue eyes, round clean-shaven ruddy face, his cheeks imprinted with webs of small veins.

"James Moody," he said. The guy must be close to sixty by now."

"He looks good for his age," Elaine said.

Decker's eye drifted to the younger lawyer. Double-breasted Hugo Boss suit, white shirt, red silk tie. Five ten, one-ninety. Strong features, slicked-back black hair with dark eyes and thick brows. "The other one is Mark Kramarze. He likes young girls."

Oliver said, "How young?"

"Pubescent but barely so."

"What were your dealings with him?" Davidson asked.

"One of my old Foothill juvey cases involved a thirteen-year-old runaway who'd been roughed up."

"Kramarze?" Oliver asked.

"Not officially," Decker said. "She dropped the charges."

Davidson said, "How much he pay her?"

"Probably five grand. That was the going rate."

Oliver said, "Chrissie has himself surrounded by some fine citizens."

"Kramarze is along as the secretary," Decker said. "Moody's the head honcho and he is *good*."

"Turn up the mike," Davidson said. "I can't hear what they're saying." Oliver cranked up the volume.

Moody said, "Comfortable, Chris?"

Whitman nodded.

"Do you want some water?" Moody didn't wait for an answer. "Officer, may we please have a pitcher and three glasses of water?"

Latimer nodded and left the room to fetch.

"How long do you think this will take?" Kramarze asked.

"Pitch a tent, Mark," Moody said. "You're going to miss the ball game. Take out the recorder and start setting up." He looked at the one-way mirror. "Can we get going please?"

Decker spoke into the mike. "We were ready a half hour ago, Mr. Moody."

"It heartens me to see LA's finest so prompt." Moody took a leather folder from his briefcase and a gold pen. "Glad to see my tax dollars at work."

Elaine turned to Decker. "Want me to set up now?"

"Please." Decker studied the men through the one-way mirror, watched Whitman's reaction when Elaine came in pushing a cart that held not only the polygraph machine but also a printer, a ream of computer graph paper, *and* a half-dozen dangling electrodes.

Whitman's eyes fell on the cart, but Decker saw that he stared through the equipment, his expression flat and vacant. Something about him was different. He didn't appear scared or nervous or even apprehensive. But he wasn't the cocky teen Decker had interviewed yesterday.

Decker studied the kid's face.

Whitman seemed *deflated*. Something—or someone—had knocked the wind from his sails.

Elaine began hooking the electrodes up to her stud muffin, separating arm hair, exposing tiny patches of Whitman's skin to get optimal conduction between body and machine.

The boy didn't flinch.

And that said a lot. Because Decker knew that electrodes on the skin *always* conjured up images of the electric chair.

To Elaine Moody said, "May I see the list of preprinted questions?"

"That isn't normal procedure," Elaine said evenly. "Besides, you couldn't read my handwriting. However, you can guide your client any way you see fit."

"Thank you for your permission."

"No need for the sarcasm, Jimmy," Decker said.

"Moody's uptight," Davidson said.

"He's trying to intimidate Elaine," Decker said. "She's too much the pro to buy into that."

Davidson said, "The kid looks guilty to me."

"He isn't acting nervous," Oliver said.

Davidson continued to peer through the mirror. "Well, he looks something."

"Not more than forty questions," Moody said to Elaine. "I'm keeping track. We've agreed to cooperate with authorities, but not at the expense of my client's health."

"I'll say," Oliver said. "Whitman looks *tired*. That's not good. Fatigue deadens the emotions. Look at how passive he is with Elaine. She's plugging him in and he's just sitting there like road kill. You don't have any anxiety, you're gonna pass the test."

"He's got anxiety," Davidson said. "Look at his eyes."

"His eyes look dead to me," Oliver said. "I'm telling you, there's no one home over there."

Elaine spoke with a seasoned air. "I'm going to do some preliminary tests on you, Mr. Whitman. Just to make sure the machine is working properly. Is that all right with you?"

Chris paused a beat, then said yes.

"Uh-oh," Oliver said. "I don't like that, either. The pause before he answered. Someone coached him on how to use the machine—to wait before answering, even if the question is routine."

"Of course someone *coached* him," Decker said. "He's being represented by the best."

"The best the mob can buy," Davidson said.

Elaine said to Moody, "These are just test questions. They don't count in the list of forty questions."

"In your mind, they don't," Moody said. "In my mind, they do."

Whitman crooked a finger at Moody. The lawyer bent over and Chris whispered in his attorney's ear.

Moody straightened up and said, "We'll let it pass."

Officer Latimer came back in with the water and three glasses. Moody said, "Would you like something to drink, Chris?"

Whitman shook his head no.

Elaine started with her test questions, Whitman answered them mechanically, his voice a soft monotone.

"He's good," Davidson said.

Decker nodded. "Yes, he is."

Elaine asked for the go-ahead. Davidson gave her the green light.

"Is your name Christopher Sean Whitman?"

"Yes."

"Are you eighteen years old?"

"Yes."

"Were you born in New York City on July first?"

"Yes."

"And were you adopted at the age of thirteen by Joseph and Donna Angelica Donatti?"

"Yes."

"Is Mr. Donatti still your legal father?"

"Yes."

"Is Mr. Donatti currently supporting you?"

Moody broke in. "Ms. Reuter, what financial arrangements father and son make bears no relevance to you or your case. Next question."

"Number-one goal of the shysters," Oliver whispered. "Get Donatti *out* of the picture."

"You got it," Decker said.

"Mr. Whitman, do you attend Central West Valley High School?"

"Yes."

"Are you a senior at Central West Valley High School?"

"Yes."

"Did you attend the senior prom at Central West Valley High School?"

"Yes."

"Have you ever been arrested before?"

Again Moody interrupted. "The police know very well that Mr. Whitman has a clean record. It was stated at his bail hearing."

Davidson looked at Decker. "Told you."

Decker shrugged.

Moody said, "What number question, Mark?"

"Ten."

"Proceed."

Elaine said, "Did you attend the senior prom at Central West Valley High School with a date?"

"Yes."

"Was your date Cheryl Diggs?"

"Yes."

"And was Cheryl Diggs your girlfriend?"

"No."

"What?" Davidson growled. "Of course she was his girlfriend! Fucking liar."

Elaine said, "Have you ever had sex with Cheryl Diggs?"

"Yes."

"Have you ever had a homosexual encounter?"

"No."

"On the night of the prom, were you aware of the fact that Cheryl Diggs was pregnant?"

Whitman paused. "I can't answer that yes or no."

"Next question," Moody said.

Oliver said, "Why can't he answer *that* yes or no?"

Decker said, "I don't know. Elaine knows what I want. She'll get it out of him."

Elaine said, "Mr. Whitman, on the night of the prom, did you suspect that Cheryl Diggs might be pregnant?"

"No."

Elaine paused. "Mr. Whitman, on the night of the prom, did Cheryl Diggs tell *you she was pregnant?"*

"Yes," *Whitman answered.*

"Good going, Elaine," Decker whispered.

"Did Cheryl Diggs tell you that you were the father of the baby she was carrying?"

"Yes."

"Did you believe her when she told you that the baby was yours?"

"No."

"Did you believe her when she told you she was pregnant?"

Whitman held up his hands and shrugged. "Can't answer that yes or no."

"Next," Moody said. "Where are we, Mark?"

"We're up to twenty-one questions," Kramarze answered.

Elaine said, "Mr. Whitman, do you believe that you fathered Cheryl Diggs's conception?"

"No."

"Mr. Whitman, after the senior prom, did you and Cheryl attend parties?"

"Yes."

"Did you have sex with Cheryl Diggs at any of those aforementioned parties?"

"No."

"*Were you alone with Cheryl Diggs at the Grenada West End Hotel in room three-fourteen the night of the prom or in the early morning afterward?*"

"*Yes.*"

"*And did you have sex with Cheryl Diggs in room three-fourteen at the Granada West End Hotel the night of the prom or in the early morning afterward?*"

"*Yes.*"

"*Did you have sex twice with Cheryl Diggs in the afore-mentioned hotel the night of the prom or in the early morning afterward?*"

"*Yes.*"

"Ah, the energy of youth," Oliver said wistfully.

"*Did you have sex three times with Cheryl Diggs in the aforementioned hotel the night of the prom or in the early morning afterward?*"

"*No.*"

"*Did you witness or hear of Cheryl Diggs having sex with any other man the night of the prom or in the early morning afterward?*"

"*Did I?*"

"*Yes, sir.*"

"*I didn't hear or see anything. But that doesn't mean she didn't.*"

"*A yes or no answer, Mr. Whitman.*"

"Skip over the question," Moody said. "It's improperly stated."

Elaine moved on. "*At the Grenada West End Hotel, on the night of the prom or in the early morning afterward, did you in any way bind, tie, or help secure Cheryl Diggs's hands to the headboard using ropes, articles of clothing, or anything else as constraints.*"

"No."

"Have you ever tied up Cheryl Diggs as part of your sexual interplay with her?"

"No."

"Have you ever tied up any person as part of your sexual interplay with that person?"

"No."

"Have you ever tied up anyone, for any reason, in the last ten years?"

"No."

"Are you a homosexual?"

"No."

"Have you ever murdered anyone?"

Moody said, "Ms. Reuter, for the second time, Mr. Whitman has a clean record for all the world to see. Your question is not only biased and prejudicial but insulting and irrelevant. If you can't keep your questions more germane to Miss Diggs's unfortunate case, we can stop now."

Elaine said, "Mr. Whitman, were you drinking the night of the prom or in the early morning afterward?"

"Yes."

"Have you ever had blackouts from your drinking?"

"Don't answer that, Chris," Moody said.

"Why'd he object?" Davidson asked Decker.

"Blackouts could be for the prosecution or for the defense. Moody doesn't know how he wants to use it, so he doesn't want to deal with it."

"Where are we, Mark?" Moody asked.

"Thirty-six."

"Four more, Ms. Reuter."

Elaine said, "Mr. Whitman, were you drunk the night of the prom?"

Moody said, "In the absence of any clinical analysis, the

question postulates a subjective state of mind which my client is neither prepared nor skilled to give. Proceed to the next question."

"Have you ever taken drugs?"

"Ms. Reuter, for the last time, Mr. Whitman's record is clean," Moody said. "I am sorely losing my patience."

"Mr. Whitman, did you murder Cheryl Diggs the night of your senior prom or in the early morning afterward?"

"No."

"Did you, in any way, do harm to Cheryl Diggs so as to cause her death the night of your senior prom or in the early morning afterward?"

"No."

"That's forty," Kramarze stated.

Elaine said quickly, "Mr. Whitman, did you in any way, wittingly or unwittingly, do harm to Cheryl Diggs so as to cause her death the night of your senior prom or in the early morning afterward?"

Moody broke in. "Again, you are asking Mr. Whitman to evaluate something subjective. How does he know what he might have done unwittingly?"

Kramarze said, "And we're up to forty-one, Mr. Moody."

"We are done," Moody stated.

Elaine said, "Mr. Whitman, have you been completely truthful in answering these questions?"

"Yes."

Elaine smiled at Moody. "Now we're done."

ᕈ 20

"He passed."

"What?" Decker said. "All of it?"

"Yep."

"You're *kidding*!"

" 'Fraid not."

Davidson grabbed the test results from Elaine Reuter's hand. "These tests are *garbage*! No wonder they're not admissible as evidence."

"I told you he was going to pass," Oliver said, combing his hair. "He's wiped out. He doesn't give a shit. No anxiety, no fluctuation in the galvanic skin response."

Elaine said, "There's some truth to that."

"Or he's a psycho," Davidson said.

"There's truth to that, too," Elaine said. "A pathological liar could probably beat it."

Decker took the test results from Davidson. "Were any of his answers inconclusive?"

"Some variation when I asked about an arrest record—"

Decker cleared his throat.

Davidson glared at him. "You got a problem with mucus, Decker?"

"No," Decker said. "I got a problem with Whitman's clean sheet. I *know* he's been caged before."

"Call New York," Oliver said. "Kid's not *that* old. Even if his records as a juvey have been sealed, someone's bound to remember a crime committed by Joseph Donatti's son."

"Anything else show up funny, Elaine?" Decker asked.

"He also had a little wiggle when I asked him about tying girls up. Betcha he's had some bondage fantasies. But nothing jumped out beyond the norm."

Davidson swore. "This is really going to put us in a one-down position when we interview him. Once the little shit knows the results, he's gonna be an impossible nut to crack."

Elaine said, "Delay it. Tell them I went for dinner, will have the results back in an hour or so."

"They'll see through it," Oliver said.

"Probably," Decker said. "But it won't hurt to increase Whitman's anxiety. Like Scott said, the kid could use a dose of nervousness."

"Goddamn mother F!" Davidson said. "How'd he pass it?"

Decker shrugged. "Maybe he didn't do anything."

Davidson glared at Decker. "He did it. You know it and I know it."

"Let's backtrack for a minute," Decker said. "Whitman admitted screwing Cheryl twice. I think that explains the two used condoms we found in the hotel room. But she also had lots of semen *inside* of her." He paused. "There's another guy unaccounted for, Lieutenant."

Oliver said, "Some of Whitman's friends told me

they'd been raging before they reached the hotel. Cheryl had been seen with a lot of guys."

Decker said, "So she had plenty of opportunity for sex before Whitman got to her at the hotel."

Elaine said, "But Whitman was with her at the parties."

Decker said, "I'm sure he wasn't with her every single moment. We're talking about teenage boys." He smiled. "I mean, how long does it take?"

"That's what pushed him over the edge," Davidson said.

"Come again?" Elaine said.

"Simple," Davidson said. "He slipped it in, realized she'd already put out for someone else. He went psycho."

Elaine said, "Except he didn't consider Cheryl his girlfriend."

"That's according to *him*," Davidson said. "According to everyone else, they were tight. Stick to polygraphs, Reuter."

Decker said, "Lieutenant, if she had had sex with another man prior to Whitman . . . and Whitman was the one who used condoms . . . there'd have been semen found on the *outside* of the skins."

Oliver nodded. "Was any found?"

"I'll check." Decker's eyes went to Davidson's. "Matter of fact, I think the best thing to do is go back to basics and check out everything about this case . . . *all* the different leads."

Davidson's eyes grew hot. "Right now, Decker, the best thing to do is lean on Whitman. You go in and interview the hell out of that kid. Grill him hard and don't let up. I know psychos and killers, and he's a psycho and a killer."

"But a tired one with no anxiety," Oliver said.

Davidson said, "That's exactly when you want to attack, Oliver. When the defenses are down and the mind's confused. By him coming in tired, he's done half our work for us."

"Loo," Oliver said, "I know wisdom states that you want to wear your suspects down . . . they become vulnerable when they're tired. But that's not *this* guy. Let him go home and sleep. Give him a chance to build up his arrogance. He's a surefooted son of a bitch. If anything trips him up, it will be his cockiness."

"Oliver, you're a good homicide cop," Davidson said. "But you're wrong." He turned to Decker. "You're going to do this right?"

"Only way I know how to work," Decker said.

"Good," Davidson said. "Now I got a couple of phone calls to make. You go get that little psycho."

Davidson left the room, slamming the door behind him. Decker turned to Oliver. "For what it's worth, I think you're right."

"I do, too," Elaine said. "Whitman wasn't my typical subject. Nothing riled him. *Way* too passive."

"Fatigue." Oliver shook his head. "Not that I personally think Whitman's innocent. I think he's guilty."

"Why?" Elaine said.

"Picture I got of him from talking to his friends," Oliver said. "A cold mother."

"He's a spooky kid," Decker said.

Elaine sighed. "The good ones are always gay or weird."

Oliver smiled. "I'd like to see him nailed. I'm just saying, if you go after someone, do it in the best way possible."

"I'll work around it," Decker said. "Got a few aces up my sleeve . . . thanks for the support, Scott."

Oliver shook his head. "I just don't understand Davidson's attitude. You don't crucify without evidence. The loo's got a real hair up his ass with this one."

Several, Decker thought. And they're all African American.

Decker walked into the interview room, taking a seat opposite Whitman. He pulled out a cigarette pack and slid it across the table. Whitman eyed the cellophane carton, then pulled out a smoke and placed it between his lips. Decker lit his cigarette.

Whitman nodded a thank you, eyes on Decker.

Decker said, "Congratulations."

Moody smiled. "He passed."

"Passed?" Decker focused on Whitman. "Oh, you mean the polygraph. Ms. Reuter took a dinner break. We'll know the results in about an hour."

Moody sat back in his chair. "Christopher, that means you passed and he doesn't want us to know about it." To Decker, he said, "Sergeant, until we can all be honest, there isn't much purpose to this interview."

Decker didn't answer. Instead, he pulled out a Xerox copy of a newspaper clipping—the sole pickings from his morning in the library. Slowly he moved the paper until it lay in front of Whitman's line of vision.

Whitman blew out a cloud of smoke, then inched his eyes to the paper. He closed his lids, then opened them, but his expression remained flat. Moody took the Xerox and read the text. He said nothing, handing the article to Kramarze.

"So when's the big day?" Decker said.

Reflexively, Moody said, "This aspect of Mr. Whitman's personal life is not germane to the case."

"I think it is, Counselor," Decker said. "According to the papers, Mr. Whitman is currently engaged to a young lady . . . from a very *prominent* New York family. Then we find out, in his spare time, Mr. Whitman's been sleeping with another girl who shows up dead *and* pregnant. This does not bode well for Mr. Whitman's future relationship."

"Is there a point to your sarcasm?"

"Last I heard, the Benedettos weren't particularly tolerant people."

"That's because you get your information from the papers," Moody said. "In fact, they are a lovely family."

"I'm sure they're salt of the earth. Being such down-home folks, I don't know if they'd approve of Christopher's extracurricular activities. Ever read a book called *An American Tragedy?*"

"Oh, don't lower yourself with melodrama, Detective."

"Do you want me to write down the name of the book, Mr. Moody?" Kramarze asked.

"No, Mark, I don't," Moody said. "Sergeant, if you have some pertinent questions that Mr. Whitman might assist you with in Ms. Diggs's terrible death, speak up. If not, I'm going home to watch the game."

Decker faced Whitman. "When's the big day, Chris?"

Whitman took another puff and turned to Moody. "Should I talk to him or what?"

Moody folded his hands and placed them on the table. "Answer his questions, Christopher."

Whitman stubbed out his cigarette and poured himself a glass of water. "October fifteenth."

"Of this year?"

"Of this year."

"Kind of young to be taking such a big step."

Whitman didn't answer.

Decker paused. "Does Lorraine Benedetto know what's going on out west?"

Whitman looked at Moody. The lawyer said, "He's trying to establish a motive for Cheryl's death. You didn't want your fiancée to find out about Cheryl so you murdered her. Answer him, Chris. Does Lorraine Benedetto know what went on between you and Cheryl?"

Whitman drained his water glass. "Yes. Lorraine knows about Cheryl and me."

Decker paused. "Your fiancée is aware of the fact that you've been sleeping with Cheryl Diggs for the past year?"

"Yes."

"Has Lorraine always been aware of this?"

"Don't know," Whitman said. "But she knows now."

"How about Lorraine's father? Does he know you've been fucking other girls—"

"Sergeant—"

Decker said, "How's your fiancée reacting to all of this mess?"

Whitman looked at Moody. The lawyer nodded.

"No one's happy about it," Whitman said. "I know there'll be hell to pay when I get back home. But we're going through with the wedding."

"You're lucky," Decker said. "She sounds like a very understanding girl."

Whitman was silent.

"I got married pretty young," Decker said. "Not quite as young as you, but twenty-one is still a baby in my book. I had a kid at twenty-two. Lots of responsibility. I always felt I missed out on my youth—"

"Is there a purpose to your biographical digression?" Moody interrupted.

"If I had known I was going to get married so *young*, I might have sown a lot more wild oats . . . done some real outrageous experimentation—"

"If you feel deprived, Sergeant, take it up in therapy. Either get with the program or we're gone."

Decker said, "You were adopted by the Donattis at thirteen, Chris?"

"Yes."

"Who'd you live with before you were adopted?"

"My mother."

"What happened to your mother?"

"She died."

"Who's your mother?"

"Who's my mother? Are you asking me her name?"

"Yes."

"Her name was Shevonne, spelled S-I-O-B-A-N."

"And do you know who your father was?"

A flash of indignation traveled through the boy's eyes. "Yes."

"Name?"

"William Patrick Whitman."

"He was married to your mom?"

"Yes."

"So you're legitimate—"

"Sergeant, I'm warning you," Moody broke in.

"And what happened to your dad, Chris?"

"He died when I was nine."

"How did Donatti come to adopt you?"

Moody said, "Next question."

"I'm just trying to get a little background on Mr. Whitman. He's got some blank spots in his bio."

"For the last time, Sergeant, make it relevant or don't ask it at all."

Decker said to Whitman, "How long were you and Cheryl Diggs sexually active together?"

"I've got to think." Whitman folded his hands and laid them on the table. "I got to Central West around a year and a half ago. Shortly after that, I guess."

"You've been sexually active with Cheryl for a year and a half?"

"Around."

"But you never considered her your girlfriend?"

"No."

"Because you were . . . still are engaged to another girl?"

"Yes."

"So how would you define your relationship with Cheryl Diggs?"

"I don't know. Sexual friends maybe."

"Sexual friends," Decker said. "I like that. Lorraine knew about Cheryl?"

"You already asked me that. I don't know."

"Did Cheryl know about Lorraine?"

"I don't know that, either."

"Did you ever *tell* Cheryl that you were engaged to another girl?"

"No."

"Why not?"

"It never came up."

"Nah, I don't imagine it would."

"Sergeant—"

"I've spoken to some of your friends, Chris. They told me that Cheryl really liked you. They told me that she considered you her boyfriend."

Moody said, "That's hearsay."

"And this isn't a court of law, Mr. Moody." To Whitman, Decker said, "Chris, did you ever correct her impression?"

"What impression?"

"Ever tell her you *weren't* her boyfriend?"

"Like I said, it never came up. We slept with each other, Sergeant. That was the extent of our relationship."

"All your interactions with Cheryl were of a sexual nature?"

"Basically, yes."

"You *never* talked to her?"

"Not about anything substantive, no."

"Well, what *insubstantive* things did you and Cheryl talk about?"

Whitman poured himself another glass of water. "You know, they were so insignificant, I can't even remember. We were *rarely* alone except when we were having sex. At those times, we didn't talk."

"How about when you weren't having sex? You ever take her to a movie . . . or to a rock concert . . . or go grab a hamburger with her?"

"No."

Decker tried to keep his face neutral, but it was a challenge. "Cheryl was a cheap date."

"She wasn't a date," Whitman said. "It wasn't a one-on-one thing. We always went out in groups. We went to parties. Sex usually took place in the back rooms of the house where the parties were. I've never been to Cheryl's house. She's never seen my apartment. We weren't emotionally close."

"So who are you close to, Chris?"

"Sergeant," Moody interjected.

"Did Cheryl have other sexual partners?" Decker asked.

Whitman remained impassive. "Yes."

"And that didn't bother you?"

"No. She wasn't my girlfriend."

Decker said, "You have names for some of Cheryl's sexual partners?"

Whitman said, "You want me to do your job for you, Sergeant?"

Moody squeezed Whitman's arm. The boy immediately stiffened. "What is the point of this?"

"Your ex-sex friend is dead, Chris. You're a suspect. I would think you'd want to help me out."

Whitman said, "I heard rumors. I don't incriminate anyone based on rumors. That's your department."

Again Moody touched Whitman's arm.

"Tell me, Chris," Decker said. "How do you know

she had sex with other guys . . . if all you have is rumors . . . and you and Cheryl never talked about anything personal?"

Whitman paused. "Sometimes when I did her, she had semen in her."

Decker paused to assimilate his words. "From a previous sexual encounter?"

"Obviously."

"And this didn't bother you?"

"As long as I was protected, what did I care?"

"I realize Cheryl wasn't your heartthrob, but still, that's pretty damn tolerant."

Whitman shrugged.

Decker said, "Just maybe you were more affected than you're letting on?"

"It didn't bother me. In fact, I liked—"

Moody interrupted, "Chris, just answer the questions."

"You liked what?" Decker said.

"Christopher—"

"I liked the fact that she had other guys," Whitman interrupted. "It meant I could walk away without a scene."

"Didn't quite work out that way. You seem to have created a real big scene—"

Moody broke in. "Sergeant, this is a fact-finding interview, not a forum for groundless accusations."

"Groundless, Counselor?" Decker said. "Your client admitted having sex with the victim in the hotel room, not once but twice—"

Whitman broke in. "So what?"

Moody said, "Chris, let me—"

"Yes, I *fucked* her. But I didn't *kill* her."

"Christopher—"

"You know, to me, sex is just no *big deal*," Whitman blazed on. "I don't carve notches in my belt, I don't have a little black book, I don't get jazzed about conquests, I don't gossip, I don't flirt, I don't talk indiscreetly, and even though girls fall in my face, I don't feel the need to put my dick into everything that moves. While we were together, Cheryl had other partners. *I* didn't. I was loyal, not because Cheryl was any great shakes but because it wasn't worth the hassle to break in someone else. A pussy is a pussy—"

"Not overloaded with passion, are you, guy?" Decker broke in.

"I have more passion in a single hair on my ass than—"

"Don't *answer* him, Christopher!" Moody said. "What's *wrong* with you?"

Abruptly, Whitman's fair complexion took on a pinkish hue. He stopped talking, sat back in his seat, and looked at his lap. Then his eyes returned to Decker's—flat and cold.

Decker stared back, keeping his own face impassive. No doubt that this time the kid was telling the truth. Behind that practiced inanimate facade lay a hotbed of pent-up emotions. Decker bet it all came out in his cello playing.

"So you're a passionate guy, Chris," Decker said. "What turns you on?"

Whitman looked at Moody.

The lawyer said, "Tell him what you like, Chris."

"Music," Whitman said. "Art."

"Literature?"

"Sure."

"Are you a good student?"

Whitman paused and Decker took it in. Something flashed through the teen's eyes, then died in a flat mask of nothingness. He said, "I get by."

"Really," Decker said. "I'd think you'd love school. That you'd be a natural since girls aren't much of a distraction for you."

Whitman didn't answer.

"What are you? Like a B student?"

"Sometimes."

"What's your GPA?"

"I really don't know."

Decker stared at him. Nothing concrete had changed in his demeanor, yet Whitman was uncomfortable.

"You're in orchestra?"

Whitman nodded.

"You like that?"

"S'right."

"Too advanced for the group?"

"It doesn't bother me."

"You're pretty damn stoic for being so passionate."

Whitman didn't answer. He had learned his lesson.

"How long have you played cello?"

Whitman turned to Moody. "Why am I answering these questions?"

"A good point." Moody checked his watch. "It's been a little while. Why don't you contact Ms. Reuter and see if she has the results of the polygraph."

Decker said, "I'll give her a little more time. But

even if he did pass, we all know that polygraphs are notoriously unreliable, Chris. That's why they're not admissible in a court of law."

"Fine," Moody said. "So now I know that Christopher passed an unreliable test. Can he go over the night of the prom for you so we can get out of here before the witching hour?"

"All right," Decker said. "Tell me your story, Chris."

"Where do I start."

"What time did you leave the prom?"

"Around midnight."

"With Cheryl?"

"Yes."

"What did you two do?"

"We went to some parties."

"How many?"

"Two."

"Did you have sex with Cheryl at the parties?"

"No."

"What did you do after the parties?"

"We went to a hotel."

"Which hotel?"

"Grenada West End."

"Go on."

"We went to a room. The gang was there." Whitman named names. "We partied a little more together."

"What does that mean?"

"Drinking . . . doping. Someone put some porno on the VCR." Whitman shrugged. "That's about it. Eventually they all left the room in pairs. Maybe that was around two-thirty, three in the morning.

When Cheryl and I were finally alone, we had sex twice. Real quick. One, two and it was over."

"Porno turn you on, Chris?"

"Don't answer that," Moody said.

"You wear a condom that night?"

"Yes. I wore two. I put on a fresh one after I came the first time."

"When did you leave the hotel, Chris?"

"Maybe three-thirty or four that morning. I drove home. I went to sleep. End of story."

"You forgot the pregnancy part."

"Oh, yeah." Whitman rubbed his eyes. "Cheryl told me she was pregnant while we were still at the prom. She told me I was the father. I told her that was impossible."

"How was it impossible?"

"I'd rather let your lab do my talking. I'll give you a sample. Fair enough?"

"You're offering to give us sperm and blood samples—"

"He's doing nothing of the kind," Moody broke in.

Decker said, "What did Cheryl say when you told her you couldn't be the father?"

"Don't recall. I *do* remember thinking that the bitch was lying. Telling me she was knocked up just to hold on to—"

Whitman stopped talking.

"What?" Decker said.

"Nothing."

Decker said, "Cheryl told you she was pregnant to hold on to you, didn't she, Chris? She didn't want the relationship—the sexual friends relationship—to end. Her clinging to you like that . . . making *demands* on you . . . that wouldn't sit well with the Benedettos or your uncle, now, would it, guy?"

Whitman said, "Sergeant, all I can tell you is I'm not the father of her baby. I'm so positive I'll give you blood and sperm samples—"

"Chris—"

"Mr. Moody, I'm *that* positive."

"Fine," Decker said. "Thank you for cooperating. We'll set something up. You said Cheryl was strung out. Did you see her doping?"

"Yes."

Decker said, "Did you see her drink?"

"Yes."

"Did she seem depressed to you?"

"I don't know. Maybe."

"She was stoned, she was drunk, she was pregnant, she was depressed . . ." Decker paused. "Why'd you leave her alone in the hotel room?"

"Because I'm not an Eagle Scout."

The room was quiet.

Whitman closed his eyes and opened them. "In light of what happened to her, I wish I hadn't left her alone. But it's too late for regrets. What else do you want to know?"

Decker said, "Anyone see you leave the hotel?"

"No."

"Did anyone see you on your way home?"

"No."

"What time did you get home?"

"Around four maybe."

"Anyone see you come into your apartment?"

"No."

"Did you make any phone calls?"

"No."

"Did you receive any phone calls?"

"No."

The catch in Whitman's throat was so quick, Decker almost missed it. "No one tried to call you?"

"No."

Decker wrote a note to himself to check calls on Whitman's telephone. "You went right to sleep."

"Yep."

"Right smack to sleep."

"Yes."

"Just dropped off like a fly."

"I was very tired."

"You slept in your tux?"

"No, I took off my tux—" Whitman paused. "I took off my tux, brushed my teeth, and then went to sleep."

The two men locked eyes. Then Decker said, "I'd like to go over a few more points again."

"Sergeant," Moody said. "Is this really necessary?"

"S'right, Mr. Moody," Whitman said. "I don't have anything better to do. And I don't have anything to hide."

🦢21

Upon entering the sixth hour of nonstop questioning, James Moody demanded a break. Decker complied, taking his breather in the viewing room. Davidson was standing in front of the one-way mirror, eyes fixed in a squint, peering at Whitman and his representation as if looking through binoculars at enemy infiltrators. Scott Oliver was slouched over the tabletop, having grown deep bags under his eyes. To Decker's surprise, Elaine Reuter had stuck around long after her job was done. She was usually meticulous in her appearance, but as the night wore on, so did Elaine. Her hair had become a straggly mane, her posture folded and wrinkled. Decker didn't feel too hot himself. He ran a hand over his steel-wool face. He was sorely in need of a shave.

He said, "We've been plowing the same ground for the last four hours, Lieutenant. What do you think?"

Davidson licked his lips, but didn't answer.

Elaine rubbed her eyes. "I liked Whitman's initial outburst about sex not being a big deal to him. Pretty big admission for an eighteen-year-old."

"Don't you believe it!" Davidson said.

"Fucking A right." Oliver picked his head up, then dropped it. "Sucker's bragging. Reverse macho. 'I'm so cool, I don't *need* it.' Meanwhile he was boffing Cheryl Diggs on a regular basis. Probably boffing others as well."

Davidson perked up. "You got names, Oliver?"

"Yeah, I'm holding back on everyone—"

"Oliver—"

"No, I don't have *names*, Loo. The kids I talked to didn't know much about Whitman, period, let alone his sex life." Oliver looked at Decker. "What about the girls?"

"Same story." Decker sat down. "But I agree with Scotty. I think Whitman has had other partners. Be nice if we dug one of them up."

"Not literally, I hope," Elaine said.

"I didn't mean it that way," Decker said. "But it's a possibility."

"A strong one," Davidson said. "He's got the look."

Decker said, "Be nice if we found a living partner. See if he has any strange proclivities."

"Like bondage?" Elaine said.

Decker said, "You said the machine wiggled when he spoke about tying up girls."

"I also said it was within normal limits," Elaine said. "Like I stated, it's probably a long-standing fantasy of his."

"Only *this* time, he made it a reality," Davidson said.

"I've still got a good three, four hours left in me," Decker said. "But truthfully, I've gone as far as I can go with him. What do you want me to do?"

Davidson looked pained. "You're telling me to spring him when I know he did it?"

Decker said, "I'm not telling you anything. It's your call."

"I need evidence, Decker!"

"Get me a warrant and maybe I can get you his tux," Decker said.

"What if he rented one, then returned it?" Elaine said.

Oliver said, "If he rented, he didn't use a local shop *or* he didn't use his real name. I've called every rental place within ten square miles of the school."

Decker said, "Being a big kid *and* Donatti's son, I'm betting he owned one."

Elaine said, "So all we have to do is find his tux, match the fibers to the bow tie found at the crime scene, and we'll have something incriminating."

"Putting it that way, it sounds so simple," Decker said.

"It *is* simple," Davidson insisted.

"Kid's smart," Oliver said. "He's probably ditched the tux by now."

Decker said, "Scotty, tuxes don't disappear. He admitted—on record—that he had been wearing one on prom night."

Elaine said, "Ah, so that's why he gave you that look. Your comment about him not even taking his tux off before he dropped off to sleep." She smiled. "Man, he sure fell into your trap."

"Yep," Decker said.

"He knew it, too," Oliver said. "What if he already went out and bought a new one?"

Decker said, "Be difficult to pull something off

the rack on such short notice, especially at prom time."

"So he'd go custom," Oliver said.

Decker said, "Scott, the murder happened Sunday morning when all the stores were closed. Today's Monday. He's had about six hours to dredge something up . . . assuming that he knew his tux could incriminate him. Though it can be done, I think it would be hard to make a tux on such short notice."

"All it takes is money, Rabbi," Oliver said. "He got fitted today, he'll pick up the monkey suit tomorrow."

"So we'll put a twenty-four-hour tail on him. See if it leads to a tailor."

Elaine said, "Pete, what happens if you find the original tux? So it matches the bow tie at the crime scene. Whitman admitted being in the room. Why wouldn't he say he just left his bow tie behind?"

"That's exactly what he will say," Oliver said.

Davidson said, "Matching the bow tie used to bind Cheryl's hands to Whitman's tux is enough to get us an indictment. That's all I care about. Because with the bow tie we've got the big three—opportunity, means, and motive, that being Diggs's pregnancy."

"His fiancée knows about Cheryl's pregnancy, Lieutenant," Elaine said. "She hasn't ditched him."

"Reuter, let me tell you how the mob works," Davidson said. "To save face in front of the police, Mafia's gonna stick up for their own no matter what. To us, they're gonna say everything's fine. But when Whitman gets home, back to Daddy Benedetto and Uncle Joey Donatti, he's gonna lose a nut."

Oliver held his groin. "Ouch!"

"We'd be doing the kid a favor if we put him away," Davidson said.

"You actually think he killed Cheryl because her pregnancy was a threat to his engagement?" Elaine asked.

"I *know* that's why he killed her," Davidson said.

"But Whitman swore the kid wasn't his."

"He's bluffing," Davidson said.

"Even though he's willing to give us blood and semen samples to prove it?" Decker asked.

"That's what he says now," Davidson said. "Bet your ass, he'll have a sudden change of heart. And even if the baby wasn't his, Cheryl threatening him was probably enough to get him riled. It don't even have to be true."

"I don't agree," Decker said.

"Course not," Davidson growled. "It's against your religion to agree with me."

"If he murdered Cheryl—even with the bondage— I don't see it as a premeditated thing. Maybe a sex game gone bad. Could be he was doing some sexual experimentation before taking the plunge. Because I don't reckon Daddy Benedetto would cotton to him tying up his daughter."

"I don't buy that," Davidson said. "Whitman's mob. All mob men have armpieces."

"Armpieces?" Elaine said.

"Mistresses," Decker said.

Oliver said, "A good-looking broad on their arm."

Decker said, "Except Benedetto is big time. He's an old-fashioned Italian daddy. His daughter's his princess."

"But the husband—the man—is still the *king*," Davidson said.

"Granted," Decker said. "He may accept Whitman getting a mistress *after* he's earned some stripes. But first Whitman's going to have to prove himself. No way at this time, Benedetto would tolerate an eighteen-year-old punk still green around the edges messing around on his daughter."

"Well, Diggs is dead whatever the reason," Davidson said. "And whatever the reason, Whitman did it."

Decker said, "We don't have a warrant now and we don't have enough to hold him. What do you want to do with him?"

Davidson rubbed a meaty hand over his face. "Go another half hour . . . should give me enough time to assign a tail until I can get the warrant."

"I'll do the tail," Oliver said.

"You're half dead," Davidson said. "I wouldn't trust you to watch my goldfish."

Decker said, "When do you think you can get a search and seizure warrant?"

Davidson looked at the wall clock. "No sense waking up a judge at one in the morning since Whitman'll have a tail on him. I'll ask Ronnie Peterson first thing tomorrow morning. We go back a ways." Davidson rolled his shoulders. "Stall Moody for another half hour, then let him go. Any questions?"

The room was silent.

"Then class is dismissed," Davidson announced.

✣ 22

Under the yellow glow of his porch light, I fell asleep, shielded from wind by a giant potted banana plant, my stack of books warming my lap. What woke me was the turn of his key. From my nestled position, I opened my eyes and whispered a hi. He jerked his head around, eyes skating through air until they lowered and landed on my face. I started to get up, but he motioned me to stay down. He put a finger to his lips and said nothing.

Chris opened his front door, stepped inside, then shut me out. I waited, and finally he opened the door a crack and told me to crawl in through pitch darkness. Once inside, he turned on the light and I was allowed to stand. Glaring at me, he backed me against his front door and leaned his face an inch from mine. His voice was eerily soft.

"I told you I couldn't see you anymore."

I waited a beat, then said, "How'd it go?"

He didn't react. Instead, he whispered, "I'm being watched. Who knows? The police might even have tapped the room. I've got to get you out of here before someone spots you. So this is what we're going to do. I'll leave here in five . . . maybe ten minutes. You wait another ten minutes after I'm gone. Then go over to the window, *imperceptibly* part the blackout drapes. If there's a brown '89 Cutlass still parked outside, you stay put. When it leaves, you go to your car, go back home, and *never* come back. Understand?"

"I don't have a car, Chris. I walked over here."

His eyes glowed hot blue lights of anger. "You *walked* here?"

"It's only a couple of miles. Besides, it was daylight when I started out."

He spoke between clenched teeth, giving equal emphasis to each word. "Well, it isn't daylight now."

"This is true."

He glanced at his watch. He talked more to himself than to me. "You can't very well walk home now, can you?"

"This is also true."

He blinked several times, his eyes lifting to the ceiling. I could almost hear him counting to himself. If he didn't see me, I didn't exist.

He spoke quietly and deliberately. "I *can't* take you home, Terry. After I leave, you're going to have to walk to the corner and call a cab."

"My parents think I'm spending the night at Heidi's house . . . we've been studying for finals together. They'd be pretty suspicious if I suddenly popped back up at one in the morning."

Chris closed his eyes and opened them. He whispered, "Remember when I told you my uncle wouldn't care if I loved you or not? I was wrong. He would care very much." He paused, then said, "I'm in serious trouble with my uncle. If he finds out about you . . ."

He blinked several times. "I don't even want to think about it."

I said, "Your engagement was called off?"

"Unfortunately, no. The marriage may have to be postponed if I do time. But for better or worse, she'll wait for me. I'm trapped in prison or trapped in marriage . . . which a lot of people say is a similar experience." He sighed. "How long have you been waiting for me?"

"Around seven hours. It's all right. I made good use of the time by studying. Not that these finals mean much. I'm already accepted into UCLA. Good grades would just round out my transcript nicely." I stopped talking. "I'm sure that's a major concern of yours right now."

"I enjoy hearing you talk. Your voice is beautiful music. Are you hungry, Terry?"

I shook my head no. "I packed a sandwich. I figured it would take you a while. Not exactly seven hours but . . ."

He was about to speak but changed his mind.

"What?"

He shook his head. I took his hands.

"*Talk* to me, Chrissie. I want to *help* you."

His smile was wistful. "My mom used to call me Chrissie."

"So we have something in common. What happened at the police station? What'd your lawyers say?"

"It doesn't matter. You take my bed. I'll bunk out on the couch." He turned and walked into his bedroom. I followed. He was in his closet, gathering up linens. I came over and touched his shoulder. He didn't stiffen, but he didn't turn around.

I said, "The questioning went bad?"

He didn't answer me.

"Christopher, *please*?"

He straightened and faced me, arms filled with bedding. "Just go to sleep, Terry."

"Didn't you pass the test?"

His face held no expression other than fatigue. "Go to sleep. I'll wake you in the morning. I'll go out first, get my tail away from you. Then you leave for school."

He shut the door behind me. I waited a moment, then followed him into the living room. He was setting up his makeshift bed on his sofa.

"You didn't pass the lie-detector test, did you?"

"I passed." He continued to spread out the sheets. "But that doesn't mean my troubles are over. Because the fat lady sure ain't singing."

I was quiet.

He tucked his sheet in between the pillows and the frame of the couch. "That's an expression—"

"I know that. Why are you still in trouble?"

"I don't want to talk about it. Go to sleep."

I didn't move.

He softened his voice. "Please, Terry."

I said, "You can sleep with me in the bed if you want."

"I don't want."

"I mean just sleep. Why should I displace you? . . . Or I'll sleep on the couch."

"No."

"Why not?"

"Terry, just get the fuck *out* of here."

Although I was hurt, I shrugged and walked back to his bed. Since I was dressed in the Seattle grunge layered look, I had no trouble finding something to sleep in. I disrobed, stripping down to my underpants and T-shirt, then slipped between his sheets. They smelled wonderful . . . smelled like him. I curled into a ball, closed my eyes, and listened to the muffled thud of his footsteps. I was just about asleep when his clops grew rhythmic and louder. The door opened, a sliver of light quickly turned into a wedge. The door shut and once again I was encased in darkness. He came to the bed and sat on the edge, feeling for my hand. When he found it, he gave me a gentle squeeze.

"I'm sorry," he said.

I said, "You break into my house less than twelve hours ago . . . beaten down . . . desperate for understanding. You tell me your innermost secrets, telling me you love me . . . goading me to *care* for you. Then when I show concern, you reject me."

Silence.

I said, "Christopher, *why* did you come to my house?"

"To tell you I couldn't see you anymore."

"If you wanted me to stay away from you, you shouldn't have come at all. I was scared of you. I wouldn't have gone near you. But after we talked, I felt for you. Now I feel foolish."

Again, the room was quiet.

"You're right," Chris said. "I shouldn't have come to see you. I told you I was selfish. I just wanted to see you one last time." He paused, "I can't believe you actually feel something toward me. I don't deserve . . ."

His words faded in the air. I opened the covers. He hesitated, then slid inside. His shoes were off, but he was still fully clothed. He embraced me, seemingly oblivious to my scant dress except there was a bulge in his pants.

"Tell me what happened with the police," I said.

He spoke softly. "The cop's clever. He . . . twisted some of my words, threw me off balance. I said some things I shouldn't have."

"Like what?"

"The specifics aren't important. What *is* important is the distortions. My own words can make me look bad."

"But they didn't arrest you, did they?"

He shook his head.

"Obviously they don't have any evidence against you."

"No, not yet." Chris paused. "Maybe it would be better if they did. Get me away from my uncle. He's livid. Pissed beyond belief. I'm fucked!"

He laughed but it was born from despair.

"I just got a sudden insight. When I shot my father, I pulled the right trigger but aimed it at the wrong head—"

"*Don't* talk that way!"

He blew out air, but said nothing. As my eyes adjusted to the darkness, I could discern the outlines of Chris's face. We locked eyes for a moment. Then he closed his lids and we kissed. Soft and magical. His hands went under my T-shirt, which he eventually slipped over my head. He caressed me, his breathing slow and steady. He took off his own T-shirt, leaving his crucifix around his neck. He undid his pants, removed them in one swift motion, then wrapped his legs around my hips. When I went for the last article of encumbrance, he jerked away and sat up.

"What the fuck am I *doing*?" He was panting. "I can't sleep with you, Terry. God knows I want to, but I *can't*. I can lie to *anyone*—you, Lorraine, Cheryl, the police . . . I can even lie to my own body well enough to pass a test. But I can't lie to Joey. He reads me too well."

He held his head.

"My uncle is crazed, not because of Cheryl but because he knows I'm in love with someone else. He's worried someone'll take me away from Lorraine. Course I've denied everything. But if my uncle finds out about you . . . Terry, he's a vicious, vicious man. You've got to get out of here. Let me get dressed and get my tail off you—"

"No."

"Terry—"

"*No!*" I pulled him back down and drew him to me, my hands passing over the rises and falls of his chest, playing with the chain of his crucifix. "I'm not a typical grungie, Chris. I'm not enamored of death. But it doesn't scare me."

"That's because you've never seen death up close."

"Not only have I seen it, I've *caused* it."

He stared at me. "Teresa, you couldn't seriously be *blaming* yourself for your mother's death."

"No, that's my father's department."

I broke into tears.

"Christ . . ." He embraced me, rocked me. "You want me to pop him for you? I'm good at popping fathers."

I talked through my tears. "Stop it."

"I'm serious. I'd pop anyone for you."

"I'm not interested in . . . popping my father, okay?"

"Whatever you want. I always said I was your pit bull. I'm a very loyal person. Beyond the point of logic."

"I'm not afraid of your uncle."

"That's because you don't know him. Luckily, I do. Nothing's going to happen to you . . . if nothing happens between us."

"You mean like sex?"

"I mean like sex. I'm going back to the couch now—"

"Since when is kissing sex?"

"No, Terry, kissing isn't sex. But it leads to sex. I don't trust myself."

"I trust *myself*." I traced the outline of his hips with my fingers. "You say no sex, it's no sex. I'll stop you."

"It's not that simple. In the heat of the moment—"

"I had a lot of heated moments with Daniel," I interrupted. "But we never did it. Because when I say no, I mean no."

He paused. "Why? What'd you do with Reiss?"

I threw my leg over his waist and pushed his hips against mine. "Stuff."

"Like what?"

"Stuff in the backseat of his car . . . in the dark . . . we'd kiss . . . we'd touch."

There was a short pause. Chris said, "Tell me more."

I kissed his mouth softly. "Sometimes . . . sometimes we'd take our clothes off. Daniel kept a blanket in his car . . . we'd get under the blanket." I slipped my fingers underneath the elastic of his underpants. "We'd touch each other."

His breathing grew stronger, purposeful. I'd heard those sounds many times in the past.

"And?" he asked.

"Sometimes I'd let him rub against me . . . until he climaxed . . . and sometimes . . . sometimes I climaxed, too."

He was quiet, his eyes boring into mine.

"You're shocked," I said.

"Surprised." Gently, he began to rock against me. "He came on you?"

"Yes."

"Where?"

I placed his hand between my groin and my inner thigh. "Around there."

"He wore a glove?"

"No. Why should he?"

"Semen's a liquid. Accidents happen."

"Well, they didn't."

"And you came, too."

"Yes."

"You're sure?"

I stared at him. "Yes, I'm sure. Why do you doubt me?"

"Just that . . ." His eyes took in mine. "Some girls think it's the real thing . . . but it isn't."

"Well, I know the real thing."

"You've done it to yourself?"

JUSTICE

241

"Don't be too subtle, Chris."

He turned silent.

"Yes, I've done it to myself. So I know what it feels like. And it happened with Daniel. Not only once, but *lots* of times. And spare me your wounded look. Compared to your crowd, we did pretty minor stuff."

"It's not a peck on the cheek, Terry."

"But it's not sex."

He stopped moving and thought a moment. "No, it's not sex." He raised his brow. "But it's pretty damn close. Certainly sounds a lot more intimate than what Cheryl and I were doing."

"That might be. We were both sober."

"Thank you, Terry. After today, I really needed another knife in my heart."

"You're jealous—"

"Hell, yeah, I'm *jealous*! It *killed* me when you started dating Reiss. I wanted to strangle the little bastard."

"Never seemed to bother you when I dated Bull."

"You despised Bull. You were like . . . in pain . . . every time the jerk tried to touch you. No one could figure it out. Course I knew what you were doing. Using him to get to me." His eyes lifted to the ceiling. "Jesus, I can't believe you and Daniel . . . Reiss must have been good, huh?"

"No, *I* was good, huh?"

His laugh was full and genuine. "God, I'm an idiot."

"No, just a pig." I grew serious. "Actually, I must be the idiot to come here . . . knowing what you're accused of. You've been deliberately vague with me, Christopher. I've thought back to our conversation this afternoon. I've replayed it in my head a thousand times. You've never, ever, explicitly told me yes or no."

"You've never, ever, explicitly asked me. So ask me. I'll tell you the truth."

"I can't."

"So you'll never know, will you?"

I was silent.

He said, "You know why you can't ask me, angel? Because it would be a breach of trust. As soon as you ask me the question . . . it says to you . . . and to me . . . that you don't trust me. Right now, you'd rather trust me than know the truth."

He began to caress my breasts.

"That's cool. I can accept that. Because the relationship has to die in the morning. But if that wasn't the case, you'd *have* to know the truth. And if you really loved me . . . the way that I love you . . . you'd accept me, no matter what. Just like I'd accept you, no matter what."

The room fell quiet. Neither of us spoke for a minute, just held each other. Leaning my head against his chest, I heard his heartbeat, felt the cool gold of his cross against my cheek. I climbed the chain with my fingers, then rested them on the back of his neck.

Wordlessly, he slipped off his chain and put it around my neck. "It's not fancy, but it's meaningful to me. It was my mother's. You'd do me an honor if you took it."

I kissed it. "It's beautiful. I love it." I kissed him softly. "I love you, Christopher. Despite everything, I still love you very deeply."

He kissed me hard, his tongue parting my lips,

then playing inside my mouth. He began to explore my flesh, his left hand resting between my legs, fingertips inching into the pleats of my womanhood. He stopped abruptly and we locked eyes. For once, his were animated. He whispered, "I'll do whatever you want, Teresa. You lead. I'll follow."

It wasn't sex but it was pretty damn close. An exquisite compromise that took us through the night.

❦ 23

Sleep had been an elusive lover—a series of brain buzzes and fits punctuated by sudden remembrances of things to do. Decker had finally given up at four in the morning, carefully rising from the bed, slipping into work clothes. He had brewed a pot of coffee, read the morning paper, walked the dog in a moonless star-studded sky, then tackled the barn—changed and pitched the hay, fed and groomed the horses.

By six, he had not only worked up a good sweat but had cleared his mind. With renewed clarity, he had put on another pot of coffee, then had taken out the Diggs file—a big envelope overflowing with official documents.

This time utility overtook vanity. Decker slipped on reading glasses, then fingered the piles of papers in front of him. The inevitable march of time took on particular significance for him because Rina was defying normal biological processes. Twelve years his junior, she looked *younger* than when they had married—a phenomenon that baffled him, but one that perhaps Einstein could have explained. Wearing magnified lens and sipping coffee, he read, made notes, diagrams, charts, and timetables.

At six-forty-five, Rina's slippers shuffled into the kitchen. "You didn't sleep, did you?"

"A couple of hours." Decker took off his glasses and stood up. "I could think of it as a poor night's sleep. Instead, I'll look at it as a refreshing nap. It's all relative."

"That may be but you look exhausted." She shook her head. "First Cindy turned you into an insomniac. Now this case. Peter, you need rest."

"Actually, I feel pretty good."

Rina began warming a bottle of milk. "That's caffeine talking."

"Speaking of which, the coffee's recent. We've got around fifteen minutes before the morning onslaught. Why don't you join me?"

Rina poured herself a cup, drowned it with milk, then sat at the kitchen table. She was blanketed in a terry robe, ebony hair falling at odd angles across her face. Her eyes were sleepy pools of clearwater blue. "Did you call Cindy?"

"Yes, I called her. Get this! Now she wants to stay in New York for the summer."

"At Columbia?"

"No, with two girlfriends. They want to rent an apartment. Can you believe that?"

"What's wrong with the idea?"

"Nothing, except I want her home."

"But she doesn't want to come home."

"So what? I'm her father and I want her home." He poured himself a refill and dropped a couple of slices of rye into the toaster. "I know, I know. Gotta let go. Let them have wings. What a truckload of crap." He frowned. "How's the rest of my family? Do they miss me?"

"They do."

"Tell the boys I'll take them riding tonight."

"Uh . . . tonight they're busy learning."

"I thought they learned on Thursday night."

"That's *mishmar* at *their* school. Tuesdays is their extra learning with Rav Schulman at the Ohavei Torah. He's been asking about you, by the way."

"I know," Decker said. "I've been terrible . . . canceling lessons right and left. I've been busy— I know, I know. You're never too busy for Torah."

"He hasn't been asking about you to scold you, Peter. He's concerned for your welfare . . . all the additional hours you've been putting in."

Decker eyed Rina suspiciously. "You haven't been talking to him now, have you?"

"About you? Of course not!" Rina got up and pulled the baby bottle out of warm water. "I'm insulted you'd think I'd talk behind your back."

"Then how does he know I'm working such long hours?"

"Because you've been canceling lessons."

Got you there, Deck. He gave her a boyish smile. Rina whacked his good shoulder. "Think you can charm your way out of everything, eh?"

"Is it working?"

"Yes, unfortunately." Rina sat back down. "I'm concerned about you, Peter. This case is taking its toll on your psyche. Do you know you've called me Marge two times?"

"That's not indicative of anything. I call her Rina

all the time. She gets peeved when I do. Are you peeved at me?"

"No. But it does show me you need some rest. Either that or you need Marge."

He parked himself in a chair. "Yeah, I do miss Marge. We talk things out, each one bringing in a different perspective. Whenever I work by myself for long stretches, I get tunnel vision."

"Can I help?"

"No, it's all right. Scott Oliver's been picking up some of the slack."

Rina smiled. "Now, how is Scott doing?"

"You mean detective drooling dog," Decker said. "I see how he acts around you."

"It's any female, Peter—*Homo sapiens* or otherwise."

Decker laughed. "Actually, he's a decent cop. If it were just Scotty and me, I wouldn't complain."

Rina took a sip of her coffee. "It's Davidson, isn't it? What's he doing to you this time?" The toaster dinged. Rina rose, but Decker gently nudged her back down. "I'll get it."

Rina watched her husband butter toast. He poured two glasses of orange juice, offered one to Rina, then sat back down with his breakfast.

"Davidson's fixated on Diggs's boyfriend as the murderer." He gulped down half a mug of black coffee. "Now, I don't like the kid. He's cold, he's calculating, he's eerie, his affect is off, and I think he's an excellent liar. I have no trouble believing that Whitman could choke a girl as easy as scramble an egg."

"Whitman's the boyfriend?"

"Yeah. Christopher Sean Whitman. He's a weird sucker and he's also Mafia."

"I didn't know there was Mafia out here."

"He's originally from the east. He's Joseph Donatti's adopted son."

"*The* Joseph Donatti?"

Decker nodded.

Rina raised her eyebrows. "No wonder Davidson is in an uproar about him."

"On the surface, the kid looks like the perfect perp." Decker took a bite of his toast, chewed quickly, and swallowed. "But there are intervening factors. Things that Davidson is point-blank choosing to ignore."

"Like what?"

"Conflicting evidence. Foreign pubic hairs not linked to Whitman. Now, that's not unusual. Lots of investigations aren't cut-and-dried. But Davidson doesn't even want to *hear* about anything that negates the Whitman-as-killer theory."

"The man is rather concrete."

"More like a cinderblock wall. He's impeding my investigative techniques. The case is moving forward, but not in a methodical way."

"What are you going to do?"

"I'm either going to find something tangible on Whitman or I'm going to move on. The homicide is already forty-eight hours old, which is nothing if you have a suspect in custody. But if it isn't Whitman, we have no understudies waiting in the wings."

Decker flipped through the stack of papers in front of him.

"I've been reading and rereading . . . I'm not having much luck. I don't know. Maybe I am exhausted."

A high-pitched plea of *momeeeeeeee* sirened through the kitchen.

"I'll get her." Decker dashed out of the room and returned a moment later snuggling a bundle cocooned in warm pink sleeper. All that was visible was a mop of auburn silk. "Someone's still very tired."

"Hello, Hannah Rosie," Rina said. "Are you hungry?"

At the sound of Rina's voice, the toddler reached out to Mama. Rina swept Hannah up in her arms, then kissed her tummy, drawing out tinkly laughter. Sitting down, she gave Hannah her bottle. To her husband she said, "Is there anything I can do for you?"

"I'm fine. Is there anything I can do for *you*?"

"As long as you asked, yes, there is."

"Uh-oh."

"*If* you have the time," Rina said, "take the boys to Rav Schulman and sit in on the lesson."

"The boys are way ahead of me."

"So they won't learn *gemara* for one night. Rav Schulman will choose something appropriate for everyone. You look upset, Peter. Maybe a little spirituality would be uplifting . . . take you away from the ugliness of your work."

A good point. Decker said, "I'll see what I can do." He let out a small laugh. "That sounds moronic, doesn't it? I should see if I can fit God and beauty and holiness into my busy schedule of murder, mayhem, and tragedy."

Rina kissed her daughter's palm—as warm and soft as eiderdown. "We all get caught up in what we're doing. Too caught up to stop and smell the coffee."

Decker smiled weakly. Rina was worried . . . and a little pissed by his preoccupation with the Diggs murder. So be it. The teen had been murdered and he wanted the perp put away for good. One less sleaze in this world to worry about.

Whitman opened the front door.

Decker pulled the paper out of his briefcase. "Hello, Christopher. I'm sure you've been expecting this." He proffered Whitman the search and seizure warrant. "You're blocking. Excuse me."

Decker entered the apartment, heading toward the boy's bedroom.

Whitman followed. "I'd like to read the warrant before you start."

"Son, you can read it," Decker said. "But I've got a job to do. And since I know it's been properly executed, I'm going to start right in so I can get out of here as quickly as possible." He smiled. "I bet that sounds pretty good to you, too."

Decker began with the closet. A quick overview: no tux. That meant going through the items one by one.

Whitman leaned against the doorframe and read. "Your warrant prohibits the demolition of anything that provides structural integrity to the building."

"That means I can't knock down walls. But if you've punched a hole in something, it's fair game."

"I haven't punched a hole in anything."

"Then there's nothing to worry about." Decker took out his pad and pen, scribbled a few notes. Whitman was *compulsive*. His shirts were arranged in rainbow-color order—red, orange, yellow, green, and blue. Same with the jackets, all the hangers facing the same way. Dress pants were pressed and folded. Tie rack on the side, again color coded. Not a thing was hung in a haphazard manner. Made Decker's job a hell of an easy task.

He said, "Where's your tux, Chris?"

Whitman didn't answer.

"You know what I'm talking about?" Decker carefully placed Whitman's apparel on his bed. "The tux you wore the night of the prom."

Having denuded the closet, Decker started tapping the walls of the empty space. "I didn't see it hanging up."

Whitman was silent.

"You didn't lose it now, did you?" Decker said.

"I can't stop you from making a mess," Whitman said. "But I don't have to talk to you."

He was aware. Decker said, "Just thought you might want to help. Get me out of here quickly."

Whitman remained quiet.

Decker knocked on the closet's ceiling, banged and checked the floorboards. Solid. He sneaked a sidelong glance at Whitman. The kid's face was flat, but his posture was stiff. He was tapping his foot, not out of impatience, but out of nervousness. His eyes kept going to the clothes piled on his bed. Had Decker missed something? Didn't appear that way. Maybe Chris just liked things orderly. If that was so, he'd do well in prison.

Decker decided to be neat and polite. If he made a mess, it might initially unnerve Whitman, but it would also make him angry and defiant. The kid probably performed well when he was mad. Rage wasn't alien to him.

"I'm done with the clothes. I'll need to toss your bed." Decker rolled his shoulders. "You want to hang up your things while I hunt through your drawers, be my guest."

Whitman started forward, then stopped himself. He wanted to put back his clothes, but he didn't want to do what Decker—i.e., the *police*—had suggested.

Decker smiled inwardly. He had put Chris in a classic double-bind. Whitman closed and opened his eyes. "Just toss the clothes on the floor. Do you want some coffee?"

"I'd love some."

It wasn't the answer he had expected. Now optionless, Chris hesitated, then left the room.

"Black is fine," Decker shouted aloud.

He started on the drawers. Casual clothes—jeans, T-shirts, polo shirts, khakis, sweats, sweaters. Lots of clothes all folded and stowed army regulation perfect. He wondered if Whitman had ever attended military school. His pants were a thirty-four extra, extra long. Decker picked up a jacket off the bed— forty-two extra, extra long. Decker wore a forty-six on good days.

Having rooted through his clothes, Decker moved on to the next bank of drawers. This one held bed linens. Decker smelled them. Freshly washed. That made sense. The stakeout had followed the kid early this morning, first to a restaurant, then to a Laundromat. Odd, though. The building had machines in the basement. It seemed to Decker as if Whitman was trying to draw out the tail.

Decker plowed through more of Whitman's drawers. One held school supplies, the other contained stereo equipment—wires, wire cutters, leads, heads, and an assemblage of doodads that Decker couldn't identify. Two other drawers were filled with CD racks—one with classical, the other with rock. Kid had eclectic tastes. More school supplies—paper, pens, pencils, calculators, a dictionary, a thesaurus, markers, crayons . . .

Decker stopped.

Crayons?

That's right. Whitman was an artist. So where did he keep the bulk of his art supplies?

More searching produced nothing of significance. Decker started in on the bed.

Whitman came back with the coffee.

"Thanks, just put it down anywhere." Decker carefully folded back the covers and searched the bedding. Then he began a careful examination of the mattress, checking the seams for signs of tampering. Finding nothing, Decker reached into his briefcase and pulled out a pocketknife.

Whitman said, "The warrant says you can't destroy anything."

Decker said, "The warrant says I can't break down walls, Chris." Carefully he cut the mattress ticking, peeled back a flap, and exposed lumpy piles of stuffing.

"Are you going to pay for that?" Whitman asked.

"You'll be compensated." Decker sorted through the stuffing. Nothing. He repeated the procedure with the box spring. Again, it was devoid of anything valuable.

Meaning he didn't stuff his tux in his mattress.

Decker opened each pillow and came up equally dry. Whitman watched it all, leaning against the doorframe, his face as expressionless as wood. Decker smiled. "Sorry about the mess."

Whitman didn't answer.

Decker moved on. He checked the floor under the box spring. He tapped the walls, the ceilings, and explored the floor on his hands and knees, looking for a trap door. Everything was intact and solid.

Rising from his knees, Decker stretched, picked up his coffee, gulped it down, then handed the mug back to Whitman. "Thanks."

Decker went into the second bedroom, Whitman his shadow. It had been set up as a music studio as well as a workout room. No exercise machines, but a rack held a dozen sets of freestanding weights. A couple of barbells lay against the walls.

Decker toed one of them. "How much weight do you have on them?"

"Don't know what's currently set up. I can bench-press around two hundred pounds. What about you?"

Decker grinned. "Buddy, I'm an old man. I look at weights the wrong way, I throw my back out."

Whitman eyed him. "I think you're putting me on."

"Chris, I never lie." Decker's eyes shifted to the cello resting on its side. Beside it was a closed case. Decker strolled over, knelt down, and examined the case. It was big, padded with a soft lining that looked to be in original condition. He took out a knife, opened a corner, and peeked inside.

"That's an antique case," Whitman said.

"I really am sorry." Decker stuck his hands inside, pulled out a clump of horsehair. He sifted through it. No clothing fibers. He did it a couple of times and came up empty. "I'll make sure it's restored properly." He walked over to Whitman's cello. "Expensive?"

"Very."

"How much?"

"It's not a Strad or a Guaneri, but it's five figures."

"Then you pick it up for me. I want to look inside."

Whitman cooperated.

Gently, Decker rapped his knuckles against the top of the wood, then against the back. Different sounds, one much more dampened than the other. He asked Whitman about the discrepancy.

"It's supposed to be like that," Whitman answered. "That's the way stringed instruments work."

"And how is that?" Decker said.

"I'm not a cello maker," Whitman said.

"Do the best you can," Decker said.

Whitman hesitated. Without emotion, he said, "The tops of stringed instruments are usually carved from soft wood—mostly spruce, sometimes pine or cedar. They are constructed to vibrate and amplify the sound wave made by the bowed or plucked string. The backs are usually hard wood—for cellos and violins it's almost always maple. They are not supposed to vibrate like the tops. They are made to support the structure of the instrument and reflect the sound wave back into the sound box. If you had two pieces of wood vibrating at different rates in one sound box, you'd have a mess."

Decker took a flashlight out of his briefcase and turned it on. "These S-shaped holes—"

"F-holes."

"Yeah, I guess they do look like cursive *f*s. These allow the sound to come out?"

"Exactly."

"They're pretty big, aren't they?"

"Cello's a big instrument."

"Turn the instrument toward me, Chris. I want to look inside."

"Can you wear gloves, Sergeant? The oils on your hands aren't good for the wood."

Decker smiled. "I was only going to take a quick peek."

Whitman's face was expressionless. "Just in case you decided to touch."

Decker slipped on a pair of gloves, then shone light inside the holes. It was hard to see inside—lots of shadows—but it looked empty except for some wood bracing along the back. He stuck his fingers in as best he could, felt along the top.

Nothing.

And that made sense. It would be hard to stuff a tuxedo inside holes meant to accommodate sound waves.

But something seemed off. Decker didn't want to let it go just yet. He looked inside the instrument again—more of the same. Again he tapped the front and the back. Decker had worked with wood before. Wood had a ring to it when knocked. The front side of his cello sounded *flat*. But damned if he could see a hint of any cloth inside.

Casually, Whitman said, "You seem to be interested in acoustics. You want to hear what this one sounds like? It's a real keeper."

Decker knew the kid was toying with him. But it seemed like a good idea to act dumb. "Sure. Play for me."

Whitman took the cello from Decker, took his bow, and brought his instrument over to his stool. He placed the bottom metal spike into a hole and eased the instrument between his knees. Flicking his wrist, he picked up the bow and started playing.

In Whitman's hands, the instrument was transformed into something animate and expressive. It was hard not to get swept away in its siren call. Though Decker didn't recognize the piece, he recognized the virtuosity. With great effort, he blinked away the right side of his brain and went back to his left side, studying the kid as he made music.

At first, Whitman was hard and stiff, the instrument a foe to be conquered. The boy seemed to attack the strings, raping it to produce sounds. But as the music evolved into something pyrotechnical, his face and posture relaxed. His wrist broke, his muscles went slack, his body almost drooped, long limbs enveloping his cello as if it were a lover. The end was lightspeed, a dazzling display of finger work that produced a crescendoed climax. When he was done, the room took on an eerie silence. Whitman's face had once again gone flat.

Decker held out his hand, asking for the instrument. "One more time?"

Whitman paused, then handed him the cello. "Be careful."

Decker ran gloved hands over the wood. "How do you do repairs on this?"

"Repairs?"

"If you drop it, for instance. How does the repairman get inside to fix it?"

Whitman smiled. "I don't know. I've never dropped it."

Decker tried to read Whitman's face. Nothing. Reluctantly, he handed back the instrument.

Whitman said, "What'd you think?"

"Thanks for the concert."

Whitman's mouth turned into a mocking grin. "That's it? I overwhelm you with my prodigious talent and all you say is thanks?"

Decker locked eyes with the kid. "You know something, Chris? You're *very* good."

"Bet that's high praise from you."

"Excuse me." Decker sidestepped around Whitman, into the room's closet. This one was filled with file cases containing sheet music. The pieces were alphabetized by composer. Tucked into the corner was another cello case. Heavy. Decker took it out. "What's in here?"

"My traveling cello. Would you like me to open it for you?"

"Yep."

Whitman took the case and opened it. "It's the same as the other, only cheaper."

Whitman handed it to Decker, who inspected it closely. Decker gave it back.

Whitman said, "I can put it away?"

"Sure."

"You know, Sergeant, I'm kind of enjoying this."

"Yeah, you look a little looser." Decker rummaged through another one of Whitman's files. "I think music's good for your soul, Chris."

"You want more coffee?"

The kid had turned cocky. Decker declined the coffee, wanting to go back and examine the cellos. But since he couldn't bust them open, he knew he'd only see the same lights and shadows. Silly to beat a dead horse.

Decker finished the second bedroom and moved on to the bathroom, then the living room. He went through the sofa, the chairs, patted down the carpeting, moved furniture, tapped ceilings and floors. He even looked behind the paintings.

Nothing unusual.

On to the kitchen. Here, once again, Decker noticed Whitman's compulsiveness. Knives, forks, and spoons neatly lay in divided cutlery drawers. All cutting knives accounted for and resting in a block. He checked the kitchen cupboards and cabinets. All the dishes had been stacked; even the towels were clean. Searched the broom closet, looked under the sinks, in the refrigerator, in the oven and broiler for signs of recent burning or charring.

Not a thing unusual.

Again he started knocking walls and ceilings, checked the floors for trap doors and squeaks.

Nothing but nothing. Or as Rina would say: *Gornish met gornish.*

Decker said, "Chris, I'm still very curious about your tuxedo. Any idea where it might be?"

Whitman held out his hands and shook his head. "I'd like to ask you a few questions about it."

"Sorry, Sergeant," Whitman said. "My lawyers hate it when you ask me questions and they're not around."

"I could take you in again."

"You could."

"Maybe I'll do that."

"Up to you."

"Let me just go through your hall closet," Decker said. "Then we'll go down to the station house."

"I should call up my lawyers then?"

"It would be a good idea."

Whitman went over to his kitchen counter and picked up the phone. Decker opened the door to Whitman's hall closet. It was cedar paneled and held a row of jackets hanging from a high top bar as well as a blocky piece of furniture tucked underneath the coats.

"Ah-ha," Decker said.

Whitman hung up the phone and walked over. "What?"

Decker smiled. "Didn't mean to make you nervous. I found your flat file and easel, that's all."

Whitman looked at him. "You were looking for my flat file and easel?"

Decker ran his hand over the flat file. "Last time I was over here, we talked about art. Rather, I talked about art; you were rather quiet. But you did tell me you were an artist. I was wondering where you kept your supplies."

"So now you've found them."

Decker opened the top drawer. It was taken up by

twenty to thirty tubes of paint. The second drawer contained brushes—small, large, fan brushes but most of them unused. It also held a set of pastels, a box of charcoals, a set of pencils, rapidograph pens, and a stack of disposable palettes.

The third drawer contained his artworks. Sixteen-by-twenty drawings stacked into piles. Decker pulled one cluster and sorted through them. All of them pencil and charcoal Matisse-like figures. "Not too shabby, Chris. You're one hell of a creative person."

Whitman was quiet.

Decker took out another group of drawings. "You like Matisse?"

Whitman didn't answer.

Decker sorted and said, "Going quiet on me, Chris? I must have touched a sensitive spot."

"You're getting on my nerves."

Decker jerked his head up and looked at the kid. Whitman closed and opened his eyes, but said nothing.

"You call your lawyer yet, Chris?"

"I'll do it."

"Might be a good idea if you do it now," Decker said.

Whitman didn't move.

"I'd like to go through your work," Decker said. "You don't mind that, do you?"

"Actually I do."

Decker said, "See, I think it's even better than your music, Chris. Though you play masterfully . . . and I'm sure you have your own unique interpretation to everything you touch . . . you're still playing someone else's compositions. But your drawings are

your own. You learn a lot about a person by what he
creates."

Whitman said nothing.

Decker peered into Chris's blues—as murky as
a muddy pond. "You don't like me looking at your
stuff, do you?"

Whitman's eyes flashed fire, which instantly dead-
ened into snuffed flames. "You know, your warrant gives you the right to look around for evidence
against me. It doesn't give you the right to invade
my privacy."

Decker stopped searching. "In fact, Chris, the
warrant gives me exactly that right."

Whitman didn't speak. Decker kept his eyes on
the boy's face. He knew he'd hit upon something, but
he didn't know *what*. He went back to his hunting.

On to the fourth drawer. More sketches, this time
crouching and hunching figures of despair with dis-
torted faces à la Francis Bacon. These were on heavy
eleven-by-eight drawing paper. All of them unde-
fined heads on nude, curled-up, damaged bodies.
"You were depressed?"

Whitman was silent.

"You like drawing the human body, don't you?"

Again Whitman was quiet.

"Guess you're not one for talking about your art."
Decker sorted through the sketches, slowly and deliberately, gauging Whitman's reaction.

It was the wrong thing to do. As the time passed,
Whitman's posture grew more relaxed.

*It wasn't the drawing, Decker told himself. It was
something else. Something in that damn closet.*

The last drawer.

Small bits of paper—lots of sketches and all of them abstract. Decker looked through every single sheet of paper, then closed that last drawer. He pulled out the flat file and easel.

Rudimentary taps on the ceiling, another check on the floor for loose boards or a trap door. Then the walls, just to complete the picture. Decker started at the bottom on the baseboard and moved toward the ceiling, his fingers rapping against the back wall, looking for unusual hollow sounds. Repeated the procedure on the right wall and then the left.

And then he felt something. Too high to be felt by a man of average height.

But Decker, like Whitman, wasn't a man of average height.

A seam. Immediately, Decker took out a flashlight and shone the beam on the top left corner of the closet. Without turning around, he said, "Did you know that there's a narrow little door up there cut into the paneling?"

Whitman didn't answer. Decker stretched onto his toes and examined the seam. "Skinny sucker. Any ideas what it could be used for?"

He turned and regarded Whitman's face—expressionless, but his posture gave him away. If Chris was any stiffer, he would have been a bronze. Again Decker shone the light on the seam. "There's a lock way on top. Do you have the key?"

Whitman was quiet.

Decker said, "You know, Chris, it would be a lot easier for you to open it than for me to pry it loose."

Whitman said, "Your warrant prohibits any de-molition that compromises the structural integrity of the building."

"We're talking about a closet, Chris."

"*I'm* talking about a closet *wall*!"

Decker thought a moment. The secret compartment wouldn't compromise the structural integrity of the building. But with enough pictures, a clever lawyer could aim the camera in such a way as to convince a judge that this was a wall. Decker didn't want to take the chance of gathering evidence only to have it be thrown out.

He reached into his briefcase and pulled out a pack of picks. "What I don't do for my job. You want to hold the light for me while I do this?"

Whitman's face was flat. "Fuck you."

"You're losing it, guy."

"I'm going to call my lawyer."

"A very good idea."

Decker tucked the flashlight under his chin. It was a hard lock to pick, taking him over a half hour. But eventually the lock gave way with a pop and the door opened. Decker reached inside and felt around.

More papers. He stuck his hand inside and emptied the compartment of its contents. Five drawing tablets. He brought them into the light and flipped off the top cover. He began to leaf through them.

They say every artist has a favorite model and Whitman was no exception. Dozens of pictures—all representational and all of the same girl. As the Bible stated, she was beautiful of face and form. She'd been posed clothed, in scant dress, partially nude, then completely nude, sitting on his bed, hunched over, arms around her knees.

Decker faced Whitman. The kid looked stunned, and for a moment Decker almost felt sorry for him. Because there were feelings here. But then he thought about Cheryl Diggs. She deserved some feelings, too.

"Who is she?"

"Nobody," he whispered.

"Chris, you're going to have to do better than that."

Whitman was silent.

"Chris?"

"Nobody," he said again. "Someone from my imagination."

"So . . ." Decker held up the picture of the girl. "So if I showed these drawings to some of your friends, they'd have *no* idea who she was."

Whitman swallowed hard, ran his hands through his hair, and said nothing.

Decker flipped through a second tablet. More of the same. He picked up a third one. Midway through, he stopped abruptly, staring at the drawing in front of him.

Same girl in very different pose, but not an unfamiliar one to Decker. The girl was lying on Whitman's bed, wrists bound to the headboard, ankles tied together and bound to the footboard. He went on to the next drawing, then the next. Variation on the face, but not on the pose. The poor girl seemed very worn, but was showing a brave face. She looked anxious to please.

Or maybe she just looked anxious. He showed the

bound girl to Whitman. "Maybe I should pass this one around, starting with the morgue."

"She isn't in the morgue."

"The pose looks very familiar and that's too bad for you." Decker pulled out the cuffs. "Turn around, Chris."

"Wait—"

"Turn around and hit the wall, now!"

Whitman did as told and Decker snapped on the cuffs. He then went to his briefcase and took out a portable tape recorder. He tested it, then, satisfied, turned it back to the beginning. "Christopher Sean Whitman, you are under arrest for the murder of Cheryl Diggs. You have the right to remain silent—"

"Can I talk to—"

"Anything you say can and may be used against you in a court of law. You have the right to an attorney during questioning. If you can't—"

"Ser—"

"If you can't afford an attorney, the state will appoint you representation free of charge. Do you understand—"

"Yes, I understand."

"Do you understand the charges read to you clearly and freely?"

Whitman said, "Yes. Let me just say something—"

"Do you wish to waive your right to an attorney?"

Whitman paused, then said yes.

"Do you understand that at any time, you may ask for your lawyer and I will stop questioning you?"

"Can you cut the crap for just—"

"Do you understand—"

"Yes, I understand," Whitman snapped. "Can I talk to you off the record for a moment?"

"No."

Whitman paused. "Then I'll just talk to you."

"Shoot," Decker said.

"Can you take off the cuffs?"

"You bench-press two hundred pounds, Chris. I think I'll leave the cuffs on."

Whitman wiped his face on his shoulder. He was showered in sweat. "I know . . ." He swallowed hard. "I know you're just doing your job. And I can appreciate that. There's nothing personal here." The kid looked at the ceiling, then back at Decker. "These are just pictures . . . made up in my head, you know?"

"Are you saying this girl is made up?"

"Just hear me out, okay?"

"Go."

Whitman took a deep breath and let it out slowly. "No, the girl isn't made up. But the poses are . . . were. She was my tutor for about . . . three months." He swallowed again. "That's all. We ran in completely different circles. I haven't talked to her in months. But she was lovely. Her face stayed with me. We had a nice working relationship. I don't want her to think of me as a sleaze."

"Well, that's up to her, Chris—"

"I realize . . ." Whitman interrupted loudly, then he stopped talking. He closed and opened his eyes. "I realize what you're trying to do, why these pictures are . . ."

Decker waited.

Whitman shook his head. "I know why the pictures are incriminating. Cheryl was found bound; you find pictures by me of girls all tied up. But that isn't proof of anything. Other than the fact that once I drew one girl tied up. You get my point?"

"There's more than one picture here."

"It was the same fantasy. That's all it was. A fantasy."

Decker said, "Well, your lawyer can argue that point to a grand jury. I'm going to call up my station house now and arrange for transport—"

"Wait!" Whitman hesitated, then said, "Suppose . . . I can get you better evidence."

Decker waited, hoping his astonishment wasn't showing.

"I'll get you better evidence against me," Whitman said. "Better evidence in exchange for these pictures."

Decker stared at the kid. What was the catch?

Whitman said, "Sergeant, I never did *anything* with this girl. You question her, she won't know what the hell you're talking about. If you parade these drawings before a grand jury, all you'll be doing is . . . *ruining* someone nice. She's a straight A student, and last I heard, she was still a virgin. Why bring her down just because I have a wild imagination?"

"Chris, that's not up to me—"

"I'll get you names, Decker," Whitman said, desperately. "Names of hookers I've actually tied up."

"You've tied up hookers?"

"Yes."

"*Live* hookers, Chris?"

"Yes, of course they're alive. I'll get you names of women I've tied up. I'll get you names and you can go down and talk to them in person. I'm talking live witnesses, Decker. Hell of a lot better than a bunch of dead drawings. You understand what I'm saying?"

Decker said, "You must really like this girl."

"Yes, I do. Now I understand that you're not going to fork over the drawings just based on my word. But if I deliver you witnesses, do we have a deal?"

"No, Chris, we do not have a deal. Unless you want to confess right now. That'd sure save your lady a lot of embarrassment."

"*Christ!*" Whitman exploded. "Don't you *goddamn* understand what I'm offering you? I'm *frying* myself in exchange for the drawings."

"If you want to confess, I'm listening."

"I'm not going to *confess*, goddamn it! I didn't *do* anything!"

Decker said, "I'm going to call transport to take you down to the station house. You can call your law—"

"*Aren't you* goddamn *listening?*" Whitman kicked a chair across his living room. It smashed against the wall and splintered into several pieces. "I'm giving you something *better*! *Open your fucking* ears, *for god-sakes!*"

It was at this moment that Decker realized Whitman was a powder keg inching toward a lighted match. He was a big, strapping boy on the verge of a violent eruption. Decker spoke soothingly. "I'm listening to you, Christopher. I hear every word you're saying. You deliver . . . and then we can talk. I'm *not* shutting you out. But I can't promise you anything. Do you understand that?"

Whitman was breathing hard. He suddenly looked very young. Decker said, "You deliver first, and then I'll talk to you. We'll all talk to you. But absolutely no promises. Understand?"

The boy bit his lower lip, then nodded.

"Chris, answer the question verbally. My tape recorder doesn't pick up nods."

"Yes, I understand."

"No promises, right?"

"Right."

"But first you've got to cooperate, Chris. Who's the girl?"

Whitman was silent.

Decker said softly, "We both want to keep this as *quiet* as possible. If you tell me the name, I can be discreet. If not, I'll start showing the pictures around—"

"*Don't* do that!"

"So tell me the name."

Whitman's knees buckled. He dropped to the floor. Decker knelt beside him. "I understand your protective attitude. She looks like a nice girl . . . very pretty."

"She's the most . . ." His voice faded.

"I'm sure I'll understand when I meet her," Decker said. "The name, son?"

Whitman was silent.

"Chris, you don't want your friends to know, do you?"

"No," he whispered.

"The name?"

"Please be nice."

"I will."

"Tell her I'm . . . I'm very sorry."

"The name, Christopher?"

"Teresa McLaughlin."

❧ 24

She spoke behind a closed door. And even when she opened it to check Decker's ID, she kept the chain on. A cautious girl, but in the end, she let him in. She kept her distance, eyes darting between the upstairs landing and the front door. Distrustful. And after what had happened to Cheryl Diggs, who could blame her?

Decker stepped into Teresa McLaughlin's living room.

Whitman had done a good job of rendering her on paper, but had fallen short. Because she was truly a stunner—a breathtaking adolescent easing with grace into womanhood. An oval face held clear, amber eyes flecked with dark chocolate. Her complexion was cream-colored except for a sprinkling of freckles across the bridge of her nose and a natural blush that outlined high cheekbones. Her hair was waist-length, thick and deep bronze, tied back and held in place with a plastic clip. She wore an oversized, long-sleeved T-shirt under a brocade vest and baggy, faded jeans.

Studying her face, Decker bet she had trouble getting dates. Because something about her was unapproachable. Her eyes, though beautiful, were stop signs that said don't touch . . . don't even *look*. Her aloofness, combined with a distinct vulnerability, must have been one powerful aphrodisiac to a cocky kid like Whitman.

Decker kept his hands in his pockets, glanced around the living room. Small and neat with conventional furniture. A six-foot sofa facing a couple of armchairs with a coffee table between them. A few nondescript floral still lifes hung on the walls. There was also a framed poster of Monet's water lilies. The carpet was oatmeal hued, marred by a couple of large, faded, amoeba-shaped stains.

"I just made some coffee for myself." Her voice was soft and wary. "Would you like a cup?"

"Black coffee would be great, thank you." Decker smiled and she returned a small one of her own. "Where should I sit?"

"How about the dining-room table?" She kneaded her hands. "My stepmom doesn't like anyone drinking coffee in the living room. Too many accidents on the carpet."

"The dining room is fine, Teresa."

"Terry, please." She looked at the table. It was covered with school papers and texts. "I'll clear it off in a minute." Again a brief smile. Then she disappeared into the kitchen. Seconds later, a child around seven came scampering down the staircase. She stopped short when she saw Decker, keeping a safe distance between them.

"Why, hello there," Decker said. "Are you looking for Terry?"

Nodding, the girl stuck her thumb in her mouth, then quickly pulled it out.

"She's in the kitchen. You can go see her if you want."

She didn't answer. A moment later, Terry returned carrying two mugs of coffee. She saw the little girl, let go with a genuine smile, then placed the coffee cups on top of a calculus textbook. Once the mugs were on the table, the child raced to Terry and hugged her waist.

"It's okay, Melissa," Terry explained. "He's just a policeman—a detective with a real gold badge."

Melissa's eyes grew wide. She muttered something. Terry bent down and the girl threw her arms around her neck. She whispered something in the older girl's ear.

"What?" Terry asked. "I can't understand you."

Melissa whispered again.

Aloud Terry said, "No, he's not going to *arrest* me. But you've got to go back upstairs because I have to talk to him, okay?"

Melissa looked scared.

Terry stood up and faced Decker. "I usually make her a snack about this time. I was about to do that when you came. Would you mind waiting while I prepare her something?"

"Not at all," Decker said. "I'll even show her my badge."

But Melissa wasn't interested. She tagged after Terry, hanging on to the hem of her T-shirt, as the teen dragged her unwittingly into the kitchen. Decker could make out soft, cooing sounds but no words. A minute later, they came back, Terry holding a plate filled with fruit slices and chips.

"I want to eat down here," Melissa said.

"I know, honey, but you can't," Terry said.

"I'll be good. I'll be quiet."

"Missy, you don't have to be quiet to be good. You're good just because you're good." Again, Terry bent down. "I have to talk to the policeman in private. You wait for me upstairs. Hopefully, this won't take too long."

The girl didn't budge.

"Come on." Terry took her hand. "I'll walk you up."

They were gone for about five minutes before Terry returned. Her expression was apologetic. "She doesn't get out much. My stepmom keeps long hours. Melissa's a little antsy around strangers. All these stories she hears at school."

"She's your sister?"

"Half sister."

A kitchen bell went off. Terry checked her watch. "That's the washing machine. Would you mind if I threw a batch of clothes in the dryer?"

"Go ahead."

"Thank you." She ran back to the kitchen, then returned and began tidying up her school papers. "Sorry about the mess. I like to spread out when I study."

"Nothing to apologize for," Decker said. "Are you studying for finals?"

"Yes . . . out of habit more than anything." She began stacking her notes. "I'm a senior so it's really all over for me. Short of a catastrophe, I should be entering UCLA in the fall as a freshman."

"Congratulations," Decker said. "I hear it's very hard to get into UCLA these days."

She shrugged. "The admissions thing is a bit over-blown. It's not that hard." She glanced at her watch. "I'm running a little late. Can I put dinner in the oven? My stepmom usually goes to the health club after work. She comes home ravenous and grumpy. It'll only take a minute."

"I've got time."

Again she flew into the kitchen. When she came back, Decker said, "You're a busy lady, aren't you?"

"It's no big deal."

"It's nice that you help out your stepmom."

She shrugged, but her face was tense.

Decker said, "Or do you have a choice?"

Terry forced herself to smile. "S'right. My step-mom works hard. She's an executive secretary at the regional offices of Filagree Drug Company. Lot of responsibilities." Then she muttered, "Or so she says."

"What about your dad?"

Terry paused. "My dad?"

Decker was quiet. He knew he'd touched a nerve.

Terry said, "Uh, sure, my dad works, too. Of course."

Lots of tension. Decker nodded passively.

"He's a maintenance engineer for several big down-town law buildings." Terry waited a beat. "That's a fancy title for a handyman."

"It's honest labor," Decker said. "Nothing wrong with that."

"It's better than flipping burgers. He did that for a while, too." Terry bit her nail, then sat down. "You're right. It is honest work. And I know my dad works very hard. I don't mean to disparage him."

"I'm sure you don't," Decker said. "You've just got your own problems, I bet."

"Who doesn't?" She folded slender hands, placed them on the tabletop and kept her eyes on her clasped fingers. "Is the coffee okay?"

Decker took a sip. "Terrific." He spoke gently. "You do know why I'm here, don't you?"

"I'm assuming it's about Chris Whitman. What are you doing? Interviewing everyone in the class?"

"Only certain people," Decker said. "You made the list."

"Lucky me." Her voice was a whisper. She cleared her throat, then spoke louder. "How can I help you?"

"Tell me about Chris."

"There's not much to tell. I know him from school. We're in the same grade."

"Is he in any of your classes?"

"Just orchestra."

"Ah . . ." Decker took out a notepad. "And what instrument do you play, Terry?"

"I play violin." She waited a beat. "Actually, I play *at* the violin. I'm terrible."

"Don't be *too* easy on yourself, young lady," Decker said.

Terry smiled and looked at him, her eyes as warm as melted butter. "I'm just being honest. I'm an excellent student, but I stink at the violin."

"You don't play like Chris, huh?"

"No, not at all."

"He's a remarkable musician," he said.

"Yes, he is."

"He's also a good-looking guy."

Terry was silent.

"A little distant, even cool in his personality," Decker went on. "But he's well-spoken . . . articulate. Classy in his own way. From what I understand, Cheryl was a real party girl. So what was the attraction between them?"

She laughed softly. "You're asking *me*?"

Decker said, "Yeah, you knew Cheryl, didn't you, Terry?"

"We knew each other by name, but we weren't friends." She began to knead her hands again. "Not that we were enemies. We weren't . . . anything."

Decker said, "What'd you think of her?"

"I didn't," Terry said. "She never crossed my mind."

"I'm sure you've heard rumors."

"I try to avoid gossip." Her voice was soft. "I wasn't friends with Cheryl . . . or with Chris for that matter. We didn't hang out in the same circles."

"But you were friendlier with Chris than with Cheryl, weren't you?"

She cleared her throat again. "He was my student . . . one of my students. I'm a tutor . . . mostly math and science, but sometimes humanities and languages, too. I tutored Chris for a while."

Decker flipped the cover of his notepad. "And when was that?"

"At the beginning of the term. Maybe seven months ago."

"How long did you tutor him?"

"About three months."

Decker looked up. "What happened?"

"What do you mean?"

"Why did you stop tutoring him?" Decker clicked

his pen. "His grades going into finals weren't exactly spectacular."

Terry squirmed. "I wouldn't know. We didn't talk much after he quit."

"It was his idea to stop the lessons?"

"Mutual." Terry fidgeted. "It wasn't a good match."

"A good *match*?"

She paused. "We both thought he could benefit better from someone else."

"Why?"

"Sometimes that's the case."

"So *you* broke it off?"

"It wasn't a relationship." Terry took a deep breath. "Why are you asking me questions? I haven't really seen Chris for months. Like I said, we didn't have the same group of friends."

"Yes, I can believe that. But that doesn't mean you and Chris couldn't have remained friends after you stopped tutoring him."

"But we didn't," Terry said.

Decker studied the girl for a moment. It seemed to unnerve her. "So you haven't seen Chris in months, right?"

"Basically, yes."

"What do you mean by *basically*, yes?"

"Just . . . I mean I've seen him in school . . . in orchestra. But we haven't really talked to each other."

"There you go again, using the word *really*—"

"I mean like we'd say hi when we passed each other in the hallways."

Decker leaned in close. "And that's been your only contact with him since you stopped tutoring him?"

"Basically, yes."

"*Basically*, again?" Decker questioned. "Terry, why don't you just tell me what's going on?"

"That is basically what's going on."

"*Basically* for a third time," Decker said. "You know what, Terry? You're a terrible liar."

She blinked back tears. "I'm not lying. I'm skirting the truth with the judicious use of modifiers."

Decker laughed and so did she until gentle rills rolled down her cheeks. Leaning in close, Decker reached over to her neck and pulled on the gold chain until a tucked-in charm was fully liberated. A gold cross dangled on the end. He showed it to her.

He said, "Two days ago, when I visited Chris at his apartment, he was wearing a crucifix exactly like this one. This morning, he wasn't wearing it."

Terry didn't answer.

Decker said, "When was the last time you saw him, Terry?"

She wiped her eyes. "It would be really silly to lie, right?"

"Right."

"I saw Chris around six this morning."

Decker paused. Whitman was being tailed at that time. The stakeout didn't mention anything about Whitman being with a girl. Something didn't jibe. "You saw Chris at six in the morning?"

"Yes."

"You met him at the Laundromat?"

"Laundromat? What are you talking about?"

Decker paused. "What are *you* talking about?"

Terry turned red. "I . . . I spent the night at his apartment."

"Ah." Decker wrote as he spoke. "Do you have a key to his place?"

"No, not at all. I came to his place last night . . . sat on his doorstep and waited for him to come home from the police station."

"How did you know he was at the police station?"

She covered her face and let her hands drop. "Is your official title Detective or Sergeant?"

"It's Sergeant. Go on."

Terry spoke slowly. "I hadn't talked to Chris in months. He stopped talking to me when I stopped tutoring him."

"Why?"

"I don't know why. I guess he was mad at me for suggesting he find another tutor."

"Why'd you tell him to look elsewhere?" Decker said. "The truth this time, Terry."

"The arrangement became . . . uncomfortable."

"Was he inappropriate?"

"On the contrary." She cleared her throat and took a drink of coffee. "Chris had been unfailingly polite."

"So what was the problem?"

"*That* was the problem," Terry said. "There were feelings between us that couldn't be acted upon. Because Chris was . . . suffice it to say that it couldn't work between us."

Decker paused. "He told you he was engaged?"

Terry breathed a sigh of relief. "*Exactly!* He was engaged to someone else. At first, I didn't believe him. He's just a kid. I thought it had to be an excuse . . . that maybe he was gay or wasn't attracted to me. Later I found out that neither was the case."

She looked at the ceiling.

"Eventually, I believed him. And that made things uncomfortable between us. I told him to find someone else."

"Then he got mad at you?"

"Real mad. He stopped . . . talking to me. I knew his behavior was childish, but that doesn't mean it didn't hurt."

"You were affected by it?"

"Of course. I liked him a lot. I wanted to remain friends. Obviously, he didn't." She laughed nervously. "Maybe he liked seeing me suffer."

She turned bright red.

"I didn't mean it like that. I was just trying to be funny. Chris was wonderful when I taught him. You know, Sergeant, I've never been attracted to dangerous boys. Lots of girls are, but not me."

"What do you mean by dangerous?"

"You know, the white gang wannabes who shave their heads and brandish weapons to impress the girls." Terry rolled her golden eyes. "Even a tame school like Central West Valley has a group of those kinds of guys. They think it's cool to terrorize, you know. They have contests who can be the first to make this girl or that girl. Once one of them came to me for tutoring. Yeah, *right*! I made up an excuse, told him I was booked. But he kept pestering me. Giving me creepy looks. Then he showed up at my *house*! That really *freaked* me out."

"What happened?"

"Luckily, he happened to come on one of the days I was with Chris. This was very early on . . . maybe I'd been tutoring Chris for a week. He stepped outside and talked to the guy. I don't know *what* he said—I never asked, Chris never said—but neither the guy nor any of his little friends ever bothered me again." She studied her nails. "I was very relieved and very grateful."

Bet you were, Decker thought. *And didn't he know it.*

"Even when Chris was mad at me, I knew he was hurting." She shrugged. "I just didn't know how to rectify it."

Decker picked up the crucifix and let it drop on her vest. "Obviously he stopped being mad at you. How did it come about?"

"It happened real suddenly." Terry thought a moment. "One minute we weren't speaking; then the next, we talked about running away together."

Decker wrote as he spoke. "When did this take place?"

"Prom night, if you can imagine that. Then this terrible thing with Cheryl happened. . . ."

There was silence.

Decker locked eyes with the girl. "Terry, did Chris call you the morning of Cheryl's murder? Answer me honestly."

Terry shook her head no. "No, he never called me. But he did come to my house yesterday afternoon."

"What went on?" Decker asked.

"We talked. He told me he was going in for questioning, and a lie-detector test. He also told me he had come to say good-bye. He said he couldn't see me again."

"He came to your house just to tell you good-bye?"

"Apparently."

"And he didn't say anything about Cheryl?"

"Yes, he talked about Cheryl. He was distraught over what had happened. His pain was like spilling over. After he left, I felt so drained. Empty. I know I should have stayed away from him last night . . . but I wanted to find out what happened at the police station. I still . . . cared for him."

She covered her face, then looked up.

"I told my stepmom I was sleeping over at a friend's house. Instead, I went to his apartment. I've never done anything like that before. But it was something that I just had to do."

Decker regarded her face. Her frank sincerity reminded him of Rina. "When did you leave for Whitman's apartment?"

"Around five in the afternoon. I walked over . . . took my books and studied while I waited."

"He came home late."

"Around one in the morning. He wanted me to go back home . . . but after I explained the situation, he had no choice but to put me up. So I spent the night at his place." She fingered the cross. "He gave me his crucifix. He said it was his mother's."

"Did you do more than just *talk* to him, Terry?"

The girl blushed.

"Did you have sex with him?"

"No," she said, quickly. "No, I didn't . . . we didn't. Honestly. It's true."

Decker regarded her face. "I think you're skirting the truth again. Terry, it's important for me to know the extent of your relationship."

"Why? Do you want to know if Chris has ever been violent with me? The answer is a resounding no. Never even a . . . a *hint* of it. He's always been wonderful with me . . . gentle, considerate, sweet."

She looked up.

"You know, it was totally my fault that he stopped talking to me. He was hurting and I didn't want to hear it."

Decker kept his face flat, but felt weary inside. Another girl willing to die on the cross for the jerk she loved. Though the teen was articulate, she was still adolescent, her grasp of reality still a mite out of her reach. He said, "Terry—"

"No, really. It was my fault. I shouldn't have broken it off right then. I should have *known* better. Because I know what it's like to hurt. To reach out and be rejected . . . over and over."

"Yes, rejection is painful, but—"

"All those times I've tried to reach out to my father. But you can't talk to walls. You know, I've worked *real* hard to nurture Melissa. Last thing I'd ever want is for her to grow up warped like me."

"You're not warped—"

"Oh, yes, I am. Chris could see it first time we ever talked. He knew damaged goods because he'd been there himself. Do you *know* what he did for me?"

Decker knew he was going to find out. "What?"

"He gave me my grandparents." Tears were streaming down the girl's cheeks. "He called up my maternal grandparents—my late mom's parents. *I* was too scared to approach them. Absolutely petrified. But he could read my heart. One day, I came to his place, expecting to tutor him. Instead, I wound up talking to my grandparents for almost an hour. He found out their number in Chicago and called them up cold. Can you imagine any boy doing that for a girl without expecting anything in return?"

The question was rhetorical so Decker didn't answer.

"My God, it was the *first* time in history anybody had ever done something for me," Terry said. "At that point, I knew I *loved* Chris more than anyone in the world."

"I understand—"

"I never knew that adults could actually be *proud* of their children's accomplishments," she went on. "You know, when I won the National Merit Scholarship, my dad didn't even come to the awards ceremony. He was sick, he was tired, he had a job interview, he was drunk, I don't remember. I was too young to drive, so I walked to school by myself . . . and walked home by myself afterward. I lied and told everyone my parents were meeting me later to take me out to dinner. Yeah, right! All I had waiting for me was a sink filled with dirty dishes. Which I washed, I might add."

Abruptly, she stopped speaking and wiped her cheeks. "So you can understand why I have a special feeling for Chris."

"Of course."

"He did *not* murder Cheryl Diggs. He didn't even care about her. Why would he kill her?"

Decker rolled his tongue in his cheek.

Terry sighed. "Yes, I know she was pregnant. It wasn't his. He was sure of that."

Decker paused. "When did Chris tell you all this?"

"Yesterday."

Decker started writing in his pad. "And you honestly believe everything he tells you, Terry?"

Terry stared at him. "He told me he passed his lie-detector test. Is that true?"

Decker paused, then nodded.

"So that says a lot, doesn't it?"

"It could be he's telling the truth." Decker looked the girl square in the eye. "Or it could be that Chris, unlike you, is an excellent liar."

"Why don't you believe what you see?"

"Trouble is, Terry, I do believe what I see," Decker said. "And I don't see Chris the same way you do."

Terry bit her lip and looked down.

Decker studied her for a moment. "Or maybe I do. You have some doubts, don't you?"

"He didn't kill Cheryl Diggs," she said, firmly.

Decker thought a moment. He hated doing it, but there was no easy way to drop a bomb. "So Chris never got physical with you?"

"Never. When we were working together, he never even uttered a cross word to me."

"So you've never seen him violent . . . or deviant maybe?"

The girl was taken aback. *"Deviant?"*

"Terry, I believe you when you say you didn't have sex with him. But you two were physical last night, weren't you?"

She blushed and nodded.

Decker kept his face devoid of emotion. "And it wasn't the first time you two have ever been physical, was it?"

Red-faced, Terry looked down. "No. Last night was the first time we ever did anything."

"Terry, please don't lie."

"I'm not lying."

"Then you're hiding something from me."

"No, I swear I'm not." The girl grew agitated. "Why don't you believe me?"

Decker shifted gears. "Last night, when you were with him, did he show any sexual deviance to you?"

"Of course not!"

"Didn't turn him on to get rough—"

"Boy, are you off base!" She looked repulsed. "I told you I don't like dangerous guys. I would never allow anything like that."

"Not even for Chris?"

"Not even for Chris!" She was adamant.

"How about if he asked a special favor from you, Terry? And he swore he wouldn't hurt you."

Panic had crept into her eyes. Decker felt terrible, but a girl had been murdered and he was determined to find her killer. He kept his voice even. "Did Chris ever talk to you about his sexual fantasies? Maybe fantasies about bondage?"

Her eyes darted from him, to the staircase, then to the front door. She was terrified as well as confused. Maybe those pictures had come from Whitman's imagination.

Decker spoke soothingly. "Terry, did Chris ever talk about tying women up?"

Her eyes suddenly got wide.

Bingo!

In a whisper, Decker said, "He tied you up, didn't he?"

Terry turned ashen. "Oh, my God, the *sketches*!" She broke out in a cold sweat. "I'm . . . I feel a little dizzy. Excuse . . ."

She stood up. Decker caught her before she hit the floor.

❧ 25

Still pale, but at least she was conscious, trembling with raw, hard shakes. Decker had dug up an old sweater from the coat closet, had placed it over Terry's shoulders. Sitting at the dining-room table, he waited while the girl sipped tea, her shoulders hunched as she gripped the mug to get warm. Not that it would help much. The house wasn't cold. Her chill was internal.

She raised her eyes from her teacup, the color as clear and gold as filtered cider. Her voice was very soft. "Can I ask you a personal question?"

"You can ask anything you'd like."

"Did you actually see the sketches?"

"Yes."

"All of them?"

"I don't know," Decker said. "I saw sketches of you nude, I saw sketches of you tied up and secured on his bed. Are there more?"

"No . . . that's about . . ." She returned her eyes to her drink. "Do you have children?"

"Yes."

"What would you have done if . . ." Her eyes lifted and met his. "If your daughter posed like I did?"

He sat back in his chair. "First thing I'd want to find out is why she did it. That's what I'd like to discuss with you, Terry."

"Would you be mad at her?"

"It depends."

"What if she told you it was art. Nothing sordid or dirty . . . or shame— . . . it was just art. Would you accept that? Or would you still be mad at her? Think that she's a whore or something?"

"Terry, I don't think you're a whore. No one does."

She lowered her head. "Thanks. But it's not something you'd want your daughter to do, right?"

Decker considered the question. "If this was an honest interpretation of what she considered art . . . if her posing wasn't coerced either physically or *psychologically* . . . and if she had considered the consequences, I wouldn't be mad at her. But as a father, I'd feel real squeamish about it. Even though my daughter is of legal age."

"Which I'm not." She covered her face. "I'm very embarrassed you had to see them."

Decker didn't know what to say. When in doubt, be a professional. He took out his notebook. "When are you going to be eighteen, Terry?"

"I'll be seventeen in a month."

"You skipped?"

She nodded. "What are you going to do with the pictures?"

"They've been filed and entered as evidence in Cheryl Diggs's murder case."

"So a lot of people are going to see them, right?"

"Some people might."

"Am I going to have to appear in a trial or anything?"

"I can't tell you any specifics, Terry, because I don't know them."

"Can you give me an educated guess?"

"It's likely the State will present the drawings to a grand jury in order to obtain an indictment."

"Will the sketches be in the papers?"

"No," Decker said.

"Not even in the tabloids?"

Decker rubbed his hand over his face. "You're a minor. They shouldn't touch you."

"Ah . . . the recklessness of youth," Terry muttered.

"Your parents will probably find out, Terry. You should talk to them about it."

"I'll pass, thank you. Let them find out. Deal with it one step at a time."

Decker said, "Tell me about the sketches, Terry."

"They were art. Chris's interpretation of Jesus dying on the cross. We're both . . . influenced by Catholicism. Him even more than me." She shrugged. "That's it."

"That's it?"

She nodded.

"You were just his model?"

"Yes."

Decker studied the girl's face. She was telling him half-truths. "After he tied you up, you two didn't become physical?"

"No. It was all very polite."

"He never touched you?"

She shook her head no. "I was his model . . . that's all."

"You told me you and Chris weren't talking for a long period of time."

She nodded.

"So how long ago did you pose for him?"

"About five months ago."

"While you were still tutoring him?"

"Yes."

Decker looked up. "How'd he get you to pose so explicitly?"

Her eyes moistened. She didn't speak.

"He told you he loved you," Decker stated.

"You think I'm an idiot."

"Not at all," Decker said. "A mistake doesn't make anyone an idiot. Not if you learn from it."

"And what's the lesson, Sergeant? Not to trust men? I already learned that from my father."

Decker kept his expression neutral. So jaded, so young. Or maybe that was just teenage hyperbole talking.

Terry said, "Yes, he told me he loved me. He also said he didn't want to sleep with me because he was engaged to someone else. He said this was a way we could be intimate without having sex. Maybe that was a line, also. But he sounded sincere. First time I posed for him, he didn't do anything weird."

Decker raised a brow. "Did he do something weird the second time, Terry?"

"No, not at all," Terry said, quickly. "I just meant that the first time, he posed me in a very normal way. You saw the pictures, right?"

"The ones with you hunched over?"

She nodded.

"Yes, I saw them."

"He had acted very respectful. So, the second time, when he asked if he could . . . tie me up for his vision of Christ . . . I did feel squeamish. But then I figured, why not?"

She took off her hair clip and shook out long strands of red-tinged mocha.

"You know, I asked him for the sketches when I stopped tutoring him. He wouldn't give them to me."

"I'm sure now he wishes he had."

Terry suddenly slumped. "That's true. The sketches are certainly more harmful to Chris than to me."

Decker said, "How many times did you pose in binds for him?"

"Just one time. That's all."

"He never asked you to do it again?"

Terry's eyes went to the ceiling. Decker regarded her face. "Or was it because of the modeling that you suggested he get another tutor?"

"One of the reasons, I guess."

"You showed very good judgment."

"I modeled willingly," she said, softly. "There was no coercion."

Decker said, "A boy as savvy and as good-looking as Chris gets you alone. He tells you he loves you. He tells you this is a way to get intimate without sex. He probably tells you to trust him, that if you really love him, you'll do this for him. Something like that, right?"

Tears flowed down her cheeks.

"Don't waste your tears on him," Decker said. "Whitman's not a nice boy. He's been arrested for murder. Consider yourself lucky."

Terry shook her head. "He didn't kill Cheryl, Sergeant."

"Terry, it's time to drop the party line," Decker said. "There is a very strong likelihood that you will be called to testify before a grand jury. I want you to tell the truth. I want you to tell how Chris manipulated you, how he used your vulnerability and emotions to get you to do what he wanted—"

"That wouldn't be the truth!"

Decker paused. "You *wanted* to be posed like that?"

"No, but . . ." Her eyes watered. "I love him—"

"Terry, you're too smart for that."

"You didn't let me finish."

Decker stopped himself. "Sorry. Go on."

"I love Chris, Sergeant. But I've got a fierce sense of justice. If I truly . . . *believed* that he killed Cheryl, I might still love him, but I'd want to see him punished."

She looked pained.

"If you put me before a grand jury, I will tell the truth. But it won't be your interpretation of the truth . . . which is a legitimate interpretation but . . ."

Decker waited. When she didn't continue, he filled in the blanks. "Terry, if Chris really loved you, he wouldn't have compromised you like that."

"He didn't compromise me. Those sketches were just between the two of us. They were very *personal*!"

"If they were so personal, why did I find them doing a simple, routine search around his apartment?"

She paused. "They were just lying around?"

"I had no trouble finding them," Decker said breezily.

"But that doesn't make sense. That he'd leave them

out in the open. They're incriminating if nothing else." She glared at him. "I thought you were honest. Now I see you're lying. All you care about is getting Chris indicted."

"Hell, yeah, I want to get him indicted!" Decker said, forcefully. "You said you don't like dangerous boys. Terry, Chris is a real *bad* egg. Do you know who his father is?"

"Joseph Donatti."

Well, so much for the element of shock.

Terry went on, "So *what* if Joseph Donatti is Chris's adopted father? So what if Chris is *from* mob? It doesn't make *him* mob. You know what Chris is?"

"A saint?" Decker said.

"Very funny!" she said defiantly. "He's a *pawn*, Sergeant! A trapped and manipulated pawn used by vicious men. And now you're manipulating me to testify against him. Look elsewhere. I won't bring him down."

"I'd try elsewhere except Cheryl Diggs is dead."

"He *didn't* kill her!"

"Terry, while Chris was proclaiming his love for you, he was sexually involved with Cheryl Diggs. The guy is not a poor little frog prince. He's a toad!"

She spoke each word with precise enunciation. "He . . . didn't . . . kill . . . Cheryl . . . Diggs . . . period."

Decker sat back in his chair. Confrontation wasn't working. The more he attacked Whitman, the more the girl dug in her heels. Because above all, there were emotions between the two of them.

He thought for a moment.

The girl had told him she had a fierce sense of justice. For her, fear and anger weren't powerful motivators. Perhaps he should be stressing kindness . . . *fairness*. He softened his expression, folded his hands, and looked her in the eye. "Would you like to know where I actually *found* the sketches?"

Terry didn't answer.

"In Chris's hall closet was this tiny locked slot that blended in nicely with the paneling in the wall. Way up high . . ." Decker stretched his arms to emphasize the point. "At the very tip-top of his closet. I almost missed it." He smiled. "But I didn't because I'm a real pro. Chris just about fainted when I found them."

Terry looked up.

"Man, I almost felt sorry for him," Decker said. "I think he would have accepted cigarette burns on his butt rather than give out your name. But I backed him against the wall. I told him if *he* didn't give it to me, I'd pass the pictures around your school until I found someone who recognized you."

Her face froze with fear. "You didn't . . ."

Decker shook his head. "No, it obviously didn't come to that." He gave her a sad smile. "Yes, he gave me your name. But he was miserable about it. He told me to tell you he was sorry."

Tears formed in her eyes.

Decker said, "You know what, Terry? I truly felt bad for him. I feel bad for you, too. But my real sympathies are with someone else. Do you know who I really feel bad for?"

Terry was silent.

"Cheryl Diggs. She died so ignominiously. Young girl tied up like a beast to be slaughtered. That's no way to die."

Wet tracks ran down her cheeks.

Decker said, "Cheryl never got a chance to tell me her side of the story. Corpses can't talk. So I have to talk for them. You understand what I'm saying, Terry?"

She wiped her cheeks and nodded.

"I took one look at that young face . . . staring at me with dead eyes . . ." Decker paused. "I swore I would talk for her . . . avenge her. Because someone viciously killed her, without regard for her feelings, for her life. And I'm sorry to tell you, I do believe it was Christopher Whitman. What do you think, Terry?"

In a whisper, she said, "Does it matter?"

"It matters to me. It'll matter to Chris. And it'll matter a great deal to a grand jury. Most important, it'll matter to *you*. It will determine how you can live with yourself after this whole mess is over."

She looked up with dry eyes. "Chris didn't do it."

Decker kept his frustration in check. He studied her face. No longer defiant. Very sincere. Calmly, he asked, "And why do you think that, Terry?"

She didn't answer.

Decker waited a beat. "Do you think Chris is capable of murder, Terry?"

Slowly, she nodded her head yes.

"So why don't *you* think he killed Cheryl?"

She took a deep breath and let it out slowly. "I used to go to the rages . . . the parties. I wasn't an active participant . . . I sat around. But I used to go to see Chris. Moon over him. It was pretty pathetic."

Decker waited.

"Chris drank like a fish! It wasn't unusual to see him polishing off an entire fifth by the end of the evening. Yet, when he left, he was always perma-pressed . . . perfectly coherent and alert."

She spoke in a soft monotone.

"Christopher Whitman is *the* most . . . controlled . . . compulsive . . . obsessively neat person I've ever met. And that's saying something. Because I'm not exactly freewheeling and spontaneous. He makes me look like a hippie. I've seen him drunk, I've seen him stressed, I've seen him angry, I've seen him . . . aroused, I've seen him happy, I've seen him miserable. I've seen him in many different emotional states. But I've never seen him *sloppy*."

She met Decker's eyes.

"Cheryl's murder was . . . *messy*. If Chris had killed her, he would have been neat about it."

Decker didn't speak. Was she serious? "Terry, even compulsives freak out—"

"Not Chris." She shook her head. "*Uh-uh, no way, not him!* For him, sloppiness is the ultimate abomination. If Chris were a killer, he'd be a ninja."

"Terry—"

"And if he *didn't* do it, Sergeant, it means someone else *did*! And if you're not going to look for him, *I* will."

Decker didn't speak right away, feeling a rise of acid in his gut. He was angered by the kid's audacity, but also forced to admit to himself that he was

worried. Whitman was probably guilty—the kid had
killer eyes. But Decker had never fully suppressed
that nagging tug in his brain.

The African-American pubic hairs found on a
routine pubic comb. The semen inside of Cheryl.

Another man.

When he spoke, he tried to appear calm. "This is
not a request, Terry. This is an order. Stay *out* of police business. Because if you get involved, you're just
going to muck things up for you and for Chris—"

"Sergeant, if you're so *sure* it's Chris, why do you
care if I ask a couple of questions?"

"Because people get scared when you imply things.
And when they get scared, they don't act rationally."
Decker made his hand into a gun, placed his index
finger at her temple and drew an imaginary trigger
with his thumb. "Now where are you, Terry?"

She was silent.

Decker said, "You're an honest kid. *Swear* to me
you won't interfere."

Terry said, "Sir, can I make a deal with you?"

"No, you cannot!"

"I won't interfere . . . sir . . . Sergeant . . . if you
promise me you'll investigate every single angle of
Cheryl's death."

"Terry, that's exactly what I'm doing."

"Sergeant, with all due respect . . . sir, I think you're
trying to put Chris away, not find the murderer . . .
sir."

Decker ran his hand over his face. "And what happens when it's proven beyond a reasonable doubt that
Chris murdered Cheryl?"

Terry blinked several times. "I'd be devastated of

course. But as long as I know that . . . Sergeant, if you promise me you'll investigate everything, I'll butt out. Because I really do think you're an honest man. Do we have a deal?"

Decker bored into her eyes. "No, we do *not* have a deal. I don't make deals with *anyone*, let alone sixteen-year-old adolescents. You back off and stay away and let me do my job. If you do that, we'll both be satisfied, all right?"

She paused, then nodded.

Decker flashed on Cindy, remembering their post-midnight marathon debates. She wore him down by sheer attrition. Such was the mission of adolescents. Turning adults into Jell-O!

"I don't know why but I *really* trust you." She looked at him with tiger-gem eyes. "I envy your daughter. I wish you were my father."

It was said so guilelessly that Decker was tempted to reach out and hug her. But of course, he didn't. Even the sweetest of faces could have an evil agenda.

Above all, Decker was a professional.

❧ 26

Flipping through the sketch pad, Oliver let go with a long whistle. "Not bad," he said. "Not bad at all, mama. You can sit on my face anytime."

Decker entered the squad room, saw Oliver ogling the drawings, and felt his temper rise. Oliver looked up and caught Decker's expression. He closed the pad and smiled boyishly. "Just checking out the evidence."

Slowly, Decker walked over, counting to ten mentally. He held out his hand. "The pad, please?"

Averting his eyes, Oliver spoke angrily. "What the hell is it to you? You've sifted through tons of shit in your years. You mean to tell me you've never taken a peek?"

"The pad, please?"

"Or is feeling horny against your born-again religion?"

Decker was impassive. "The pad, Scott?"

Oliver paused, then handed it to him.

"You have the evidence-slip number?" Decker said.

"Yeah." Oliver sorted through his desk drawer. "Here it is. Also, here's the numbers for Whitman's other sketch pads. They've already been entered and filed in the evidence room. Davidson told me to go through this one since it's the most incriminating. Make photocopies of all the sketches that resemble the Polaroids taken at the Diggs crime scene. To me, they all resemble the postmortem snaps."

"Have you done anything?"

"Oh, fuck off, Mr. Holy Roller!"

"I'm not being sarcastic," Decker said evenly. "If you haven't done it yet, I'll do it."

Oliver blushed. "Sorry. I'll do it."

Decker was quiet.

"No, really, I'll do it," Oliver said. "You've got more pressing business. Whitman's been asking for you for the last half hour."

"Has he contacted his lawyer yet?"

Oliver said, "First thing after he was booked. He and Moody must have conferred for an hour. Bail hearing's set at Van Nuys."

"And Whitman's still here?"

"Yeah. Moody wanted to hold him at Van Nuys jail, but the kid refused transfer until he'd talked to you. We've penned him solo, holed up in one of the padded numbers. High-profile case plus he's a mafioso's son. Davidson wanted him segregated."

"A good idea."

"You talk to the girl, Deck?"

"Yep."

"And?"

Decker said, "The pictures aren't from Whitman's imagination. She posed for them at Whitman's request."

"She *admitted* it?"

"Yep."

"She actually told you that he had tied her up?"

"Yep."

Oliver clapped his hands together. "Prosecution's gonna tongue your ass. You got her to admit that Whitman tied her up, now Whitman's got a history of bondage. Defense can't say that Diggs was an impulsive first-time thing because Whitman was raging drunk. We got a good case for a calculated homicide."

"Yeah, he's used binds before."

"And so much for Elaine and the polygraph." Oliver did a raspberry. "No wonder the tests aren't admissible."

"No, they're not foolproof." Decker paused. "But they *are* hard to beat. Whitman was good."

"Real good," Oliver said. "Did she pose willingly?"

"Yes and no. If I were the State, I could make a case that she was manipulated and psychologically coerced."

Oliver smiled. "Little Chrissie is up to his balls in quicksand. No wonder he wants to talk to you. Cut some sort of deal."

Decker said, "If he had deal in mind, his lawyer would be talking to the prosecution. He wouldn't be asking for me."

"Ah, c'mon," Oliver said. "You know how it works. They always try to cut deals with us first . . . like we got some magic power to kiss the boo-boo and make it go away. First we're their worst enemy, then we become their best friend. We've seen it a hundred times before."

Decker shrugged.

"The girl must be pissed at Whitman."

"Not really." Decker scanned the sketch pad and winced. "Mostly, she's embarrassed . . . really embarrassed."

"Nice girl?"

"Yep."

"So what's she doing posing like that?"

"Nice girls can screw up." Decker raised his brow. "He told her he loved her. He told her it was art . . . Jesus dying on the cross. Who the hell knows? Maybe in his own sick mind, it was the truth."

"Yeah, and I'm a horse's ass."

Decker glanced at him and said nothing.

Oliver let out a soft laugh. "I set myself up for that one." He ran his hand over his forehead. "How old is she?"

"Sixteen."

"Was he violent with her?"

"Nope." Decker closed the top of the pad and gave it back to Oliver. "Not at all. But she knew something about him was kinky. She suggested he find another tutor after he tied her up. She told him she didn't want to model anymore."

"In other words, she smelled a fart and didn't call it perfume. Give the girl a point." Oliver made an imaginary notch with his index finger in the air. "Her quivering antenna may be the reason she's alive today."

"Still, she's not out to fry him."

"Don't tell me," Oliver said. "She still loves him."

"That's probably part of it," Decker said. "But I think she honestly believes he didn't do it."

"Christ! They just don't learn! Why don't you show her the postmortems of Cheryl Diggs. See how deep her affections run."

"It's up to the prosecution now. I've done my job." Decker smoothed his mustache. "I think the best way to approach this sketch versus Polaroid thing is by points of comparison, like doing a fingerprint match before we got the computers. Methodically go through the pad and photos and mark the similarities. Look at the angles, the hand position, the wrist position, head positions, the way the feet were bound, the crossing of the ankles, and so on and so on. Anybody else call me?"

"No."

"Then I'll see you later." Decker started to walk away, but Oliver called him back.

Decker turned around. "What?"

Oliver said, "Deck, *you've* got the beautiful wife, *you've* got the perfect kids. Have a little patience with the less fortunate going through hard times."

Decker was quiet.

Oliver made popping noises with his lips. "You know it's gotta be bad if evidence makes me salivate."

Decker was careful with his words. "Anything at home to salvage?"

"I thought so. But Patti has different ideas." Oliver sliced air with the side of his palm. "She wants a clean break. I'm looking for a two-bedroom, but I'd take a large one-bedroom. You think Marge might have any rentals in her building?"

"You can ask her when she gets back."

"Patti wanted me out by the weekend."

"What about your girlfriend temporarily?"

"No A-effing way I'm moving in with her. I don't want to give her any ideas."

"How about friends?"

"I'll find someone."

No one spoke for a moment.

Decker said, "It'll get better, Scott."

"Not in the short run." He rubbed his eyes. "You ever meet my oldest kid before he left home?"

"Your son? No."

"Yeah, he cut out about six months ago. I think that was the final blow. I kept trying to tell Patti that it was no big deal. Kids have to find themselves. But she didn't want to hear it. Easier to blame me."

Decker was quiet.

"He's doing okay," Oliver said. "He's hoping to get a contractor's license in about six months."

"That's great."

"Yeah, I think it's fine, too. Patti's disappointed. She wanted him to go to college. Of course that's my fault, too."

Decker didn't answer.

Oliver said, "He's a great-looking kid, Deck. Real popular with the girls. Occasionally he brought a few home for us to meet . . . little cutie-pie nymphets. . . ." He looked up and laughed. "They'd call me *sir.* Man, do I feel old! Worse, I can't seem to grow old gracefully. How do you do it?"

"Scott, my wife is twelve years younger than I am."

Oliver smiled, then laughed out loud. "Son of a bitch, you're just as bad as I am."

"I wouldn't go that far—"

"Twelve years younger!" Oliver clapped his hands. "You big, horny bastard."

"Now that you've reduced me to a typical middle-aged dick, do you feel better?"

"Yeah." Oliver took out the Diggs Polaroids and opened up Whitman's sketch pad. "Sure, I feel better." He took out two sheets of paper, labeled one POLAROIDS, the other SKETCHES. "I feel a *hell* of a lot better."

After depositing his gun in the weapons dropoff and filling out the required forms, Decker was led to Whitman's cell by Ramirez the jailer. Whitman had been stuffed in a cell usually reserved for high-profile criminals or violents. The detention chamber was hermetically sealed, had no windows except for a wire mesh, double-thick glass pane cut into the door. Inside, the space was padded and painted yellow, the only article of furniture being a bunk chained to the wall.

When Ramirez opened the door, Whitman was quietly lying on the flat board, hands behind his head, long legs crossed at the ankles and falling over the bed. He turned and sat up when he saw it was Decker.

Ramirez said, "Stand up, face the wall, put your hands on your head."

Whitman moved quickly. From behind, Ramirez brought down Whitman's left hand behind his back, slapped on the handcuffs. He brought down Whitman's right, then cuffed the hands together. He said, "He's a big guy. You want me to link him to the bunk?"

Decker said, "No, that won't be necessary."

Ramirez wasn't fully convinced. But he left anyway, closing the sealed door. The chambers were eerily quiet.

Decker said, "You can turn around now, Whitman, but keep your back to the wall. Slide down until you're sitting on your butt, legs crossed, spine plastered to the wall."

Whitman did as told.

Decker studied the boy. He actually looked healthier than when Decker had arrested him. His eyes were clearer, his skin looked less mottled. Sometimes perps were like that. At peace, because they had finally gotten what they deserved. He shifted his position and grimaced.

Decker said, "Cuffs too tight?"

"I'll live."

"I'm done with you, Chris," Decker said. "Any deal you want to cut should come from your lawyer to the State."

Whitman maintained eye contact. "Did you talk to her?"

Decker didn't answer.

Whitman looked at the ceiling, then back at Decker. "You remember what we talked about when you arrested me?"

"I think you should be talking to your lawyer, Chris."

"Look, do you want this collar or what?"

"I've *got* this collar."

"You want to make it stick, don't you?"

"That won't be a problem."

Whitman threw his head back and whispered, "Terry, Terry, Terry." He shook his head. "The girl couldn't lie to save her soul."

"Looks like she ain't gonna save yours, either."

"She has no idea what she's in for . . . so damn innocent." Whitman blew out air. "I'll give you those hookers now. I remember four specifically, but I know there were more."

"Busy guy, were you?"

Whitman bit his lower lip. "In my community, you take a wife for your family, a girlfriend for regular sex, and hookers fill in the blanks. It's just the way I've been brought up."

"You're starting young."

"Engaged at seventeen, I'll say." Whitman paused. "Maybe I bought it a dozen times this year. Not exactly a world's record. Anyway, they'll tell you shit, Decker. Much more *interesting* shit than Terry. All I want in exchange is suppression of the sketches as evidence . . . if it pans out like it should."

"Talk to your lawyer, Chris."

"Decker, *why* do you want to bring her down, when you can get the same evidence against me *without* her? C'mon, you know the deal. Prosecution and press'll turn her into hamburger. She doesn't deserve that when her only crime was trusting an asshole like me."

"Nobility wears well on you, kid."

Whitman's cheeks pinkened. "In another world, I was a knight. Look, these cuffs are cutting the hell out of me. Talk to me, Decker. I'm serving you my head on a platter."

"So why not go all the way and confess?"

"Because I didn't *do* it." Whitman lowered his voice. "I didn't do it, Sergeant. Yes, I have kinks in my circuitry, but that doesn't make me a homicidal maniac."

"Your kinks sure as hell make you a liar," Decker said. "Because you lied during the polygraph. You told us under oath that you never tied anyone up."

"I lied because I knew what admitting it would mean. I was real surprised I beat it."

"Looks like you're an excellent liar."

"Being an excellent liar doesn't make you a murderer. If that was true, all politicians would be behind bars." Whitman swore under his breath. "I'm not going to screw myself unless I have your . . . *promise* for lack of a better word . . . that you'll follow up on this. Do you want the names or not?"

Decker said, "Whitman, you can give, but I'm not promising you anything. It's your call."

Whitman paused. "Looks like I'll take my chances."

Decker pulled out a pad. "Shoot."

"First one's black, around eighteen, about five four, one-fifteen, maybe one-twenty—"

"Does she have a name?"

"I'm sure she does, but it was a kind of a 'hey you, brown sugar,' type thing. But I used her twice, maybe even three times. If you find her, she'll remember me. I'm big with and without clothes. Let's see . . . she was one-fifteen, one-twenty. Big floppy tits. She wears leggings, a low-cut tank top and fuck-me backless shoes. Lots of makeup and jewelry, hangs out on Sunset—"

"Well, that narrows it down."

"I'm doing the best I can," Whitman said tensely. "Next one I think went by the name Pearl. She was

Asian, long straight black hair, smaller . . . about five
if that. Enormous tits—real firm, probably implants.
Around eighteen, maybe even younger. Also lots of
makeup and jewelry. I found her on hookers' row on
Sepulveda. Next girl I remember was also black,
eighteen years old, around one-fifteen—"

"Sounds like the first one." Abruptly, Decker
stopped writing. "Chris, I don't have the time or in-
clination to start checking out hookers that all sound
alike."

Whitman banged the back of his head against the
wall. "What the hell do you want from me? I'm describing them the best I can."

"Sorry, buddy. It's not good enough. Get me a
name."

Whitman suddenly straightened his spine. "Free
up my hands and give me your pen. I'll draw them
for you."

Decker looked at him. "You can draw them from
memory?"

"In a snap."

Decker thought a moment, then knocked for the
jailer. Ramirez opened the door. "Had enough, Sergeant?"

"Not yet. Cuff him in front for me. I want him to
be able to write something."

Ramirez grudgingly did as requested. After the
jailer left and Whitman was immobilized, Decker
slid his pen and pad over to the teenager.

"Don't shit around with me," Decker said.

"Pissing you off is the last thing on my mind."
Whitman sat, legs bent at the knees, feet on the
ground. He placed Decker's pad on his legs, using

his thighs for an easel. He picked up the pen and began to make strokes. "God, I can't believe I'm *doing* this. I didn't even bust her cherry."

Decker said, "So why are you doing it?"

"'Cause I'm crazy." Whitman studied the drawing and spoke in a mock Viennese accent. "Ker-razy in de head." He sketched furiously, then flipped the paper. "One down, three to go."

"You're fast."

"I've got a good eye."

Decker said, "A good eye like that. Yet you can't remember seeing anyone when you left the Grenada West End."

"It was like three-thirty in the morning, Decker. The lobby wasn't teeming with bodies." Whitman paused. "You know, I did see the night clerk when I left. But he didn't see me."

"Go on."

"There's nothing else to tell." Whitman turned to a fresh page. "Two down. I saw him at a distance. He was in the back room."

"You said you've got a good eye. Would you recognize the clerk if you saw him again?"

"I *knew* the clerk," Whitman said. "One of Cheryl's numbers. Henry Trupp."

Decker said, "What do you mean, one of Cheryl's numbers?"

"She had an adult fan club, if you know what I mean. She didn't exactly hook . . . more like bartered for favors . . . a certain male teacher who gave her As when she deserved Fs . . . the car mechanic . . . the Korean papa for groceries. A cop when she got busted for drugs—"

"A cop?"

"That's what she said."

"Who?"

"Never mentioned a name."

Decker had heard that one before. Seems like every hooker in the world boasted a cop in her pocket. Rarely did it pan out. "Did Cheryl have an honesty problem?"

"Yeah, she lied a lot. But I know she did Trupp when she needed a place to crash . . . whenever she ran away from her alcoholic mother . . . which was often. We were all comped rooms prom night because Cheryl visited Trupp the day before."

"You told me you and Cheryl never talked."

"*She* talked. Sometimes I even listened."

"What does Trupp look like?"

Whitman paused. "You never grilled the guy?"

Trupp still hadn't been located. But Decker couldn't tell Whitman that. So he said nothing.

Whitman raised his brow. "Middle-aged, bald white guy with a paunch. You want me to draw him, too?"

White guy. Decker said, "Sure, draw him for me. Could you see what Trupp was doing in the back room?"

"Watching TV . . . tee*vees* actually. Guy had two, three sets going at the same time."

"Could you see what was playing? Get a time frame for yourself?"

"I wasn't paying attention. I just wanted to go home and start a new day." Another flip. "Three down. You're gonna be amazed by how good I am at rendering."

"I saw your sketches of Terry."

"Those were garbage," Whitman announced. "I couldn't get her right. Too beautiful to capture on paper. How'd the interview go with her?"

Decker was silent.

"Ah, the inscrutable detective." Whitman grinned, then turned serious. "She hates me, doesn't she?"

Decker remained quiet.

Whitman looked miserable. "I'm writing brief descriptions at the top. You *are* going to check this out?"

"No promises, no guarantees."

"Yeah, yeah," Whitman said. "I'm finished with the whores. I'll give you Trupp now." He sketched a few moments. "Too bad I'm so messed, because I got so much raw talent."

"The world bleeds heavily, Chris."

Whitman sighed, drew a few moments more, then closed the pad. He slid it and the pen back to Decker. "Take a look."

Decker picked up his pad and nodded.

Whitman said, "The blacks worked Sunset. Pearl and the other one—the white girl who called herself Luscious—worked Sepulveda. You may want to check them out first because they're closer."

"I told you, Chris. No promises, no guarantees."

Whitman said, "You're going to check it out. Not because of me, and not because of Terry, but because I *know* you'll do it. You're just like me."

"Son, I'm *nothing* like you."

"Yeah, you are. You don't like loose ends." Whitman pointed to the pad. "You know what those are, Decker? Those are loose ends."

ᕽ 27

The bail was set at a half million on a 10 percent bond. A fifty-thousand-dollar check graced by Moody's sweeping signature, and an hour later, Whitman was a free bird. Daddy Donatti had come through with the requisite pocket change. Decker passed it off with a shrug. Onward and upward.

Sepulveda Boulevard had never been known for designer architecture. But the shift from basic thoroughfare to hookers' row had been sudden. A ballooning population in the San Fernando Valley required lots of new goods and services. Sepulveda was well trafficked and had several rows of cheap motels. The ladies were pragmatic. Why travel to Sunset when there were accommodations in the backyard?

The girls came out at twilight. Armed with Whitman's sketches, Decker began his hunt. He was a cop and made no attempt to hide it, so the girls made him in an eye blink. But his profession didn't stop their strutting. A UN's worth of trollops boogied over to him, all of them way too young for their work, way too old for their years. Within minutes, he was surrounded by two Asians, four blacks, and four whites.

The guys who had been cruising the boulevard must have thought Decker some awesome stud.

He showed them Whitman's drawings. The girls giggled and shook their heads no. Some seemed more truthful than others. Decker studied them, one face at a time, his attention slowly shifting to an Asian girl. He shooed the others away and took her aside. Maybe she was eighteen, but probably not. Her ID told Decker her name was Mae. He showed her one of Whitman's sketches. Then he looked her square in the eye.

"Her name is Pearl," Decker said. "Where can I find her?"

Mae cracked gum. "What'd she do?"

Broad Brooklyn accent. Decker said, "She didn't do anything."

"So den why should I help you?"

"I can make it worth your while."

"Whatchu have in mind?"

Decker peeled off a twenty and flicked it in front of her face.

"Dat's it?"

"Mae, let's get along, okay?"

The girl shrugged and snapped up the bill. "Her name's Tachako Yamaguchi. She's Japanese. I saw her go into the Royal Crown Motel 'bout twenty minutes ago with some ugly, pumped-up dude. Now how about a tip for being so nice?"

Decker palmed her another ten. "Get out of here."

She took off. The motel was a block away. Decker started walking. As luck would have it, he hit upon the entrance right as some ugly, pumped-up dude with a small Asian girl stepped outside. Decker grabbed the girl's arm and told the dude to disappear. He saluted, backed away, then turned and ran.

She was very small and thin except for enormous breasts as big and round as cantaloupes. Dark protruding nipples were visible under a cotton gauze tank top.

Whitman was right. Girl had implants.

She wore crimson latex short shorts, black backless high heels, and her nails were dragon red inset with rhinestones. Through the layers of foundation, blush, lipstick, and eye goop, Decker could make out a pretty face. Her ID said her name was in fact Tachako Yamaguchi. According to the DMV, she was nineteen. According to Decker, she was a child. Hoping to expedite things, he slipped her a ten, then dropped her arm. She remained rooted to the spot, looked at Decker with expectant eyes. A good sign. Maybe he wouldn't have to work too hard.

He fished in his pockets and pulled out mug shots of Whitman that were taken at his booking. "You know this guy?"

Tachako's eyes went from Decker's face to the sketch. "What'd he do?"

"Just tell me about him."

She tapped her foot and shrugged. "Quiet. He paid well."

"How'd his taste run?"

"Nothing I've never done before."

Decker pulled out four fives and showed them to her. He gave her one. "Talk to me, Tachako."

Her eyes went to the ground. "Blow-jobs."

Decker frowned. "That's it? Blow-jobs?"

She waited.

"C'mon, c'mon," Decker said. "You've got to work for the money, even with me."

"Head with him was enough." Tachako studied her nails. A rhinestone winked in the moonlight. "Did him two separate times. Third time I saw him coming, I ducked in the alley. Enough's enough, you know."

"What's *enough*, Tachako?"

"He was real big. Liked to use it all."

Her eyes were uneasy. There was more. Decker gave her another five.

She said, "He liked me on my back. Liked to kneel over me and do it."

"Straddle you?"

She nodded. "Just picked up my head and shoved it in. Second time, he did it so hard and deep, I had a sore throat for a week. I kept gagging and gagging. Didn't stop him. Kept going till he came. After, he gave me double my usual. But who needs it, you know? Plenty of others not so big."

Her eyes flitted from spot to spot. Decker gave her a third fin. Tachako buffed her nails on her latex hotpants. "He was into control. Bondage."

"He tied you up?"

She nodded.

"Just the hands?"

She shook her head.

"Hands and feet?"

She nodded.

"Gags?"

"Be hard to suck him if I was wearing a gag."

Decker laughed and so did she. He said, "You do a lot of regular bondage?"

"No."

"So why'd you do it with him?"

"Like I said, he paid well." She flicked imaginary dirt off her sweater. "And he was cute."

"He ever knock you around?"

"No. He just liked bondage." She paused. "I think he used old ties."

Decker pulled out his notebook. "He tied you up with neckties?"

She nodded.

"Tight?"

"Not tight enough to kill, but tight enough."

"Would you be willing to testify to a grand jury that he tied you up with neckties?"

"You crazy? He'd kill me."

"He gave me your name, Tachako. He drew me your picture. Want to see it?"

The girl was quiet. Decker took out the sketch and showed it to her. Her eyes widened. "Why's he drawing me?"

"So I could find you. He drew me a few others as well. You know any of these girls?"

He gave her Whitman's drawings. Tachako sorted through them one at a time, then she shook her head. "Is he like one of these like whacko . . . serious killers? Am I on some kinda hit list?"

Decker said, "Tachako, he drew you so *I* could find you. He wanted you to tell me just what you told me."

She took a baby step backward. "Why'd he want that?"

"He's being held for murder. If you tell a grand jury about your bondage, we may not need evidence we have to indict him. He doesn't want us using that evidence. He's trying to protect someone."

"He wants *me* to mess him up so's he can protect another girl?"

Decker nodded.

"I don't believe you. That kind of guy don't do *nothing* for other people, even girls they say they love."

"Tachako, I'm telling you the truth. You testify against him, you'll make him very happy."

"I still don't believe you."

Decker raised his eyebrows. "Fine. Don't believe me. If I can't convince you, maybe Whitman can. He's out on bail. I know he'll be looking for you."

The girl's eyes widened. "Wha . . . what do you want from me?"

"How about an official statement?"

Davidson read the two sworn affidavits and said, "Where the hell did these come from?"

Decker said, "The names of the girls are on the bottom—"

"That's not what I meant, Decker. How'd you find these girls?"

"From Whitman."

The lieutenant jerked his head back. "What?"

"Whitman gave me the names of the hookers."

Davidson paused. "You're telling me the guy is deliberately screwing himself?"

"He wants a deal."

"A deal? What kind of deal? Solicitation instead of Murder One?"

"He wants to suppress the McLaughlin sketches—"

Davidson burst into laughter. "He *can't* be serious."

"He's very serious."

"Then he's not only dangerous, he's delusional. State won't deal with him. The shit's got nothing to trade."

Decker paused. "McLaughlin's a nice girl. Why put her through an ordeal if we have other evidence to convict him?"

The Loo glared at him. "What the fuck happened to you? You didn't promise him or her anything, did you?"

"Of course not."

"You know, Decker, even if I was psychotic and agreed to the *possibility* of a deal, State would never take hookers' testimony in exchange for those sketches we found at his apartment. We need those drawings to make a definite case."

Decker smoothed his mustache. "I know."

Davidson grinned. "You sly bastard." He hit Decker's arm in camaraderie. "You weren't really thinking exchange. You were just trying to squeeze him, weren't you?"

Decker paused. "I was just trying to see what I could do. Like I said, McLaughlin's a nice girl."

"Not that nice."

"She made a mistake. So have I."

Davidson said, "I've lived with my mistakes, let her live with hers. At least you should be convinced the fucker's guilty."

"Loo, I can't help but ask why this piece of shit is screwing himself up to protect this girl."

"He knows he did it," Davidson said. "He knows

he's going down for it. He knows he's fucked. You said he liked this girl. Maybe he don't want to take her down with him."

"Maybe."

"Definitely." Davidson gave Decker back the hookers' sworn statements. "Give those to the State. More evidence against Whitman, the better. From your perspective, Diggs is done, you can move on."

Decker said, "I'd like to check out a few more things—"

"Waste of time. Let it go, Sergeant. If you don't, you're gonna screw yourself."

"That sounds ominous."

"Not ominous." Tug raised his head and gave him a mean smile. "Just a friendly word of advice."

❦ 28

Another bad night's sleep coupled with a nagging piece of evidence brought Decker into work around seven. He had sneaked out of the house before Rina had arisen. He hadn't wanted to deal with another one of her lectures. Especially because he knew she was right. His first appointment was a court case at ten.

He glanced around.

Davidson hadn't checked in yet. Decker took out his notebook and pulled out the Diggs file, sorting through the now familiar pages with practiced speed. Within moments, he found what he was looking for. He clicked a ballpoint pen and copied down the phone numbers of the three identified black males who had been in the Grenada West End the night of the murder. He also took out Whitman's sketch of Henry Trupp and copied down the night clerk's address and phone number.

Scott Oliver got off the horn and managed to get his body upright. He trudged over to Decker's desk, his feet shuffling against the linoleum floor. "Tell me you had a fight with your young lady. Make me feel better."

"Leave me alone, Scotty," Decker barked. "I'm not in the mood."

Immediately Oliver backed off. "What are you working on, Rabbi?"

"Diggs. I can't shake those unaccounted-for pubic hairs. I've got to know where they came from."

"Maybe they came from Whitman," Oliver said. "Maybe he screwed a black female before he got to Cheryl and transferred them onto her."

"They're male hairs."

"He was dead drunk. Who said the black had to be female? Why don't you ask him about it right now? He's waiting for you."

"Whitman's here? Christ, what the hell does he want?"

"Maybe mercy from his arresting officer." Oliver clasped his hands. " 'Please don't fry me. I'm so young and have so much to offer. I'm a musician, I'm an artist, and I'm an expert in knot tying.' "

Decker rolled his eyes. "Why me?"

"It's in the script," Oliver said. "Kid's out by the front desk."

Decker plopped his hands on his desktop and pushed himself up. He went through the secretary's office, passing the assignment board. Yes, it was true. Marge was still on vacation. He thought of her tanning in Hawaii, feeling a twinge of envy. Then he remembered he never tanned anyway, only burned, UV rays being the bane of a redhead's existence. Plus, Decker hated sand, which always settled in his crotch. Furthermore, he detested poi and papaya.

He came into the front station. Officers Gerrard and Belding were manning the desk today. They peeked at Whitman, then gave Decker an inquiring look. Decker returned their silent questions with a shrug.

Whitman had parked himself next to the candy machine. He wore a starched white shirt tucked into black jeans, a black wool blazer, and black leather high-tops. His posture seemed tense, his eyes were unreadable. He stood when he saw Decker, but remained fixed to the spot. Decker loped over to him, looked him in the eye.

"What's up, Chris?"

Whitman maintained eye contact. "I thought we had a deal. A trade—evidence for evidence."

"News to me."

Whitman's eyes went dead. "I talked to the girls last night. They told me they talked to you." He lowered his voice until he was whispering. "They said they told you everything. From the blow-jobs to the binds. You know they're telling the truth. Because you got to them before I did."

Decker said nothing.

Whitman said, "You've got sworn statements, Decker. Their testimonies are far more damaging to me than a couple of stupid sketches. I came through. Now you do the right thing, Decker, and let her go."

"It's not up to me, Chris."

"That's bullshit!" Whitman blurted out.

Gerrard and Belding picked up their heads. Belding said loudly, "Everything okay, Sergeant?"

"We're fine." To Whitman, Decker whispered, "You're cruising for a bruising, son. Keep your temper in check."

Whitman opened and closed his eyes. "Are you telling me that your input has no influence on how the State handles this case?"

"Whitman, the sketches have already been entered as material evidence—"

"So *unenter* them, dammit!"

"It doesn't work that way."

Whitman clenched his jaw and made tight fists with his long fingers. "Why does the State need drawings when they have more incriminating statements?"

"Statements made by hookers—"

"*Sworn* statement by hookers." A desperation rose in the kid's voice. "You *know* they're telling it true. You got to them before I did. You got good shit against me without the drawings. Why bring Terry down when you don't need her?"

"The State needs the sketches, Chris."

"Aw, *c'mon*!" Whitman did a half turn and swung back. "You can't actually *believe* that crock of shit?!"

"You never heard that a picture's worth a thousand words?"

Whitman glared at Decker, nostrils flaring, blood vessels pulsating in his neck. "You *met* her. I can't believe you're gonna waste her just like that."

Decker was quiet. His silence only increased Whitman's frustration. "You're washing your hands in her blood. You feel good about that?"

Decker's eyes bored into the teen. "Chris, you're arched like a cornered cat. Go take a walk and blow off steam."

Whitman threw back his head and stared at the

ceiling. Then he flashed Decker an eerie smile. "Man, I don't know what I was thinking when I gave you those names."

"Get a grip on it, kid. Take a walk *now*!"

And even though Decker had anticipated it, even though he saw it coming, Whitman was still too fast. The best Decker could do was take a giant hop backward so the punch failed to make full contact. But there was enough impact in the solar plexus and Decker doubled over. He gasped for air and told himself that *if* he breathed normally, the sparkling mobile of stars and tweeting birds behind his eyes would go away.

By the time he recovered his vision, Decker could make out Whitman subdued on the floor, his hands behind his back, a pile of uniformed and plainclothes officers cuffing and clamping him. Watching the melee put on by LAPD were the civilians—a Latina with a tattooed arm holding a drooling baby, two acned, overweight, busty biker ladies wearing bustiers and torn jeans, and lastly, two teenagers, one black and pregnant in cutoff shorts and Rastafarian curls, the other white and *very* pregnant in cutoff shorts and Rastafarian curls.

Decker was not only surprised he could speak but also shocked that his voice could carry. "Let him go," he shouted.

The officers looked up in amazement.

Decker stood up straight. Man, it hurt bad. "Get off of him," he ordered. "I can handle the bastard myself."

Nobody moved.

"Get off of him!"

Slowly, layers of blue began to peel off and Whitman came into view. When there was enough clearance, Decker went in, grabbed the kid's jacket, and jerked him to his feet. One ankle was dangling chains, the other ankle was metal-free.

Decker said, "Who has the keys to the leg press?" He took a deep breath and let it out slowly. The sharp, jabbing sensation had turned dull and throbbing. "Take the chains off his feet, but keep the handcuffs on."

As soon as Whitman's ankles were liberated, Decker twisted Whitman's collar, dragged him into the squad room, then threw him inside one of the interview rooms, banging the kid against the wall.

"Sit!" he commanded, slamming the door.

Whitman obeyed.

"Well, that was real smart, Chris. Now you're in a heap of shit."

"Sorry."

"You're sorry?" Decker paced as he spoke. "You think an apology's going to prevent me from hauling your sorry ass into jail? You think an apology is going to sit well with your bondsman? Or with your uncle after he just forfeited fifty grand worth of bail money? Let me tell you something, Whitman. Sorry doesn't cut it. I thought you were smart. I thought you were clever. Now I realize I'm dealing with a garden variety dumbshit."

Whitman said nothing, as quiet as a chastened puppy.

Decker stopped treading the floor and ran his

hands through his hair. "I *told* you no promises. If you heard different, you heard *wrong*! Your girl is going down and it's your own damn fault! Stop looking for villains. Instead, look in the mirror."

"You gonna arrest me for assault?"

"Hell, yeah, I'm going to arrest you for assault. And, buddy, that's a charge that'll stick like tar."

Whitman's eyes darted about the room. "Call up the prosecution. Get them down here. I want to cut a deal."

"Cut a deal?" Decker was incredulous. "Cut a *deal*?! Whitman, you got rocks between your ears? You've got *nothing* to deal with."

Whitman tried to make eye contact, but couldn't sustain it. He blinked again. "I . . . I want to . . . confess. Get the State down here. I want to plea-bargain."

Decker paused, unsure if he had heard right. His ears were still buzzing from his whack in the stomach. His head was pounding. He lowered his voice. "Did you just say you wanted to confess?"

Whitman nodded. "Yes."

"Confess to what, Chris?"

"To Cheryl . . ." Whitman bounced his leg up and down. "To Cheryl Diggs's murder."

"All right." Decker felt himself panting and reminded himself to breathe normally. "All right, that's fine with me. I did hear you right. You said you wanted to confess to the Diggs murder. Am I correct?"

Whitman licked his lips and ran his hand over his face. "I want to plea-bargain. If I get what I want, you'll get what you want."

Decker said, "Okay, Chris. I'll set it up as fast as I can. You want to call your attorney?"

Whitman shook his head. "He wouldn't let me go through with it. He . . . my uncle . . . no. No, I don't want my attorney."

"You're waiving your rights to an attorney?"

"Yes."

"And you'll sign a waiver card?"

Again, Whitman nodded.

"Okay, Chris," Decker said. "Just hold that thought until I can get everything arranged."

"You're still going to book me on assault?"

"Yes," Decker said softly. "Yes, I have to do that. But who knows what kind of a deal you can cut? Maybe we can get the assault thrown out. But no promises, okay?"

"Okay," Whitman whispered.

Decker said, "I'm going to take you downstairs to booking until I can get everything squared away. I'll bring you back up just as soon as I do."

He nodded.

"You're not fucking around on me, are you?" Decker said. "Because if you are, I'm going to be pissed."

Whitman shook his head mechanically. "I'm not fucking around. I want to deal. I want . . . I'll give you what you want. Just as long as I get what I want."

"That's what cutting a deal is all about," Decker said. "I'm going to bring you down now. No more stunts, okay?"

He nodded. "I'm sorry I hit you."

"S'right. No harm done."

"If it's any consolation, my hand hurts."

Decker clamped his hand on Whitman's arm and helped the kid to his feet. "Chris, it is no consolation for me whatsoever."

Since the Diggs case had made the news as well as the papers, Prosecution was not just Erica Berringer but also her boss, Morton Weller. He was a rail-thin man in his fifties with over two decades of experience with the DA's office. White tufts of hair sat atop his long face, which held a beak nose and deep-set eyes. A birdlike neck housed a big, bobbing Adam's apple. Weller had a deep voice.

State had brought a video camera. Decker put the DAs in a small interview room, giving Weller and Berringer time to set up. Davidson joined them a few minutes later. He had caught wind of the action and had demanded inclusion. As long as Davidson was going to be there, Decker figured Scott Oliver also had a right to know what was going on.

By the time everyone was ready, the once barren room was filled to capacity. Decker hoped the crowd wouldn't scare Whitman off. He brought him from holding, and after making the introductions, he asked Whitman if he still wanted to forgo his rights to an attorney. Whitman nodded and signed a waiver card.

Decker said, "I'm going to turn on a tape recorder, Chris. We also want to videotape this interview. Any objections?"

"No," Whitman said. "But there won't be anything worth taping unless I get what I want."

"Which is?" Davidson broke in.

Weller said in an undertone, "Lieutenant, we can't

afford to rush. Please." He looked at Erica Berringer. "Are you all set?"

Erica made final adjustments with the camera controls. She turned on the switch and peered through a viewfinder. "We're rolling."

Decker turned on his tape recorder and stated the identification of all the parties involved. Finally, Weller sat back in his chair. He said, "Tell me what you have in mind, Mr. Whitman."

"I'll plead guilty to Man Two, three to six. In exchange, I want the assault charge dropped, plus I want suppression of any and all evidence found during Sergeant Decker's search of my apartment."

The room went quiet. Weller flashed him a hard look. "You've thought about this, have you, Mr. Whitman?"

"Very much."

Weller looked Whitman in the eye. "Sir, I don't know where you've learned the legalese . . . I suspect it's from the electronic school of TV law . . . but something or someone has steered you in the wrong direction. Because I know the evidence against you. And I know what I can do with it. Manslaughter is out of the question."

Whitman said, "Mr. Weller, if we go to trial, and if I'm convicted, the *most* I'll get is Involuntary Manslaughter."

"You think so?" Davidson blurted out.

"Lieutenant, I know so. With time served in jail prior to trial, I won't do a day in prison. And that's *if* I get convicted, which is a big question mark. I'm offering a break not only to *you* but also to the taxpayers of LA."

Weller and Berringer passed a sidelong glance to Decker. He tried to make his shrug invisible.

Weller said, "And what's your proposed defense, sir? Abuse or Diminished Capacity?"

"Either/Or."

"Don't tell me," Erica said. "A little birdie told you to strangle her."

"Not a birdie, just the voices in my head. And believe me, Counselor, it'll fly. Because unlike certain rich-kid brothers in this city who *almost* got away with murder based on *nothing*, I've got documentation—a solid, psychiatric history of mental illness *prior* to Cheryl Diggs's murder."

Weller glanced at Berringer, then at Decker.

"Why are you looking at Sergeant Decker, Counselor?" Whitman seemed annoyed. "He doesn't know anything. Because it's not the kind of stuff that one advertises. But I will if I have to."

Again the room went silent. Oliver broke it. "This defense save you from being shitcanned in the past, Whitman?"

"Well, it won't work now," Davidson said.

"My record's squeaky clean." Whitman looked at his hands. "What you have is an abused kid with mental problems, and no prior record of antisocial behavior." He looked up and grinned. "I guess I just snapped."

Everyone waited a beat. Then Decker said, "Tell me your history, Chris."

"Pick a condition, Sergeant . . . one from column A, one from column B. You want verification of my voices, I'll send you my files from the Northfolk

County Psychiatric Hospital. I was an inpatient there for three months when I was twelve."

Nobody spoke.

Whitman said, "Or how about depression and despair? I'll give you the dates of my two suicide attempts as well as the names of each mental hospital where I was subsequently committed. A month in each."

Davidson said, "Kid's a nutcase!"

Whitman flashed him rage from hot blue eyes. "You said it, Lieutenant! And I'm betting a jury'll feel the same way." He looked at Erica. "Are you getting all this on tape, Counselor?"

She said nothing.

Whitman said, "As long as we're doing true confessions, I might as well tell you about my prior drug and alcohol condition. Six-week inpatient stay at the Clinic Care Hospice in upstate. I voluntarily checked in right before I came out to Los Angeles. Unfortunately, I've had relapses. People saw me drinking the night Cheryl was murdered. Of course, I don't remember too much."

"I'll bet," Davidson muttered.

"How much of a wager, Lieutenant?" Whitman retorted. "You short on cash, I'll take a marker."

"Shut up, Whitman," Decker snapped.

"Yes, sir!"

Again, the room went dead.

Whitman said, "Out there are lots of notes about my mental state. The picture isn't pretty. Looks like I'm never going to run for office. Unless mental illness suddenly becomes PC."

Decker said, "Is that all, Chris?"

Whitman's eyes went dead. "It isn't enough for you, Decker?"

Decker rolled his eyes. "Whitman, I'm just trying to get a total picture."

The teen seemed mollified. "You want to hear about the abuse?"

Decker was impassive. "Yes, I do."

"The usual. Cigarette burns in the back and butt along with scars from some slashing across my lower back and thighs. Now, the missing spleen. That's a good one. Courtesy of a sucker punch from my old man when I was eight. Nice emergency surgery done at Lenox Hill in Manhattan. I'm sure they keep excellent records. My father did time for it. I was taken away, put in foster care for a couple of months. Then my old man swore he had reformed. I was sent back home and . . . what can I tell you? Old habits are hard to break."

Whitman sat back in his chair and blew out air. But his expression was anything but smug. Decker realized he'd been tensing, even cringing as the kid told his tale. And if this was the gut reaction of a seasoned cop of twenty-odd years, he could only imagine how the boy's story would play to civilian jurors.

"You said I'm nuts, Lieutenant? You're absolutely right."

Again, there was silence.

"Matter of fact, I'm about this close . . ." Whitman measured out a tiny space of air between his erect thumb and forefinger. "About this close to a breakdown. I can feel this . . . this buzz in my brain that keeps getting louder and louder and louder . . . I mean I've *been* there before. The only reason I'm maintaining is because someone else is involved. So do we deal or what?"

Weller was quiet.

"Speak to me, Counselor," Whitman said. "I'm getting very uptight."

Weller said, "Any deal we cut is predicated on your telling the truth. And that's a *big if* since you're a known pathological liar."

"Fine," Whitman said. "Check it out. I'm not worried. I accept your conditions. So let's talk about pleas. You heard my offer. Are we done?"

Weller said, "If you're telling the truth—and that's a big if—"

"You're repeating yourself, Weller."

The DA said, "On a confession and a plea of guilty, I'll give you Man One, six to twelve. Best I can do, Whitman."

"That's shit."

"Take it or leave it."

"That's shit."

"Now who's repeating himself?"

Whitman buried his hands in his face, then looked up. "Let's see. Even if I should receive max . . . with prison crowding and time off for good behavior, I should be out in what? Around six, seven years?" He looked at Decker. "That sound about right?"

"Something like that."

"I'll be twenty-five. . . ." He nodded. "I can truck with that. But you've got to drop the assault charge. And most important, I want my drawings back before I get shitcanned."

To Weller, Decker said, "If you have the plea, State doesn't need the drawings."

Davidson said, "Whose side are you on?"

Decker said, "What difference do the sketches make once we've settled on a plea? You want to hear what *I* care about? I care about Cheryl Diggs. Before you bargain, I want to hear his story."

Whitman said, "Too bad. Because I'm not going to confess anything until I've got a deal."

"How can we deal until we hear what happened?" Decker said.

"That's your problem," Whitman said. "And even when I talk, I want it off the record."

"What good does something off the record do?" Davidson said.

"It gives me a sense of completion," Decker said. "How about this, Counselor? We hear Whitman's story off the record. If it sounds plausible, we deal. If not, I send Whitman back to jail, we go back to what we already have. No harm, no foul."

"Not a chance," Whitman said. "Bargain first, confession later."

The room turned silent. For a moment, the only sound was the whirring of the video camera.

Weller tapped his foot. "I like Decker's solution. We hear you off the record first. You don't talk, we don't deal."

Whitman banged the table with his fist. "I don't believe this shit!"

"Believe it!" Davidson said.

"Oh, fuck—"

Decker said, "Chris—"

"Fuck you, too!"

Davidson said, "Send him back. We're through."

"*I'm* not through," Decker said.

Davidson said, "You bucking me, Decker?"

"Looks that way," Whitman said.

"Whitman, *shut* your fucking mouth!"

The teen went quiet. Decker took a seat next to him. He leaned into the kid's face and spoke softly. "You want your friend dragged into your mess, Chris?"

Whitman was quiet.

Decker spoke in the kid's ear. "You can save her, guy. But first you've got to tell me your story. Just the two of us, okay?"

"You and me and the rest of the vultures looking through the one-way mirror."

"No. Just me and you and the video camera, all right?"

Whitman was silent.

"We talk in privacy," Decker said aloud. "Later, I play it back for Mr. Weller and for Ms. Berringer."

"Then what?"

Decker looked at Weller. "How about this, Morton? If we like the story . . . and if the kid's history checks out . . . if he passes both tests . . . you'll agree to Man One, six to twelve, no assault, no drawings."

Weller swallowed, his Adam's apple bobbing up and down like an erratic thermometer. "All right."

"Whitman?" Decker said.

The kid buried his head in his hands, then looked up. "Why should I trust you?"

"So who are you going to trust, Chris?" Decker smiled. "You want to trust your lawyer? You want to trust your uncle? Tell me what you want."

The teen blew out air and nodded.

"That's a yes?" Decker asked.

"It's a yes." Whitman shook his head. "You like what I say, we deal. Let's get this over with."

Davidson said, "It better be good, Whitman."

"Don't worry, Lieutenant. It'll be good. Because it'll be the truth."

☙ 29

Erica said, "You push this button here when you're ready. This red light should go on. That means it's recording."

Decker said, "I think I can handle that."

Erica glanced at the blanket hanging over the one-way mirror. Decker knew that the crew on the other side would be straining to see or hear something. They'd get their opportunity later on.

The young DA left the interview room and closed the door. Decker made final adjustments through the viewfinder, then pushed the record button. He pulled up a seat opposite Whitman, took out a pack of cigarettes, lit one of the smokes, and handed it to him. The kid inhaled deeply.

"Thanks."

Decker poured him a glass of water. "Anything else?"

Whitman shook his head.

Decker waited.

Whitman leaned his elbows on the table, clasped his hands together, placing his forehead on his knuckles. Wisps of smoke swirled to the ceiling, hairspraying the room. "In order to get with the program, you've got to know the history."

"Shoot."

"Right before I came out here, I was six weeks in detox for drug and alcohol abuse."

"What drugs do you do?"

"Did. Past tense. I did lots—reed, coke . . . popped a little scag. Also, I had lots of legal drugs—imipramine, Prozac, Xanax, Haldol. But mainly, it was booze. Like all boozehounds, I've got a really high tolerance for drinking. It takes a lot before I feel a buzz. I don't have a good stop mechanism until I'm blitzed out."

Decker kept his face flat. "You just can't help yourself. It's an illness."

Whitman looked up, cigarette between his fingers, and broke into a smile. "Yeah, these hospitals aren't too big on personal responsibility. They say the lines—gotta pull yourself up and take charge—but not *too* loud. Because if being self-indulgent isn't an illness, they don't get their insurance money."

Decker waited.

"It's all pretty irrelevant," Whitman said. "All I'm saying is, when I'm drunk, I'm basically comatose. Which means I don't remember anything."

"You ever get DTs?"

"Couple of times. But that was right before I was committed to County for hearing voices. So I don't know which caused which—the psychosis or the booze."

"What did your voices say?"

"I don't remember much, but I don't recall anything violent. Stupid, repetitive things. 'Tie your shoes, tie your shoes, tie your shoes' . . . over and over. But it was a real pain in the ass because I listened to them. You have any idea how miserable it is to tie your shoes a million times a day?"

"Do you remember your official diagnosis at County?"

"Something like Acute Episodic Self-Limiting Paranoid Schizophrenia—Adolescent Onset. I might have gotten a couple of words out of order. Anyway, the voices went away after I took medication. Eventually, I was weaned away from the Thorazine and that was that. But even after I was discharged, I still drank."

"You were admitted when you were twelve?"

Whitman nodded.

"You were an alcoholic at twelve?"

"I can walk away before I get drunk. But that's only because it takes a lot to get me drunk. When I don't walk, things get very hazy. Couple of times I woke up in a strange place and didn't know how I got there."

Whitman took another drag on his cigarette.

"One of my suicide attempts? I woke up in my bed, blood leaking out of a hole in my stomach, a twenty-two in my hand. I don't know what happened. Only thing I remembered was I'd been drinking. It could have just been an accident. But because of my history, they labeled it suicide."

"Was that the first or second attempt you were talking about?"

"Second."

"What'd you do the first time?"

"Pills. I tried to OD on my mother's Demerol.

Her death was an ugly one . . . painful to watch. Suddenly, I didn't want to live anymore."

Decker waited a beat, then said, "Let's talk about you waking up in strange places."

"There's a psychological term for it—fugue states. I know it happened at least twice—it's on my record at County. And there was my second suicide attempt. That was like a fugue. I'd use that as my defense if this mess about Cheryl went to trial."

"Meaning?"

"Meaning I have no idea how Cheryl happened."

Decker took in the kid's eyes—flat and dimensionless. "You don't remember anything?"

"I remember some things. But I don't remember killing her."

"You remember tying her up?"

"Sort of. I'm sure I did it. Because whenever we had sex in the past, I'd tie her up. Originally, I used to just pin her down with my hands. But she didn't like it. Said it hurt her too much because of my weight, and it was too much like rape. She'd been raped several times by one of her mother's ex-boyfriends."

Whitman sucked his smoke.

"I told Cheryl I wouldn't do her unless she was pinned. So she agreed to the binds. After a while, I think she liked it. Because she trusted me. On the rare times the sex wasn't working, I never forced her. Never forced a girl in my life."

Decker scratched his temple. "Why wouldn't you do her unless she was tied up, Chris?"

"I like being in control. Trouble is with sex . . ." Whitman took a drink of water. "When you're into it, you're not in control."

Decker waited for more.

Whitman took another hit of his smoke. "If the girl's tied up and I lose control, I know she can't hurt me."

"You thought Cheryl might hurt you?"

"Once you've been a piñata, Sergeant, you never trust again."

"Not even your friend Ms. McLaughlin? Is that why you tied her up?"

"No, that was different. That was art. I never had sex with her."

"Art?"

"My rendition of Jesus on the cross."

"You tied her up for art?"

"I couldn't exactly peg her to the cross."

"Why'd you tie up Cheryl?"

Whitman said, "I told you. I didn't trust her. I don't trust anyone. You're in ecstasy, coming inside a woman . . . next thing you know she has a knife in your back."

"You thought Cheryl was going to kill you?"

"Call the binds insurance." Whitman stubbed out his cigarette in an ashtray. "I need to be in control. When I'm not, there's always a chance that I'll freak. You want an ogre for my weird behavior, blame my father."

"How old were you when your father died?"

"Nine."

"How'd it happen?"

"He was murdered. Gangland hit."

Decker studied the kid's eyes. Again, they were unreadable. Even though everything was on tape, Decker still took out his notebook. His own scribblings reminded him of the salient points of the case. "What happened after your dad died?"

"My mother and I went to live with Joey Donatti."

"Did Joey ever beat you, Chris?"

Whitman's eyes went to the camera. "No."

"At least not when you're on film."

"Joey never beat me."

"Donatti adopted you."

"After my mom died, yes."

"Is Joey Donatti a blood relative of yours?"

Whitman shook his head.

"Why'd he adopt you?"

"Deathbed promise to my mom."

"What was their relationship?"

"My mother was his mistress."

"Ah." Decker took a sip of water. "You remember tying up Cheryl the night of the prom, Chris?"

"Like I told you, I was real drunk. But I'm sure I could have."

"You weren't too drunk to put on condoms."

"Habit. I always use rubbers."

"In the heat of passion, you can stop, evaluate the situation, then calmly put on a rubber. That takes a lot of discipline."

Whitman shrugged. "I never allow myself to be in the throes of passion unless she's incapacitated and I'm wearing a rubber."

"Even when you're drunk, and you don't remember doing too much, you remember to put on protection?"

"For me, putting on a condom is like zipping yourself up after you take a piss. No matter how drunk you are, you just do it."

Decker said, "How about with your friend Terry? Did you wear a condom with her?"

"I told you, I never had sex with her."

"Never did anything physical with her?"

"Nope."

"She tells it differently," Decker said. "She tells me the two of you were quite physical. You know what, Chris? I believe her."

"We kissed," Whitman said. "Maybe to her that's physical."

"So what's kissing her to you, Whitman?"

"A heartbreak."

"She said you did more."

"I didn't have sex with her."

"You climaxed."

Whitman looked at Decker. "She told you that?"

"She also told me you weren't wearing a rubber."

"We didn't have intercourse, *okay*?"

"Don't get peeved. I'm just trying to sort fact from fiction. You say you don't remember things. You say you always wear a rubber. And you didn't with Terry, that's all."

"Because we didn't make love . . . we didn't . . ." He sat back in his chair. "You and Terry must have had quite a little talk. What *else* did she tell you?"

"I'm running an investigation, Whitman. I ask lots of questions, and nothing's too personal when it comes to murder. You tell me you don't remember anything. But I tell you that you were aware enough to put on protection."

"I told you that's habit."

"Except with Terry."

"Decker, I don't use rubbers when I don't screw.

Hookers give me head, I don't use rubbers. Why would I bother? Give me an effing break!"

"Tell me what you do remember about that night in the hotel room."

"Not much. I remember waking up the next morning in my bed with a thrashing headache. Of course, I was out of Advil. I went to a twenty-four-hour drugstore and bought a bottle. When I came home, I found your card on my doorstep. I called. You came over with your pictures." He looked pained. "I knew I was in deep shit. Because the whole scene at the hotel was pretty sketchy in my mind."

"When I showed you the postmortem pictures of Cheryl, you were sober?"

"Unfortunately, yes."

"Then you saw Cheryl had her hands bound with a bow tie."

Whitman didn't answer.

Decker said, "What happened to your tux, Chris?"

Whitman paused. "Everything's off the record?"

"Not exactly. But what you're telling me now can't be used against you if we go to trial."

"Whatever that means."

"What happened to your tux?"

"Yeah, I saw the bow tie. I knew it was evidence against me. I stuffed my monkey suit in my cello . . . cellos. You looked carefully, but I hid it really well. Since I knew you couldn't take them apart, I knew I was safe."

"How'd you get them apart?"

"Cellos are held together by glue joints. Loosen the glue, the top pops off." He poured himself a glass of water and drank it up in a few gulps. "I forgot about the sketches of Terry. She wanted them back after she stopped tutoring me. I'm sorry I didn't listen to her."

"Why'd she stop tutoring you?"

"I guess I scared her. But even so, I knew she still liked me. She would have taken me back—as her student or something more intimate. Chemistry is chemistry. It was hell holding back from her."

"Why'd you do it?"

"Because I was engaged to someone else. Believe it or not, I didn't want to hurt her."

"What about Cheryl? You didn't mind hurting her?"

"I meant I didn't want to hurt Terry *psychologically*. As far as Cheryl was concerned, I would never hurt her physically on purpose."

"How about by accident?"

"Look, maybe I did something nasty to her. But if I did, I don't *remember* it! I was *blitzed*, don't you understand?"

"Chris, you remembered seeing the night clerk watching TV in the back room when you left. How can you remember seeing a night clerk . . . remember what he was doing . . . but not remember murdering someone."

"When you're drunk, it's weird how the mind works."

"You're selling, I'm not buying." Decker kept his face flat. "What's the last thing you recall about the hotel?"

Whitman ran his hand over his face. "Can I have another smoke?"

Decker gave him another lit cigarette.

"Thanks." Whitman took a deep drag. "What do I remember about the hotel? I remember watching fuck films in the room. I remember Bull Anderson loading me up with shots of Jack Daniel's. I recall feeling horny, vaguely recall having sex. And now that you mention it, I do remember leaving and seeing Henry Trupp in the back room watching TV. The desk was unattended when I left."

"Do you remember Cheryl telling you she was pregnant?"

"Yeah, but that happened way earlier in the evening."

"How'd you feel about that?"

"I told you it wasn't mine."

"And you were positive?"

"Yes. I'm still positive. Enough to give you blood and semen."

"Go on. What else do you remember about your night in the hotel?"

"That's really it. Next thing I can *actually* recall is getting up with a headache the next morning—"

"What?"

"Nothing."

Decker ran his hands through his hair. "Chris, I'm tired. Don't give me shit. What do you suddenly remember?"

"I think . . ." Whitman flicked ashes from his cigarette. "I think Terry might have called me. I'm not sure because it was a hang-up. But I seem to remember a phone call waking me up. It might have been her."

Decker said, "What time?"

Whitman shrugged. "Three, four, five in the morning. She'd know better if she made the call. She wasn't pickled."

"You tied Cheryl up that night, Chris?"

"Probably . . . because tying and fucking are routine things for me."

Decker said, "It's the killing that sticks in my craw. Unless killings are routine for you, too."

"I was shitfaced drunk. I don't remember killing Cheryl. Just like I didn't remember blowing a *hole* in my stomach. And yet here it is." Whitman stood, lifted up his shirt, pulled down his waistband, and pointed to a small circle of glistening white flesh above his pubic bone. "While I'm stripping, want to see my scar from my spleenectomy? Or the cigarette burn—"

"Sit down, Chris."

Whitman sat. "Can we stop now? I've got a hell of an ordeal facing me. Namely, my uncle's in town. He's going to *nail* me as soon as he finds out I dealt with the police without my lawyer and behind his back."

"Why'd you do it, then?"

"Because I had to." He pointed to the camera. "Turn the fucking thing off. I'm tired of my ten minutes of fame."

Decker went over to the video camera and turned it off. He sat down next to Whitman. "Okay, Chris. Now we're *really* off the record. Tell me what happened."

"You don't believe me." Whitman's eyes went flat. "You're going to recommend against a deal, aren't you?"

"I'm going to play the video and leave it up to the State."

"And if they ask your opinion?"

"They won't."

"But if they did?"

Decker studied the boy. "With your mental history, Man One is about as good as we could get if it went to trial. Why waste time and money?"

Whitman closed and opened his eyes. "Thank you, Jesus, for sending me someone with a brain."

"But that doesn't mean I believe a word you're saying."

"I'm crushed."

Decker glared at him. "Shut your friggin mouth, kid. I'm tired of this case and I'm really tired of *you*!"

Whitman licked his lips. "Sorry."

Decker ran his hands over his face. "We both know you're doing more time than if the case went to trial. I can't figure out if you're being noble or if you want to settle this quickly because there's some major shit I've overlooked."

Whitman took another drag on his cigarette. He spoke softly. "Unless you're Catholic, you couldn't understand. All the shit they brainwash you with. But she can't escape it. Truth is, neither can I. To pose like she did for me . . . flaunting her body . . . her nakedness. Decker, I let those sketches go public, I screw up her head for *life*."

He shook his head.

"Man, I *swore* that no one but me would ever see the drawings. I owe it to her to keep my promise as best I can."

"It's worth being shitcanned for?"

Whitman gave a careless wave in the air. "In my family, doing time is a badge of honor. After a five-year stint, I come out, I got notches on my belt. Believe me, there are worse things than the hole."

The kid turned slightly pale.

Decker said, "Like your uncle's temper?"

Whitman shook his head. "God . . . what a fucking *mess!*"

"I'll give you one thing, Chris. You must really care for her to go against Donatti."

"Sergeant, for that little girl, I'd take a bullet between my eyes with a smile on my face."

Decker regarded the kid. For once, he knew that Whitman was telling the truth.

❧ 30

Seeing his uncle, Whitman suddenly realized how short the man was. Short but muscular with hands like leather paddles. His face had grown fleshier . . . jowlier. Once a lean pit bull, Joey was now more like a bulldog. But his eyes . . . man, they never wavered once they hit their target. And today the poisoned darts were aimed straight at his face. Whitman forced himself not to look away.

Joey didn't dress like the rest of them. He went for flair, not flash—designer from tip to toe. Even with his squat size, he somehow pulled it off. Today he had on a slate-colored double-breasted suit, white shirt, and a muted, rust-patterned tie. His breast handkerchief was a pleated flower and exactly matched the hue of the dominant color of the tie. His shoes were burnt almond loafers, polished to a mirror surface.

The jailer opened the cell and told Donatti a half hour. Joey nodded. As soon as the door slammed shut, Whitman felt his heart in his chest. He stood up from his bunk, but his uncle motioned him back down with a flick of the finger.

Whitman sat.

Slowly Donatti walked over to him. As Joey stood above him, Whitman knew that he could take his uncle down with a single well-placed punch. It was all a psych game. Because he knew better than to *ever* lay a finger on his uncle. He was a well-trained machine, just like Joey's Neapolitan mastiffs—all three of them over two hundred pounds of vicious fighting dog. Yet a look from Joey sent them whimpering in the corner.

The smack across his face was so hard, Whitman felt it in his toes. Instantly, blood gushed from his nose, but he kept his hands in his lap and maintained eye contact.

Softly, Joey said, "That's for disobeying me and moving without my permission."

Another slam of dried beef against his jaw.

"That's for wasting my money!"

A wood-hard backhand across his cheek.

"That's for disobeying your lawyer and acting stupid."

Another thwack.

"For getting yourself into this fucking mess and wasting my time and energy!"

A final crash over his face. Whitman felt something crack, felt pebbles in his mouth. Blood was pouring over his lips, down his face, dripping onto his chest and lap.

"And that's for doing more time than you should have just to save a cunt some trouble."

Whitman said nothing, did nothing. How the hell did he find out about Terry that *quickly*?

Donatti shook his head. "What am I gonna do with you, Christopher? Bad enough you fuck yourself up.

Now you start fucking me up, too. What am I gonna *do* with you?"

Whitman didn't answer.

"You're lucky you got your mother's face. Without your mother's face, you got nothing, you know that? Benedetto's ready to drop everything, ready to call everything off. You know what that means to me in manpower, Christopher? You know what that means to me in profits?"

Whitman was quiet.

"Benedetto don't want no jerk-off like you as a son-in-law. Just lucky for you that Lorenza likes your face. Or maybe it's your dick, I don't know . . . but that don't mean it ain't gonna cost me. I don't want to even think about what it's gonna cost me."

Donatti flexed the fingers of his right hand and shook them out, eyes glued to Whitman's face.

"I shoulda junked you when you came out of the loony bin. Even your own *mother* was ready to junk you. She was dying, she didn't want to think about no fuck-up son. It was your aunt, God rest her soul, that saved your faggoty ass. She felt *sorry* for you. Well, now she's gone. And lucky me . . . I inherit the problem."

Donatti frowned, threw Whitman his silk handkerchief.

"Clean up your face. You're a disgustin' mess. I heard somethin' snap. I break anything?"

Whitman took the handkerchief and forced his hands not to shake. He wiped his face, spit a mouthful of blood and enamel into his handkerchief. He ran his tongue across his mouth, felt razor-sharp edges. "Chipped a couple of teeth."

"Front? Back?"

"Front ones, I think."

"Good! I put a dent in that perfect, faggoty-ass smile of yours. You got a dentist out here?"

Whitman looked at the handkerchief—it was drenched in blood. He examined his jail blues, found a clean spot, and swabbed his face. "No, I don't have a dentist. I ruined your handkerchief."

"Fuck it." Donatti held his son's chin and examined his face. Whitman snapped his head back. "I'm bleeding like a slaughtered pig. I'll ruin your suit."

"So I'll buy another one. Don't jerk away from me like that."

Donatti untucked his white shirt, spit several times on the tail, and began to clean Whitman's face. "Your nose don't look broke. Used to be I could crack a face in a single punch. I must be gettin' old."

"You didn't punch me, you slapped me."

"Good point." Tenderly, Donatti dabbed his son's bloodied lips. "You cause me nothing but grief, Christopher. First, you pork the school's whore and she winds up dead—"

"It was stupid—"

"Shut up! Don't interrupt me when I'm talking! Then you screw yourself up to save some nobody *girl*? What's she do to you? Suck your brain out through your pipes?"

"I never even slept with her, Joey."

"Then you're *real* stupid! Make a smile."

Whitman smiled.

"Yeah, I got both your front teeth."

"Bad?"

"Nah, just small corner chips. Girls'll think it's kinda cute." Donatti spit another wad of saliva onto his shirt. "Hold still."

Whitman didn't move.

Donatti said, "You put me in a bind, Christopher. You put yourself in a bind 'cause you know what I gotta do. I gotta mess her up, that's what I gotta do. Except I don't really feel like messin' up a sixteen-year-old girl. Especially her. She's very pretty."

"You saw her?"

"Course I saw her. Moody tells me about the sketches, first thing I say to Tony is find the girl. I really should mess her up." Donatti stood, studied Whitman's face, then tucked his bloodied shirt back in his pants. "You pull shit like this, I gotta teach you a lesson big time."

Calmly, Whitman said, "Tell Benedetto that as punishment for disobeying you, I'll marry Maria."

Donatti took a step backward. *"What?"*

"Tell Benedetto that as my punishment for moving without your say-so, you're making me marry Maria."

Donatti stared at him. "You seen Maria lately, Christopher?"

"I know what she looks like, Joey."

"The girl's moving to four hundred pounds. You're my son! Benedetto knows that even *I* wouldn't do that to you."

"It'll get you back in Benedetto's good graces. And it's proper. The older daughter should marry before the younger one, right?"

"Except when the older daughter's a retard."

"She's not a retard, she's just simple. That's all

right. She can cook, she can clean, and she can probably make decent babies."

"How you gonna screw her?"

"With my eyes closed. If I marry Maria, you won't have to pay Benedetto grievance money, will you?"

Donatti shook his head. "He'll owe *me*!"

"So do it."

"What are you after, Christopher?"

"You know what I want, Joey."

"Leave your pussy alone."

"That's all I'm asking."

"How do I make sure you don't bolt on me?"

"Joey, I swear on my mother's grave, I never even slept with her. Never."

Donatti peered into his son's eyes. "Tell me that again, Christopher?"

"I never slept with her. I knew I had to leave her. I figured, what was the point?"

"What was the point?" Donatti squinted. "What was the point? The point is to *fuck* her, that's the point. What the fuck is wrong with you? You been hearing strange voices again?"

"No."

Donatti studied Whitman's eyes. "Maybe you didn't fuck her. But she did something to make you crazy. She gives that good a blow-job, I'll take a round with her."

Whitman blinked several times. "She didn't give me head, okay?"

Donatti gave Whitman a firm slap across his swollen face. "What the hell is wrong with you? All of a sudden sucking's too good for your faggoty ass?"

"No. Not at all."

"You spent too much time out here. All these faggoty-ass Hollywood types."

"They like blow-jobs, too, Joey."

Another slap. "Don't wiseass me. What's this girl to you if you didn't do nothing with her?"

"I love her, plain and simple."

"So how do I know you won't bolt on me? It was bad enough worrying about Lorenza. I know you hate her guts."

"I don't hate her."

"You hate her. Don't argue with me. I know you hate her. She's a bitch and a half, but at least she's cute, right?"

"Lorenza is very cute."

"At least she's got a body. At least she ain't a re-tard. So what do you got after you get out of the hole? Four hundred pounds of fat waiting to smother you in the sack? And you're telling me you won't bolt, Christopher?"

"I won't bolt."

"*I* gotta be a retard to buy that."

"I won't bolt because I know better. I know what you'd do to me. I know what you'd do to *her*."

"She's so special, maybe I'll screw her myself."

Whitman closed and opened his eyes, but said nothing.

Donatti grinned. "You fuck on me again, that's exactly what I'll do, Christopher. I'll do it right in front of you."

"I swear I won't. I get out of the hole, I go straight to the altar with Maria. You've got my word."

"That's worth shit. You're a liar."

"What can I do to convince you? You want me to sign my name in blood?" He swiped his nose with the back of his hand. "I certainly have an ample supply right now."

"And what about your piece of ass?"

"She's out of the picture."

"I'm supposed to believe that?"

"Yes. Because I love her. I don't want her hurt."

"You didn't screw this girl?"

"No."

"What'd you do with her?"

Whitman put his hand to his face and grimaced with pain. Every facial bone was sore to the touch. "Not much."

"She give you a hand-job . . . maybe a little tongue along the rim—"

"Joey, *please*!"

Another slap. But this one was gentle. "You're stupid for testing me. But I gotta say I don't blame you. She's a pretty one."

Whitman was quiet. Then he said, "You'll leave her alone?"

"She's a pretty girl, Christopher," Donatti said. "Pretty and lucky. And as long as you show up at the church, she'll stay pretty . . . she'll stay lucky."

Whitman closed and opened his eyes. "Thank you very much, Joey."

"In the meantime, you're stuck in the hole for at least five years. That's not great for me, Christopher."

"I'll make it up to you."

"Damn right you will." He waved him off. "What the hell? Five years won't hurt you none. Maybe even give you some spine . . . a few points with the guys back home. They think you're a closet queer."

"They think anyone who listens to classical music is queer."

"They got a point." Donatti grinned again. "Where are your cellos?"

"At the apartment."

"I'm gonna send Davey down there. He's good with an ax."

"The Rowland Ross is worth money, Joey."

"I need money? What *I* need is to teach you a lesson."

"It's worth about ten grand."

"Well, it ain't gonna be worth firewood by the time Davey finishes up."

Whitman closed his eyes and shook his head. "Whatever you want. You know best."

"I hope you really love her, Christopher. Because you just bought yourself five years extra service."

"Two."

Donatti furrowed his eyebrows. "You arguing with me?" Spittle sprayed from his mouth. "You got the nerve to *argue* with me?"

"Five years is outrageous. You wouldn't respect me if I didn't argue. Two years is fair. Especially because you won't have to pay Benedetto grievance money."

Donatti glared at him, then broke into laughter. "You may be something yet if I can train out all the faggoty-ass things that Donna, God rest her soul, trained into you." He looked around the cell. "I can talk to some people if you want. Have you transferred back east. I got more pull over there."

"I'd rather stay here."

Donatti took in Whitman's face. "You hate me, don't you, sonny?"

"No. Not at all. I know you're doing what you have to do. I know it's nothing personal."

"Ah, such beautiful words from your beautiful lips." Donatti smiled. "You are so full of shit, Christopher. You hate my guts. That's okay. You also fear me. That's even better."

Whitman was quiet.

Donatti took a seat on the metal bunk chained to the wall. "Okay. I'll go with two years extra service. What do you say?"

"Thank you."

"Kiss me."

Whitman planted a kiss on each of Donatti's sagging cheeks. Donatti took Whitman's chin and kissed his son's forehead. Then he let go of his face and threw his arm around Whitman's shoulder, rubbing it as he talked. "Okay, I won't hurt your girl. You feel better?"

"Yes, I do. Thank you very much."

"You know, you're not a total fuck-up, Christopher."

"Thank you."

"I know you can do good when you put your mind to it. We both know that."

"Thanks."

"I do appreciate your help."

"It's nothing."

"Yeah, but I still appreciate it."

"Thank you."

"I do love you. You know that, too, don't you?"

"I know."

"It just makes me mad when I blow fifty grand. It also makes me mad when you sucker-punch a cop. Last thing we need is the law mad at us."

"It was stupid."

"Real stupid." Donatti checked his watch. "I got about ten minutes before someone comes to get me. Your face looks like something out of a funhouse."

"I'll tell them I fell."

Donatti smiled. "You're trying hard, aren't you?"

"Very."

"I appreciate that, too." Donatti paused. "I really do, Christopher. And you know what I think? I think you've done enough penance. So I'm gonna do something for you."

Whitman waited.

"This girl, Teresa Whatserface . . . you really like her, don't you?"

Whitman felt his heart race. He was silent.

"They'll probably send you to Piedmont." Donatti massaged his son's shoulders. "I got some pull there. For the right price, I can arrange something."

Whitman didn't speak.

"Once a month, I could maybe arrange something. Get Moody to hire her on, get her a paralegal license. That way you could see her alone . . . attorney/client privilege." Donatti grinned. "It'll get you . . . about thirty minutes, maybe an hour alone with her . . . guards looking the other way. Make your stay in the hole a little less . . . frustrating. You know what I'm saying?"

Whitman nodded, swallowed dryly.

"You're gonna marry Maria, I gotta get you some good memories. Want me to set something up, Christopher?"

"If . . . if she's interested, I'd like that very much."

"Course she's interested. A stud like you." Donatti ran his fingers through Whitman's thick hair. "She's interested, believe me."

"Don't sic anyone on her, Joey. Nothing by force."

"I'll handle it myself." He wagged a finger in front of Whitman's face. "But no more movin' on your own. As soon as you're out, Terry's gone. You marry Maria, you hear me?"

Whitman nodded. "Yes, I hear you, Joey."

"I figure, in the meantime, why not make you happy?"

"Thank you, Joey."

"Kiss me, Christopher." Donatti leaned in close. "Kiss me like you love me."

Whitman kissed one cheek, then the other, then gave him a long, closed-mouth kiss on his mouth. Donatti held his face, stroking Whitman's puffy cheek, then broke it off. He peered into Whitman's eyes.

"You're lucky you have your mother's face, you know that?" Again, Donatti kissed him. "If you was a girl, I'd marry you tomorrow."

"I'm not a girl."

"I know that. But that's not all bad. You got other uses." Donatti gave him a final kiss on the mouth, then stood and straightened his tie. "Yeah, you got lots of other uses. But the only reason I keep you is because you got your mother's face."

"God bless Mom."

"Don't be rude, Christopher."

"I loved my mother."

"I know that, son." Donatti closed his jacket to hide the bloodstains. "I know you loved her deep. So did I."

❧ 31

Without ever seeing the man before, I knew instantly who he was. He fit the stereotype—central casting of the Mafia don, except his eyes weren't acting. Cold and assured, they told me he meant business. I knew that if this was *it*, there wasn't anything I could do to dissuade him. My heartbeat quickened and I broke into a cold sweat. He waved his hand, signaling me to step aside. I did and he walked into my house, closing the door softly. Then he turned the deadbolt. It clicked and I jumped.

He wasn't tall, maybe five seven or five eight, but he was very muscular. Big hands and wrists and a wide bull neck that strained his collar. His hair was a dense nest of steel wool but cut stylishly. He was swarthy and saggy, his cheeks shadowed despite a recent shave. But he was dressed nicely—a black wool crepe suit over a white shirt and tie.

He glanced around my living room, then zeroed in on me.

"Where are your parents?"

His voice was surprisingly gentle. I tried to answer his question, but it took me time to find my voice. "Working."

"Christopher tells me you got a little sister."

"She's not here," I said quickly.

He smiled. "What? You think I come here to hurt you?" He smiled again. "Like in the movies, huh? I rip out an automatic and start turning your walls into Swiss cheese?" He laughed. "Sit down. I just wanna talk to you."

Slowly I made my way to the dining-room table. Out of habit, I asked him if I could get him something to drink.

"Someone with manners." Again he smiled. His teeth were white and capped. "I like that. No, I don't want anything to drink, thank you. Sit down."

I sat.

"So you know who I am, huh?"

I nodded.

"You been expecting me? Christopher must have spooked you good. The kid has more sense than I thought."

I was silent.

"So I don't have to introduce myself, do I?"

I shook my head no.

"Christopher told you all about me?"

"I guess."

"You guess? What do you mean, you guess? It's a yes or no question."

"He . . ." I swallowed hard. "He told me a little about you."

"Like what?"

My head was ringing. "Like . . ." I cleared my throat. "He told me you adopted him after his mother died. He told me that you took him in when he had nowhere else to go."

"Yeah, only the good stuff, right?" He laughed again. "He also tell you I was a son of a bitch?"

Again I shook my head no.

"Nothin' like that, huh?"

"Only that you shouldn't . . . be messed with. He really loves you a lot."

"You're a terrible liar."

I shut up, waiting for the bomb to drop. But he seemed unhurried—calm and relaxed. Of course, he had all the power. Why shouldn't he take his time?

He examined his knuckles. "Tell you one thing, little girl. Christopher means the world to me. This whole business about this dead girl . . . what was her name?"

"Cheryl Diggs."

"Yeah, Cheryl Diggs. I know my son. Christopher didn't do nothin' to her."

I nodded.

"Not that Christopher doesn't have some growing up to do. But why would he bother wasting a whore? It's stupid and pointless, and Christopher isn't stupid or pointless. I'm not saying this Diggs deserved to die. But it ain't Christopher's fault if the little whore took some bum chances. So I'm not shedding tears for her, you know what I'm saying?"

I nodded.

"Some cop had something against the name Donatti; next thing I knew, my son was arrested, booked, and arraigned. Pissed me off, but I coulda lived with it. That's why I got my lawyers on retainers. You wanna know what *really* pissed me off?"

I waited, didn't dare move.

He said, "What really pissed me off was what

Christopher did for you. Taking all this heat and time just to bury a couple of pictures of you spreadin' your legs. You know what that means, girlie? It means I don't like you much."

I felt sweat dripping off my forehead. He beckoned me closer with a crooked finger. I moved in until I was inches away from his face. I expected to be overwhelmed with the smell of garlic or cigar smoke. Instead, he was perfumed with good cologne. He waved his finger in my face.

"You owe me, Teresa. You took my son from me. That means you got a debt to pay."

I was starting to feel dizzy. Sparks of light pinpricked my brain and I made a big push to breathe deeply. If he noticed my distress, he wasn't worried about it. He was back to studying his hands. His nails were short and clean. No pinkie ring.

I waited, too frightened to speak.

Softly he said, "But I'm a decent man, Teresa. Despite what you heard about me, I'm a fair person. You owe me. But I'm willing to let bygones be bygones, for Christopher's sake. Because I really do love my son."

I licked my lips and waited for him to continue.

"I want Christopher happy," he said. "And that isn't going to be easy, girlie. Because he's going to a shithole. As pens go, Piedmont ain't all that rotten. But it isn't the best place for him. There aren't enough blood brothers and way too many niggers. *I* wanted to transfer him back east, but *he* didn't want it. Kids. Try to do them favors . . ."

His eyes went back to my face.

"Christopher's a very strong boy. Resilient is the

fancy word for him. He'll do okay wherever he is. But that don't mean I don't want the best for him. You should too if you love him."

I felt my eyes well up with tears. I managed to stave them off. "Yes, of course."

His eyes took on a menacing squint. "My sonny loves you very much, Teresa. Too much in my opinion, but I can't control his heart. So you know what he's doing? He's doing time for you. Least we can do . . . both of us . . . is try to make his time at Piedmont as good as possible. You with me?"

"I'll do anything you want."

He seemed to be examining my face. Apparently I met with his approval because he gave a slight nod.

"Glad to hear you say that. Because I've arranged something for him . . . for *you* and him. Just the two of you. You understand what I'm saying?"

I didn't and my face must have reflected my confusion.

"Time alone with him, Teresa. I expect you to be nice to him, girlie. Real . . . *real* . . . nice."

The light bulb went on, but I didn't respond.

"You do understand me, don't you?"

"I think so."

He threw back his head in frustration, a mannerism I'd seen in Chris. "You *think* so? Do I gotta spell it out for you?"

Quickly I shook my head no.

"Good. So we understand what's expected?"

I nodded.

Donatti smiled. "Now that wasn't so bad, was it?"

Again I shook my head no.

"So here's the deal, Teresa. Christopher's being

transferred in a week. Give him a month or two to
settle in. When he does, I'll send someone by here to
drive you to Piedmont. He'll call you a couple days
before. Give you time to work around your parents.
You don't tell them nothing. This is between you
and me!"

"Yes, of course."

"Now I got some very important advice for you.
So listen up."

I waited.

Donatti said, "I'm gonna try to get you in as a
paralegal. Maybe it'll work, maybe it won't. Either
way, you're a natural beauty and that's a *big* problem. When you go to the hole, you wear an old-lady
dark, loose dress with long sleeves and a high neck.
Nothin' bare showing, little girl, not even your feet.
Wear some old slippers with socks or something.
They won't let you in if your shoes got laces. Are we
together so far?"

I nodded.

"Good. No makeup, no perfume, and braid your
hair up. You keep your mouth shut and your eyes
plastered on the ground. If I get you credentials,
you show them at the desk, then some guard'll take
you through to my sonny. Now it's true I'm calling
the shots. But in real terms, you're gonna be at the
mercy of some guard I bribed. Which means he's
got the principles of a turnip. If he happens to get it
in his mind to hit on you, if he backs you into a corner, just let him do whatever the hell he wants. I'll
make him sorry later. But that won't help you in the
short run, will it?"

Slowly, I shook my head.

"Remember, you're going to a place that houses nothing but cutthroat son of a bitches who haven't been with a woman in a very long time. You make a wrong turn, Teresa, you're gonna be history." Donatti moved in close. "You think you can handle that?"

I whispered a yes.

"Look at me when you talk."

I managed to meet Donatti's eyes. "I can handle it." My eyes remained on his, locked in ocular combat. "I can handle it, sir, and I will handle it. This is not a punishment for me. It is a privilege."

Donatti pursed his lips as he continued to stare at me. "Good answer. You really love my sonny, don't you?"

"Yes."

"That's too bad. Because he's marrying someone else."

"I know."

"Pity," he said without emotion. "But that's life. Sometimes it's good. And sometimes it sucks. Like I told you, my man'll call a couple days in advance. Expect it."

He stood and so did I. But he motioned me back down. "I can see myself to the door. I'm not as old as I look." He said, "Off the record, Teresa. You think he did it?"

I shook my head no.

"Why not?"

I looked down, then back at his eyes, remembering how he liked eye contact when I talked. Just like

Chris. It made me wonder. In actuality, how dissimilar were father and son? "He didn't do it . . . because the murder was too messy."

Donatti stared at me. "That's a reason?"

"It's a good one if you know Chris."

"You saying I don't know my own son?"

I shook my head no. "I'm just . . . Christopher is very neat, that's all."

Slowly he nodded. "You got a good eye, little girl." He stuck his hands in his pockets. "You're a tough one. Tough, but you don't know it. It makes you appealing. That and your face. You got one hell of a face on you. Goddamn edible. You want to keep it that way, you be good to my boy. No complaints, you understand?"

"Yes."

"You won't hear from me again directly unless something goes wrong. Make sure it don't happen."

He closed the door. I felt an unimaginable relief as if I had suddenly found shelter from a blistering rainstorm. I prayed the refuge wasn't temporary.

❧ 32

Time passed quickly, time dragged its heels. An overcast June and July suddenly burst into a smog-choked, sweltering August. It seemed as though the call would never come. Then when it did everything happened too quickly. I made hasty arrangements with a voice on the phone line. Two days later, nine A.M. sharp, I was picked up by two men in dark suits. Neither spoke as they flanked me, both gently guiding me with a soft hold on my elbows. I was led to an air-conditioned midnight-blue Lincoln with smoked-glass windows, ushered into the back with its plush leather seats. I was offered water or soft drinks, which I declined, before I was whisked away.

I dressed just as Donatti had told me. If my escort's face was a mirror reflecting my sex appeal, I was in good shape. He lowered his shades for a millisecond, then slipped them back on. His attitude said I was a stick of wood. Most of the time I kept my eyes on my lap. But I did manage an occasional glance out the window.

The prison was about a three-hour drive away. A medium-security correctional facility, Piedmont was built about twenty-five years ago. It was located one hundred and fifty miles northeast of Los Angeles, erected inside an isolated pocket of hell-hot desert and water-starved scrub. The ride was long and monotonous—endless miles of blacktop passing through Joshua trees, gnarled oaks, and chaparral, which eventually gave way to tumbleweeds and pincushions of cacti. In another time, I might have fallen asleep, lulled by the breeze of the car's airconditioning, rocked by the Lincoln's suspension. But I was too nervous to doze.

As the hours passed, I grew hotter and hotter. My backseat companion must have noticed me wiping my damp forehead. Without a word, he turned up the blower. It cooled my skin but did little to relieve the internal heat. He reached under the seat, pulled out a small cooler, and handed me a can of Coke. Someone must have instructed him to take good care of me. I took a couple of sips, then elected to cool off my hot cheeks with chilled aluminum.

Three hours later, we were in the county of Piedmont. There were no residents or businesses to speak of—the county was the prison. There were lots of posted warning signs along the roads. The unsuspecting should beware, though I couldn't imagine *anyone* traveling these sinkhole roads unless they had business with the prison. Indeed, the only vehicles we'd passed in the last hour had been a blue prison bus with metal-grate windows and black-and-white sheriff cars.

The Lincoln signaled right, exiting on a well-worn turnoff to the prison. The road was two lanes—a streak of pitted asphalt. On either side was an endless bleak horizon.

The sun was close to its high point, the outside heat pouring through the darkened windows. Despite valiant efforts from the Lincoln's cooling system, the desert proved victorious. The inside temperature had turned tepid. My dark clothing was ringed with moisture despite liberal applications of morning antiperspirant.

Off in the distance, I could make out a speck of gray. As we drove farther, the speck grew and grew, eventually materializing into a concrete, impenetrable mountain jungled by vines of laser-hot barbed wire. If I looked up and squinted, I could make out the turrets of the guards' towers rising into the sun's glare. My head was pounding, I felt sick to my stomach.

We parked as close as we could to the entrance. As soon as the car door opened, I was smothered by a relentless, broiling heat. I was helped out of the car, but I felt light-headed. I must have stumbled because both men tightened their grip on my elbows. Slowly, I was led to the prison.

Once inside, I was aware of the drop in temperature but that was all I was able to take in. Sweating and shaky, I didn't notice much because my eyes had been bleached by the hot, outdoor light. Once they did adjust, I kept them focused on the floor tile. I have some fuzzy recollection of showing some papers, of signing into a logbook. Then I was handed over to a female prison official dressed in khakis, a gun riding her hip. She took me in back, into a supply closet, and closed the door, leaving both of us in pitch darkness. Then she turned on a dim, bare light bulb.

My eyes hadn't left my feet.

She frisked me thoroughly over my clothes. Then she reached up onto a high supply shelf and pulled down a suit of prison blues and a pair of paper slippers and told me to change my clothes. I wasn't looking at her face, but I know she was watching me as I disrobed. Then she frisked me again, examining every crevice I had. But that was as bad as it got. Satisfied, she told me I could get dressed, then to put my hands behind my back. When I did, she handcuffed me. The cuffs were loose. I could have wiggled out of them, but I said nothing. She clutched my arm and opened the door to the supply room.

She poked her head outside. Another guard—this one male—was standing watch. The two of them sandwiched me just like Donatti's men. Same walk, different uniforms. They told me to keep my head down. I obeyed without question.

They led me down a series of poorly lit corridors that stank of urine and grime. Eyes on my feet, I had no idea where I was going. My sense of direction was scrambled. I was vaguely aware of solid-steel meat-locker-type doors on either side of me. I could hear things in the background—angry shouts, screams, curses in several languages, and even laughter.

Abruptly, we stopped in front of one of the doors. The female guard took out a ring of keys and opened it. The portal was as thick as a bank vault's. Suddenly I was pushed inside. My handcuffs were removed and I was instructed to wait. The door slammed shut and I was encased in semidarkness. I was happy to be alone. But I was also terrified of being left alone.

For a brief moment, I was seized with panic. The shakes came on in waves. I forced myself to relax, managed to block off an anxiety attack. I couldn't even fathom what Chris must have gone through the first couple of days . . . the fear and depression . . . the singular lack of freedom.

This was it for him for at least five years.

I grabbed my body as if it were a life preserver and looked around. A hermetically sealed padded cell, except there was a beam of light from a small, single-grated dormer window above. The pen couldn't have been larger than six by eight. But at least I could stand. That was good because I was too scared to sit.

I strained to hear something . . . anything. But all I could make out was the sound of my own breathing. To keep from going crazy, I started counting mentally. Three hundred and fifty-two beats later, the door reopened. The same guards escorted someone else in blues. But unlike me, this body was taller than either of the officials.

They told him to face the wall, which he did. One of the guards whispered something in his ear. He nodded, then his handcuffs were taken off his wrists and he placed his hands atop his head. The guards told him to hold the position until the door closed. When it did, he dropped his arms to his sides and turned around.

Chris.

At least I thought it was him.

I had known a lanky teenager. What I now saw was a developed man. His upper body was fuller, his biceps pronounced under his short sleeves. His hands had somehow enlarged in two months. They were big, his smooth musician's knuckles roughened by some sort of manual labor. His thick golden hair had been nearly shorn to the scalp, leaving only peach fuzz. His cheeks and chin had been obliterated by a reddish-blond lawn.

I found the strength to look at his eyes. They were as unreadable as ever. I took comfort in that familiarity. Anything I could grab. He massaged his wrists.

"Are you all right?" he asked me.

The same voice. I felt better. I said, "I should be asking you that."

He didn't answer me. His eyes hadn't left my face. I said, "How are you . . . managing?"

He spoke quietly. "It doesn't matter. Nothing matters now. Nothing except you and me."

He was leaning against the back wall. I was standing next to the closed door. But the cell was so small, we were within touching distance. Even so, I made the first move. I came to him, slipped my arms around his waist, hugged him tightly. Coiled steel. For once, he didn't tense in response to my touch. He closed his eyes and drew me into his embrace.

From that moment, what we did became a series of blurs—tossed clothing, heavy breathing, hard kissing, a tangle of hot, wet bodies followed by searing, stabbing pain as he pushed his way inside my body. It all happened so fast that I didn't have time to formulate an expectation. I wouldn't have known he had climaxed except for the change in his breathing. Afterward, he managed to sit up and flip me onto his lap. My legs were still around his waist. He gripped me tightly as he thrust himself deeper into my body. I grimaced, biting my lip to keep from screaming. I had to let it out some way so I raked his back. He stopped, but didn't pull out.

"Hurt?"

"A lot."

"I won't move then. Kiss me, Terry."

I did. We kissed over and over, my nose tickled by his facial hair. His lips traveled from my mouth to my sweat-soaked breasts. True to his word, he didn't move. But the lack of motion didn't stop him from growing inside of me. But it was a pain I could deal with. And because he wasn't actively hurting me, I began to relax. As I did, I could feel my body opening up. He felt it, too. He pried his mouth away from my nipples and looked at me expectantly. I nodded, and he began to rock inside of me.

This time the pain burned more than stabbed and sliced. Probably because I was lubricated with wetness from my own once virginal body as well as from his seed. It took him a little longer, but he was still quick. Both times couldn't have taken more than five minutes apiece.

He remained inside me when he was done. I knew he wanted more, but I was in too much pain to comply. He didn't push it, but he didn't back off. He continued to hug and kiss me, exploring my body with calloused hands. He held my face and kissed me hard. I broke away.

"Chris, we have to talk."

He shut me up with another kiss. "Later."

He started to move inside of me. I clutched his arms in agony, making deep red fingerprints on his triceps. He stopped moving.

"I need you," he said. "But I don't want to hurt you anymore. Do it with your mouth, okay?"

I smiled weakly and nodded. He wiped himself off, using his prison shirt, then directed my mouth to his groin. I'd never done this before even with Daniel. I closed my eyes and hoped for the best. It must have been good enough because he had no trouble climaxing, pushing my mouth away before he came. Even in this state, he was showing me consideration. It brought tears to my eyes. Afterward, he finally allowed me respite. Slumped against the wall, he brought me back on his lap, but left my loins unencumbered.

He was still breathing hard, his eyes on the ceiling. "God, it was worth everything." His gaze lowered to my face. "Worth . . . everything."

His chest heaved as he spoke. "You all right, Terry?"

I told him I was fine.

He kissed me softly, then hard, his tongue dancing inside my mouth. He cupped my breasts as we kissed, rolling my nipples between his fingers.

"Just pull the plug now," he said, between kisses. "It can't get better than this. I can't believe you actually came out here to this pisshole." He suddenly stopped kissing me. "Or didn't my uncle give you any choice?"

"He didn't," I said. "But I would have come anyway. I love you."

"I love you, too. I love you so much, it hurts. Kiss me, baby doll. Kiss me, kiss me, kiss me."

I brought my mouth to his, ran my tongue across his teeth, felt something sharp against my taste buds. I broke away and looked at him. "What happened to your front teeth?"

"Accident—"

"Oh, God—"

"Nah, not here. My uncle did it. It doesn't matter."

"He *hit* you?"

"It doesn't matter." He kissed my breast. "It doesn't matter at all. Like my beard?"

"Very much."

He sucked my nipples. "How about the haircut?"

"You're handsome no matter what."

"Meaning I look like a fuckin' skinhead." He came up for air. "It's because of the lice. Rampant little critters." He looked up and ran a hand across his denuded head. "Shampoo they use here burns like hell. Send me some decent stuff when you get back home, okay?"

"Do you need anything else?"

"No, nothing. At least nothing available in a store. Kiss me, angel." Once again, his mouth attacked mine. "Let me give you satisfaction . . . like we did in my apartment."

"I'm too sore. Besides, I want to talk to you. I'm ready to know the truth."

"It's over, Terry. Let it ride."

"Just tell me yes or no."

He kissed me and didn't answer.

I pulled away. "Chris—"

"It won't change anything. Drop it."

"I know it won't change anything. It certainly won't change the way I feel about you. But I still want to know."

"God, you're beautiful—"

"Chris—"

"Drop it!"

"Chris, did you kill her? Yes or no?"

His face contorted in anger. Abruptly, he pushed me away. "Yes, Terry. I killed her. I didn't mean to do it. But that doesn't make Cheryl any less dead. Are you happy now?"

I stared into his eyes, trying to decipher their muddied look. "I don't believe you."

My answer made him madder. "And *why* don't you believe me, Terry?"

"I . . . just don't."

"It certainly won't change the way I feel about you," he imitated me. "What a crock of shit—"

"Chris—"

"You know why you don't believe me?"

"Chris—"

"You know why?" he said louder. "You don't want to believe it. You can't *allow* yourself to believe it. Because that would mean you just gave your cherry to a lowlife. And what would that say about you?"

"It's not that at all."

"Yeah, say it enough times and maybe you'll convince yourself."

"Why are you getting so angry?" I said. "You *told* me to ask you."

"That was then, this is now." He glared at me with furious eyes. "So now you know. And you're *disappointed*! Too fucking bad I didn't meet your expectations—"

"Chris, it doesn't matter—"

"Oh, cut the *shit*, Terry! You just got *fucked*! Cool

it with the Goody Two-shoes virgin bit and get real, okay?"

I blinked several times. Then I whispered, "Please don't talk to me like that."

His eyes engaged mine for a moment, then they broke contact. He shook his head and blew out air. His voice turned soft. "We'd better get dressed. Gestapo'll be here soon."

I covered my face and broke into sobs. He took me in his arms and rocked me gently.

I said, "I wanted to make this perfect for you."

"It was perfect." Chris hugged me tightly. "God, I'm sorry. *Please* don't cry."

I bit back tears, kept my head against his chest, my hands resting against his newly developed pectorals. His new body . . . a shorter fuse, so unlike the Chris I knew. I said, "You're on steroids, aren't you?"

He didn't answer right away. Then he said, "I needed bulk in a hurry."

"I understand completely," I said, wiping my eyes. "I don't blame you."

He didn't answer me.

"Do you need more stuff?" I asked. "Do you need anything at all?"

"No, I'm all right." He broke away from me and began feeling around for his clothes. "I've got money . . . some clout. I can get the illegal stuff. Just can't get decent shampoo."

"I'll send some right away." I found my shirt and slipped it over my neck. "So you're surviving okay?"

"Surviving's a good word. Mafia still carries weight." He put on his pants and shirt. "Not that I haven't been tested, but simple shit. Nothing I couldn't handle. They've got lots of jail bands here. So I'm okay."

"What instruments are you playing?"

"Headbangin' ax for the Aryans, mandolin for the shitkickers, and bass for the soul brothers. Rest of the time, they leave me alone. They got me doing foundry work . . . lots of ore under the desert. It's as hot as hell but I don't mind. I like sweating and the work builds up muscle. Foreman's an okay guy . . . meaning you can buy him. When the shop is closed, he lets me fool around with the scrap. I've done some interesting sculpture. Let me help you on with your pants."

I nodded.

He raised my legs and slipped them into my pants. "Terry, you're all bloody and red down there. You should see a doctor. Just to make sure you're all right."

"That would be a first. Death by deflowering." I paused. "Unless you meant something else."

He looked blank.

"We didn't use protection, Chris. I'm about midway through my cycle."

He shrugged carelessly. "Nothing we can do about that. We're both Catholic. If it happens, it happens. You know I'd take care of you. You sure you're all right? I tried to be gentle, but I got carried away. I'd feel better if you saw a doctor."

"If I need to, I will. Don't worry about it."

He raised his brow. "You're a lot cooler than I gave you credit for. I thought you'd go ballistic when you found out I was using."

"Chrissie, I understand that there are different laws here."

"Man, ain't that the truth. You know what, Terry? There are different laws everywhere . . . even in our so-called civilized society. We all think we live under one big Constitution, but we don't. We're influenced by our own cultures. In my family, extortion is a time-honored trade—"

"Chris—"

"I'm not saying *I* believe it's good. But really, when you think about it, my uncle's only doing what comes naturally. Where he grew up, paying the don was just a fact of life. *His* community thinks it's normal. Among his people, he's well liked and well respected."

"But he's living under American law—"

"Which is arbitrary at best. In Texas and Florida, they fry people. The death penalty's outlawed in Massachusetts. There's no consistency. Laws are broken every hour of the day by lawmakers, why should we expect the criminals to behave?"

"So we should just chuck it all and live in chaos?"

"I'm just saying laws work in a context, that's all. In my uncle's community, a law against extortion is not only meaningless, it's just plain silly."

I looked at him. "You've thought a lot about this."

"You're the legal son of a big mafioso, you think about these things. Look, I'm sure I'm trying to justify in my own mind what my uncle does. But I do understand where he's coming from."

Not wanting to get him mad, I nodded in agreement. It seemed to satisfy him.

"Anyway, I'm sorry I spoke to you like that. It won't happen again." Chris kissed me softly on the cheek. "I'm sorry if I misjudged you."

"I do love you, Chris."

"I'd sure like to believe that."

I whispered, "Please tell me what happened with Cheryl?"

"Terry, I was drunk—"

"Chris, I've seen you drunk. You've got more memory than a pentium chip. That line satisfied the lawyers. But it doesn't satisfy me. What happened?"

He didn't answer.

"Christopher, *talk* to me."

He ran his hand over his face. "Terry, you know when I leave this place, I've got to go home." He sighed. "We've had a change of plans. I'm being married off to Lorraine's older sister, Maria. She's fat, she's ugly, and people call her retarded—"

"When did this happen?"

"It was my punishment for copping a plea instead of letting my lawyer handle the case."

"Chris, why'd you *do* that? I didn't ask—"

"I know you didn't ask," he said. "But I wanted to do it for you. Because the sketches were my fault. So here I am and here you are. We're *together*, Terry. This arrangement is the best thing that ever happened to us. As much as I hate it here, I don't want to get out. Because what do I have *waiting* for me?"

"Me."

"Oh, baby doll." He shook his head. "You've met my uncle. You want to mess with him?"

"You're changing the subject."

"I'm telling you what's important to me. Are you going to come back and visit me again?"

"Of course."

"Swear?"

"Swear."

"No matter what?"

"No matter what. Did you kill her?"

"Terry, I'm not going to answer you. Because I'm screwed either way. I tell you, 'Yes, I did it,' you're destroyed—"

"Chris—"

"If I tell you, 'No, I didn't do it,' you'll start hunting around for some psycho sex killer—"

"You didn't do it, did you?"

He ignored me. "If you care about *my* feelings, you'll just drop it. What's done is done. Let's just enjoy the time God has blessed us with."

I was quiet.

"Come here." He patted his lap.

I climbed back on top of him. He took my face in his hands and kissed my lips. "I love you. I want you to know that. Promise me you'll let things ride."

"Meaning?"

"Meaning you won't go around being my avenging angel. Swear to me you'll let things be."

Before I could answer him, the door opened. Chris gripped me hard, his face a mask of despair. "Just five more minutes, please."

"Wouldn't chance it, buddy. Lock-down's in fifteen minutes. They don't count your head, you bought yourself thirty days in the hole."

"Chris, you have to go!"

He held me tighter. "Oh, God—"

"Please!" I begged him, pushed him away. *"Please!"*

He swallowed dryly, then stood up. Gave me a heart-wrenching smile. We exchanged vows of love, then he left.

The door slammed shut and I was alone. I wept bitterly. My face was beard-burned and I could barely walk. But a long hot bath and *I'd* be close to normal. *I'd* be back home. But the boy I loved would remain in hell.

And he did it all for *me*! Donatti was right. I owed him . . . I owed both of them. At least I could look the old man in the eye and say that I'd handled it. But it wasn't enough.

The guards came back for me. Procedure was identical except in reverse. I checked out of the logbook, and by two in the afternoon, I was in my old hot, stuffy clothes and once again traveling isolated desert roads. My eyes drooped, my body ached for sleep, but I refused to succumb. There were things to think about.

True, I had promised Chris *I* wouldn't avenge him. But that didn't mean that someone else couldn't. Because, really, how much control did I have over other people's actions?

❦ 33

She stood up when he came in, said she was sorry to be bothering him. Being a polite kind of guy, Decker told her it was no problem. He pointed to one of the orange plastic chairs attached to the floor, but she didn't sit.

"Could we speak where it's a little less . . . public?"

Decker studied the teen. She wore a floral strap dress over a white cotton tee. Her legs were encased in nylons, her feet housed in white, polished flats. Her cheeks were tinged with blush, her lips coated with something glossy and mauve. She had dressed for the occasion. Her eyes were bright and purposeful. They accepted his scrutiny without a flinch.

She reminded him of Cindy—scared but tough. He thought about his daughter living off campus in New York. At first Decker had thought Cindy wanted to stay to prove herself strong. No rapist was going to chase her away. Now he was thinking it was something much more mundane.

How's it going, Princess?

Fine, Daddy. I can't talk. Someone's waiting for me.

A long pause. *A girl someone or a boy someone?*

Oh, Daddy!

And with that, she had hung up on him.

Cindy had a boy up her sleeve. Dear Lord, please make him a nice guy and not a scumbag like Chris Whitman.

The thought brought him back to the present. To Terry he said, "Would you like to talk at my desk?"

"If that would be okay."

"Come." He led her through the door marked SQUAD ROOM, passing through the detectives' ante-room where two dees were fielding calls. He brought her into the working area proper. For once, Decker's desktop was clear. He pulled up a chair for her, then motioned her to sit. After she did, so did he.

"I forgot what you like to be called—Terry or Teresa. Or we could go very formal and I could call you Ms. McLaughlin."

She let out a small laugh. "Terry's fine."

"So what can I do you for, Terry?"

Her eyes were anywhere but on him. "I saw Chris the other day."

"You did?"

She nodded.

Decker said, "How's he doing?"

"He's . . . coping."

"Good."

She said, "He seemed depressed."

"I'd be depressed, too, if I were in prison."

Neither spoke.

Terry said, "Can I ask you an honest question?"

"Sure, although I can't guarantee an honest answer."

She looked at her lap, then at his eyes. "Do you think he did it, Sergeant?"

"Are you asking me if I think Chris killed Cheryl Diggs?"

She nodded.

Decker said, "Yes, I think he did it."

"Not even a little doubt in your mind?"

Decker rolled his tongue in his cheek. "Are you here to proclaim his innocence?"

"I know, I know," Terry said. "You think I'm dumb and naive."

"You're not dumb."

"I'm not naive, either. I asked Chris straight out. I asked him if he did it."

"And?"

"He was . . . vague. Deliberately vague."

"It's hard getting the words out," Decker said.

"Except we both know that Chris is a great liar."

Decker raised his brow and waited.

Terry shrugged. "I think he's testing me . . . will I still love him even if he did do it? I told him I would. It's the truth. But I don't think he believes me."

Decker didn't speak.

Terry said, "You're probably wondering why I'm here."

"Yes, I am."

"I respect you. I just wanted to know if there was ever a little, teeny . . . minuscule doubt in your mind about Chris being the one."

"Terry, there's always a little, teeny, minuscule doubt."

She looked up. "Really?"

Decker was about to explain, then thought better of it. But she was sharp and caught it.

"What is it, Sergeant?"

Decker said, "Nothing."

She became animated. "You do have a little, teeny doubt, don't you?"

"You forgot minuscule."

"Do you have any doubts?"

Decker didn't answer. He noticed her facial muscles tighten. She said, "What is it? Some sort of code of silence? You can't admit your doubts to us ordinary people?"

"Terry, Chris Whitman is a murderer."

She looked at him sharply. Then her eyes grew heavy with sadness. "So I guess I got what I came for. Like they say . . . the truth hurts." She shrugged. "Maybe Chris is right. Maybe I am better off not knowing."

"I would think so."

She started to get up, then changed her mind. "You can't tell me anything to make me feel better?"

The statement, said with such blunt innocence, tugged at Decker's heartstrings. "Did Chris send you here, Terry?"

"No." She shook her head vigorously. "As a matter of fact, he'd be really angry if he knew I came. He wants me to let the whole thing ride. See, once he gets out of prison, he has to go back home and marry some girl he doesn't love . . . or even like. Some sort of arranged thing with his uncle."

Decker said, "Is the girl's last name Benedetto?"

"Yes, but it's not Lorraine," Terry said. "It's her older sister who's apparently fat and ugly and stupid. His punishment for not consulting his lawyers before he confessed to the police."

Decker said, "Chris must trust you to talk so openly about his family."

"Of course he trusts me. He loves me. I love him."

Casually, Decker asked, "What else did he tell you about his uncle?"

Terry shrugged. "Just that Benedetto is a rival of his uncle. I guess the Mafia works like old royalty. They use marriages to keep peace. So you can see why Chris isn't anxious to be freed."

"I don't know, Terry." Decker said, "Prison seems like a funny kind of haven."

"Except in prison, he has me . . . visiting him."

"How many times have you gone to see him?"

"Just once so far. But it was really intense."

Decker focused on the girl's face. "Intense?"

She looked down and nodded.

"Whitman's uncle . . . Donatti arranged some kind of special visit for you?"

Again she nodded.

"A conjugal visit?"

She looked away, her cheeks crimson.

"Ah," Decker said. "So this is how you're spending your summer vacation."

"You're making fun of me."

"Not at all." Decker waited a beat. "Well, maybe a little. I'm sorry."

She smiled with moist eyes.

Decker spoke gently. "Terry, the case was closed two months ago."

"Can I look at Chris's file?"

"First of all, it's not Chris's file, it's the Diggs murder file. Secondly, no, you can't look at it."

"You'd let Chris's lawyers look at it, wouldn't you?"

"You're not Chris's lawyer."

"Suppose I can get a release from Chris that allows me to look at his files."

"But of course he wouldn't do that," Decker said. "Because he'd be real mad if he knew you were here."

"Yeah, you're right." She sat back in her chair. "He wouldn't permit it."

Decker thought a moment. Perhaps the girl did come in on her own.

Terry said, "Then I guess I'm going to have to look into the case on my own."

"Be my guest."

"Because I think there's a person out there who got away with murder."

"Uh-huh."

"Doesn't that bother you?"

"Can't say that it does."

"You think Chris killed Cheryl."

"Yes."

She looked pained, but she didn't stop. "Any hints on how I should start an investigation?"

Decker sat up. "Terry, enough."

"Do I just start asking people questions or what?"

Decker reminded himself to be patient. "Terry, we've had this conversation before. You put your nose where it doesn't belong, you get people mad. If you're really hell-bent on retribution for your boyfriend, hire a private detective. I'll even cooperate with him, how about that?"

"I can't afford a private detective."

"So approach Donatti. The man has some powerful connections."

"Chris would be furious if he found out I went behind his back. Sergeant, *please* help me out!"

"Terry, I'm not Whitman's advocate. I'm his adversary."

"But we're all on the same side, aren't we? The side of truth and justice."

"You forgot the American Way."

"I'm being *serious*!"

Again her eyes had turned moist—bright and shiny like rain-slicked stones. Decker said, "Terry, I know you're hurting. And I feel bad for you. But *I* can't help you."

She wiped tears away from her cheek and nodded. "I know. It's my problem."

Decker said, "If Chris really told you to let the case ride, *listen* to him. It's good advice."

She nodded, but wasn't hearing him. She said, "Every case starts from square one. So I'll start from square one. Besides, I know all the people involved . . . I'll just ask around."

Decker's expression remained flat, but inside he was steeped in frustration. "It would not be a good idea for you to poke around. If you respect my opinion, now's a great time to start showing it."

Terry sighed. "Sergeant, did you have any other leads before you arrested Chris?"

"No," Decker lied.

"So it was always Chris?"

"Yes."

"Did you interview all of his friends?"

"Yes."

"How about all the hotel personnel?"

"Yes," Decker fibbed.

"Each and every person who was at the hotel?"

"Are you casting aspersions on my thoroughness?" Decker said, smiling.

"Oh, no, not at all. I'm . . ." She stopped, saw the look in Decker's eyes, and smiled. "I'll just start from square one."

Decker rubbed his mustache. "You're wearing me down."

"That's the idea."

Decker stared at her. "Why do you care so much, Terry? He wasn't even your boyfriend in high school. What happened?"

She looked down. "You're thinking that Chris found a real sucker in me."

That's exactly what Decker was thinking. But there was more to it. He said, "Chris is bright. Why did he need a tutor in the first place?"

"It was a ploy . . . a way to get to me since we didn't hang out in the same groups."

"Ah . . ." Decker said. "That sounds like the Chris Whitman I know."

"But I don't think the extra push I gave him hurt. Because he missed a lot of school."

Without thinking, Decker took out a notepad. "How so?"

"He traveled a lot, did a lot of gigs . . . playing with orchestras, ensembles . . . sometimes even solo work."

"There's a national shortage of cello players?"

"A shortage of players of his caliber."

Decker said, "So he missed a lot of school."

Terry nodded. "One minute he'd be totally caught up. Then he'd miss a week or two and fall behind."

"How often did he play gigs?"

"I think he had . . . maybe two gigs during the time I was tutoring him. Why do you ask?"

"Just trying to get some background."

Her eyes brightened. "You're going to help me?"

"I didn't say that," Decker backtracked. "While you tutored Chris, did you two talk about other things?"

"Sometimes."

"Did he ever talk about his family?"

"Sometimes."

"Did he ever mention doing work for his uncle?"

"Just the opposite. He made a point of telling me he had nothing to do with his uncle's activities."

"And you believed him?"

"At that time, I had no reason to doubt him."

"How about Cheryl?" Decker scribbled. "Did you talk about her?"

"I brought her up once or twice. He said she was no big deal. They went together because it was easy."

"Easy?"

"She was promiscuous. That kind of easy."

"And you accepted that?"

She sighed. "Sounds crazy but yes, I did. He was engaged to someone else. He felt it was better not to even start."

"Looks like you've both changed your minds."

She smiled but it was a weak one.

Decker knew he was mining old fields. Still, a

pinprick nagged his brain. Something Terry had told him the first time he interviewed her. About prom night.

We talked about running away together.

Why would Whitman kill Cheryl when he was planning to run away with the girl he truly loved. And he did love her. Guy was scum, but he went to the hole for her.

And then there were those African-American pubic hairs. . . .

But was Decker curious enough to pursue it? Whitman was a cold mother. Why should Decker care if the kid rotted in jail? Then Decker realized something. He didn't care about Whitman. But he did care a great deal about the process.

He said, "I'm going to cut you a deal, Terry—"

"You're kidding!"

"If for no other reason than to get you off my back. Promise me you won't do any homespun investigating, and I'll reread the Diggs files. If something pops out at me, I'll look into it—quietly and discreetly."

"And if nothing pops out?"

"You drop the whole thing."

"Will you let me know if you find out something?"

"No. You'll just have to trust me on this one."

"You won't even keep me updated?"

"Probably not. That's what quietly and discreetly means."

"So I have to sit back and wait? I don't know if I can do that."

"Yes or no, Terry. I'm getting tired."

"Yes."

"Great." Decker stood. "I'll walk you out."

"What about—"

"Gosh, it's so noisy in this room. Can't hear a blessed thing." He took her elbow and prodded her upward. Then he led her out the door into the front reception area. "Good-bye."

"Can I call you?"

"No."

But Decker knew she would anyway. The teen was a very beautiful girl. And a smart one, too. But she was a pest. Like a fly, she seemed attracted to garbage.

~ 34

"I'm going to be working late," Decker said. "But I'll be here. So call if you need anything."

"A new case?" Rina asked.

"No. Just tying up loose ends. If tonight's not good, I can do it tomorrow night."

"No, tonight's fine. Maybe I'll ask the boys to pitch in with some baby-sitting. I'd like to go over to the yeshiva and catch one of the Rebbitzin's *shiurim*."

"What's the Rebbitzin lecturing about?"

"*Shyalahs* and *Tchuvahs*—questions and answers. She's a good speaker."

"When's the lecture?"

"She usually starts around eight."

"You know what, Rina? I'll meet you there. If the lecture isn't over, I'll learn in the study hall. Then maybe we can go for a ride afterward . . . get some ice cream."

There was silence over the line. Then Rina said, "A ride? *And* ice cream?"

"I'll bring the Porsche. I'll even put the top down."

"Just the *two* of us? With the top down?"

"Yes. Can your heart handle the excitement?"

"I don't know. This is an untested event."

Decker laughed. It had been awhile since they'd stolen some quality time together. He didn't count the times his insomnia had brought her to the kitchen in the wee hours of the morning. "Love you, kid."

"Are you all right, Peter?"

"I'm great. My business shouldn't take more than an hour or so. Old stuff. So I'll see you soon."

"You promise?" Rina quickly added, "No, don't promise me anything."

"Why not?"

"Don't make promises you can't keep."

"You don't trust me, huh?"

"Of course I trust you." Rina paused. "It's your job I don't trust. A truly seductive mistress."

Decker was quiet. "That's an odd way of looking at my work."

Rina said nothing. "You'll be home in an hour?"

"Of course." Decker was peeved. "Bye."

"Bye."

She hung up. Tension in the air. Screw it. He'd handle it later. He was good at handling things.

Just an hour, though the case didn't deserve even that much. He opened the folder and scanned the pages for an overview, refamiliarizing himself with the facts, the figures, and the autopsy report. All the lab tests had been completed. The semen inside Diggs hadn't matched Whitman's. As far as the fetus Cheryl had been carrying . . . no one had ever tested Whitman to see if he had been the father, hadn't been necessary since Whitman had confessed.

Back-to-basics time. Decker fished out his old checklist. First name on the roster was Henry

Trupp—the night hotel clerk. A handwritten scrawl in the margin that Decker had called the house three times, but Trupp hadn't answered.

He dialed the number. After two rings, he was told the line had been disconnected and there was no new listing. He hung up, asked directory assistance for a new number. But there wasn't any listing—not anywhere in the Valley.

Decker tried the city directory. No luck there. Aloud he sang, "Oh where, oh where has Henry Trupp gone?"

He rang up the Grenada West End, and spoke to a desk clerk named Caroline. First identifying himself, Decker then asked for Trupp. His request was followed by one of those pregnant pauses.

Caroline said, "Excuse me, Sergeant, I'm going to transfer your call to my supervisor."

Decker said, "Is there some sort of problem?"

But she had already pressed a button, sending him into the great electronic void. Another voice came through the receiver—Joe, the supervisor.

Decker said, "I'm trying to find an employee . . . or maybe a former employee of the hotel—Henry Trupp. He used to work the night desk at this location."

Joe was suspicious. "What is this about, sir?"

"Just want to talk to the man, that's all. Do you have his current phone number?"

"Sergeant, Mr. Trupp is . . . deceased."

Decker sat up. "He's dead?"

"Yes, sir. About two months ago."

"What happened?"

"We've already made our statements to the police, sir."

Statements to the *police*? Decker said, "Trupp was murdered, Joe?"

"Sergeant, if you are who you say you are, you should know all this. If you have any questions, contact the hotel attorneys."

The phone disconnected. Decker's mind was reeling. *Two* months ago. That would have put it around the time of the Diggs murder. It was obvious that Trupp hadn't been whacked at the hotel. Otherwise, Devonshire would have fielded the call. He looked down at his notes. Trupp's former address was on Sepulveda near Roscoe.

Decker called up the Van Nuys Substation, asking for Detectives. A CAPS dee named Bert Martinez answered the line. Briefly, Decker told the man who he was and what he wanted.

A hesitation over the phone. Martinez said, "I'm missing something here. I thought the Diggs case was closed. As I understood, it was a mob case."

"Not exactly. The kid who confessed had Mafia connections. And yes, the case is closed officially, but—"

"So what do you want with Trupp?"

"Just wanted to go over a few minor things. Was the case solved?"

"Unfortunately no," Martinez said. "It's my case and it's still wide open."

"CAPS is picking up homicides?"

"No. I used to be in *Homicide*. Funny how that works."

Decker hesitated. The man was sitting on some holy anger. "What can you tell me about Trupp?"

Martinez said, "Why exactly do you want to know?"

Decker said, "I'm sensing reluctance, Martinez. What am I doing to make you squirrely?"

Slowly Martinez said, "It's just weird to find the principal homicide detective in a major case reopening his own investigation after it's been solved."

"I'm not reopening anything," Decker said.

"So what are you doing?"

"Tying up some loose ends."

"What's *really* going on, Decker? You doing Cosa Nostra a favor or something?"

Instantly, Decker felt ire well up inside, but kept it in check. Martinez was making sense. Decker said, "I'm at Devonshire. Give me twenty minutes, I'll meet you at Van Nuys, all right?"

"You'll meet me here? At the station house?"

"You've got something else in mind?"

"I'm hungry. There's a coffee shop a couple of blocks from here." He gave Decker the address. "Twenty minutes?"

"Make it thirty." Decker felt his stomach tighten, his words mocking him. *Just an hour.* "I've got to call my wife. I have a feeling it's going to be a long night."

The place was so old, it was a wonder it hadn't come tumbling down in the '94 earthquake. It held a half-dozen booths and a Formica lunch counter hosting ten swivel stools. The vinyl used to fabricate the booths and stool tops must have been brown at one time, but now it was so faded and cracked, it looked like beef jerky. The floor was washed-out linoleum, something between an ivory and gray. Decker trod carefully, grateful that his shoes didn't stick to the tiles as he walked over to someone he assumed was Martinez.

The guy was stocky, his complexion mocha-colored, a dense, black mustache providing an awning for a thick upper lip. He had black hair and coffee-bean eyes, and wore a white shirt loosened at the neck, a thin, out-of-date paisley tie, and a pair of gray slacks. He was eating a bowl of soup, dipping a French baguette into the tomato-based liquid. He looked up at Decker. "Have a seat."

Decker sat.

The men shook hands. A waitress came up, automatically poured Decker a cup of coffee. She asked if he wanted anything to eat, but Decker shook his head. After she left, Decker said, "I didn't appreciate your comment."

Martinez gobbled up half of his soggy roll. "So tell me why you're opening the case."

"Long story short? I was never happy about the way the investigation was handled."

"Why weren't you happy if you handled it?"

"It was a big case. Lots of people involved. My superior and I had differences of opinion. You might guess who won out."

"You got your conviction. What's the problem?"

"No problem," Decker said. "I just don't like being told how to do my work. But sometimes it's unavoidable. The Diggs case was one of those times. Now that it's over, I want to satisfy myself that I did everything right."

"Your caseload's that light that you got time for Monday morning quarterbacking?"

Slowly Decker appraised the detective. "Martinez, I take shit from the upper brass, I ain't gonna take it from you. I'm not in bed with anyone. I'm working for my own personal reasons. You doubt my motives, I can live with that. Bottom line—are you going to help me out or not?"

Martinez looked up from his soup. "You're not going to eat anything?"

Decker sat back in his chair. "You've got an agenda here, Bert. Fill me in."

The waitress came over again, took Martinez's empty soup bowl and placed in front of him a roast beef dip and a plate of fries. Decker felt his mouth begin to water.

Martinez said, "Give the man the same, Mimi."

"No, no, no," Decker said. "Nothing . . . well, maybe a scoop of cottage cheese."

"Sugar, I've seen them all." Mimi winked at Decker. "Believe me, you don't need to diet."

"Thank you. But cottage cheese is fine."

"Want me to throw some fruit on it for you, sugar?"

"What do you have?"

"Lots of melon balls. I'll throw some on for free."

"Fine."

Mimi left. Martinez said, "I think she likes you. She's never offered me free balls."

Decker said, "Speak to me, Detective."

Martinez took in a mouthful of roast beef. " 'Bout

two months ago—when I was still in Homicide—I caught a two A.M. call . . . a Saturday night special." He swallowed and took another bite. "Some geezer was found dead in the parking lot of the Chopperhouse. Are you familiar with the place?"

"No. Sounds like a biker bar."

"An ex-con, biker bar . . . which is probably a redundancy. It's about six blocks from the station house, which makes our job easy. From the bar, they go to the joint. Released from the joint, they go back to the bar. It's quite a scene. Shitkicking scumbags on heavy metal transportation and girls with big knockers wearing leather vests."

"You forgot ZZ Top booming out at earsplitting volume."

"On the nailhead," Martinez said. "Anyway, I got called down. We IDed the victim. His name was Henry Trupp."

"Trupp was a *biker*?"

"One of them old, skinny, used-to-be types turned pathetic lush."

"Did Trupp have a record?"

Martinez nodded. "Cat burglary."

"Well, that's confidence inspiring," Decker said. "Trupp worked for a major motel chain. He had passkeys to all the rooms."

"Motel help . . . we're talking four-figure incomes. Some of the dives take whatever they can get, no questions asked."

"He wasn't working for a dive."

"Then I guess he could fake it well enough to work."

"When was Trupp's last arrest?"

"About two years ago."

"He was working for the Grenada for about a year and a half. Wonder if he did some pilfering there?"

"Could be. But dig this. His last arrest *wasn't* for burglary."

"Morals charge?"

"Very good. They caught him with some thirteen-year-old runaway who was rooting his pipes."

"Cheryl Diggs supposedly got free rooms for herself and friends in exchange for head."

"How old was she?"

"Seventeen . . . maybe even eighteen."

"Mr. Trupp must have matured in his tastes."

Decker smiled.

Martinez said, "Anyway, you get called down to a ex-con bar for a murder . . . how do you figure the guy's been done in? Maybe shooting, most likely a stabbing—a broken beer bottle across the jugular. Maybe even a fatal beating, right?"

"Trupp was strangled," Decker said.

Martinez stopped himself mid-chew. "Exactly."

"Not garroted. It was done manually. You found imprints around his neck."

Martinez didn't answer.

Decker said, "Had Trupp been tied up?"

Martinez shook his head no. "Parallels to your girl?"

"To Cheryl Diggs, you mean? A few. Go on."

Martinez sipped his coffee. "Now, Trupp had enough booze in his blood to preserve him in a specimen jar. So it wasn't hard picturing someone going up to him and snapping his neck. The question was, why would someone do it that way?"

"And?"

"Well, Decker, that's about as far as I got. Because I suddenly got word from my superiors that this guy was the night clerk at the Grenada, where the prom queen was murdered. I also got word that Devonshire was on the verge of arresting a suspect. Because of the publicity on the Prom Queen Murder, I was told to keep my investigation quiet so as not to complicate your shit before your suspect was arraigned. A week later, I got a promotion and a raise. But I also got bumped to CAPS. Someone shut me down."

"Wasn't me," Decker said. "I would love to have known about this."

"So why didn't you follow up on Trupp?"

"Why do you think, Bert? I had the prime suspect in custody and a legit confession. Whitman said he did it, I'm going to tell him he was mistaken?"

"Well, all I knew was that some mafioso kid was plea-bargained down to a Man One. You've got to take a look at it through my binoculars, Pete."

"You're figuring the kid whacked the girl, then whacked Trupp because he saw something?"

"Exactly. But then I blink and the kid's lost to me. I'm moved *out* of Homicide—"

"With a raise and a promotion."

"Hush money. I was taken off Trupp and told to move on to something else. So I'm wondering if the loose ends you're talking about is the Mafia trying to clean up its paperwork. Or somebody upstairs covering his tracks. Because from my point of view,

I see a Man One conviction that maybe shoulda been two counts Murder One. For all I know, you've been hired to give me motivation for forgetting about Trupp."

"I'm not working for anyone, especially the mob."

"Look, at the time of the murders, I asked around about you. You've got a rep as an honest guy. But I'm clearing the air just so we understand each other."

"Not a problem." Decker shook his head. "So they booted you out of Homicide. No wonder you're testy."

"With the raise I'm not bitching. The shift just seemed like a coincidence to me. Then I get your call . . . that you're reopening your own case. Sort of gets my dander up. Why are you doing that?"

"A half-dozen black pubic hairs."

"What?"

"They did a pubic comb on the murder victim," Decker stated. "They found pubics that matched the convicted perp—"

"The mafioso. Donatti's kid, right?"

"Yeah. Christopher Whitman. The ME also found African-American pubic hairs. I want to know where they came from."

"Didn't the girl get around?"

"Yes. But none of the witnesses or friends recall Cheryl being with a black the evening of the prom. According to what *I* knew of the girl, she wasn't actively involved with any blacks, period."

"Maybe it's not the type of thing a nice white girl would advertise."

"Cheryl wasn't a good girl. She was rebellious

and sexually promiscuous. I think it would be the first thing she'd advertise."

Mimi brought Decker over a white mountain of curds covered with boulders of green, orange, and pink melon balls. She cocked a bony hip and squinted at Decker, further creasing her wrinkled face. "Sure I can't get you a cheeseburger?"

"Positive."

She refilled their coffee cups. "Holler if you need me." She let out a cackle. "For *anything*."

Martinez smiled. "Yeah, you're all talk, Mimsy."

Mimi threw her head back and laughed, disappearing behind the doors to the kitchen.

Martinez said, "This is getting very interesting. Trupp's clothing was combed for transfer evidence. Guess what *we* found?"

Decker's heart quickened. "You found African-American hairs?"

Martinez nodded. "Which never made a lot of sense to me. Because the Chopperhouse is white boy only."

"Maybe they belonged to a hooker."

"They were male black hairs," Martinez said. "And they weren't pubis, they were head hairs."

"Did you do a DNA on them?"

"No. Didn't have a suspect. Why? Did you?"

"I was going to but then Whitman showed up. We can order the tests now. Quietly, of course. Find out if yours match mine."

"Opening up a closed case just for curiosity?"

"Your case is open, Bert. And if they match, we have something more than just curiosity."

"It's gonna take time," Martinez said. "But right now, the hairs are all we got. Because we didn't find any blood at the scene. How about you?"

Decker thought a moment. No blood was found *at* the scene. But after reexamining the autopsy report, Decker recalled Craine's stating that there had been trace amounts of blood inside Cheryl's vagina. That blood had matched the semen from the unidentified source, the ME postulating that the blood might have come from a wound on the penis.

"There was some blood work. Of course, that's not going to help if you don't have anything for me to match it against."

"We'll just have to wait for the DNA." Martinez studied Decker intensely. "You sit on this case for a couple of months. Now you decide to open it up. What gives?"

"Like I told you, I was never satisfied with how it was handled."

"So why now?"

"Someone gave me a push. Not the mob. For now, that's all you need to know."

"Why'd your superior shut you down in the first place? Does he have a hard-on for the Mafia?"

"No, I think it was the riots," Decker said. "It scared him a mite."

Martinez's eyes widened. "Ah . . . the thought of a black boy killing a white girl . . ."

"Especially when the white girl had a rich, white, mob boyfriend with kinks. He's also a pathological liar and a cold mother-effing SOB."

"Capable of murder, then."

"Absolutely."

"So why start?"

"Because either the system works or it doesn't. And if the system doesn't work, I'm in the wrong profession."

✒ 35

The house was dark and quiet. At one in the morning, Decker hadn't been expecting a party. But he had hoped to see that welcoming crack of light peeking out from under his bedroom door. It was not to be. Quietly, he walked through his shadowed living room and dining room and into the kitchen. He turned on a small-wattage lamp resting on the kitchen table and started to boil some water. While the kettle heated, he sat down in one of the two chairs, his body slumped and tired.

A moment later, the kitchen door opened.

Rina's face was flushed, her cerulean eyes darting with confusion. Her long black hair was loose and wild. She wore a long white gown and a matching peignoir. She looked like something the moors had blown in.

"I'm fine, Rina," Decker said. "Go back to sleep."

She sat down at the kitchen table. "What time is it?"

"A little past one. Did you attend the Rebbitzin's lecture?"

"Huh?"

Decker laughed softly. "Go back to sleep."

"What did you say?"

"I asked you if you attended the Rebbitzin's lecture."

"Oh . . . yes . . . yes, I did. It was good. Not as good as what we had planned, but I enjoyed it."

Decker felt his stomach tense. "You're mad?"

"No, I'm not mad."

"Disappointed?"

"Not really."

"Resigned?"

Rina rubbed her eyes. "Keep throwing out enough adjectives, you'll find one that fits." She sat down. "It's okay, Peter. I'm not complaining."

The kettle began to whistle. Rina stood, but Decker held her arm. "I'll get it. You want some herbal tea?"

"Sure."

Decker smiled. "With honey, honey?"

"With honey, honey."

Decker got up and made two mugs of tea. He sat down and took her hand. "So the Rebbitzin's lecture was good, huh?"

"Yes, it was fine." She sipped tea. "She had a pretty good-sized turnout. Over thirty women. I was surprised."

"Were they all from the yeshiva?"

"No. About half were from the community. Women interested in exploring their roots . . . what Orthodox Judaism is all about."

"That's great."

"I thought so. We had quite a lively discussion . . . not all the women were pro-Orthodox but everyone was respectful. It made for interesting conversation."

"I'm sure."

"Afterward, the Rebbitzin and I went to her house for coffee. We talked. Apparently the Rebbitzin has developed quite a reputation. She's going to be doing some kind of lecture circuit for the next month. She asked me if I would fill in for her while she was gone. I told her sure."

"Wait a minute." Decker sat up in his chair. "Wait a minute. What did you agree to?"

Rina squinted over her teacup. "I told the Rebbitzin I'd help her out. Is that a problem?"

"Uh, no . . ." Decker sipped his tea. "No, not at all. Just what does it entail?"

"Four lectures, Peter. I think I can handle that."

Decker laughed, but he wasn't happy. "Of course. I wasn't implying you couldn't. I'm just . . ."

"Irritated?"

"No, Rina, I'm not *irritated*," Decker said. "I'm just surprised you didn't discuss it with me first, that's all."

"It's only four lectures, Peter—"

"I know, I know. It's fine. I think it's great."

"Thank you. But I don't need your permission."

"I'm not *giving* you my permission. Christ, Rina, why are you acting so touchy?"

"Because I tell you I'm going to be filling in for the Rebbitzin, the *normal* response is for you to say, 'Great. What are you going to talk about?' Instead, you're asking me what it entails."

"I don't think that's an abnormal response. I just want to know how it's going to affect our family."

"You mean how it's going to affect *you*."

"Rina, it's not going to affect me—"

"Of course it won't. You're never home."

Decker put down his teacup, blew out air, and placed his forehead in his hand.

The room turned quiet and cold. Rina sipped her tea and waited. Decker waited.

Finally, she whispered, "I can understand the pressing nature of your current cases. What I can't understand is why you had to cancel our date for an old case you closed months ago. A case where the guy confessed and is currently doing jail time."

"I told you it could wait for tomorrow."

"Then why didn't you put it off until tomorrow? Why does something *always* come up?" Rina shook her head. "It's late. We're both tired. I'm going to bed."

"Wait a minute," Decker said. "Let's thrash this out, all right?"

"Fine. What came up that was so important on a case you closed two months ago?"

Slowly, Decker recapped the Diggs case. When he was finished, he said, "I didn't reopen the file because the girl asked me to. I did it because I was never happy about the way the whole thing was handled, you know that."

"I know that."

"The girl just more or less jogged my memory, reminded me that I was unhappy. So . . . I pulled out the file, figuring it shouldn't take more than an hour at most. Next thing I knew, a major player in the story had been murdered and I was talking to some pissed-off dee in Van Nuys who'd also been shut down."

"You became intrigued."

"What can I say? It could have waited. But I got caught up in the situation. It was very inconsiderate of your feelings. But beyond that it doesn't mean anything—"

"Not for *you* maybe."

"I'm just saying it doesn't mean I prefer my work to my family. You and the children are the most important—hell, you people are the *only* important things in my life."

"How nice to be valued."

"I'm going to ignore the sarcasm. Rina, I'm very sorry."

She sighed. "It's all right. Another time."

Decker felt low. "I ruined your evening. I missed out, too. I know I need to prioritize. I'm human. I screw up."

Rina sighed. "You can't check up on the case during working hours?"

"If Davidson sees me working on a closed case—any closed case, but this one in specific—he'll have a full-blown snit. I don't want to deal with him right now."

"So what exactly do these African-American hairs mean?"

"There was another man involved."

"But Cheryl was wild."

"Her friends never mentioned her being chummy with a black. Whitman never mentioned it, either."

"I'm sure neither her friends nor Whitman knew everything about her."

"Whitman knew quite a bit. He knew she was having an affair with a teacher. He knew she got free rooms at the Grenada in exchange for sexual favors. I think she might have told him if she was having relations with a black. If for no other reason than to try to get a rise out of him. He was real apathetic toward her."

"Not that apathetic. He murdered her." Rina paused. "Or don't you believe that?"

"I don't know. All I'm saying is, the hairs should have been looked into a long time ago. Now I've got Martinez telling me that the ME found Afro male head hairs on Trupp's clothes. It got me curious. I had some choices when I finished up with Martinez. I could have gone home. But the evening was shot anyway."

"I'll say."

"Rub it in."

"Go on, Peter."

"I didn't want to wait till tomorrow morning for an analytical officer. So I decided to do my own computer work. I fed the basic stats of the Diggs case into the Crime Analysis Detail program. The software compares major crimes in the department from the different substations. That's one of the ways we see if there're any pattern crimes."

"Serial killings?"

"Serial anything. Could be robbery or rape. Anyway, I wanted to see if there were any other LA cases in the last couple of years that matched any of the particulars of mine."

"You must have gotten back a ton of read-outs. There are lots of rapes and murders in this city."

"Not too many where the victims had been strangled and bound ritualistically like Cheryl Diggs. Only about a dozen including my own. Most of them didn't fit. But there was this one case. I don't know. Intuitively, I think I may have something. It was about two years ago in West Bureau, Wilshire specifically."

"A black area."

"Racially mixed—black, Hispanic, Asian, and white. A gradation area, not a salad bowl. Farther south you go geographically, the blacker it gets. You go north, it's where the whites live."

"So the perp could be black or white."

"The victim lived in a black area. And the biggest victims of black crime are blacks themselves."

"But Cheryl was white, Peter."

"Rina, felons are opportunists."

"Meaning?"

"Meaning, if he's a black guy, the girls he sees the most are black. So he's going to rape blacks. But suppose . . ."

Decker paused to formulate his thoughts.

"Just suppose he gets a job in a white hotel that services white people . . . white *girls*. Then one night, he sees a bunch of drunken, zonked-out teenagers checking into some rooms for an evening of debauchery. He waits, he bides his time. Then he sees them all leave. Except this one girl who stays behind in her hotel room. She's all alone. Maybe she's sleeping. Maybe she's so stoned, it doesn't matter if she's awake or not. He goes in there . . . and ties her up . . . and bam . . . make any sense?"

Rina raised her brows. "This is all very far-fetched."

"All I want to know is why Cheryl had African-American pubic hairs on her. If this Wilshire case is similar to mine, they'll have physical evidence, too. I'll take a look at the lab work, see if anything matches. Simple enough."

"Except that you're completely discounting an uncoerced confession by the victim's boyfriend."

Decker rubbed his neck. "I think Whitman was protecting his girlfriend."

"She's dead."

"Not Cheryl. The other one . . . Terry."

"The girl who asked you to reopen the case?"

Decker nodded. "Whitman drew nude sketches of her. The poses in the drawings were similar to the way Cheryl Diggs was found. The sketches incriminated him in the Diggs case. He knew that the drawings would be presented to the grand jury as evidence. He knew that the girl would be called up to testify. I think he was trying to save her embarrassment. They're both Catholic, and overt nudity outside of procreation is a big sin for them. First she put herself on the line for him. Next it became his turn to put himself on the line for her. And he did. He plea-bargained his crime down to something he felt he could handle."

"Now *that* doesn't make any sense."

"It does if you had seen Whitman's reaction when I found the pictures. Kid had been totally cool. I pulled out the drawing . . . Rina, he absolutely crumpled. I'm telling you, he *loves* this girl."

"I'm supposed to believe that the son of a crime boss willingly went to jail for a murder he didn't commit . . . just to prevent some nude sketches from being made public?" She shook her head. "Peter, you just said that Whitman was a sociopath."

"No one is immune to feelings," Decker said. "I've heard the kid play cello. He's got passion for what he loves. And Rina, he loves this girl. This is his one shot at martyrdom. I think he's feeling quite saintly about it."

"This is all very spurious."

"Granted," Decker admitted. "But at least I'm using some kind of logic to explain the confession away. I haven't come up with anything to explain away the unidentified semen and pubic hairs found in and on Cheryl Diggs."

"Did you have any black suspects in the case, Peter?"

"I have a list of people who were at the Grenada when Cheryl was murdered. A few of them were black. I never got a chance to question them because Davidson kiboshed the whole thing. And truthfully, Whitman came forth and at the time that was fine with me. So I'm not about to start calling up innocent blacks and grilling them. That would just be lighting unnecessary fires."

"They could construe your actions as police harassment."

"Absolutely. But if I find a match with this Wilshire case, I'll do what I have to do. I've already let one small-minded superior stop me. I'm not going to let it happen again. Still, I know what you're saying. There are many ways to do the same things. I can poke into things quietly."

Rina leaned over and kissed her husband's face. "I admire your sense of principle, Peter. And for what it's worth, I agree with you. There are absolute rights and wrongs in this world. I just get . . . worried sometimes."

"I know." Decker rubbed his face. "And I wish I could say I'm doing it out of a strong sense of principle."

"You're not?"

Decker shrugged. "Rina, Whitman's a psycho—a pathological liar with eyes like a dead fish. I don't care if he rots in jail."

"Are you doing it for his girlfriend?"

Decker laughed. "Well, she does have a way of making you feel guilty. She reminded me of you."

Rina punched his shoulder.

Decker said, "Actually, she seems like an okay kid—smart and responsible in her own way. But, man, she's one very confused teenager. I don't know if I'm pursuing this out of spite for Davidson or just out of a sense of what's right . . . or maybe it's something deeper."

Rina waited for him to elaborate.

Decker looked pained. "I think I screwed up, Rina. I might have let my anger about Cindy's ordeal in New York get in the way of my professionalism."

"What are you *talking* about?"

"Whitman. I knew there were some doubts. Maybe . . . just maybe I went after him because I couldn't get my hands on the shopping-bag rapist."

"Peter, Whitman confessed!"

"But I never fully bought it."

"So what were you supposed to do? *Argue* with him?"

Decker smiled. "Putting it that way, it does sound

stupid. All I know is, I won't rest until I'm satis-fied."

"A man with a mission."

"That's me." Decker leaned over and kissed his wife's forehead. "For what it's worth, I'm glad you decided to fill in for the Rebbitzin. What are you going to lecture on?"

"I don't really know." Rina seemed to shrink in her chair. "One of the reasons I got so mad at you was because you hit a sore spot. I agreed a bit impetu-ously. Now I've got to think up four lectures. And these women are bright. I can't snow them with the usual lines."

"I'm sure you'll come up with something great."

"Maybe I'll talk about the weekly Torah reading."

"That's always appropriate."

Rina laughed at his enthusiam. He was trying so hard. She said, "During the Rebbitzin's absence, we'll read *Parashat Pinchas*. He was quite an interest-ing character."

"Which one was Pinchas?"

"The zealot. He was the one who took a huge spear and skewered Zimri and Kozby, the Midianite princess, while they were in the act."

Decker smoothed his mustache. "Uh . . . I bet the women would have lots to say about that."

Rina smiled, too. "The *parashat* addresses moral-ity, yes. But it's also about Pinchas and his zealotry. Which was a double-edged sword. It was something to be admired but always something that needed to be reined in." She looked at her husband. "But isn't that always the way it is with fanatics?"

Decker gave a slow grin. "Are you talking about me?"

"Heaven forbid."

"No hidden references beneath your scholarly words?"

"None." She tousled his head. "Let's go to bed."

"A very good suggestion."

"I'm just full of them tonight."

❧ 36

First came the shot of staticky music followed by hyperspeed radio talk. A press of the snooze button and Decker silenced the unwelcome intruder. He longed to pull the covers over his head and wake up at a reasonable hour. But doubts roused him to consciousness and he lumbered out of bed, throwing on a bathrobe as he tiptoed to the kitchen. Ginger was curled up on her blanket. She lifted her head when Decker came in, then buried it back into the folds of her front legs when she realized it was still dark outside.

He turned on the table lamp and reached for the phone. Wilshire's front desk put him through to the Detectives squad room. The phone rang and rang until someone finally picked up.

"Detectives. Bellingham."

Decker identified himself, then said, "You're not in Homicide by any chance?"

"Grand Theft."

"Anyone there from Homicide?"

"Not yet."

"Maybe you can help me anyway. I'm looking for the primary Homicide detective on a two-year-old case. The victim was an African-American female, seventeen years of age, found raped, bound, and strangled in her bedroom."

"The Green case," Bellingham said. "I remember it. Real terrible thing. She was alive when nine-one-one caught the call. Still going when the cruiser and ambulance got there, but was pronounced DOA. Harold Creighton was primary. He retired a year ago. Moved to Arizona."

"Who inherited his files?"

"They were split up. I think Marty Crumb got Green."

"Do you have his phone number?"

"Marty's on vacation."

Decker swore to himself. "Any way of getting hold of the file?"

"I could probably . . . help you out."

Meaning he could pick Marty's desk lock. Decker said, "I'd certainly appreciate it."

"You want the entire thing or just something specific?"

"Lab reports would be nice."

Bellingham said, "I'll see what I can do."

While Bellingham was doing his bit for petty crime, Decker made coffee. He was on his second cup when the Grand Theft detective came back on the line. "I got the file." He paused. "There's lab work here. I don't know if that's all of it but it looks pretty complete."

"What was done?"

"Uh, semen, blood, saliva . . . looks like they did a fingernail and toenail scraping. Foreign hairs, foreign fibers."

"Don't suppose anyone did a DNA analysis?"

"I don't see it here."

Decker said, "If you could fax me what you have, it would be helpful."

"Sure thing. Hold on. Let me get to the machine."

"I'm going to have to hang up and put my machine on fax mode. Just dial this number and I'll let you know if it came through."

"You bet."

Decker hung up and adjusted his phone fax machine. He waited, tapping his toe, slugging down coffee by the mugful, the hot liquid burning his throat. But he didn't even feel it. Five minutes later, he heard his phone ring once. The fax machine kicked in. Thank God for modern technology. He promised he would never curse his computer again. The machine seemed to go on forever. Decker couldn't wait that long. He tore off what was there and began his comparisons.

In bright light that hurt his eyes, he laid down papers crammed with scientific data he didn't fully understand. But he knew how to read charts and numbers and that was all the start he needed. He took out the Diggs files, specifically lab analysis taken from Diggs's fluids.

He laid the sheets with the numbers and the substrates side by side.

Granted, he was no lab expert. There were so many figures and facts, he knew he was only doing preliminary scanning. But damned if there weren't enough matching markers to hurry his heartbeat. Blood groups, proteins, isoenzymes, antigens. Between the coffee and his excitement, his chest was thumping.

He called Bellingham back. "Got the information. Thanks."

"Helpful?"

"Very. I'm coming down."

"I'm just about to leave. But I'll leave the file on top of my desk in a manila envelope with your name on it. Take good care of it. I don't want Marty pissed off at me."

"I hear you. Does the file mention which uniforms were originally sent out?"

A pause. Then Bellingham said, "George Ridley and Wanda Bontemps. I'll transfer you to Day Watch commander."

Decker said wait, but it was too late. A flick of the phone, a moment later he was talking to Sergeant Lopez.

Lopez said, "Ridley's on midafternoon, but Bontemps's on the morning shift. She should be strolling by in a half hour or so. You want to talk to her?"

"Yes." Decker looked at his watch—five-twenty A.M. Wilshire Substation was on the far side of the mountain. He said, "It'll take me about forty minutes to get out there."

"That would put you here at roll call. You want me to tell her you're looking for her?"

"Please."

"What do you want with the Green case?"

"Just general information. I've heard it was a tough one because she was alive when the uniforms arrived."

"Yeah."

"She was actually breathing?"

"More like twitching . . . convulsing. Seeing that was hard on my officers."

"I can believe that. Was the victim ever conscious?"

"Not to my knowledge. A real, real sad thing all the way around. The victim was an honor student. A good kid from an intact family."

"Her death must have destroyed her parents."

Another pause. "Her parents were . . . not exactly uncooperative. More like . . . withdrawn. I know everyone grieves in different ways. But truthfully, I don't think they ever fully trusted us. Anyway, I'll grab Bontemps at roll call . . . tell her you're looking for her."

" 'Preciate it."

Decker cut the line, juiced up and ready to get a jump on the day. He said his morning prayers, adding his own personal benediction for the welfare of his family. Then he took a quick shower but didn't bother shaving. The result was a clean but sinister-looking face. But hey, too damn bad. Two dead teenagers were calling his name. It had just taken him a while to hear the summons.

Making record time, Decker arrived just as Day Watch Commander Lopez announced the last item on the rotator. It had been a long time since Decker attended roll call. At six in the morning, looking out at the sea of uniforms, he found he didn't miss it. The room, built as a lecture hall with long wooden slab tables fronting plastic butterscotch-colored seats, was about two-thirds full. The officers were busily scratching notes as Lopez talked, because who knew which data byte might lead to the apprehension of a suspect or, even more important, what bit of trivia might save a life. Lopez pointed, spoke a few minutes more, then dismissed the group. The officers got up, gulping down the last of their lukewarm coffee, and filled the hallway, descending the staircase en route to the kit room. Decker briefly scanned the crowd, then walked up to Lopez.

He was average height but thin, with a smooth, caramel-colored complexion. He wore a pencil-line mustache and had a wide, open smile. He shook hands with Decker. "Detective Sergeant, sir. Welcome."

"Thanks."

"A minute for me to gather my papers."

"Take your time."

Lopez shuffled some loose leaves, then stuffed them into a briefcase. "Let me introduce you to Officer Bontemps." He talked as they walked down the flight of stairs. "I sure hope you make some headway with the Green case. It's been bothering a lot of people over here. I know Homicide will want to speak to you if you have anything new."

"Nothing yet, but who knows?"

When they reached the bottom, the hallway was jammed with officers waiting in line to receive their equipment—shotguns to be anchored inside the patrol cars, batons, mace, tazers . . . the war packs. Lopez crooked a finger at a black woman near the back of the line. She appeared to be about five seven or eight, well built and well proportioned with muscular arms and big wrists. Her complexion was midnight, jet-black hair cropped very short, a few calculated loose strands straightened and plastered to her forhead. Her eyes were wide, lashes thick and long. Her nose was broad, her mouth was serious with thick lips that were slightly pursed.

Lopez said, "Officer Bontemps, this is Detective Sergeant Peter Decker from Devonshire Homicide."

Decker and Bontemps shook hands.

"Sergeant Decker would like to speak with you for a few moments . . ." Lopez looked at Decker. "In private?"

"Just somewhere quiet."

Lopez smiled. "I think there's an empty interview room in the jail."

"How about the snack room?" He smiled at Bontemps. "I'll even buy you a cup of stale coffee."

Bontemps's face remained grave.

Decker dropped his smile and smoothed his mustache. He thanked Lopez for his cooperation, then turned to Bontemps. "You want to lead?"

"Certainly, sir."

They went back up the stairs into a small snack room replete with several cheap tables, mismatched chairs, and overused vending machines. A wall-mounted TV was making some electronic noise. Decker flicked off the power button. The room fell quiet. A good place. Comfortable but they were still alone.

"Have a seat." Decker dropped a couple of coins in the coffee machine and pulled out a steaming paper cup. "How do you take your coffee, Officer?"

"Nothing for me, sir."

Decker took his coffee, sat down, and pulled out

his notebook. "Sergeant Lopez tell you why I'm here?"

"Yes, sir."

"You and Officer Ridley were the first to arrive on the scene of a murder about two years ago."

"Yes, sir." Her voice was soft. "The Green murder. We arrived about a minute or two before the ambulance."

"I heard the victim was still alive."

Bontemps winced. "Yes, sir. She . . . was alive, yes."

Decker looked up. "The victim have a name, Officer?"

"Deanna." Bontemps spelled it for Decker. "Deanna Lark Green."

"The victim was convulsing when you arrived, Officer?"

Again Bontemps winced. "Yes, sir."

"Where was the victim when you arrived?"

"In her bedroom."

"What'd you do for her?"

Bontemps looked distressed. As if whatever she had done hadn't been enough. "The victim . . . was tied to her bed. We cut the constraints. Her complexion was very . . . bad. She didn't appear to be breathing. Officer Ridley and I . . . attempted mouth-to-mouth resuscitation until the paramedics arrived."

"Then what?"

She pursed her lips. "Officer Ridley began to secure the crime scene for the detectives . . . I stayed with the parents . . . Deanna's parents."

"Did they place the nine-one-one call?"

"Yes."

Decker smoothed his mustache. "Where was the actual crime scene, Officer?"

"In her bedroom . . . Deanna's bedroom."

"And there was no sign of a perpetrator?"

"No, sir. Not when we arrived."

Decker took a moment to write some notes. "So someone broke into Deanna's bedroom, bound and gagged her in an unusual way, then raped and choked her to death. And this all happened while the parents were sleeping?"

Bontemps thought about the question. "It's a large house. Two stories. The master bedroom is on one side of the hallway; the kids' rooms are across the hall. Maybe the parents were heavy sleepers."

"How many children are in the family?"

"Two—a son and a daughter?"

"Who's the elder?"

"The son."

"What's his name?"

"I think it was Steven, sir."

"Do you know how old he was?"

"I think a couple of years older than Deanna."

"So he would have been what? Nineteen?"

"I suppose."

"Where was he when you arrived, Officer?"

"I don't know, sir. He wasn't at home."

"He wasn't home the night his sister was murdered?"

"That is correct."

"Was anyone else in the house at the time?"

"Not to my knowledge, sir. But I don't know everything. The case was turned over to Homicide and I wasn't kept up to date."

Decker paused. "You weren't kept up to date?"

Her eyes were unwavering. "Homicide likes its privacy."

Sipping coffee, Decker locked eyes with Bontemps. "Was there a special reason why you wanted follow-up on the case, Officer?"

"No, sir. Except it was a . . ." Finally, she looked away. "It was a very difficult case, sir. It would have been nice to get some resolution."

Decker nodded. "Who was the primary detective on the case?"

"Harold Creighton."

"Who else was assigned to the Green case?"

"Detectives Taylor, Brody, and Crumb. I think there was a fifth person. I don't remember his name."

Decker finished his coffee. "By any chance, did you have any contact with Deanna's parents after the case was turned over to Homicide?"

Bontemps pursed her lips, her eyes focused somewhere over Decker's head. "The parents did call me a few times—inquiry phone calls. Nothing beyond that."

"What were the inquiries about?"

For the first time, Bontemps squirmed. "The usual, sir. A laundry list of complaints. Why weren't the police doing more? I assured them that we were doing everything we could be doing."

Decker scratched his cheek. "Did you tell Homicide about the calls?"

Bontemps bit her lower lip. "Pardon?"

"Did you tell Homicide about the calls?"

"No, sir." Bontemps stiffened. "They . . . were grieving parents. Their calls had much more to do with rage and frustration than with actual facts. I didn't feel the need to disturb the detectives."

Decker said, "Sergeant Lopez told me Deanna's parents were withdrawn almost to the point of being uncooperative. You're telling me they were venting their spleen to you. There's an inconsistency here."

Bontemps didn't speak.

Decker said, "So . . . Detectives Creighton, Brody, Taylor, and Crumb were assigned to the Green case, is that correct?"

"I believe so, sir."

"I don't know the gentlemen . . . or ladies."

"They're all men."

"Are any of them black?"

A pause. "No, sir."

Decker rubbed his stubble. "Deanna's parents complain to you about that?"

Bontemps's sentences stopped and started several times. "The parents felt the police weren't doing their job. I told them—"

"Did the parents use words like *racism* or maybe *police racism* or *anything* like that, Officer?"

This time, the woman sighed. "Yes, sir."

"Well, we got the R word out in the open. Tell me about the conversations, Officer."

She became animated. "They were real angry."

"I'm sure they were enraged. Their daughter was brutally murdered."

"It was more than that. They didn't like how the detectives were treating them."

"How were the detectives treating them?"

"Condescending . . . patronizing . . ."

Decker said, "Was that an accurate perception in your mind or were the parents just blowing off steam?"

"Not knowing the details, I couldn't judge."

"Did they complain about anyone specifically?"

"I don't see the point in naming names."

"Did you know Harold Creighton's retired, Officer?"

"No, I didn't know. Like I said, the detectives like their privacy." Bontemps licked her lips. "It was Creighton. They hated Creighton. Claimed he was a racist and had it in for them. That he kept making unfounded accusations."

"Against whom?"

"Against them, against their *son*. They thought Creighton had it in for their son because the boy had some past trouble with the law."

"Such as . . ."

"I don't know, sir. I was trying to remain neutral—defending us while trying to console grieving parents. It was a tight squeeze."

"What did Creighton tell them that got them so angry?"

"That it had to be an insider. Because to do all that shi . . . all that stuff to Deanna so quietly . . . it had to be someone familiar with the routine. He felt it was someone in the family."

"He had a point."

"Yes, sir. Of course." Excited, she waved her hands as she talked. "But the family claimed Creighton didn't bother looking anywhere else. Kept hammerin' away at them. Hammerin' and hammerin'. He was treatin' the parents like they were on trial."

"Where was Deanna's brother the night of the murder?"

"He was sleeping at his girlfriend's house."

"A very nice alibi."

"Or maybe it was the truth. They never arrested him, Sergeant. Creighton tried, but . . . you should have heard that man cuss. How impossible it is to find evidence against 'these motherfucking people' when the 'motherfuckers' *live* there, blah, blah."

Her voice had turned curt and angry. Decker kept himself impassive. "Did the parents complain about the other detectives as well?"

Bontemps crossed her arms in front of her chest and sat back in her chair. "Creighton was in charge. He set the tone for the group."

Decker said, "There's an old Jewish expression. Fish rots from the head down."

Bontemps's eyes narrowed, but she didn't speak. Decker sensed immediate hot hostility that took him by surprise. Was it possibly because he mentioned something Jewish? A big problem if that was the case. But one that would have to wait until later on.

"I haven't read Deanna's Homicide file," Decker said. "But I hope to do that by the end of the day. I want to learn what went down from the cops' point of view. But I'm also going to need to talk to the parents. They didn't like five white males before; there's no reason to think they're going to warm up to me. Now I'll make the appointment. But I want you to come along with me. They trusted you in the past; you'd make an ideal liaison."

She waited a beat, her hands clasped and resting in her lap. "Certainly. What time, sir? Now?"

"No, it's going to have to be after hours for both of us. Around seven in the evening. It's going to cut into your free time. Is that a hardship for you with family or kids?"

"Nothing I can't manage. Seven is fine."

"Good." Decker sat back in his chair. "Now I'll tell you the problem."

"Problem?"

"Yes, there is a problem. Officer, I need you to do this quietly and on your own time. Because I'm working on this case on *my* own time."

Decker gave her as concise a recap as possible, studying her face as he laid out the facts. She tried to keep a poker face, but twitches and mannerisms gave her away. By the time he had finished, he knew he had put her in a terrible dilemma, working with him on the sly. At the end of the story, Bontemps didn't say a word. She seemed shell-shocked.

Decker kept his voice even. "All I'm trying to do is solve some murders . . . two, maybe even three murders if Henry Trupp, the night clerk, is tied into any of this mess."

Bontemps spoke between tight jaws. "Sir, one of the murders has already been *solved*!"

"Not to my satisfaction. Look at these, Bontemps." Decker laid down some scientific papers. "These are some of the lab tests run on Cheryl Diggs. Now these . . ." Decker spread out more sheets of figures and graphs. "These are Deanna Green's tests. Compare the blood results."

Bontemps picked up one of the piles. "There're over twenty pages of tests here."

"Skim them. Just tell me what you see."

Bontemps said, "I'm not an analysis expert."

"Nor am I. Just tell me your impression as a layman."

Reluctantly, Bontemps began studying the papers. The more she read, the more absorbed she became. After five minutes, she said, "It looks like we may be working with the same person . . . maybe." She looked at Decker. "But maybe not."

Decker said, "Bontemps, this semen analyzed here isn't Whitman's semen. The pubic hairs aren't Whitman's either."

"Doesn't mean he didn't kill her."

"No, but it does mean we're working with two men, one who's a missing link. And that link just might have raped and killed before. And if he killed before, he can kill again. Now do you understand why I'd like a handle on Mr. Mystery Man?"

She tried to get the words out, but stumbled. Finally, she formulated her thoughts. "Forgive my . . . uppitiness, Sergeant, but it sounds like you're trying to pin a murder on a black man."

Decker's eyes bored into hers. "Uppitiness?"

Bontemps spoke earnestly. "You know what I mean."

Decker said, "Just for a moment, can we forget about race? I have a victim here, Officer. She was raped and murdered, swimming in unexplained evidence. And that evidence is similar to lab work taken from a crime that occurred two years ago. I'm not going to ignore facts that jump in my face. Yes, I have a confessed killer. But I know someone else was involved."

"Were they in on it together?"

"A good point. But I don't think so. Whitman doesn't seem like the type to work with a partner. Look, I'm just running a thorough investigation. Like I should have done in the beginning. Are you in or out?"

"I'm in." Bontemps tried to be calm, but her face was tight with tension. "Yes, I'm in. But I got doubts. Sir, I am a sworn officer of the law. But I hesitate because you're working on a solved case without the blessing of your superior. That puts me in a fix."

"It does indeed," Decker admitted. "And I do see your point. Maybe if my superior had seen these papers . . ." Decker began stowing the lab tests back in his briefcase. "Maybe if he had studied these, he would have had second thoughts about Whitman. But probably not. Because my loo was truly *relieved* when Whitman confessed to the crime. He just didn't want to have to deal with any sort of black issue."

Bontemps was quiet. Decker studied her face. Frozen, like a deer caught in headlights.

Casually, he said, "It's a tragedy to let race get in the way of a murder investigation. But sometimes I guess that's inevitable. We all have our preconceived notions. All I can say is thank you for helping me, Officer Bontemps. Thank you very much. You're doing the right thing."

"I just hope this doesn't blow up in our faces."

"Officer, the last thing this police department needs is another incident. That being said, *nobody's* going to hold my conscience hostage. And it looks like you feel the same way."

Again, Bontemps didn't speak.

"What I want to do is go over the file notes . . . compare Deanna's case to mine." Decker folded his notebook. "Let's meet before we visit the Greens. Around six?"

Bontemps nodded.

"And like I said, it might be a good idea if you kept a low profile about this."

"No problem there."

Decker smiled. But Bontemps's expression was sour—as if she had just stepped in dog turd. After a few moments Decker said, "I've got nothing more to say, Officer. You can go whenever you want."

Bontemps started to speak, but changed her mind. She turned on the heels of spit-polished black oxfords and walked out the door.

❧ 37

As expected, Oliver was already at his desk. Decker had to shout to be heard above the roar of traffic.

"It's Deck. I'm not coming in. There's something I've got to do and it's going to take the better part of the day. I've got plenty of sick leave. Figure I better cash in on it before someone takes it away as part of a police-package compromise."

"You sound groggy, Deck."

"Could be. Got up early enough. I'm at a pay phone outside Wilshire Substation."

"Wilshire Sub . . . What are you working on?"

Decker rubbed his forehead, feeling a heavy pounding behind his eyes. "The Diggs case. You know I was never satisfied with how it was handled. I just found out some new developments. Tell you about it later."

Oliver paused. "It's those black pubic hairs, right?"

"You've got a good memory, Oliver. Do you also remember the night clerk?"

"Henry Trupp."

"I found out he was murdered outside an all-white, ex-con bar in Van Nuys. Strangled. There were African-American hairs found on his clothing."

Quickly, Decker filled him in. About Bert Martinez and how his investigation was curtailed, along with the matching evidence with Deanna Green.

A long pause. Then Oliver said, "Obviously someone shut us all down! It's crappy, Deck. But that doesn't mean Whitman didn't kill Diggs. You're treading thin ice because you have Whitman's confession. And you'll look like a dunce by opening up your own case—"

"Thanks for the support."

"I'm being honest. So I'll also tell you something else. *I* never liked what went down with Whitman, either. I understand what you're doing. But our loo's going to have a shit fit, you working on your own closed case. Davidson knows you're never sick, Deck. Let me dodge him for you."

"Thanks, Scott."

"Where're you off to?"

"Prison."

A long pause. "To Whitman?"

"He was there."

Oliver said, "You start pumping him for info on blacks, you're handing the kid an appeal on a silver platter. Not to mention getting other community members up in arms."

"I'll be discreet."

"That's a good word. Not that I like Davidson, but I see his point. Between the riots, and our own bigoted dees on high-profile trials . . . ahem, ahem."

"Very high-profile trials . . . ahem, ahem."

Oliver said, "Last thing we need is more accusations of racism being tossed our way."

"I'm in the kitchen," Decker said. "I can obviously stand the heat."

Long stretches of dusty road. In his head, Decker was in jeans, T-shirt, and high-tops, speeding in a four-by-four supercharged truck, dirt bikes in the back bed. In reality, he was in a suit and tie, sweating buckets, chugging along in the Volare whose air-conditioning couldn't keep up with the searing temperatures. Heat waves radiated off the asphalt. Periodically, Decker had to roll down the window just to get some circulation. But the outside air was so damn scorching, it stabbed the car like a hot needle.

He made good time, though, reaching the penitentiary before eleven. Inside, the air was more tepid than cool, but any old port in a storm. Decker checked in his gun, passed through a sally port, and presented his credentials to a civilian clerk at one of four bulletproof glass windows. She told him to wait a moment. A few minutes later, Decker signed the logbook, then was buzzed inside the offices. He was met by a khaki-uniformed prison guard named Brackson. The guard led him to an empty interview room, turned on the light, and closed the door.

The area was tiny and stank of urine. Yellowed acoustical tiles on the walls and ceiling, a sticky black linoleum floor. There was a built-in table sided by two bolted benches under which dangled loose handcuffs. Decker managed to squeeze his legs under the tabletop. If he and Whitman were to sit at the same time, they'd be playing kneesies. Decker elected to stand.

Ten minutes later, Brackson brought in a cuffed Whitman in prison blues. Decker studied the teen who had made a rapid transformation from high school senior to hard-timer, indistinguishable from the other cons who made up the institution's population. He'd grown a beard, his head was nearly shaven. More impressive was Whitman's girth. Kid must have put on twenty-five pounds and all of it was muscle.

Decker said, "Just anchor his right hand. I want his left hand free."

Brackson nodded, told Whitman to sit, hands down, head and chest against the table. The guard then took a pair of cuffs from underneath the bench and secured the teen to his seat with his right hand. He then removed Whitman's other manacles and told him he could sit up now.

Whitman sat up and stared at the wall in front of him. After the guard left the cell, Decker leaned against the door. "You making a statement with your hairdo Chris?"

Slowly, Whitman turned to Decker, his eyes as flat as ever. He said, "Yeah. My statement is I don't like lice."

"Nothing to do with the Aryan brotherhood?"

Whitman rubbed his neck. "What are you doing here, Decker? Wait. I know the answer. Terry." He blew out air. "Stupid bitch. What the fuck she tell you?"

Decker was quiet for a long time. Then he said, "You sound awfully hostile toward a girl you went to prison for."

Whitman drew his hand over his face. "I really love that girl. I swear I'd die for her. But man, she is a *girl*. Talk, talk, talk, talk, talk. I got nothing to say to you."

"You want a smoke, Chris?"

Whitman shrugged. "Sure."

Decker lit up a smoke and gave it to Whitman. The teen inhaled deeply a couple of times, then sat back in his chair.

Decker said, "Tell me about Cheryl Diggs's other sexual partners."

"It's over, man. Let me serve my time in peace."

"And catch a little satisfaction while you're at it?"

Whitman's eyes widened. Then he let out a small laugh and said nothing.

"She's trying to help you. Why don't you help yourself and talk to me?"

Whitman was silent.

"Listen to me, Chris," Decker said. "I know what's going on. So that explains a lot of your behavior to me. I know you're engaged to a girl who's fat, ugly, and stupid. Right now, you're in a hellhole. But you're willing to put up with it because you get time with the girl you love. How long do you think that's going to last?"

Whitman's eyes sparked fury.

"I know you love her, Chris," Decker went on. "Terry's *beautiful*. She's beautiful and smart, and truly, she loves you, too. But she's also one very young puppy, guy. She jumped into your arms because you're a strong, good-looking dude who gave her a shoulder to cry on. How long before she finds another strong, good-looking guy who'll give her another shoulder to cry on. Some college stud who won't be locked up in this pisshole—"

Whitman threw his cigarette at Decker's face. "Get the *fuck* outta here!"

The lit end stung Decker's face; then the butt fell to the floor. Calmly, Decker wiped the hot spot on his cheek and crushed out the smoke. He lit another cigarette and placed it between Whitman's lips.

"Son, she's good for about a year. Then she's going to start missing visits. So where will that leave you? And before you open your mouth to cuss me out, just *think* about what I'm saying. Because by talking to me, you may be helping yourself."

Staring at the wall, Whitman said, "She meet someone new, Decker? Don't shit me."

"Whitman, your girl is head over heels in love with you and that's no lie. But the future is a queer bird, know what I'm saying?"

"You're sounding like my uncle." Whitman sucked on his smoke. "He buy you or something?"

"No."

"Then what's all this to you? You hate my guts."

Decker didn't answer.

"I don't get it," Whitman said. "What do you want?"

"Tell me about the men in Cheryl's life."

A long pause. Then Whitman said, "I'm sure Cheryl didn't tell me everything. I don't even know why she told me anything. I didn't give a damn."

"Maybe that's why she told you."

"To make me jealous?" He shrugged. "Didn't work. I didn't care what she did. Too busy stalking Terry."

"Stalking Terry?"

Whitman's eyes were far away. "After she blew me off, she started dating this . . . nerd. But I could tell she liked him." His breathing became rapid. "Outside I was pure cool . . ." Short breaths. "But inside . . . in my brain . . . I was slipping . . . on the cliff's edge with sweaty hands . . . started thinking up plots of revenge. First it was killing him . . . then it was kidnapping her . . . keeping her in a basement . . . like in the book *The Collector*. John Fowles. You ever read it?"

Decker nodded.

"I could have done it, you know. I'm real good at hiding things." Whitman smoked down to the butt, then he crushed it with his shoe. "Got another one?"

Decker gave him another cigarette.

Whitman took it, blowing hard, leaning back and staring at the ceiling through a carcinogenic cloud. "You know why I didn't do it? Because I know the difference between having monstrous thoughts and being a monster. It's the difference between me and my uncle."

He was absorbed in his nightmare, but Decker steered him back to the present. "Cheryl's partners, Chris."

Whitman clucked his tongue. "I know she was having an affair with one of the teachers at the school—Tim Gobles. He was head of the prom committee. Big surprise when she made prom queen."

Decker flipped out his notepad and started writing rapidly. "Go on."

"I know she did everyone in the group at one time or another."

"The group being . . ."

"Steve, Tom . . . Steve Anderson, Tom Baylor, Blake Adonetti. But I know she did other guys at school, too. She liked sex. Simple as that. She was pretty good at first. Then she got real stale real quick. I think that's why she started bartering for sex. Something different. Added a little thrill."

"Trupp?"

"Yeah, Trupp. In exchange for rooms whenever her mom or one of her mom's boyfriends kicked her out. She did Gobles to get the queen title and for an A in his class. She did this grocer for food . . . anyone who had something that she needed. Mostly old guys. She liked their . . . desperation."

"Any other men?"

Whitman looked up at Decker and smiled. No longer toothpaste perfect. His two front teeth had been chipped and stained yellow from coffee and tobacco smoke. "She told me she'd done a cop."

Decker managed to keep his face flat. "You have a name?"

"Never said. Just that he was an old fart."

"You think she was blowing smoke?"

"Could be. Who knows?"

"Guy married?"

"According to her, yes."

"Say anything else about him?"

"Nope . . . not really."

"Did he have children?"

Whitman shrugged.

"White guy?"

"I would assume. Cheryl didn't have much fondness for the brothers. Used to call them monkey dogs."

Decker hesitated just a moment. "Why the antipathy?"

"I guess she was a bigot. She certainly didn't have any real experience with blacks. Somehow . . . I don't remember how . . . she found out I did a black whore. After that, she made me wash myself off with alcohol before she'd have sex with me. As if being black was like AIDS. You could get it from intercourse. God, that girl was *stupid*!"

"You see any blacks the evening of the prom?"

Whitman shrugged. "Sure. School has about a dozen black seniors. Everyone was at the prom."

"How about at the hotel?"

"Don't remember. Why are you asking me questions about blacks?"

"Did you see any blacks at the hotel?"

"Let me think . . ." He shook his head. "No, I don't think so."

"Anyone from the hotel come up to Cheryl's room that night?"

"What do you mean? Like Trupp?"

"Did Trupp come up to Cheryl's room?"

"Not when I was there. Too busy watching the boob tube in the back room."

"Did anyone else come into Cheryl's room?"

"Just the gang."

"Besides the gang. Someone from security? Maybe a maid came in to turn down the sheets?"

"Not in *that* place. They don't even have real room service. You want something, you call up their seedy coffee shop and some stoned-out dude—" Whitman looked up. "Shit. I forgot about him."

"Who?"

"After I was done with Cheryl, I called the hotel coffee shop and ordered up some coffee. So damn drunk I had to get something into my stomach. Guy who brought it was black . . . light-skinned but definitely black."

Decker remained calm. "Did the server come into your room."

"No," Whitman said. "Cheryl was zoned out and I didn't see the point of letting anyone see her like that. I told him to put the coffeepot down in the hallway and leave."

"So how do you know the server was black?"

"I opened the door to tip him."

"Then what happened?"

"I drank the coffee and left."

"And Cheryl?"

"By that time, she was out like a light. I remember thinking she looked dead." He shrugged. "Maybe she was."

"Was Cheryl still tied up at that point?"

Whitman blinked hard. "I must have taken off the binds. I wouldn't have left her up like that."

"You don't remember?"

"It's all real hazy. I was drunk."

"Describe this man from room service."

"I only saw him for about two seconds."

"The best you can."

"He was . . . maybe a few years older than me. Light-skinned guy. Brown eyes, kinky hair . . . big surprise, huh?"

"Go on."

He stared at Decker, but seemed to be looking through him. Concentrating on an image that was visible only in his brain. "A mustache . . . a tuft of hair under his chin. I don't know what they're officially called. We call them juice mops." He continued to gape at nothing. "A couple of like little moles over his eyes . . ."

"How can you describe a man so clearly, Chris, when you were so drunk you can't even remember if you untied Cheryl?"

"I'm an artist." He shrugged. "I'm good with faces."

Decker paused. "You could draw this guy for me, Chris?"

"Yeah, I could draw him." Whitman hesitated. "What's the catch?"

"No catch."

"I don't believe you."

Decker said, "You might as well trust me, Chris. You can't get much lower than where you are now."

Whitman ran his hand over his face. "Give me a pencil and paper. I'll give you the guy. Then kindly get the fuck outta my life."

ᔰ 38

Decker managed to squeeze in dinner with Rina and the kids before hurrying to meet Bontemps. It was a rushed meal that no one enjoyed, his family listening to his attempts at casual conversation while watching him gulp down food. He knew he needed to slow down, but he couldn't seem to find the brakes. His stomach was in knots by the time he reached Wilshire Substation. He parked in the back lot and reached the snack bar by a quarter to six. That gave him just enough time to wash down some antacids and Advils with bitter black coffee.

At six, Bontemps walked through the door. She was wearing a camel-colored suit over a loose black blouse and carried a big leather bag over her shoulder. She bought coffee and sat down next to Decker. She looked tired, her eyes telling him anywhere but here.

"Everything okay, Officer?" Decker asked.

Bontemps said, "I'm fine, sir."

"Okay," Decker said. "I'll take you at your word. I had a chance to read Creighton's files on the Green case. Lots of men were questioned—relatives, neighbors, friends. Deanna didn't seem to have a boyfriend. Do you know anything different?"

"I don't recall her having someone special, Sergeant. From what I remember, the parents said she put most of her energies into her studies and lessons."

"Did she date at all?"

"I don't remember."

"Bright attractive girl . . ." Decker shook his head. "She must have had some sort of social life." He looked at his notes and moved on. "According to the autopsy report, whoever strangled Deanna broke her windpipe. There was nothing you could have done to save her. The convulsions could have been reflexive. She was gone by the time you came."

He waited for Bontemps to say something. She didn't.

Decker said, "Unfortunately, you had to witness her last moments. I've seen people die. It's horrible. Only satisfaction I can offer you is, maybe we can drum up a new lead . . . find the monster who did it."

Bontemps looked at Decker, then her eyes went to her coffee cup.

Decker pulled out a sheet of paper and laid it on the table. "Look at this face, Officer, then put it in your bag. If this guy is known to the Greens, just maybe we'll be a baby step closer to resolution."

Bontemps eyeballed the paper. "Doesn't look like a police-artist sketch—too much detail."

"You've got a good eye. Christopher Whitman drew it. He's an artist. Whitman saw this man at the hotel the night Diggs was murdered. I'm not saying it means anything but maybe it does."

"What's preventing him from making someone up?"

"Nothing. But with this much detail, if the face is

fictitious, the Greens won't recognize it as anyone familiar."

"Unless they happen to know some poor guy who looks like the drawing."

"Bontemps, the sketch isn't conclusive. We'll use it as a possible tool, all right?"

"Yes, sir. Of course." Quickly, Bontemps checked her watch. Decker caught it.

"Are you pressed for time?"

The woman blushed. "No, sir. I just need to call home before we go. Check to make sure the babysitter arrived. My big daughter's watching my little one."

Her big daughter? The woman appeared to be in her late twenties. Decker said, "How old is your big daughter?"

"Seventeen." She started smiling, but held it back. "She's going to be entering the academy next year."

Decker studied the woman, trying to find hidden signs of age. He couldn't. "Congratulations. You must be very proud."

"More relieved than anything. Can I make my call?"

"Of course."

In Bontemps's absence, Decker thought of Cindy. Relief was a biggie in the emotional repertoire of parents with teens. Wanda was back in five minutes. "I'm ready whenever you are."

Decker finished his coffee. "You know, Bontemps, before we go, I want to clear the air about something. This morning I made an offhand comment about being Jewish. Is that something you have trouble with?"

Slowly, Bontemps answered, "Like you said, sir, we all have our preconceived notions." She looked at Decker. "I apologize if I offended you."

At least the woman was honest enough not to fake it. Still Decker was skeptical. "I'll give you points for being truthful. But we need to have a professional attitude here. You can't let your notions get in the way."

"Absolutely. You have my word on that, sir." Bontemps stowed the picture in her purse. "It's good you caught me. If I want my dream, I'd better learn to keep it all inside."

"What's your dream, Bontemps?"

She kneaded her hands. "Detectives, sir. It's been my goal from the start. I'm very qualified, Sergeant. Overqualified if I have to say so myself. I've been applying for six years. Somehow there's always a reason why they can't make it work."

"Who's they?"

"The brass." Bontemps mashed her lips together. "It's one excuse after another—there's no opening, there's been cutbacks, there're people out there with more seniority . . . meaning 'We got our quota of black women so you're outta luck, sweetheart.'" Abruptly, she stopped talking, looked at Decker. "There I go again. Shooting off."

Decker stood. "I asked you a question, you answered it. No harm in that. Let's go."

Decker drove the Plymouth, Bontemps sat shotgun. A five-minute ride from the substation put them in LaFayette Park, a genteel neighborhood of homes and children squeezed between blighted industrial thoroughfares. Most of the avenues were lined with stately palms that fronted turn-of-the-century Victorian or Craftsman-style houses, the driveways filled with twenty-year-old Caddies and Oldses. Mixed in with the homes were a few fraternity houses. While the University of Southern California wasn't within walking distance, the area was apparently close enough for some to set up camp.

The Greens lived in a pale-blue, two-story, wood-sided Victorian house loaded with white-painted gingerbread. It held several peaked roofs inset with shuttered dormer windows, parapets, and cornices. The bottom story was symmetrical—a big bay window on either side of an arched doorway crowned with a keystone. The wooden porch held a swing. Four steps down was a rose-lined walkway that bisected a front bed of impatiens and begonias as well as a newly mowed lawn.

Decker parked the car but didn't get out. He rolled up the window, then turned to Bontemps. "You'll have to sneak some glances my way to pick up my cues. I can't tell you how to do that. It's an intuitive thing. And nothing confrontational. No good cop, bad cop here, Bontemps. We're both good cops, okay?"

"I understand, Sergeant. Do you want me to introduce you?"

"No, I'll handle that. Just try to look like you're supporting me."

"I am supporting you."

Decker wondered about that as he got out of the car. He recognized hostility in his own voice. He was irritated at the woman—for her honesty, for her prejudice. It was his own damn fault. What he got from breaking professionalism. He should just have ignored her and moved on.

Then again, how can you deal with notions unless you deal with them? Professionalism was a hard, hard thing. Decker was still plagued with self-doubts. But Rina was right. He couldn't exactly have argued with Whitman. Maybe he should have argued a little more with Davidson.

They walked up the pathway and climbed the creaky steps. Decker knocked on the front door. The woman who answered appeared to be in her forties, kinky black hair flecked with gray pulled back into a ponytail. Her face was coffee mixed with cream, crow's-feet webbing from the corners of her dark brown eyes. Her cheekbones were high, her lips full and thick. Her hands were slender, her nails painted natural, the tips painted white. She had on a gray silk pantsuit and a sleeveless white blouse, a metal cross hanging from around her neck. Her feet were housed in sandals.

Decker said, "Mrs. Green? I'm Sergeant Decker. We spoke over the phone."

The woman appraised him with a cool eye. "Yes. Come in, please." She offered Decker a smooth hand. "And call me Tony."

Decker shook her soft hand. She retracted it into the folds of her silk suit and looked at Bontemps. "How are you, Wanda? It's been a while since we've spoken."

Bontemps appeared to shrink under the woman's scrutiny. "I'm fine, ma'am, thank you."

Tony stepped aside, granting permission for Decker and Bontemps to come in.

The room was paneled in walnut, light streaming through the mullioned bay windows in round, dusty beams. The muted-patterned furniture was over-stuffed and old—faded fabrics, scarred wood. But at one time, it had been top quality. Heavy and durable, not a rip or a tear in any of the pillows or seams. The room held shelving units and bookcases. The Greens appeared fond of knickknacks. Lots of glass or porcelain objects, not only in the cabinets but also resting on tables and on a vintage upright piano. The wallpaper was heavy and gold-flocked, some texture rubbed from the pattern. No pictures or photographs anywhere. If there ever was a family, it was now as distant as the faded, square spots on the wall.

"My husband just called. He's going to be a bit late. He told me to start without him." Tony pointed to the couch. "Do sit. Would you like something to drink? I just made a pitcher of iced tea."

Decker said, "Thank you, that sounds great."

"Wanda?" Tony asked.

"Yes, thank you."

"Excuse me, then."

Decker and Bontemps sat on opposite ends of the couch. In front of them was a salver of canapés on the coffee table. Decker whispered, "Are we supposed to eat these or are they just for show?"

"No, you're supposed to eat 'em. But wait till she offers us the tray."

Decker grimaced. "What looks vegetarian?"

Bontemps said, "Are you vegetarian, sir?"

"Kosher."

"Oh." Bontemps stared at the tray. "These look like smoked ham, these look like turkey. This one here seems like egg with a slice of cucumber. Or is egg not okay?"

"No, eggs are fine. What's this? Watercress and tomato. That's okay, too."

"That isn't plain lettuce?"

"Watercress is a type of lettuce."

Bontemps shrugged. "Guess you'd know about that better than me."

"Yeah, this certainly ain't soul food," Decker said. "Was this for my benefit?"

"Probably."

"Was she more natural when she was alone with you?"

"More natural? You mean more black?"

"I meant less affected."

Bontemps thought a moment. "Maybe a little less snooty. But there's still a distance. She's educated. She lets you know about it right away."

Before Decker could ask what she meant, Tony reappeared from the kitchen, carrying a tray of three iced-tea glasses garnished with mint sprigs. She set it down on the coffee table.

"Here we go." She doled out the glasses, then picked up the plate of canapés. "A little something to go with your drink?"

Decker thanked her and popped a sliced cucumber topped with egg into his mouth. Bontemps reached for the smoked ham.

Decker said, "This was thoughtful of you."

Tony smiled. "Thank you."

"Especially because . . ." Decker took a sip of iced tea. "Because I'm sure your previous contact with the police was less than satisfactory."

Tony's eyes went to Decker's face. He picked up a watercress and tomato appetizer, then said, "Not that I'm blaming anyone. I was just talking about the outcome. It's terrible when everyone tries their hardest and there's still no resolution."

Tony seated herself ramrod straight in a wing chair opposite the couch. She gave Decker an angry eye. "Assuming everyone tried their hardest."

Decker appeared casual. "You thought the police could have done more?"

"My daughter's murder is still unsolved," Tony said icily. "Of course I thought the police could have done more. The police *should* be doing more."

"Did you have any problems with the detectives, ma'am?"

"Not really." Tony gave a sharp look to Bontemps. "I suppose everyone was . . . *respectful* enough. I'll just chalk it up to . . . incompetence more than anything."

Bontemps flinched, but Decker was impassive. He took another hors d'oeuvre. "Let me explain to you why I'm here. I'm working on a case far away from here. We have a computer system in the department. You can program in the specific details of your case and ask the computer if there are any similar cases on file with the LAPD. Are you with me so far?"

"Yes, Sergeant, I'm *with* you."

Decker ignored her sarcasm. "Your daughter's murder had some common details with my file. That's why I'm here."

"So my daughter's murder is . . . secondary to your solving your case."

"Mrs. Green, we don't consider Deanna's murder secondary to any other," Bontemps said.

"All very good and fine, Wanda. But certain murders are more . . . high-profile than others. I mean, what's so special about another black teenager being . . . brutally assaulted? Certainly no cause for alarm around these parts."

Bontemps said, "To Sergeant Decker and me, murder is always cause for alarm."

Decker said, "Mrs. Green, if your daughter's homicide had nothing in common with my case, I wouldn't be here today. Because I wouldn't have been aware of it. But the fact is, now I *am* aware of it, everyone would benefit if we worked together."

Tony said, "And what happens if . . . ah, Parker's home. Very good. If you'll excuse me, I'll tell him you're here." She got up and left.

When she went out the door, both Decker and Bontemps sat back in the couch. Bontemps blew out a gush of air. "Jesus, that woman is tough. I forgot how difficult . . ." She rubbed her face. "So full of *rage*."

"Her daughter was murdered."

"No, it started long before that, Sergeant. Believe me, *I* know the type." Bontemps moved closer to Decker and whispered, "She and her husband . . . clawing against everyone to make it through the system. Now that they've arrived, there aren't lots of places for them. They can't go back . . . too much jealousy and resentment from the have-nots. And they can't really go forward 'cause they're not quite big enough to break out into the white world. So they've got their little bit of success here. And that's about it."

"What does she do?"

"She's a paralegal for a corporate firm. He's a civil engineer. Together, they do well. In this neighborhood, they do very, very well. But put them in Beverly Hills, they aren't worth squat."

"Put me in Beverly Hills, Officer, and I'm not worth squat, either."

For the first time today, Bontemps gave him a genuine smile. "Yeah, I keep thinking all white men are rich. And if they aren't, what's their excuse?"

"Unfortunately, being male and white isn't enough."

"Yeah, but you're—" She stopped herself.

Decker said, "Yes, Wanda, even being white and male and *Jewish* isn't enough to guarantee wealth. But believe it or not, I understand what you're saying. White men don't have the built-in barriers, so what's holding them back? Or are you really asking, what's holding *me* back?"

"I think you're doing fine, sir."

"Yes, I am, Officer. But I'll tell you this much. If I knew the secret to wealth, I sure as hell wouldn't be doing this . . . shhh, she's coming back."

Bontemps nodded. "Anything you want me to bring up for you?"

"Just keep filling in the blanks. You're doing good, by the way."

"Thank you."

Tony led her husband over to the sitting area. Parker Green had heavy-lidded dark eyes and a wide mouth. His head held a shiny bald spot surrounded by a ring of close-cropped black and silver fuzz. He wore a white shirt, loosened at the collar, a striped tie, and a pair of tan slacks. His sleeves were rolled up to his elbows, his coat was draped over his shoulder, a worn briefcase in his right hand. Tony took her husband's coat and briefcase and told him to sit. Parker took the unoccupied wing chair. He looked at the tray of canapés and took a couple of crackers topped with turkey.

He said, "Tony said you've reopened my daughter's case."

Decker said, "It's never been closed."

"Officially," Green said. "Unofficially, we haven't heard a damn thing in over a year." He looked at Decker's face. "You got something new or are we going to be rehashing the same old shit?"

"Probably a bit of both," Decker said.

Tony came back into the room with a glass of iced tea for her husband. She sat down and reached for her husband's hand. Fingers interlocked, both parents waited.

Decker said, "I've read your daughter's file. I didn't see any notes about a boyfriend. Did your daughter have a boyfriend?"

The Greens looked as if they'd just sucked on lemons. Tony said, "We've answered these questions before."

"I'm sure you have," Decker said, "but not to me."

"Don't aggravate yourself, Tony. They're not worth it." Green ate a smoked-ham appetizer. "No, she didn't have a steady. Of course, she went out. Deanna was very popular. But no one in particular could hold her interest."

Tony said, "Deanna was a serious student. Her studies always came first."

Green said, "Not like some of these kids today . . . too damn lazy to work—"

Tony squeezed her husband's hand. "Just what kind of new developments do you have?"

Decker said, "I'd like you to take a look at a drawing. Just tell me if the person looks familiar."

Again, the parents exchanged glances. Bontemps fished the sketch from her purse and handed it to Tony. Green got up and stared at the face by looking over his wife's shoulder. They studied it for at least a couple of minutes. Finally, Tony shook her head. She raised her eyes to her husband. "Parker?"

"Don't know the kid." Green's eyes went to Decker. "Is he the bastard?"

"I don't know," Decker said.

"Where'd you get this drawing?" Tony asked.

"It's a long story," Bontemps said. "Does he look familiar to you at all, Mrs. Green?"

"No, he doesn't."

Decker tried to read their faces. From what he could decipher, they were telling the truth.

Tony handed the picture back to Wanda. "Anything else?"

" 'Fraid not," Decker said.

"That's it?" Tony's disappointment was palpable.

"Mrs. Green, all I have is some matching physical evidence. Unfortunately, I don't have a suspect—"

"Who is this monster you're investigating?" Green broke in. "Some kind of serial killer?"

"I'm not sure," Decker said. "You've never seen

this face in the neighborhood or around Deanna's school?"

Tony said, "You came down here just to show us a single *drawing*?"

"We work with what we have," Bontemps said. "Sometimes it isn't a lot."

"I'll say!"

Green sighed, disgusted. "Try the picture at her school. Maybe you'll get lucky. 'Cause that's the only thing that's going to solve this case. Luck."

"I'll try the school." Decker stood and so did Bontemps. As he reached out to offer Green his hand, the front door opened.

The young man appeared to be in his early twenties, tall and lithe, but very well defined. He had hazel eyes, high cheekbones, and a small mustache underneath a broad nose. He wore a black muscle shirt, black running shorts, and high-top athletic shoes. His body and face bathed in sweat, he was panting when he came in. His eyes immediately went to Decker's face.

Green rose from his chair. "Come here, Stephain. I want you to take a look at a picture." Almost as an afterthought, he added, "This is my son, Stephain."

"What's going on?" Stephain said.

"Police," Tony said. "A *supposed* new lead on Deanna's murder."

The young man stood at the doorway, eyes darting from parent to stranger. "What new lead?"

Green said, "Come here and take a look at this."

"Lemme wash my face first," Stephain said.

"For godsakes, Stephain, it'll only take a minute."

Stephain glared at his father. "So will washing up."

He stomped into the kitchen. Tony followed. Green was about to stop her, but changed his mind.

Nobody spoke for a moment. Then Green muttered, "Boy should get a damn job . . . something . . . anything! Mother isn't helping at all. So damn clingy to him since Deanna . . ." He lifted his arms helplessly and then dropped them to his side. "When I was his age I was working two jobs and going to night school. Yeah, it's hard, but I've tried to tell him that nothing is imposs—Aw, hell with it!"

Green marched into the kitchen. Seconds later, muffled conversation could be heard. No words, just angry, disjointed vocalizations.

Bontemps whispered, "He's not the face in Whitman's sketch."

Decker nodded in agreement.

A minute passed, then Stephain stormed back into the living room, his mouth screwed in anger. His parents followed, looking upset and embarrassed.

To Decker, Stephain said, "Lemme see the picture."

Tony blushed. "Stephain, these people are trying to help—"

"Cut the crap, Ma. They don't give a damn about us. And what are you trying to prove with this *shit*?" He gave the tray of canapés a gentle kick. Bontemps managed to rescue the salver before it fell to the floor. "You think this is what white people do, Ma? Serve little crackers and iced tea to the police? You think that's gonna stop the beatings?"

"Stephain!" his father rebuked him. "Remember who you're talking to."

The young man went nose to nose with his father. "And you remember who you're talking to—"

"Hey!" Decker said forcefully. "Enough, all right!"

The two men looked at Decker. Stephain shouted back, "No, it's not all right! Just who the *hell* do you think you are?"

"Buddy, my sister wasn't murdered. But yours was. Think you can pause a minute in her memory to maybe get a little justice done?" Decker shoved the drawing in front of the brother's face. "You know this guy? Yes or no?"

Angrily, Stephain grabbed it from Decker's hands. The change in his eyes was instant. From naked hostility to a look of surprise.

Decker kept his face flat. "Who is he?"

Stephain handed the picture back. "Don't know him."

Bontemps blurted out, "Now who should cut the crap! You know who he is. Tell us!"

"Get lost, Aunt Thomasina!"

"Stephain!" Tony yelled. "I'll not have—"

"Yeah, start defending the cops, Ma. Maybe if you defend them hard enough, you'll turn white—"

Again, Decker shoved the sketch in Stephain's face. He whispered. "Do us a favor, Stephain. Look again."

Enraged, Stephain batted the sketch away. "Man, I already *told* you—"

"I know that, sir," Decker said, quickly. "And I respect that. But I also respect the *dead*. A monster removed your sister's earthly body. But he couldn't touch her soul. I know that for a fact because your sister, Stephain . . . her soul's been talking to me."

Stephain opened his mouth, then closed it, glaring at Decker. But he held his tongue. The entire room fell quiet. Out of the corner of his eye, Decker could see the perplexed look on Bontemps's face, the Greens exchanging glances, the husband rolling his eyes. So they thought him strange. Anything to break the tension. He dropped his voice a notch.

"Your sister sent me here. She woke me up last night and said, 'Sergeant Decker, you go out and talk to my family . . . talk to my brother, too.' That's what she said. Now I've got to respect that. So please . . . take a look at this picture . . . and tell me if the man looks familiar to you."

Decker held out the sketch. Stephain didn't bother to look. He spoke softly. "I think his name is Kalil Ashala."

Decker's expression remained fixed. As unobtrusively as possible, he took out his notebook. "Do you know how to spell that?"

Stephain stared into space. "Your guess is as good as mine. I only met him once."

Decker said, "What do you know about him?"

"Not anything really," Stephain said. "He's an asshole. A typical gangbanger . . . you know, a dude with a 'tude looking for a free lunch."

Bontemps said, "Does he live around here?"

Stephain shook his head. "South Central."

Green took a step forward. "Where do you know this . . . person from, Stephain?"

"I don't *know* him, Dad, I just met him once—"

"So how did you *meet* this person, Stephain?" Green said, speaking through clenched teeth.

"Through Deanna."

The room fell quiet.

Dad tried to keep his voice even. "This boy was a friend of Deanna's?"

Stephain shook his head. "His sister. His sister and Deanna were . . . friends."

Again the room was quiet. Tony cleared her throat. "Stephain, please. This is no time to protect your sister. Was this man a . . . secret boyfriend?"

Stephain shook his head. "No, Mom. Nothing like that."

"Nothing going on between them?" Decker asked.

"No."

"You're sure about that?" Bontemps said.

"Positive," Stephain answered.

"How do you know?" Tony persisted.

"I just *know*, Mom. I just know."

"We believe you," Decker said, calmly. "So Kalil Ashala lives in South Central. Do you have an address?"

"In the seventies or eighties, east of Fig . . . I drove Deanna there once."

"Why did you drive Deanna there?" Tony asked.

Stephain seemed subdued. " 'Cause she asked me and you weren't home."

"I meant, what business did she have there, Stephain?"

"I told you she was friends with this guy's sister."

"What's the sister's name?" Bontemps asked.

"Fatima."

"Fatima?" Tony asked, holding her cross. "Where did Deanna *meet* this girl?"

"I don't know, Mom. I didn't asked her. I just drove her to the house. I stopped in for a minute." He looked at Decker. "Did this guy mess up my sister?"

"I don't know," Decker said. "So *don't* get any ideas."

Stephain averted his eyes. "You're telling me that you're doing this . . . because my sister talked to you in your sleep?"

"Exactly." Decker folded his notebook and shook hands with the Greens. "Thank you very much. I'll be in contact soon." He paused, turned to Green. "Please, sir, don't do anything that might jeopardize my investigation."

Green said nothing, his jaw working overtime.

"Did you hear me, sir?" Decker said.

"Yes, I heard you." His eyes met Decker's. "I heard you."

But neither Decker nor Bontemps was convinced. Wanda raised her eyebrows and picked up her purse. Decker said, "Walk us out, Stephain."

When they got to the curb, Decker's eyes zeroed in on Stephain's face. "You are going to let me handle this, right?"

The young man paused. "You know I could cut through it a lot faster than you."

"Stephain, we got a concept in this country called due process. I've worked very hard on this case. I want to bring this bastard to justice. Don't mess me up."

The brother looked down, said nothing.

Decker said, "And while you're watching your manners, keep a watch on your father for me. Last thing your mom needs is your dad in jail for acting impulsive."

"Now that we're alone," Bontemps said, "are you still sure that this guy, Kalil, and your sister weren't—"

"Yes."

Softly, Decker said, "How about your sister and Fatima? Did they have something going?"

Stephain jerked his head up, but said nothing.

Decker said, "Like Officer Bontemps said, your parents aren't here. Tell me about your sister's relationships."

Stephain looked away and said nothing.

Bontemps said, "If this guy's involved, it's going to come out, Stephain. Might as well tell us your side of the story."

Stephain sighed, then sighed again. "Deanna . . . she belonged to this . . . there was a group of them at school. She probably met Fatima through them . . . one of her lezbo buddies. Dumb bulldyke bitch." He looked up, eyes burning with ire. "This kind of shit wouldn't have happened if she'd had a *man* to protect her."

Bontemps was about to speak, but Decker threw her a look that silenced her. What was the use of quoting statistics? That on average four women a day are killed by exes, husbands, or boyfriends. No, no, no. They weren't here to debate or educate. They were here to solve a homicide.

Decker said, "Thanks for your help, Stephain. I really mean that."

Stephain gave a weak smile. He started toward the house, then backtracked to Decker. "What was this bullshit you were feeding my parents about ghosts—"

"Souls."

"Whatever. It's still bullshit."

"Not to me."

"I can't tell whether you're putting me on." Stephain rolled his eyes. "I can't believe I'm saying this but . . . but *if* Deanna contacts you again . . . if she talks to you in your dreams . . . you tell her I say hello, okay? Tell her I miss . . . I really . . . miss her."

Abruptly, Stephain turned around and jogged back into his house. Decker smoothed his mustache, then headed toward the unmarked. There was work to do.

❧ 39

Decker put on his seat belt and started the Plymouth's motor. From the corner of his eye, he saw Bontemps twisting her hands. "You did good, Officer. You can relax now."

Immediately, Bontemps clasped her fingers together and buried her united fists into her lap. "Thank you, sir."

Picking up the mike, Decker called in Kalil Ashala's name to dispatch, asking for pertinent ID—address, phone number, make and model of his car, and any outstanding wants or warrants. While he waited for a response, he put the car in drive and headed east toward Figueroa. It was dusk. He flicked on the car lights and hoped the night would be a dove rather than a vulture.

Bontemps said, "Sir, I was . . . impressed with how you diffused the tension between the Greens."

"They never taught you the séance method of anger deescalation in the academy?"

Bontemps gave him a fleeting smile. "No, sir."

"Today it was souls. Tomorrow it may be a Puccini opera aria. Anything that works." He paused. "Actually, I wasn't putting them on. The eternal soul is a

Jewish concept. Deanna did speak to me, as bizarre as it sounds."

He glanced at Bontemps. She was taking it all in. He rolled down the window and caught a solid whiff of heavy grease, onions, and garlic. It smelled unhealthy and satisfyingly good. The air on his cheeks was like a shot of caffeine.

Bontemps said, "I was too . . . confrontational with Stephain. I should have handled it better."

"Didn't help that he called you an Aunt Thomasina."

"Yeah, but that was afterward. I let my excitement get in the way. It could have turned into something ugly."

"It didn't."

"It just made me mad, Stephain being so angry at the world. Couldn't see past his own rage to help us find his sister's murderer."

"In the end, he came through."

"Not before blaming the victim. 'Wouldn't have happened if she'd had a *man* to protect her.'" She shook her head. "Good thing you gave me a look. No sense in telling domestic crime numbers to someone as pigheaded—"

Abruptly, she stopped talking, the silence filled in by distant horn honks and the chirping of crickets.

After some thought, Bontemps said, "I guess he's hurting bad if he's telling *us* that he misses her. Feeling guilty that he wasn't home to protect his sister."

"Yeah, he's hurting, all right." Decker waited a beat. "Hard to admit that some things are out of your control." He made a series of turns, heading deep into the inner city. He said, "Well, maybe we'll get a break in Deanna's case. That would sure be spiffy."

"Sir, exactly what is our status regarding this case?"

A good question, Decker thought. "I'm not looking to horn in on Wilshire's case . . . steal anyone's collar. But if that happens in the process, I can live with it."

"In the process of what?"

"In the process of solving my case."

"I see."

Decker hesitated. "No, that's not entirely true. Initially, I was interested in Green only as it related to Whitman. But Deanna has taken me in. I'd sure like to find the sucker who murdered her."

"Are you going to contact Wilshire Homicide?"

"Now?" He shrugged. "Be better if we had something definite to tell them, don't you think?"

Bontemps gave him a conspiratorial nod. "Yes, sir. Definitely."

"Our evening is already shot. Why disrupt theirs?"

"I agree."

Dispatch called back. Immediately Bontemps pulled out her notebook, jotting down the data as Decker drove. Ashala had managed a brief but active criminal life—a dozen arrests for felony drug possession, grand theft auto, and burglary. No assaults, rapes, or murders. At least nothing was on the books. The radio transmitting operator gave out Ashala's address and Decker was on his way.

Warm summer nights in the 'hood. The sun goes down and people come out for air. The living becomes alfresco as the sidewalk swells. Mothers pushing

strollers while their older children run ahead, their
steps punctuated with shouts and laughter, hand-
holding couples out for strolls, groups of bored teenagers out for trouble. The din of traffic was often
drowned out by bass-heavy music coming from car
stereos and boom boxes. Old apartment buildings
were temporarily emptied of their residents. Lots
of lawn parties, lots of drinking—ergo, lots of problems.

It had been a long time since Decker had worked
the inner city. His area, although not without its
trouble spots, was considered a plum. Looking at the
street life, he felt it was good to see what Bontemps
and his other colleagues dealt with day after day.
Gave him perspective and maybe more than a hint
into the woman's frustration and anger.

Decker turned down Ashala's block. It was poorly
lit, an area of single-family bungalows, some of them
in sad disrepair but others well preserved—compact
and standing proud. The lawns had been baked to
yellow straw by the heat, wilting plants craning their
stalks upward. Most of the homes held barred windows and fenced yards; behind the barriers were snarling dogs, straining at their leashes. They were called
bandogs—tying the animals up all day drove them
crazy, made them mean.

Ashala's house was somewhere in the middle on the
scale of neglect—a fried lawn, a couple of punched-
out spots in the wall that once had been overlaid with
stucco, a single boarded-up window. It was fenced,
the dog who patrolled it a mixed-breed of around
sixty pounds. The front-door grate was closed, but

the door it protected was wide open. Decker could see flickering colored movement from a TV screen. He parked the car, rolled up the windows, then took out his Beretta, readjusting his shoulder harness so his gun would be in easy reach.

"Don't know how much it will actually help if they start raining down on us," Decker said. "But it makes me feel better."

Bontemps opened her purse and pulled out her service revolver. "I didn't bring my belt."

"I've got a war kit in the trunk."

"How are we going to get past the dog?"

Decker opened the glove compartment and removed a small plastic Baggie and a leash. He sniffed the contents of the bag and made a face. "Dried liver—better known as canine pâté. My setter loves it."

"And if that doesn't work?"

"We have Mace. Twilight is on our side. We won't be as visible. Let's go."

They got out of the car, Decker popping the trunk to retrieve the utility belt for Bontemps. As they approached the house, the dog leaped at the fence, greeting them with a hostile bark. Decker dangled the treat in front of the dog's snout, then threw it up and over the wrought-iron pickets. The dog caught it airborne. Softly, Decker called the dog over, holding out another liver treat. The animal stopped barking and trotted over to investigate.

"Hey, there . . ." Decker looked at the dog's rear end. ". . . girl. Are you a good girl or what?"

The dog stuck her snout out through the bars.

"Yeah, you're a nice girl." Decker held out the desiccated liver. "Kinda ribby, too. Bet they don't feed you too much." The dog continued to sniff vigorously, then let out a bark. Slowly, Decker stuck his hands through the bar, feeding her while feeling for her collar. Finding it, he quickly snapped on the leash and gave her another treat. Then he tied the leash to the fence, reinforcing her cooperative behavior with more treats. Decker got up from his crouch and spewed the treats over a two-foot-long diameter.

"That should keep her busy for a while. A well-trained guard dog would never accept food from a stranger. Nice that someone got lazy. Let's go."

Decker unlatched the gate. Bontemps stowed her canister of Mace, resting her hand on the butt of her gun. It felt weird, wearing silk cinched by a utility belt. Maybe she'd make a new fashion statement. The sophisticated garb of urban living.

They went to the front door, peered through the metal grate. The living room appeared empty.

They knocked. A moment later, a porch light came on. A woman wearing shorts and a bikini top appeared behind the grate.

"Police," Decker said, presenting his ID. "Can you open the door, please?"

"Depens on whatchu want."

Bontemps stepped in. "Girl, open the door and quit buying trouble."

"I'm not buyin' nothin'. Last time you come in here, you tear the place apart. Take me five days to clean up the mess."

"No one's going to tear up the place," Decker said.

From behind the grate, a male voice said, "Who is it, Mama?"

"Police."

An ominous scurry of movement. Decker said, "I'll take the back door. Call for backup *now*!"

He raced around the rear of the bungalow just in time to see a figure jump over the bushes into the next-door neighbor's yard. Without thinking, he followed, cursing his age, catching a glimpse of the runner, who was scaling a fence. Before Decker could scream out "Police," a staccato burst of fire suddenly flew his way. He hit the ground and swore, the bullets whizzing past him as he reached for his Beretta. When Decker looked up again, the sprinter was at the top of the fence, face shining in the moonlight, eyes peering down on him. The mother had a semi-automatic aimed at Decker's heart. It spit molten lead as Decker rolled furiously for cover. He managed to fire a round in return.

A moment later, the sprinter was gone.

Decker didn't move. In the distance, he heard screaming sirens. He looked around, saw Bontemps falling into the neighbor's brush, cursing like a sailor.

"You okay?" she shouted when she landed.

"Fine."

"I heard shots."

"Yep." Decker got up. "Lost the fucker but I got a good look at his face."

"Is it—"

"Let's go meet backup."

They both started to run.

Bontemps's gait was unsteady. "Goddamn shoes!" She swore as she limp-sprinted. "I broke a heel. Last time I dress up for *any* assignment. I requested a canine unit, by the way."

"Good."

Within minutes, six black-and-whites were at the scene, a dozen uniforms spread out down the block. A low-flying helicopter chopped up the sky. The air became saturated with the sounds of motors and deep barking—police dogs on the hunt.

Decker returned to Ashala's house, stationing himself on the front porch, absorbing abuse from the woman who had answered the door. She hurled one obscenity after another, finally ending her complaint with a wad of spit directed at Bontemps.

"That's it!" Decker turned her to the wall. "Hands up now! You're under arrest for assault upon a police officer."

"Whachu say—"

"You have the right to remain—"

"I didn't touch no one—"

"Spitting is an assault."

Before the woman could resist, Decker had clamped on the cuffs. The woman let out a streak of swear-words, kicking and cursing adding to the soundtrack of barking dogs, rotary blades, police sirens, angry shouts, curses, and rap music. The commotion was gathering too much momentum. Neighbors were pouring out for a better look. Hostile epithets were thrown in their direction.

Decker ignored the crowd, hoping they would stay put. But the woman's shouts and screams were a magnet for problems. Several men took steps forward, crossing the street. Bontemps took a step forward herself, ordering them back. The woman continued to flail about and yell. Decker tightened his grip on her, then discreetly leaned in close, whispering several sentences in her ear.

Immediately she went slack. She stared at Decker and he nodded. Bontemps looked at him quizzically, but Decker kept his face flat. He turned to the handcuffed woman and said, "Was that your son, ma'am?"

The woman shrugged. "Mebbe. What's it worth?"

Decker said, "Why'd he take off like that?"

Before she could answer, the air came alive with thunderous roars that echoed down the block. Decker and Bontemps exchanged looks.

"The dogs," Bontemps said. "They got him?"

"Sure sounds like it."

A few minutes passed, then two panting uniformed officers returned to Ashala's house. One was black, the other was white. The white one said, "What are you doing here, Bontemps?"

"Helping me out," Decker said. "You find him?"

"We got someone," the black man said. "Do you want to take a look, sir?"

"Did you get his gun?"

"Yes, sir."

"Then I'll take a look." He threw Bontemps the keys to the Plymouth. "In the trunk of the car are evidence bags, plastic gloves, and a flashlight. Go back to the spot where the assailant fired at me, try to retrieve the bullets, then call it in to Ballistics." To the officers he said, "Take my friend here down to the station house." Happily, he transferred his prisoner. "I'll deal with her in a little while."

"Remember whachu tole me," she shouted out.

"I never lie," Decker said back.

As the uniformed duo escorted the woman to a cruiser, Bontemps turned to Decker. "What *did* you say to get her to cooperate, sir?"

"Nothing much." Another pair of uniforms were walking toward them. Decker said, "Ah, my escorts. Go get some evidence, Bontemps."

Wanda didn't move.

Decker smiled. "I told her that if she behaved herself, there was money in it. What's a hundred bucks to the department if it prevents a scene? Get to work."

"She gets a C-note and I'm doing this for nothing?"

"Life isn't fair. But to show you what a sport I am, I'll pay for your broken heel."

"I'd rather have the hundred bucks."

Decker laughed. "You came through for me, Officer. Thank you."

Bontemps licked her lips. "You're welcome, sir." She paused. "The man, sir. Was it Kalil Ashala?"

"I believe so."

There was a moment of silence.

Decker said, "The bullets, Bontemps?"

"Right away." She raced toward the next-door neighbor's backyard, limping as she galloped.

Decker jogged toward the waiting officers. A moment later, he was whisked down the block in a cruiser. An agitated but restrained man was lying spread-eagle on the ground. Surrounding him, but not touching him, were a team of at least a dozen police officers, two German shepherds, and one over-sized, snarling male rottweiler.

Decker made the ID.

~ 40

Decker had originally planned to jail Ashala until the search warrant came through for the house. Since he knew what evidence he needed, he wanted to comb the place before taking a crack at Kalil. But right now the fleeing felon seemed excessively chatty. Not one to waste an opportunity, Decker booked him, then placed him in a four-by-six interview room. Since Ashala had waived his rights to an attorney, it was just the two of them in a cubicle about as big as a gym locker. Smelled like one, too. As Decker studied Ashala, he realized what a good artist Whitman was. The same high cheekbones and upward-slanting eyes almost giving Ashala an Asian look. Whitman had captured not only the face but kinetics in the expression—from the small, sneering mouth to the dark, jumpy eyes.

Decker turned on the tape recorder, stating all the necessary identification. Then he poured Ashala a glass of water and placed it in front of him. He said, "You want to tell me why you bolted, Kalil?"

"I wasn't boltin'," he said. "You was chasin' me, so I be runnin'."

Decker waited.

Ashala squirmed. "You was scarin' me."

"Scaring you?"

"Stompin' in like you did. I was afraid you was gonna bust up the place again. Take a crack at my head while you was at it."

"I never entered your house, Kalil. Why were you shooting at me?"

Ashala pursed his lips. "Self-defense. You was scarin' me. I thought you was tryin' to kill me."

Decker said, "Let's try this again, Kalil. Why'd you bolt on me?"

"I didn't bolt—"

"You didn't hear the question right, Kalil. You did bolt. That's a given fact. Now *why* did you do it?"

"You was chasin' me—"

"Kalil, you were climbing the fence before you even saw my face. I wasn't chasing you, you ran away. Tell me why."

Ashala's eyes went to the ceiling. Decker looked upward at a dozen white acoustical tiles that had seen better days. He returned his attention to the arrestee.

"Kalil, you shot at an officer of the law. That's attempted murder under special circumstances. You're going to do time for that. But that's not the only stick up your butt, sir. I've got stuff on you. *Lots* of stuff linking you to nasty things. And I'm sure we'll find more stuff once we search your house. So if you've got a story to tell, I suggest you tell it now."

"What kind of shit you got on me?"

"Good shit."

Ashala drank his water, asked for a cigarette. Decker

handed him a smoke. That was all he needed—bagged up in a cell under a nicotine cloud twice in one day.

"If I talk to you, I first be needin' a deal, you dig?"

Decker played along. "What do you want?"

Ashala's dark eyes darted from side to side as he blew out smoke. "What do I want?"

"Yeah, tell me what you want."

"You gonna get me what I want?"

"I can't answer that, Kalil, until you tell me what you're after."

"I don't want to do no time, dig? Maybe like community service. That kind of shit."

Decker said, "Kalil, tell me about Deanna Green."

Ashala's face went flat. "Deanna who?"

"Deanna Green."

"Don't know her."

"Don't know her at all?"

"Nope."

"Think again," Decker said.

Kalil stuffed out his cigarette, curled his lip, and shook his head no. "Don't know her."

Decker stared at Ashala for the longest time. Then he said, "I know you from somewhere."

"Well, I don't know you."

Mentally, Decker counted to one hundred. Then he said, "*I* know where I know you from! You used to work at the Grenada West End in the West San Fernando Valley, didn't you?"

Immediately Ashala looked down. He said nothing.

"You worked in the coffee shop, right?"

The felon looked up, eyes darting from side to side. He remained silent.

"Or was it room service? Maybe it was both."

Again Ashala looked down, this time to ostensibly study his nails. He shook his right leg up and down.

Decker said, "Were you working the night of that big murder . . . that prom queen? Man, that was something—"

"I want a—"

Decker pressed against the tape recorder as he leaned over the tabletop. "You want to know something, Kalil? You are fucked beyond *fucked*! Because you know who is sitting in jail for the murder *you* committed—"

"Didn't do no murd—"

"A *white* boy, Kalil. But not just any white boy—a *Mafia* white boy. And not just any Mafia white boy, the *crime boss's son*! Do you know anything about the Mafia, Kalil? They were the original Cryps and Bloods—"

"You're bullshittin'—"

"Ever seen any of the Godfather movies, Kalil? The decapitated horse head in bed . . . that's just warm-up—"

"I want—"

"You know they're making a Godfather Part Four movie? Guess what. You're gonna be in it." Decker aimed a finger gun at Ashala's head. "Ker-*boom*!"

Ashala broke out in a cold sweat. "I can take care of myself. I got *friends*, man."

"Kalil, you'd better have *lots* of friends. Because if you piss off the Mafia, you're not safe anywhere and I do mean *anywhere*. Not a jail or a country around that's gonna save your ass. I drop your name and you're maggot meat—"

"Fuck you. I'm not afraid of no one."

"That's good, Kalil, because the Mafia has lots of friends, too. And you know what their motto is. *Everyone* has to sleep."

Ashala shuddered, mopping his soaking brow with his shirt sleeve.

Decker said, "Buddy, if you want to deal with me, then talk to me. If not, take your chances and deal with *them*!"

Ashala was silent.

Decker sat back in his seat. "Ah, would you *look* at what happened. I accidentally depressed the pause button on my tape recorder. Careless of me." He flicked the cassette player back on record. Calmly, he said, "Are you sure you don't want a lawyer, Mr. Ashala?"

Ashala turned off the tape recorder. "What do you *want*?"

Decker turned the recorder back on. "Cheryl Diggs."

Ashala started to sweat. "Diggs the white girl who was offed?"

"Yes."

"I didn't do nothin' to her."

"Don't give me that bullshit. You screwed her. I know it, you know it."

A long pause.

"Maybe I did," Ashala said. "But that don't mean nothin'. She already be dead."

Decker felt his blood pressure shoot up, but he kept a stoic demeanor. "Try again, Kalil."

"But that be the truth."

"You tied her up, Kalil."

"'Cause I got nervous. That maybe someone be

watchin' me leave the place. So I tied her up like the boyfriend did."

Decker paused. "Like her boyfriend did? Did what?"

"He tied her up. I knowed because Trupp's got hidden video cameras in the rooms."

"Henry Trupp, the night clerk?"

"He be the one."

"He placed hidden video cameras in the rooms?"

"That's the truth. See, we had this thing goin'. I watch for him while he does his thing. He watches for me while I do my thing."

"What was his thing?"

"Watchin' people fuck."

Trupp was in the back room, watching TV . . . rather teevees. Decker groaned inwardly. No more hotels *ever.* From now on, vacation would be sleeping bags and a Winnebago. To Kalil, he said, "What was your thing?"

"B and Es while the people slept. Henry be my lookout. Sometimes Henry be wantin' a cut, but that's okay. 'Cause sometimes I'd watch the action with Henry." Ashala smiled. "Lots of nasties goin' down. Better than rentin' a video 'cause it's *live*, know what I'm sayin'?"

"Did you watch the action on the night of the white girl's murder?"

"They was puttin' on a show so I watched." Ashala played with his water glass. "Got me too hyped up for the girl. I only did her 'cause she was already dead."

"How do you know she was dead?"

"She wasn't movin'."

"So why did you strangle her?"

Ashala didn't answer.

"Why'd you strangle Cheryl Diggs, Kalil, if she was already dead?"

Ashala shrugged. "Just in case."

Decker ran his tongue over his teeth. "Is that also why you tied her up?"

"No, I tied her 'cause that's what the boyfriend did, you dig?" Ashala shrugged. "Anyway, it looked like fun."

"You like ropes, Kalil?"

"Sometimes. And sometimes the bitches like it, too. She sure liked it when he did it . . . howling like a hound dog. So why not me?"

"Why not indeed."

"Yeah. Right. So what if Henry was lookin' on. He was a perv hisself. See, Henry didn't care what I did to the ho. Except then things got heated up."

"Go on," Decker prodded.

Ashala squirmed in his seat. "I ain't sayin' no more."

"Kalil, Kalil, Kalil . . ." Decker took a drink of water. "How can I do anything for you if you don't *talk* to me? Tell me about Henry Trupp. Was he nervous . . . maybe saying things that made you nervous?"

Ashala blurted out, "I did all those people a *favor*, man. See, Henry got a collection. He not only watched, he *taped*! Got money from it 'cause like I said, there was lots of nasties goin' down in the hotel . . . old men doing thirteen-year-old girls, you dig? I did everyone a *favor*."

Ashala sat back, feeling very self-righteous. Decker

kept his expression flat. "So Trupp was a peeper and a blackmailer. Yes, he was a bad guy. What kind of favor did you do for all those people?"

Ashala was silent.

Decker said, "You want any kind of deal, you're going to have to cooperate."

"I didn't *do* the white girl," Ashala said. "Like I tole you, she already be dead."

"But you strangled her."

"Just in case. She was dead."

Decker formulated his thoughts. "Tell me about Trupp."

"I don't say nothin' about him unless we deal."

"We found physical evidence to stick Trupp on you, Kalil. Cooperate and maybe you won't sizzle."

Again, Ashala said nothing.

Decker said, "You don't want to talk about Trupp, how about Deanna Green? Tell me about Deanna Green."

"I tell you I don't know no Deanna Green."

"Kalil," Decker said, "you've met her. I've got witnesses saying she was in your house."

"That don't mean I've met her."

"I have witnesses saying you've met her."

Ashala jumped out of his seat. "Then they're *lying*!"

Decker stood. "*Sit! . . . down!*"

"No problem." Ashala held his hands up, then sat down. "No problem."

Slowly, Decker settled back in his seat. "Tell me about Deanna Green."

"You give me a deal?"

"No, I can't do that. That's up to the district attorney. But cooperation may earn you brownie points. You know Deanna Green. Tell me about it."

Ashala scratched his chin. "I knowed her, yeah. But I didn't kill her."

"You didn't kill her?"

"No."

"Did you have sex with her the night she was murdered?"

Ashala looked away.

"Look at me, Kalil," Decker said. "I got you pinned to Deanna, too. Physical evidence doesn't fib."

"I didn't kill her!"

"You didn't kill her, you didn't kill Cheryl Diggs. Man, you are just in the wrong place at the wrong time, then."

"You're right!" Ashala cried out. "That's essackly it."

Decker said, "Kalil, did you have sex with Deanna Green the night she was murdered?"

He looked down and nodded. "But I didn't kill her."

"You raped her, but didn't kill her?"

"No, I didn't *rape* her. I was just help teachin' her a lesson, that's all."

And then the light went on. "You were just helping to teach her a lesson," Decker paraphrased. "What was the lesson? You don't mess with your sister?"

Ashala looked down. "I didn't kill Deanna Green."

"Tell me who did."

"If I give you Deanna, I don't want to do no time for rape or murder or . . ." He looked up. "Something like community service shit, dig?"

Decker said, "You are in *dreamland*, my friend."

"I didn't do Green, I didn't do Diggs. She be dead."

"You strangled her, Kalil." Decker ticked off his fingers. "I got you for Diggs, I got you for Trupp—"

"Man, I did everybody a favor with that motherfuck."

Bingo! Got him for Trupp, Decker thought. Calmly, he said, "Tell me about your sister and Deanna. Whose idea was it to teach Deanna a lesson?"

"Not mine. I hardly knew the bitch."

"Whose idea was it, Kalil?"

Resigned, Ashala slumped in his seat. "Fatima was mad 'cause Deanna didn't want her no more. Deanna be thinking herself as a real classy bitch 'cause she was Catholic and her parents were rich. Looking down her nose at us 'cause we were poor and didn't accept her *Jesus*. Pissed Fatima off. She axed me to help her teach the bitch a lesson."

"How'd you do it?"

Kalil leaned in close as if talking to a friend. "The way it work was this. Fatima threw a rock at Deanna's window and Deanna open the door to let her in. You know. 'Cause Deanna thought they still be friends even if they weren't *that* kind of friends, you dig?"

"Go on."

"Fatima kept the door open for me. While Deanna and my sister were talkin' in the bedroom, I came in. And then we both jumped her."

Decker waited. "I need details, buddy."

Ashala looked away. "I held her down, but it was Fatima who tied her up like her holy Jesus. Fatima liked that. Bitch lived by her God, she be dead like her God."

"What about you? You told me you like using ropes."

"Yeah, it's fun."

Decker paused, collecting his thoughts. Quirk of fate that both Kalil and Whitman liked ropes. So who *really* was responsible for Cheryl's death?

"What happened after Fatima tied up Deanna, Kalil?"

"I tole you. Fatima axed me to really teach her a lesson. Deanna was good-looking." Kalil shrugged. "I didn't mind."

"You raped her?"

"I teached her a lesson. It just got outta hand."

"She died, Kalil."

"'Cause it got outta hand. Deanna started making noise. We tried to make her be quiet. To save her. We didn't want her dead, just to shut her mouth. But she kept making noise. Bitch gonna wake up her parents. It just got outta hand. If she wasn't so stupid, she be alive today."

Decker exhaled very slowly.

Ashala said, "I want a lawyer."

Decker said, "I can arrange one for you."

"Are you gonna arrest Fatima?"

"She'll be brought in for questioning based on what you've confessed."

"The bitch is gonna tell you I did it all by myself. It's not true. Why would I do Deanna? I didn't give a shit about Deanna. So if Fatima tries to hang this all on me, she is lying, lying, *lying*! Don't fall for the slut. The bitch is a bad, *bad* actress. Fatima be all in tears after it happened. 'Oh, poor Deanna, poor Deanna!' And she pull it off real good 'cause she know how to talk and ack real white when it suit her. Had the cops holdin' her hand and pattin' her back. All *I'm* saying is I didn't kill her. You believe me, don't you?"

"You tell your story to your lawyer, Kalil. It's important that he believes you."

"It be the goddamn truth, man. I didn't kill her!" Ashala shook his head indignantly. "Besides, I did the bitch a favor. If it had just been Fatima and her friends . . . if I hadn't done her that night . . . Deanna woulda died a virgin."

🐍 41

This time Decker bypassed Davidson and went directly to Strapp. A thirty-year veteran, the captain was in his fifties, medium height but thin. He had small eyes, a long face, a sharp nose, and thin lips. A thoughtful man, Strapp never spoke without weighing his words. His deliberative nature made him acceptable to the people under him as well as the brass above him.

As Decker laid out his investigation detail by detail, Strapp sat at his desk, his pointed chin resting on clasped fingers. He didn't take notes. He didn't need to. After everything was recounted, Strapp spoke.

"There's a lot going on here. First, we've got a major sticking point with Diggs. Was she really dead or not?"

"Objectively, all we can do is go back to the autopsy report. The coroner stated that Diggs most likely died by strangulation. And Ashala admitted to strangling her."

"What about Whitman? Could he have strangled her, too?"

"One set of imprints was found around Cheryl's

neck. The impressions seem to line up with Ashala's handprints."

No one spoke.

Decker said, "But that isn't conclusive. The autopsy report also noted confounding factors. Diggs's system was overloaded with drugs and alcohol. It's possible that she died from an overdose. Possibly in Whitman's presence, possibly with his help."

"Before Ashala strangled her."

"Exactly."

"If that's true," Strapp said, "State might have been able to stick Whitman with a Manslaughter . . . like the Belushi thing, correct?"

Decker nodded.

"So if Whitman had been tagged with that, he'd be serving the same sentence." Strapp unfolded his hands, ran them through his thinning hair. "There's no problem sticking Diggs on Ashala. Even without it, Kalil's going to do time. The problem is with Whitman. Would your new findings change his current status? The way I figure, we've got several options."

He began to enumerate.

"One, we could let Whitman serve his present time in jail and forget about these recent developments. Two, we could recommend reduced jail time to the warden because of the new evidence. Three, we could cut our losses before Whitman's legal eagles get wind of all the details. Just go ask the governor to commute Whitman's sentence. Maybe even pardon him."

Again the room fell quiet.

Decker broke the silence. "One thing is for certain, Captain. Whitman's attorneys will get wind of it."

"Yes, they will. And when they find out, they're going to create a stink. Which could be a big problem for LAPD if the lawyers say that the case was insufficiently investigated in the beginning. Certain right-wing groups could claim that the police used reverse racism to placate minorities and purposely pinned Diggs's murder on a white man."

"That isn't what happened."

"What does reality have to do with anything? It's all perception. Lot of discontented people in this state. Look at what's on the ballots, Decker."

"You mean Prop one-eighty-seven," Decker remarked.

"Not only the illegals. Affirmative action is under fire. And Whitman's team is going to zero in on it. And if the blacks riot, we all know that, unlike other groups, the Mafia isn't afraid to take anyone on. We could have a real disaster here."

"We had a legitimate confession from Whitman, our prime suspect. At that time, it didn't seem necessary to look for other possibilities."

"It didn't seem necessary *then*? So you explain to me why you reopened your own case three months later."

"I was curious about certain things."

"And you think that answer will satisfy America's top crime boss? Not to mention how that's going to play to the blacks . . . or the media."

"I realize my actions could be misconstrued."

"I like that, Decker." Strapp made a teepee with

his fingertips. "Your actions could be *misconstrued*. Reopening your own case looks like you were bought off by Donatti."

Decker kept his face flat. "Lieutenant Davidson, as lead investigator on the case, made a choice, sir. He followed one avenue before another. Given what we knew at the time, it was a logical decision."

"But it wasn't the right decision. You proved that yourself."

"What can I say, Captain? If I had had the final say-so in the Diggs case, I would have checked everything out before taking it to the DA. That's the way *I* work. But that doesn't mean we screwed up. We had Whitman's confession."

"I've reread his confession, Sergeant," Strapp said. "He never said he did it. He simply expressed a willingness to concede that he *might* have done it. He stated specifically that he didn't remember one way or another."

"But he copped a Man One plea. Everything that was agreed upon was done without coercion and of his own volition."

"Granted." Strapp paused. "Still, Whitman's lawyers could file a motion to invalidate the confession because the defense wasn't ever made aware of the conflicting evidence. Furthermore, our current case against Ashala is heavily predicated on his confession—"

"Now *that* was all done by the book."

"That doesn't matter, Sergeant. He can claim coercion. He talked without representation."

"He waived his rights to representation."

"He didn't understand them, Decker. You know how it works. Besides, there's a funny gap in the tape. Know anything about that?"

Decker shrugged ignorance. "We've got solid evidence against Kalil to back up the confession."

"True," Strapp admitted.

Decker said, "So what's his lawyer asking for?"

"He'll give us Diggs and turn State's witness against his sister, Fatima, in the Green case, *if* we give him something in return. That being the case . . . if he gives us Diggs in a deal . . . we can maneuver Whitman quietly."

"What are you giving him in return?"

"Man One on Diggs and Trupp, nothing on Green—"

"You can't be serious—"

"If it prevents a race riot, yes, I am serious. Decker, if Ashala doesn't give us Diggs, we can't do Whitman without the press catching on. The whole thing could blow up in our faces."

"The bastard *murdered* three people. Son of a bitch tried to *shoot* me."

Strapp didn't speak.

Decker said, "I don't believe this."

"Cool your indignation. You did it to yourself. If you had a problem with the way Davidson was handling things, you should have come to me immediately."

Decker held his temper and said nothing.

"I know," Strapp said. "You didn't want to go above a superior. I respect that. But that doesn't mean we don't have problems. Namely, your own chain of events regarding Kalil Ashala could be shot down with a single arrow. You found out about Ashala through a drawing from *Whitman*."

"I didn't find out about Deanna Green through Whitman's drawing. I discovered her through *police* work—the Crime Analysis Detail. Both Diggs and Green were strangled and bound in the same manner. That's why we have the comparative service."

"Whitman also bound women in that same manner."

"But Whitman wasn't associated with both Diggs and Deanna Green. Kalil Ashala was!"

"Sergeant, between these walls, Ashala did both of them. But we've got political overtones that could disrupt. If we think Ashala did Diggs, then we owe it morally to Whitman to get him out of jail without blowing up the city. Nothing's carved in stone yet. Let me think about this for a few days . . . what to do with Whitman. In the meantime, you have plenty of other paperwork to keep you busy."

This was true. Decker said, "Yes, sir."

"Did you put in the papers for your overtime?"

"I was doing this on my own time, so . . . no, I didn't."

"Go ahead and do it. I'll authorize the hours for you."

"Thank you, sir. I'd also like to see that Officer Wanda Bontemps in Wilshire gets her overtime as well."

"Not a problem. We'll talk later. Anything else?"

Decker paused for a long time. Strapp wasn't the only one who thought before he spoke.

"Sergeant?" Strapp said.

"No, sir," Decker said, "there's nothing else."

* * *

Softly, Rina closed the door to Hannah's nursery. She came back to the dinner table and noticed her husband's untouched plate. Peter was staring at his food; his eyes were moving back and forth as if he were following a tennis match. He drummed a tea-spoon against his dinner napkin, creating a beat for his rolling eyes.

The rest of the table was devoid of people. It was very late, the boys having gone to sleep hours ago. Peter sat alone, engrossed in his rhythm, his thoughts, and his meat loaf. Rina sat down, but he didn't notice. She stood back up, went around from behind, and placed her hands on her husband's shoulders.

"Are you done?" she asked. "Or did you even start?"

"Huh?" Decker looked up. "Uh, no, I didn't start. I was waiting for you." He loaded his fork with meat loaf. "Great. Wonderful." He tossed her a phony smile. "You want any wine, darlin'? I'd like a glass." He stood suddenly. "Sit down, Rina. I'll pour."

He disappeared into the kitchen and came back with a bottle of wine and a corkscrew. His cheeri-ness had all the gaiety of a comedian laying a bomb. "Just a few quick . . . damn, the cork fell in the bottle. You can't get a decent hold on it with this contrap-tion. I don't make a fortune, but I think we can spring for a real corkscrew."

"Relax. A little dead matter never hurt anyone. Sit down, Peter. You're making me nervous."

Decker poured the wine, cork and all, then sat.

Rina said, "Do you want to tell me what's go-ing on?"

"What do you mean?"

"What's bothering you?"

"Oh, that." Decker smiled. "No big deal. I'll handle it. How's Hannah's cold?"

"She's snorting like a warthog, but she'll survive." Rina nibbled on a green bean. "The question is, will you?"

"I told you I'm fine."

"But you're not. You're not eating. I'd like to think it's because 'something's on your mind' rather than 'you don't like my meat loaf.'"

"Your meat loaf is delicious." Decker took three quick forkfuls. "I love it."

"If you won't talk to me, at least talk to someone—"

"I don't need to talk to anyone. Besides, sometimes talking does more harm than good." Decker sipped wine. "Sometimes it can even get you fired."

Rina paused with her fork in the air. "It's that bad?"

"Put it this way," Decker said. "You keep it inside, it burns your hide. You let it out, everybody thinks you're a whistle-blower or a political butt-kisser."

Rina put her fork down and touched her hand to her mouth. Decker looked at her expression, then felt his stomach sink. He silently cursed his big mouth.

"See! That's why I don't like to talk. I just overstated myself. Forget about it! Don't worry. I'll handle it."

"Peter, you did what you thought was right," Rina said. "That's all that matters."

"After I screwed up in the first place by listening to Davidson."

"Did you have a choice?"

"You always have a choice."

"So you made what you considered the wrong choice first time out. But you corrected yourself, which shows integrity—"

"Call me Saint Peter."

"Jews don't believe in saints."

"Neither do I."

"Peter, we've *all* made bad decisions. It doesn't mean we're incompetent at our jobs or that we're bad people—"

"Rah, rah, sis boom bah!"

"I can't stand to see you flagellating yourself."

"I love it when you use words like *flagellating*."

"You're hopeless." Rina took a sip of wine. "By the way, before I forget, Detective Martinez from Van Nuys called the house."

Decker looked up. "He called the house?"

"Yes."

"What did he want?"

"I don't know. Why don't you call him back and ask him? I left the number on the kitchen counter."

Decker started to rise, then caught himself. "After dinner. How was your day, darlin'?"

Rina gave him a disgusted look. "Peter, go ahead and make the call."

He smiled, genuinely this time. "I know. You want to get rid of me. I'm about as useful as a lump of butter."

"Actually, I have use for butter."

Decker laughed and went into the kitchen to make his call.

The conversation was a quick one, not more than five minutes and a dozen sentences on both sides. But the exchange was more than enough to jolt Decker into action. He told Martinez he'd come down right away. After he hung up the phone, he grabbed his jacket and car keys, kissing his wife hard on the mouth as he raced out the door.

Rina was definitely right. Sometimes it does help to talk things out. It just has to be talk with the *right* person.

❦ 42

The lieutenant's office was not a big one, but it did have its own walls and it did have privacy. Decker wondered what Davidson was thinking as he stared from across his desk. A formidable figure of a man with a solid history of police work to back him up.

The lieutenant said, "Are you drawing me a line in the sand, Sergeant? Is this the purpose of this little secret get-together? You going to warn me off your ass?"

He leaned over his desktop.

"Let me tell you something, Decker. You think you did the right thing by spitting in my face and going on your own? You know what you did, Sergeant? You fucked up. It may have worked out for you this one time. But no one upstairs . . . and I mean *no one* . . . will ever trust you again. Nobody here respects a snitch who cozies up to the Mafia."

Davidson's eyes held Decker's.

"Sergeant, I hope you like your rank. Because that's as high as you're ever going to get."

Decker said nothing.

"So if you think you did the right thing by going over my head, think again," Davidson continued.

"And if you called this meeting with me to try and smooth things over, *really* think again. Because it ain't going to work. Everyone *knows* who really screwed up."

"I'm not going to make excuses for me. But I'm not going to make excuses for you, either. I came here to do you a favor, Loo. To give you some dignity by allowing you to resign quietly."

Davidson's eyes narrowed. But he didn't talk.

Did he know? Decker wondered.

"I screwed up," Decker said. "I'll say it to anyone who asks me. But you screwed up, too—"

"After what happened to our city with the King verdict, I did what I thought was best. If you didn't agree, tough shit. I've had many more years than you, Decker. That's why I'm your superior."

"And that's why I *listened* to you, Loo. You had a good point, you had a good rep, and I honestly thought you were handling the investigation to the best of your ability—"

"You have a punch line, Decker?"

"I listened to you, Davidson, because I thought you were doing what was in the city's best interest. In reality, you didn't give a good goddamn about the city. You were trying to save your own ass and you *used* me in the process! And that really pisses me off!"

"You're demented, Decker—"

"And you deliberately mishandled the investigation, pushing me and Oliver and everyone else involved toward a quick conviction on Whitman. Not because you believed he was guilty, you just wanted a stooge—"

"Get out of—"

"You were *fucking* her, Davidson! We found *pictures,* for chrissakes!"

The room fell cemetery quiet, the only sound heard was the ticks from the clock.

Decker couldn't look at Davidson's face. He averted his eyes and talked quietly. "Did you really think that no one would find out about it?" A pause. "I guess that's exactly what you thought. And for a while it worked."

Decker rubbed his tired eyes. He finally managed a quick glance at his superior, then looked away. Davidson's complexion had turned waxen.

"Why didn't you just come *out* with it in the first place, Loo? Strapp would have handled it. He could have gotten you out of here with a sideways promotion."

Davidson remained silent. Decker wiped his forehead.

"You think politically, sir. Thinking that way, you know what your indiscretion could have done to this department. If I hadn't gotten a confession from Whitman, I would have been forced to go back and look around. You know what would have happened if I had caught you second time out. You would have been one of our *prime* suspects."

Decker finally managed to look at Davidson's face.

"Did you ever think about what might have happened had Whitman's lawyers found out? Whole mess would have blown up in our faces!"

Davidson didn't respond, his eyes staring but not seeing.

Decker spoke quietly. "Not only did you shut me

down, you had Detective Bert Martinez from Van Nuys shut down as well. You know, for just a moment, I entertained fantasies about you whacking Henry Trupp—"

"I had *nothing* to do—"

"I know that," Decker interrupted. "That was Ashala, too. But once I found out about the videotapes, I thought maybe you had something to do with Trupp's death."

Davidson paled immediately. "*Videotapes?* You said *pictures*—"

"I meant videotapes."

The lieutenant's cheeks took on a greenish tinge. "You have *videotapes* of Cheryl and me . . ."

Decker nodded.

Davidson broke into a sweat. "Cheryl took secret videotapes?"

"Not Cheryl," Decker said, "Henry Trupp. He had hidden video cameras in the rooms. Used to watch people screwing for kicks. If he came across someone big, he'd dabble in blackmail."

Davidson stumbled with his words. "He never called me."

"Obviously he didn't know who you were. He probably thought you were just one of Cheryl's regular nobody Johns. She did some hooking on the side."

Davidson looked away.

"It was Martinez who recognized the official badge in one of the tapes. It was blurred . . . buried off to the side. Lucky for you Martinez had a good eye."

Davidson buried his head in his hands. "I got a wife and kids."

For just a second, Decker felt pity for the man.

Davidson asked, "Who has the tapes?"

"Martinez. After we arrested Ashala, he got the go-ahead on the Trupp investigation. He went back to Trupp's house to look for further evidence that could tie Ashala to Trupp's murder. That's where he found the videotapes."

"Why'd he look at them?"

"Because we both knew that Trupp videotaped the rooms on prom night. We thought that maybe we'd be lucky and find a video of Ashala strangling Diggs. No cigar. Ashala probably tossed Trupp's place long ago. If there ever was a video, Kalil probably destroyed it."

"The remaining videos . . ." Davidson's voice was a ghost whisper. "They've been bagged and filed as evidence?"

"You mean your video, Lieutenant? Rather, video*ohs*?"

Davidson was quiet.

Decker sighed. "Martinez pulled them all as soon as he saw the badge. He doesn't know who the cop is, just that it's someone in my department. Because he saw the look on my face when he showed me the videos."

"What does Martinez want?"

"Nothing. He's leaving it up to me. And I'm giving you this choice. You can either retire . . . or you can fight me and take your chances. But I'm not going to bury this. Not because I care what you do in bed . . . even though she was only seventeen—"

"Eighteen. We were consenting adults, Decker."

"She was barely eighteen when she died, Davidson."

"That's not what she told me."

"Loo, for godsakes, hookers aren't known for their honesty . . . or their discretion. Diggs had a big mouth, sir. Matter of fact, she actually *told* Whitman she was doing a cop—"

"And you believed that little psychopath?"

"He didn't say she was doing you . . . just that she was doing a cop. And yes, I believed him. Damn lucky for you, Whitman didn't give Cheryl much thought. Otherwise . . . if he had put two and two together . . ."

Decker exhaled forcefully.

"Davidson, you let your personal problems get in the way of your police work. Even so, I'm giving you an out. Martinez is giving you an out. Because we all make mistakes. Sometimes we make *bad* mistakes. And we have to correct them, look like friggin' idiots. Anyway, it's up to you how you handle it."

Softly the lieutenant said, "How about what you suggested in the beginning? How about a sideways promotion?"

Decker shook his head no. "You've got over twenty-five years. You've got a good pension—"

"Deck, how do I explain it to my *wife*?"

"I don't know, Loo. However you explain it, it's got to be easier than explaining Cheryl Diggs."

Davidson looked up, regarded Decker with mean eyes. "The empty lieutenant's spot is going to look mighty good to you, isn't it, Decker?"

Decker paused. Silly to deny his intentions. Let the poor slob think the worst of him. He could live with it. "I just want to make sure nothing like this ever happens again. So, yes, after you announce your retirement, I'm going to Captain Strapp and ask him for your position—"

Davidson turned florid with rage. "You mother-fucking, grasping Jewish bastard—"

"Think what you want if it makes you feel better," Decker said calmly. "I didn't screw her, you did. And *if* Strapp gives me the promotion, and *if* I fuck up in my position like you did, then by all means, let some other motherfucking grasping bastard kick my ass out, too."

"You self-righteous shit."

"Not only am I going to ask Strapp for my promotion, I'm also going to recommend Bert Martinez to fill my vacated spot in Homicide—"

"You two little shits are in it together—"

"Just letting you know what's going on. You want to charge Bert and me with conspiracy, go ahead. The only true conspiracy Bert and I are in is saving your ass from a very *embarrassing* situation. Because the last thing this department needs is media on another asshole who can't keep his zipper closed. Any other questions?"

Still red-faced, Davidson was about to strike back. Then suddenly he shrank in defeat. Quietly he said, "I'm surprised you didn't force me to recommend you as part of this deal."

"There is *no* deal here, Loo. We can chuck the videotapes because they're immaterial. No one's out to screw you. But I don't ever want to get screwed by you again. Just stay out of it. Let Strapp make the decision, all right?"

"Do I have a choice?"

Decker smiled to himself. Rina had asked him the same question. "Hell, yeah, sir. We all have choices."

Davidson looked down, talked as much to himself as he did to Decker. "I know this is going to sound corny, but . . . I liked her . . . Cheryl. And she liked me, too. It wasn't like a . . . midlife crisis thing, Decker."

"I do believe you. But that's irrelevant."

"It's not *irrelevant*. Because it explains why I acted like I did. She *talked* to me, Decker. She talked to me about Whitman. He's a motherfucker . . . a cold, cruel son of a bitch who used to *abuse* her."

"But he didn't kill her—"

"He killed her, Decker. I don't care what kind of confession you got from Ashala, I know what I know. Whitman's a fucking bastard who deserves to fry. If ever justice was done, it was putting that psycho behind bars. Instead, you go ahead and save the son of a bitch. You let him *walk*."

Decker stared at Davidson, unable to come up with an adequate defense. Because much of what Davidson said had struck a resonant chord in Decker's heart.

Whitman was a bastard. And now it appeared that the bastard was going out a free man.

The air had turned slightly cooler with the nip of fall, but her smile was pure sunshine, her eyes were golden rays. Delight was etched into her face when she opened the door. When she saw it was Decker, she brought her hands to her mouth and blushed.

"Omigod!" Terry stepped aside. "Oh please come in. I'm so embarrassed. I've been meaning to call you—"

"It's fine." Decker entered her house. His smile was gentle. "I'm sure you've been busy. College is what . . . a week away? UCLA usually starts around October, doesn't it?"

"I guess so. I haven't thought about it much." Terry clasped her hands. "You've done so much . . . you've done everything." She breathed out air and looked at the ceiling. "I can't believe you actually came through. No one has ever come through for me. Except Chris of course. I don't know how to thank—"

"I didn't do it for you, Terry."

She turned red. "Oh, no, of course you didn't. You helped Chris because it was the right thing to do. I didn't mean to imply—"

"S'right," Decker cut her off. "Anyone home?"

"Nope." Terry smiled. "It's wonderful to have some solitude. There's so much to think over." She made eye contact. "Even if you didn't do it for me, thank you anyway. Thank you, thank you, thank you."

"Wait until I leave. Then if you want to thank me, be my guest."

As expected, she gave him a puzzled look. But she was too polite to question him.

"Please sit down," Terry said. "Can I get you something to drink?"

"Nothing, thanks. But I will take a load off for just a moment." Just like the last time he had been here, he sat at her dining-room table. "You sit, too."

Terry sat down. "So much has happened these

past six weeks. I can't believe it's really over. Chris is being released in three days, you know."

"I know."

The room was quiet.

Decker said, "Are you excited about starting college?"

"Uh, that may be delayed for a semester or something like that."

"What happened?"

"Just a change of plans. I'm not going to be going to UCLA." She looked down. "I'll be going to New York instead."

Decker paused. "Back with Chris?"

She nodded.

"What about his upcoming marriage?"

Her smile broke into a grin. "His uncle is having second thoughts about Chris getting married. It may not be what he wants . . . what his uncle wants. It may not be the right family. So he's postponed the wedding. And he's letting Chris take me along with him."

Decker kept his face flat and said nothing.

"They're paying for me and my education and everything else . . . until his uncle decides. It's like a dream come true for me."

Decker raised his eyebrows, but said nothing.

Terry looked down. "I guess I shouldn't expect you to understand."

Decker said, "You know what his family is, Terry?"

"Yes, sir." She nodded. "Yes, sir, I know everything. It's what Chris's family is, and I know that Chris is close to his uncle. I also know that Chris has to obey certain rules. He has to look the other way. But that's not the same as doing it, Sergeant. Chris is *not* his uncle."

"And you're sure about that?"

Terry closed her eyes and opened them. She said, "I know Chris has had a few problems in the past."

"A *few* problems?"

"All right. I know about his breakdowns. I know about his brushes with the law. I know lots of things that even you don't know about. But the past is the past and it's time to move on. I refuse to let him look back. I owe him that much."

"You know lots of things that *I* don't know?"

Again, Terry opened and closed her eyes. Decker wondered if she'd picked up the habit from Whitman. "Yes. And don't ask me about it anymore. Because that's all I'm going to say."

"Good for you, Terry. A tight lip will serve you well in that family."

The sarcasm angered her. Still, she was overly polite. "Thank you for what you did. I'll always appreciate it even if you don't understand certain things."

Decker kept his face flat. "Terry, maybe you do know everything. And if that's the case, what I have to show you will be pretty meaningless."

He handed her a manila envelope.

Her eyes clouded. "What is this?"

"Some newspaper clippings."

She broke open the seal with her fingernail and pulled out two articles—the sum total of Decker's library research over the past month. But he felt it was enough. Her expression was a question mark.

"Go ahead," Decker said. "Read them."

Terry's eyes flitted over the print. Her face registered distaste but not horror. "They're articles about murders."

"Not just any homicides, Terry. The murdered men were rivals of Donatti."

She looked at him. "I told you, Sergeant. I know what his uncle is . . . what he *does*. I *hate* it!" Her face was branded with rage. "But it's not *Chris*!"

"You're sure about that?"

"Yes!"

She was barely controlling her temper. Decker stood up. "I'm glad you're sure. Because I wasn't. Because Chris has always been kind of a cipher to me."

She kept her eyes on the articles and said nothing.

"I just thought it was odd that . . . here was this guy, old for a high school student—"

"He missed a lot of school because of his problems. There's nothing wrong with that."

"I agree. Except Chris is a real bright kid. And he was hanging out with dolts. He didn't seem to fit the mold."

"Is there anything wrong with individuality?"

"Of course not. But like you said, Chris is close to his uncle . . . his father actually. And here he was in LA while all his family was back east. At first I thought he might have been running from something."

"He wasn't."

"Yeah, I scratched that idea. But I wasn't satisfied. I get a little obsessive sometimes, even Chris noticed it. So I got to thinking about how he supported himself . . . by playing cello all over the country."

"Is there a problem with that?"

"Not at all if that's what he was doing."

Her head shot up.

"You were his tutor, Terry," Decker said, softly. "I assume you had a schedule of his sessions with you. If you still have your appointment book, you might want to check the dates. See if any of his . . . gigs corresponded with the dates of those newspaper clippings. See, you'd have a record of when he was here in town . . . and when he was absent."

Her eyes darted from the shreds of newspaper to Decker. Color suddenly drained from her face. Her hands started shaking.

Gently, Decker said, "Terry, I have no proof. And I'll never get proof. If I investigated his whereabouts, I'm sure he'd come up with an iron-clad alibi. Because that's the way it works with them. They take care of each other."

Decker tried to make eye contact, but she kept averting her glance.

"The question is," he whispered, "who's going to take care of you? I only told you this . . . showed you this . . . because I think you should know what you're *really* getting into."

Slowly, she lifted her head to look at him. And in her, he now found the expression that he'd been dreading.

Because now her eyes registered horror.

❧ 43

He was surprised to see me because that wasn't the plan. I didn't know if it was my sudden appearance or my expression, but something caught his attention, judging by the way he was scrutinizing me. I walked into his apartment.

It had been stripped bare, all the furniture removed and shipped back east. This room, which once represented to me adult independence, now looked lonely and rejected. I didn't go into his bedroom, but I knew it was the same. The only personal item left was Chris's sleeping bag lying like a twisted corpse on the white living-room carpet.

Two packed suitcases rested on the kitchen counter. He said, "What are you doing here? I thought I was supposed to pick you up in an hour."

I clasped my hands, then let them fall at my sides. "I finished early. I thought I'd come over and see if you needed help."

His smile was slow to come, but bright. "I'm fine, Terry. How'd you get here? Did you walk?"

I nodded.

"Where're your bags?"

"At home."

"Well, I'm almost done." He eyed me hungrily. "How 'bout if I take a break?"

I looked down and shrugged. He came to me, cupped my chin, and raised my face. "I know it's been an intense couple of days for you. Are you real sore?"

I nodded.

"So how about doing me with your mouth?"

I managed a weak smile. "Sure. Whatever you want."

My focus met his expressionless eyes. Softly, he said, "Think you can fake a little more enthusiasm?"

I walked away and leaned against the counter, staring at his empty cupboards. I felt my throat go dry. A moment later, his hands were on my shoulders.

"It's just that I love you so much, Terry. I want you to want me."

I turned around and nodded, tears in my eyes.

"I know I should back off, give you a break." His hands went over my shoulders, around my neck. "I just can't seem to do it. You've got to remember where I've been, angel. I'm not adjusted yet. Seeing any female . . . let alone you . . . so incredibly gorgeous . . . delicious. Have a little patience with me. I promise I'll be more patient, too."

We kissed, softly at first, then more passionately, his hands taking what he considered rightfully his.

And perversely feeling so good for me.

He led me to his sleeping bag and drew me down. We never stopped kissing, even when he undid his pants and lifted up my dress. Another repeat of the last couple of days—pain mixed with bits of pleasure.

I knew I could erase the physical soreness within a month's time. And then it would be wonderful. He was beautiful and gentle, and was trying so hard to make it good. He was everything I'd ever imagined in a boy, but so much more.

It would take only a month.

If I'd give him another month.

When he was done, he rolled off my stomach and put on his pants. I stayed curled up in his bag. His oversized hand began to rub the back of my neck. It felt like a block of ice and I shuddered.

"What is it, my love?" Chris asked. "Are you scared?"

I nodded.

"Moving three thousand miles away . . ." His voice was hypnotic. "A new town, new school, new people, and a lover who wants your body every fifteen seconds." He laughed. "I guess it's normal to be a little scared."

I didn't react. He rolled me over and looked me in the eye. "Terry, I swear I'll take care of you. Won't let anything or anyone hurt you."

I couldn't take my eyes off his. For the first time I noticed soft specks of pale green floating in the aqua pools. We kissed, then he pulled away and stood up, hoisting me to my feet with him.

"I'll be ready in about ten minutes," he said. "You'll feel better once you're on the plane."

"My parents are real mad," I said quietly. "Especially my stepmom. She's lost her baby-sitter."

"She's not mad enough to prevent you from going."

"That's because you're paying for my schooling." I gave out a nervous laugh. "Anything to save a buck."

"They'll get over it. Let me finish up."

He tousled my hair and went into the bedroom. I rubbed my hands together, then called out to him. He didn't answer. I went into his bedroom. His clothes were neatly piled on his floor—shirts with shirts, pants with pants, jackets with jackets, and all of it color-coordinated.

"Chris?"

He kept his back to me. "What?"

"Did . . ." I cleared my throat and tried again. "Did you ever keep a . . . a playbill . . . from any of your concerts?"

Still in a crouch, he pivoted around. His eyes met mine and were expressionless. "A playbill?"

I laughed nervously. "Not a playbill." I hit my forehead. "I mean a program . . . did you ever keep a program from . . . from any of your cello performances?"

He stood, suddenly appearing enormous in bulk as well as height. Chris's beard was gone, but his head was still nearly shaven, reminding me of where he had been just a few days earlier.

"Why do you ask?"

"It's for my grandparents in Chicago . . . remember them?"

He didn't answer me.

"I told them you were this big-shot classical musician. I thought they might get a kick out of . . . seeing your name in print."

He stood as still as stone. "I stopped collecting them about two years ago. Just too many to bother with. I think I still have some old ones at my uncle's house. I'll try to dig a few up for you when we get back east, okay?"

I felt my heart racing. "But you do have them, right?"

"I'm pretty sure I kept a few of the early ones." He laughed, but his eyes remained dead. "Why is this so important to you?"

"I just want . . . to impress them. I want them to like me."

His eyes went gentle. "Terry, they'd have to be idiots not to like you."

I felt my emotions crumble. I burst into tears, burying my face in my hands. He came over and drew me to his chest, shushing as he hugged me.

"It's going to be okay," he whispered. "Nothing is ever going to hurt us anymore, Terry." He kissed the top of my head, then caught my eyes. "You know why my uncle changed his mind?"

I didn't answer.

"'Cause he really, really *likes* you." Chris smiled. "He thinks you're beautiful, he thinks you're brilliant, and most important, he admires your loyalty. Course he'd *never* tell me that outright. Doesn't want to make me feel too secure. But I can tell. You know what he told me the other day?"

I shook my head.

"He said you'd make me good babies—"

"What?" I laughed despite myself.

"'Cause you have big hips."

Again I giggled. "They're not *that* big."

"They're *perfect*!" Chris laughed with me. "They're beautiful. I just *love* to watch them move."

I looked away, embarrassed.

He brought my face back to his. "It's his dumb way of letting me know that he approves of you." He brushed hair out of my eyes. "And don't worry about the baby comment. My uncle's an old-fashioned guy, but I'm not. I know how important your education is to you. I'll put you through college . . . through medical school, too. Set you up in practice if you want. Hell, I'll get my uncle to buy you an entire hospital—"

"That's not necessary," I said.

"Terry, I'd do *anything* for you. All I ask is that you love me in return."

I nodded, wiping tears from my cheek.

Chris kissed my lips, then said, "I need to finish packing. You keep standing around me, looking so fine, I'm going to get distracted. Why don't you go and splash a little cold water on your cheeks, baby doll? It'll make you feel better."

"Good idea." I threw my arms around his neck and kissed him passionately. "I love you."

"I love you, too." He extricated himself from my grip. "Go freshen up."

I nodded and went to the bathroom. I turned on the faucet and let it run for a long time. Bathing my face in a baptism of tap water.

It felt good.

Thinking pure thoughts even as his seed swam inside my body.

Trying to block out sentences of newspaper print.

Drowning out the potency of the sergeant's words that rang in my brain.

Erasing old memories . . . Chris's beeper going off . . . leaving his apartment to return the call.

Wiping away new memories, too. The stench of burned leather that once was my old appointment book.

Because the dates matched and I didn't want to think about it.

When I came out of the bathroom, Chris wasn't in the bedroom. I found him leaning against the kitchen counter. My purse was open. He was reading the newspaper clippings that I had stashed in my wallet.

I stopped in my tracks. He looked at my face and held up the articles. "Where'd you get these?"

"Why . . . why were you looking through my purse?"

"You answer my question first . . . then I'll answer yours."

I stood mortified.

He said, "Okay, *I'll* go first. I went through your purse because you were acting funny and asking me strange questions. Now it's your turn."

I couldn't talk.

"Cat got your tongue?" he said playfully. He pocketed the clippings and sat on his carpet adjacent to his sleeping bag. He patted the spot next to him. I forced myself to walk over and sit. He put his arm around me. "I'm not mad. Just tell me where you got them."

"From . . ."

"Go ahead. From where?"

His voice was soft like a faraway echo.

"From Sergeant Decker."

"When did you see him?"

"About a week ago. He came to my house."

"Why didn't you tell me?"

My eyes started getting misty. "I don't know why."

"He spook you, Terry? Spook you about me? Truth now."

I paused, then nodded.

"Do you know why he did that?" Chris flipped hair from his eyes. "Because the prick hates my guts. This is his final revenge on me."

"He got you out of prison."

"No, you got that wrong, angel," Chris stated. "He got me out of prison to save his *own* ass. Because he screwed up the first time around. If he hadn't done something, my lawyers would have brought incompetency charges against him and sued the entire LAPD."

I looked down and said nothing.

"Did he tell you I had something to do with these murders?"

I started crying. Chris pulled me close. "Terry, I need you to tell me the truth. Did Decker tell you I had something to do with these murders?"

I blurted, "He just told me he thought it was funny that you were out here going to high school. And he thought that your cello gigs didn't make any sense—"

"How did he know about my cello gigs?"

My voice got small. "I guess I told him about them. In the beginning. When he first interviewed me. Like why I tutored you . . . you know, to explain why you missed so much school."

"You talk a lot, don't you?"

I looked away and didn't answer.

Chris said, "We'll have to work on that. But first, I want you to listen carefully. Did he say *anything* about investigating these murders?"

"He said he didn't have any proof about . . . about who did them. That even if he . . . if he investigated them, he'd probably come up empty. Because these guys take care of each other."

Chris closed his eyes, then opened them. "Terry, look at me."

I did.

Chris crossed himself. "I swear to Jesus, I didn't have anything to do with this shit. Decker told you things to discredit me."

"But why would he do that?"

"I told you why. Because I fucked up his investigation by being *innocent* of Cheryl's murder. He had to go back and retrace his steps and hope that my lawyers didn't catch on. To save face, he tried to snow you with this garbage. And that's what it is, Terry. It's garbage!"

He fished the articles from his pocket and ripped them to shreds.

"I don't *kill* people, Teresa. If we're going to make this thing work between us, you can't doubt me. Because I don't want to have to spend the rest of my life proving that I'm not Joseph Donatti."

I didn't react.

"Look at me, Terry."

Again, I looked at him.

"Do you believe me?"

I averted my eyes. He picked my head up. "Nuh-uh. You can't run away from me now. Do you believe me?"

"I . . . I don't know."

"You don't *know*?"

I said nothing.

"Look at me, dammit! I went to *prison* for you!"

I looked at him, my eyes swollen with tears. "I know you did. I'm sorry, Chris. I'm sorry about everything."

"What does *that* mean?"

I looked away, stared at my lap, and couldn't speak.

Chris let out a soft laugh. "Oh . . . now I get it. You need another break from me, right? A temporary separation, right? Just like the first time you blew me off. I'm not perfect so that gives you a right to rip out my heart."

Anything I said would have angered him. We sat in utter silence, my eyes glued to my lap, until I heard something click. I looked his way. My mouth dropped open.

A gun in his hands. It must have been tucked away in his sleeping bag. He showed it to me, then pressed it against my temple.

I was trembling so hard, I bit my tongue. But Chris's hand was steady—a flesh extension of his weapon. His face was as dead as if he were embalmed. He said, "They were bad men, Terry. You believe that, don't you?"

Icy rills were running down my cheeks. I felt faint, but managed to keep conscious.

"Answer me," Chris said, quietly.

"Yes, I believe you."

"Very bad men—dealers, murderers, extortionists. Got in my uncle's way. Just . . . bad men killing bad men. No concern of yours . . . unless *you* get in the way."

Chris's voice turned very soft.

"I'm not stupid, Terry. I know you don't believe a word I say. And you shouldn't, because I'm a pathological liar. All you had to do was fake it . . . minimally fake it. Why didn't you do it?"

I hugged myself to prevent the spasms from over-taking me.

"You hurt my feelings," Chris said.

"I'm . . . sorry," I whispered.

"I'm sure you're *very* sorry now. Look at me."

I did, the gun moving from my temple to between my eyes.

His eyes were red and moist. "Calm down. I'm not going to hurt you. I love you too much. Except right now I hate you an awful lot. You know why, don't you?"

I nodded.

"You keep quiet about all this, you hear me?"

"Yes."

"Very quiet. You talk, you're dead. Understand?"

I nodded.

Slowly, Chris lowered the firearm and rested it on his lap. My eyes stealing a glance at the hunk of metal, shocked to see such a little weapon, almost comical-looking because the barrel seemed to be wrapped with Brillo. Looking at the ceiling, he said, "Let me ask you a philosophical question."

I waited.

"Suppose you have a pit bull—a good specimen. Strong, quick, and a real fast learner. Suppose it gets in the hands of the wrong owner. If it listens, it gets rewarded. If it doesn't, it gets the shit kicked out of it. The owner teaches it to attack. And it attacks. And it does it real well. Matter of fact, it gets rewarded big time because it does it so well. Is it the dog's fault he's like that?"

"No."

"Terry, I'm not going to hurt you. Answer me *honestly*! Is it the dog's fault?"

No, it isn't the dog's fault. Still, it's a vicious animal and should be destroyed. I said, "We're people, Chris. We can walk away."

"Not true," he said. "Just maybe . . . maybe I could hide from my uncle. But I could never hide from the entire organization. I'm stuck." He looked at me. "Do you see that?"

I told him I understood, praying the pit bull wouldn't turn on me.

"God, how I *love* you," he whispered. "Love you enough to give you a head start. So get out of here, Terry. *Run* out of here! And don't let me ever see your face again. Because if I do, I swear to Jesus, I'll blow your head off and give you a mirror to watch."

Slowly, I stood up on shaky knees and managed to get to his door. I opened it, was about to leave. Instead, I turned to him. "You didn't kill Cheryl Diggs, did you?"

In a flash, Chris fired off shots in my direction—soft, *zvitt* sounds that sent clouds of steel wool in the air and made me jump and gasp. Two bullets flew over my left shoulder, two over my right. All of them hit the wall, but left me quivering. I almost dropped to the floor. But some inner strength kept me upright.

"Perfect double taps." Chris smiled eerily. "I'm a real pro. Don't work unless I get paid. And I didn't get paid with Cheryl." He clicked the gun. "Next set won't miss, Teresa. Go before I change my mind and *never* let you go."

I closed the door and ran all the way home.

❧ 44

The autumn flower arrangement practically covered his desk, the card in it congratulating Decker on his new promotion. The entire squad room had signed it, but he knew that Marge was behind the whole thing.

He started unpacking, settling himself into his new office. His official duties would begin five days from now, on Halloween. He had considered coming to work dressed up in costume but a) Halloween wasn't a Jewish holiday, b) dressing in costume wasn't him, and c) with his new position, he already felt like an imposter.

Because along with the position came the title— Lieutenant Decker.

The one thing he would sorely miss was working in the field every day with Marge. Not that he couldn't work with her directly on the big cases— actually, he could work with anyone on any cases he wanted—but that wasn't his main job anymore.

Everything that went down in the Detectives department was now his responsibility. Being the kind of person he was, he knew that would mean a major personality adjustment. His obsessive nature made him focus on detail. One of the reasons he was such a good detective. Rarely was something overlooked.

Now he'd have to approach everything with a broader outlook, a bigger lens. But that was okay with him.

Because nothing ever stayed the same.

First thing up was the picture of the wife and kids. He smiled at Rina's face, wondered how she'd put up with his miserable moodiness the last couple of months. Ah, well, maybe the increase in his paycheck would make up in part for his grumpiness.

Next came the picture of the boys riding bareback in the woods, followed by a snapshot of Hannah on her swing. Lastly, Cindy's senior picture. She had moved back to the campus dorm. Last time Decker had spoken to her she had sounded depressed. Things hadn't worked out between her and the boy. So she'd be going it alone for a while longer.

Alone.

Nothing new on the shopping-bag rapist. The bastard had taken his own summer break. Every time Decker talked to his daughter, he reminded her that the madman was still out there, lurking around, just waiting . . . waiting. By now, Cindy was probably growing weary of the lectures. But Decker wouldn't ever let up until the bastard was caught.

Someone knocked.

"Door's open," Decker said aloud, arranging the pictures on his desk.

Wanda Bontemps stepped inside his new office. She was dressed in civies—a gray suit offset by a white blouse with a frilly collar. She wore makeup and had had her hair done.

"Have a seat," Decker said. "You don't mind if I keep unpacking, do you?"

"Not at all." She regarded his working space, looked at the empty walls. Then she sat in one of the two folding chairs. "I just stopped by to congratulate you on your promotion."

Decker stopped working and smiled. "Well, that was nice of you."

The room went quiet.

Wanda said, "I got a promotion myself—Detectives."

Decker offered her a handshake. "Congratulations."

"Thank you. You didn't know about it?"

"May have heard something floating around. Anyway, that's great. Good luck!"

"It's in Van Nuys."

"Quite a commute for you."

"Yes, but that's okay. That's where the opening was."

"You take what you can get."

"There was an opening in Van Nuys because Detective Bert Martinez was moved here."

"That's the truth."

"So that left an opening in Van Nuys Detectives."

"Yes, I can see where it would work like that."

Wanda kneaded her hands. "Was Martinez moved here at your request?"

Decker stopped unpacking, tossed her a smile and sat down. "You're prying, Detective Bontemps."

"Did you go to bat for me?" Bontemps blurted out. "Please. It's important for me to know."

Decker smoothed his mustache. "I mentioned you

to some people. And I'm sure it didn't hurt that you're a black woman. But you got the promotion with your own scores and your own record."

Bontemps was quiet, looked at her lap.

"Detective," Decker said, "don't worry how you got there. Instead, start looking at what you have to do. I think you'll do great."

She looked up and smiled sheepishly. "I'm nervous."

"It's a big step. I'd be nervous, too."

"You just got promoted. You don't look nervous, sir. You look like you own the place." She suddenly blushed. "I just wish I could be so calm."

"I hide things well." Decker stood up and continued to unpack his belongings. "They give you a detail yet?"

"Juvenile, naturally."

"I worked juvey for eleven years. Great detail . . . and a good one to cut your teeth on."

"Any advice?"

"No."

Wanda laughed. "Well, that was to the point."

"You're honest and so am I."

Bontemps paused. "I've done some thinking, sir. I realize that you don't have to be white to be prejudiced. And I apologize for my own biases. My grandparents had problems with some Jewish people. Big problems. A Jewish man owned the apartment building where they were living. Then my grandfather hit on hard times. The Jewish man didn't want to listen."

Decker nodded and kept unpacking.

"I loved my grandparents. And I felt real bad for their pain." Wanda sighed. "But that was then . . .

and this is now. We're all adults and we all make our own beds. It's time to move on."

"I have an uncle that I dearly love," Decker said. "Still calls blacks niggers. No matter how many times people correct him—and lord knows, my mother alone has corrected him more times than I can count—he won't stop. Bugs the heck out of me, but the old bastard ain't going to change. We all have baggage in our closets. Unless we deal with it, we're not going to change it. You and I working on the Green case . . . it was instructional for me."

"For me, too." Bontemps stood. "Thank you, sir. Thank you very much. I won't forget it ever."

"See, the way I figure it, a veteran mother should outrank her incoming daughter."

Bontemps grinned. "Yes, sir. Definitely need to keep the rookies in check."

Decker laughed. "Bye, Detective."

"Want me to close the door, sir?"

"You can't. It's warped."

"Shouldn't be too hard for someone to fix that."

"I could take a plane and do it myself." Decker paused. "But why bother? I think I'll just leave it that way."

❧ 45

She looked burdened but somehow that only added to her beauty. It made her look older and wiser. Her complexion was paler than Decker last remembered, her cheeks a bit thinner. She wore a flowing dress; the miniprint held hundreds of pink roses. Her long, auburn hair was pinned back by a flower clip. She could have been a Victorian noblewoman.

Decker pointed to a chair at the side of his desk. "You didn't go with him, Terry?"

"Appears that way."

"Are you in UCLA?"

She nodded. "For the moment, yes."

"Are you mad at me?"

The question took her by surprise. "I never thought about it. Maybe."

Decker smiled gently, but she didn't smile back. Her eyes moistened. "I thought you might be interested in this," she said. "I got it in the mail yesterday."

She handed Decker a newspaper article.

Society page.

A black-and-white photo. The bride was a heavyset girl with an ordinary, round face. But somehow her expression of joy offset her God-given plainness. The groom looked less than thrilled but not grossly unhappy. More relieved than anything else. As if he had hit rock bottom and things *had* to get better.

Decker read:

DONATTI AND BENEDETTO EXCHANGE VOWS.

He skimmed the article as he spoke. "Christopher Sean Donatti . . ." He stopped. "Chris changed his name?"

"Guess so. After all, he is Joseph Donatti's son." Terry took the article back and stowed it in her purse. "Chris's subtle way of telling me to screw myself."

"I don't think he's overjoyed, Terry."

"Who knows? He's more addicted to revenge than to love. He once told me that. Now I believe it."

"You're much better off."

"I'm not so sure. I'm pregnant."

Decker kept his expression flat, but inside, his stomach dropped. He waited for her to speak, but she didn't. So he said, "Did you tell your parents?"

"First thing," Terry said. "That's me. Responsible to the last drop."

"And?"

"Well, I have a few options. I can give it up in a private adoption—my parents' first choice. They're Catholic and still consider abortion a major sin. And if I go private, they can get the prospective adoptive parents to pay for all my medical care."

She looked down, then up.

"I can abort it with my own money of course. But *I'm* too Catholic for that. And if Chris found out, I do believe he'd literally kill me. Last option is I can keep it and raise it. But then full-time school would be out. Because I'd have to work. My parents flatly stated that this is my problem, I'd better learn to deal with it."

No one spoke.

She finally said, "Of course, they'd give me a discount on room and board if I stayed with them."

"How far along, Terry?"

"Around twelve weeks." She stared at him, dry-eyed. "In the meantime, being the creative person I am, I've come up with my own solution. I'm moving to Chicago at the end of the quarter . . . right before Christmas. I have my maternal grandparents there. We've been talking quite a bit this past year. They're wonderful people . . . retired but not all that old . . . in their late fifties."

She wiped her eyes.

"I told them the situation. They insisted I come live with them. Told me they'd help me out if I wanted to keep it . . . baby-sit while I went to school part-time, while I worked. They said it would be their pleasure. I hope they mean what they're saying."

She smacked her lips together.

"So I'm going to keep it. I guess I came here to say good-bye."

Decker was silent.

Terry laughed softly. "Ironic. It was Chris who got me in contact with my grandparents in the first place. Never know what life has in store for you. I'll be okay. I'm smart, a hard worker, and I wear adversity well. And even though Chris is damaged, he's got some impressive raw talent. Mixed in with all that psychopathology are some good genes. I'm going to have a wonderful baby."

"I'm sure you will."

"At least I won't be distracted by social things. I think boys are out of the picture for a long time."

Again, the room was quiet. Decker said, "Are you going to tell him, Terry?"

"No." She shook her head. "I thought about it, but it's out of the question. Our parting wasn't amicable. I'm scared of him . . . what he'd do to me . . . to the baby. Some things are better kept to oneself."

"He sent you the article, Terry. You're still on his mind."

"That was for spite, telling me he *doesn't* need me. A knife in the back. Chris can totally drop things when he wants them to be totally dropped. I remember how he completely tuned me out in high school. Not so much as a nod when we passed each other in the hallway."

"You think so?"

"I was there, Ser—It's Lieutenant now, right?"

"Right."

"Anyway, I don't think Chris cares a fig about me."

"I'm not so sure, Terry. He told me he was obsessed with you. Spying on you in high school when you weren't looking."

She said nothing.

"Terry, he's going to find out. Might be better if it came from you directly."

She looked up at the ceiling. "He won't find out."

Decker didn't answer.

She shrugged. "And if he does, *que será, será*. I can't exactly protect myself against a professional hit man."

Decker felt her anguish. As if the girl sensed it, she smiled.

"I'll be okay. Somehow, I'll get through this mess—raise my baby . . . get an education. I'm smart. And I'm tenacious."

"I'll second that," Decker said.

She laughed with wet eyes. "Thank you for seeing me. I learned from you, you know."

"From me?"

"From you. I learned you can make mistakes . . . big mistakes, even . . . and still go on to do what's right. Even though you knew what Chris was, you freed him anyway. Because you believed in something higher."

"That's giving me an awful lot of credit," Decker said. "But I'll take the compliment anyway."

She stood up. "I'd better get going."

"Do you need anything, Terry?" Decker asked. "I can set you up with Social Services."

"No, thanks. I'll slug it out my own way. Can I write to you from time to time?"

"Absolutely."

"Congratulations on your promotion."

"Thanks."

She gave Decker a tiny wave, then left, trying to close the door behind her.

"Just leave it," Decker said. "It's warped."

Terry gave him a dazzling smile. "Aren't we all."

Decker laughed, his eyes following the sway of

her dress as she left the squad room. Decker sighed. A strong girl, not unlike Rina, not unlike Cindy. Given some breaks, she'd do just fine.

If Whitman didn't kill her first.

Coming soon in hardcover from

WILLIAM MORROW

the next book in

FAYE
KELLERMAN's

thrilling Decker/Lazarus series

gun games

New York Times Bestselling Author

FAYE KELLERMAN

FALSE PROPHET
978-0-06-199933-8

When Lilah Brecht is beaten, robbed, and raped in her own home, L.A.P.D. Detective Peter Decker finds it hard to put too much credence into the victim's claims that she has psychic powers that enable her to see the future. But when Lilah's dark visions turn frighteningly real, Decker's world is severely rocked.

THE BURNT HOUSE
978-0-06-122736-3

A small commuter plane crashes into an apartment building. Among the dead inside the plane's charred wreckage are the unidentified bodies of four extra travelers. And there's no sign of an airline employee whose name was on the passengers list.

THE MERCEDES COFFIN
978-0-06-122737-0

Lieutenant Peter Decker resents having to commit valuable manpower to a cold case, but when the retired detective who originally investigated the murder case commits suicide, Decker realizes something evil has returned.

BLINDMAN'S BLUFF
978-0-06-170241-9

Peter Decker is summoned to investigate the brutal murders of a billionaire philanthropist, his wife, and four employees. At the same time a chance meeting puts Decker's wife, Rina Lazarus, directly into the path of the relentless killers.

Visit www.AuthorTracker.com for exclusive information on your favorite HarperCollins authors.

Available wherever books are sold or please call 1-800-331-3761 to order.

FK1 0411

New York Times
Bestselling Author

FAYE
KELLERMAN

SACRED AND PROFANE
978-0-06-199925-3

MILK AND HONEY
978-0-06-199926-0

SANCTUARY
978-0-06-199935-2

JUSTICE
978-0-06-199936-9

PRAYERS FOR THE DEAD
978-0-380-72624-0

SERPENT'S TOOTH
978-0-380-72625-7

DAY OF ATONEMENT
978-0-06-199927-7

THE RITUAL BATH
978-0-06-199924-6

JUPITER'S BONES
978-0-380-73082-7

STALKER
978-0-380-81769-6

THE FORGOTTEN
978-0-380-73084-1

MOON MUSIC
978-0-380-72626-4

THE QUALITY OF MERCY
978-0-380-73269-2

GRIEVOUS SIN
978-0-06-199934-5

Visit www.AuthorTracker.com for exclusive
information on your favorite HarperCollins authors.

Available wherever books are sold or please call 1-800-331-3761 to order.

FK2 0411